1929

Also by Frederick Turner

When the Boys Came Back: Baseball and 1946

*A Border of Blue: Along the Gulf of Mexico
from the Keys to the Yucatan*

*Of Chilies, Cacti & Fighting Cocks:
Notes on the American West*

*Spirit of Place: The Making of an
American Literary Landscape*

*Rediscovering America: John Muir
in His Time and Ours*

*Remembering Song: Encounters with
the New Orleans Jazz Tradition*

*Beyond Geography: The Western
Spirit Against the Wilderness*

Edited by Frederick Turner

Into the Heart of Life: Henry Miller at One Hundred

The Portable North American Indian Reader

Geronimo: His Own Story

FREDERICK TURNER

COUNTERPOINT
A MEMBER OF THE PERSEUS BOOKS GROUP
NEW YORK

This is a work of fiction. Though it draws on American history of the 1920s, its characters and incidents are the author's own inventions and are not intended to represent actual figures and events. The work, in other words, is an imaginative narrative, not an historical one.

Text design by Trish Wilkinson
Set in 12-point Adobe Garamond

Library of Congress Cataloging-in-Publication Data
Turner, Frederick W., 1937-
    1929 / Frederick Turner.
       p.   cm.
    ISBN 1-58243-265-1 (hardcover)
    1. Beiderbecke, Bix, 1903–1931—Fiction. 2. Jazz musicians—Fiction. 3. Cornet players—Fiction. I. Title.
PS3620.U765 A616 2003
813'.54—dc21   2002154007

Counterpoint
387 Park Avenue South
New York, N.Y. 10016

Counterpoint is a member of the Perseus Books Group.

03 04 05 / 10 9 8 7 6 5 4 3 2 1

For Elise
The Song Is You

Contents

1

Hudson Lake

*O*n the anvil of the cornbelt's summer sun the crowd sizzles at the riverfront park in Davenport. The gaunt-framed old man stands slightly separate from them, his back turned on the bandshell where the Natural Gas Jass Band races through Muskrat Ramble. His hand rests on the curve of the yellow limestone wall with its inset tributes to Bix, his gaze on the bust of the man himself—the batlike ears winging off the slicked-back, center-parted college kid haircut; the bow tie; the eyes staring down at some spot just in front of him or maybe at nothing at all. Behind the bandshell the iron hoops of the Centennial Bridge skip through the brown muscles of the Mississippi to Rock Island on the Illinois side where the old man keeps his solitary rooms in a house whose upper floor he rents to the area's rootless young. Beneath his John Deere cap sweat beads on the long upper lip, catches in the thickets of the eyebrows he no longer suffers the barber to prune. He is indifferent to the sounds all around him, to the band, even to the heat that pours out of a sky that is like tarnished brass, dimensionless. Instead, his attention is on the blackened bronze of the bust, wondering once again where it was that the sculptor missed getting Bix, though the ears are certainly right and the hairstyle, too. Still, it isn't Bix, and maybe it's so simple a thing as the material the sculptor had to work with, just a handful of old photographs, and most of these oddly indistinct and blurred, as if even in the random, improvised midst of his life Bix had wished to reserve some part or essence of himself from the pitiless inquisition of his peculiar, unpremeditated fame and the camera's eye, managing in whatever circumstance that shy,

3

long-lashed, down-looking attitude that precluded definitive image. And now as the old man known locally as Henry Wise casts his mind back over these aging images, trying to arrange them in memory's long, echoing gallery, he finds Bix looking so different in every one that you had to wonder after a while whether you were looking at the same guy, or whether the guy had any essential sameness to him that the camera could catch.

There was, of course, the famous Young Man with a Horn, the shot in which the eighteen-year-old kid on his way to his first professional gig—rented tux, third-hand horn propped upright on knee—had run into old man Rau's corner studio, just across the tracks from here, and paused a few fleeting ticks while Rau had ducked beneath the black hood and squeezed the shutter bulb, fixing Bix forever as exemplar of the Twenties' Flaming Youth. That kid is full of face and soft-featured as a child. Only a year thereafter, there he is in a too-tight sports jacket in a group shot at the prep school outside Chicago where his desperate parents had sent him, hoping to drive that terribly trivial music out of his head, and this kid doesn't look like a kid anymore, looks like he's picked up some miles in that short span, traveling fast, his features harder of line and edge, eyes narrowed against the onrush of experience, all roundness left somewhere behind him. Yet the Bix who posed with his band in Cincinnati in '24 looks as young if not younger even than the kid in the hometown studio shot of three years earlier, and neither of these Bixes bears much more than an extended-family resemblance to the sleekly assured man in a St. Louis band in 1925. In a photo the old man keeps hidden with the one picture he has of his mother and his paternal grandfather's death certificate from Bregenz, Austria—these buried beneath a layer of neatly folded suits from the Twenties and Thirties that is settling imperceptibly in the brass-bound steamer trunk in his basement—Bix poses with the Jean Goldkette band on an autumn tour of New England in 1926. Sitting casually atop the band's bus in his light-toned three-piece suit, this Bix is a dead ringer for

F. Scott Fitzgerald. And there is in this same photo the dark image of another young man, obscure within the overhang of the cab, the young man Henry Wise had been in that existence, unsuspected by any here in Davenport, or maybe anywhere else for all he knew: Herman Weiss, the band's road manager, mechanic, driver, general factotum.

As Natural Gas races into the reprise of Muskrat's melody Henry Wise tries to reconstruct what Bix looked like when they first met at Hudson Lake the summer of '26 and can't. He remembers plenty of details, all right. Remembers the temporary false tooth Bix kept losing up on the bandstand so that the other band members would have to get down on all fours to look for it while the youthful dancers waited with the mingled high-spirited humor and ungovernable impatience of that post-war generation. Remembers him also for the astonishing personal slob he was, wearing elements of his tux all day, sleeping in them at night—when he slept at all. He sees the slightly popped right eye, the bat ears and slicked-back, center-parted hair the sculptor got right, the shy, crooked grin like a boy with a secret he might share with you sometime. But these details don't make up a face somehow, don't cohere, and maybe there isn't anyone left alive who could say what Bix really looked like. Except Hellie, and maybe Hellie isn't alive, either. So, he feels a sort of sympathy for the sculptor.

Natural Gas swings into their final number, Waitin' For The Robert E. Lee. They are the festival's penultimate act and like the sun they're still belting it out and the crowd is still absorbing these happy, ricky-ticky re-creations of the white jazz that eighty years earlier had been new, nervous, jagged with the explosive energy of those years following the Great War. And when they finish and wipe their shining faces they get sustained, satisfying applause from a crowd that's still big enough to extend all the way to the park's outer reaches where the casino steamboats are moored and where the blackjack dealers and croupiers, the floorwalkers, the bartenders, cocktail waitresses and security personnel are just as glad about Bix in their detached, gimlet-eyed way as the motel managers and restaurant owners and barmaids as far out as Cedar Rapids and Galesburg. The annual Bix Fest is big business.

The long weekend's last act is out at the gravesite, where a band from Germany plays a few of Bix's famous numbers, and when the last notes of Copenhagen have arisen from the shining horns into the late afternoon air, it's over. The faithful begin to drift and break apart while camera and sound crews reel in and pack up. One of the Bix Society board members catches sight of Henry Wise moving with stiff resolution in the direction of his car and calls after him, inviting him back to the Blackhawk for a valedictory drink, but Wise barely pauses in his slow retreat, only waving a declining hand. "Strange guy," the board member says to another. "Helpful and all. But what's he do with himself all day, anyway?" The other shrugs. Nobody knows much about Henry or even where he came from, except he once told them he used to be a mechanic up in Chicago. And so they simply stand there a moment, watching Wise shuffle up the gradual curve of the white-graveled drive, deeper into the cemetery, until the sight of his cheap striped shirt is lost among the time-stained tombstones and the umbrageous overhang of the oaks and hemlocks. And while they turn back to their affairs the old man moves on, still deeper, his purpose obscure even to himself, knowing only that he wants the place to himself and is killing time until the crowd has cleared out.

He passes the markers of the old German families who settled this place and put their stolid stamp on it forever—Stouffer, Schaeffer, Toerring, Schmidt—pauses at the curiosity of a mausoleum the size of a cottage, paper flowers slotted into the grillwork defending dirty windows nobody could see out of anyway; and then the tomb of a doctor that proclaims him to have been AMICUS HUMANI GENERIS; coming to a halt finally at a plot devoted to the Civil War dead where he glances along the ranks of identical stones, each bearing the same word, "Died," and wondering what it really meant. Where did you go when you did that? What could it possibly mean that Bix Lives! as the festival caps every year proclaimed? He'd seen plenty of dead men and women in his day and some who'd died violently but none that ever looked deader than Bix.

His shuffling steps bring him around the oval from the Civil War plot with its flag hanging limp in sunset stillness, back to the gravesite, deserted now except for a flock of big crows that caw his entrance and flap heavily upward through the lowering shafts of sunlight into the oaks where they settle to watch the solitary figure and wait for his departure too. Around the grave the grasses are already springing back, blade by blade, in secret resurrection, and except for a couple of cigarette stubs in the pathway there remains no sign that anything had ever disturbed the Sabbath's sepulchral hush. He stands there with that hush rising up around him like an invisible mist, regarding with a slow, steady concentration the family monument that presides with its ponderous one-word declaration over the gathered graves beneath it: BEIDERBECKE. He doesn't ask himself what after all these years impels him to do what now he does, lowering himself with careful calibration to sit on the low curve of the granite block that is all of Bix that remains above ground, feeling its raised letters imprinting themselves in his undefended haunches: LEON BIX BEIDERBECKE. And sitting there thinks of what's down there beneath him, staring up perhaps through coffin lid and dark, intervening feet of earth. At least, he thinks, he's with family here and has his own name, more than could be said for himself, he with all his known family dead or disappeared and the name he now carries a late improvisation, the last in a process begun before his birth when his Austrian father for unknowable reasons had changed his name from Hartmann Weissmuller to become Herman Weiss in America and then had conferred this new name on his only son. Nor was this the end of the paternal changes of identity—though his namesake was never to know this—since after Weiss Senior's wife died in the epidemic of 1918 he had abandoned his son and an older daughter and gone just over the Illinois line into

*Wisconsin, Kenosha, to found another family under the name Hart—
the name he lay under in the Green Ridge Cemetery there.*

*He tips his feet onto their outer edges, peering beneath them, won-
dering if Bix might be doing his bit to build the earth here, adding to
history's heap. These days undertakers promised eternal preservation.
Not back then. And he knows for sure a hasty job was all they had time
for in New York on that roaring summer's day when Bix, striking out
at his demons, had flung himself out of the gray twist of his sheets and
then out of life itself. He knows this because Hellie had called him from
the room, begging him for old time's sake to get over there and help her
get Bix cleaned up for the undertaker and for the mother and brother
who were at that moment steaming for Penn Station on the through
train from Chicago. And he can hear now that telltale crack her voice
made over the wire and himself muttering, "Okay," and can see with a
clarity astonishing in the blurred world in which he now moves that
little corner apartment, crowded with the building's super and the
next-door doctor and his doctor wife who seemed so unprofessionally
upset, and Hellie, her platinum hair plastered to the forehead and
cheeks of her ruined face with its long scar running like a crack
through alabaster from eye to the knot of scar tissue just under the jaw,
fiercely guarding Bix like some sort of stately animal, made half-feral
by grief, might its fallen master and finally succeeding in driving the
strangers from the room. And then he had raised the gummy windows,
the sad, short curtains sucking briefly in the new cross-draft, stirring
air heavy-laden with a long season's accumulated heat, with grime,
sloth, body fluids, and with something else he couldn't put any name to
then, except Death itself. And that done, he had been forced to turn
back to the room, making himself look at what, entering, he'd been
able to avoid. And there was Bix, back in his sheet-shucked bed and
stiffening by the second, his right eye opened on Nothing. He remembers helping Hellie remove the soiled underwear—shirt and drawers—
and while she went over the body with soap and warm water, he*

washed the underwear in the sink, moving the material about in the thin, sudsy slosh, thinking back on similar scenes in other, anonymous hotel rooms when he'd had to clean up after Bix and even clean up the man himself, dropping him into a cold bath, dunking his head under a full-force faucet, throwing shirt and tie and coat on his unprotesting form, raking a comb through his hair—"Christ, Bix! You got rehearsal in twenty minutes—!"

Bix's letters continue to cut deeper into his parchment skin and his back is protesting, but maybe it would take a greater effort to get up from the gravestone than to stay put. Looking up, he finds it deep dusk and the oaks gathered into a black and shapeless conclave with the fireflies winking and winking, and in their brief incandescences he is vaulted suddenly away from all this in the kind of unpredictable shift an old mind will make, back to the Chicago Loop of more than seventy years ago when the electric lights of outdoor signs were still a novelty: those little bulbs in rows that popped on and off in ordered succession like ranks of soldiers, so that when you looked at the sign the white dots marched endlessly around its borders until at dawn they turned it off and the thing went suddenly dead. He'd seen this transformation plenty of times back then, can even feel at this moment the peculiar sense of loss and abandonment it always brought him, as if it really had signaled a kind of death instead of merely the end of another brutal night of business in a city that knew far more than its share of true sadness and loss and death. At that hour when they turned the signs off, when the chairs were stacked for the brooms and mops, keys turned in locks, bolts thrust, till counted; when the flappers had been taken home and the men who'd played for their pleasure had packed their pieces; when the wickets and windows rang shut and Chicago took a deep breath and blew it back in a stale belch of bootleg booze and cheap cigars: then he might still be at work, chauffeuring some middle-echelon gangster somewhere, maybe with his sodden girlfriend snugged up tight to him in the upholstered gloom of the backseat. Or maybe he was waiting at a *warehouse on the South Side while men filled the bed of a truck with cans of alcohol or cases of beer. Or under the chassis of one of those trucks, or under its side-opening hood, yanking at the end of a wrench. Or maybe, if he'd been lucky, he'd been in bed a couple of hours and hadn't seen the signs go black and dead, heard the heavy* whomp *of the bulldog edition of the* American *or the* Tribune *hitting the greasy black pavement at the corner newsstand under the El, the coarse twine cutting into the stack and the topmost copy in tatters—LEOPOLD, LOEB GET LIFE IN FRANKS THRILL SLAYING! BIG BILL— LOVE THIS CITY WITH ALL MY HEART. But damned few nights when he hadn't witnessed all this and more, damned few, and back then in his broad-shouldered youth, his vigor, there had come unbidden moments when he'd allowed himself to feel how truly tired he was and to wonder,* How can I ever get caught up? *Because he was very handy around autos and trucks, he was young and tireless and steady, and his services were in demand almost around the clock, and the Big Shot was paying him three hundred a week when other guys driving delivery in Indiana and Michigan and downstate were lucky if they were drawing forty. Plus, he lived rent-free at the Calvert where Jake Greasy Thumb Guzik had told him he could also take his meals, which, so he had quickly learned, was the cruel kind of joke his employers went in for because he almost never had time for a sit-down meal. Virtually the only sit-down meal he might have in a week would be behind the wheel of a touring car, waiting for one of the Outfit to finish his business inside some South Side building: paying off a copper; getting paid off; putting the blocks to a mistress with the wife and kiddies safely stashed elsewhere in a modest bungalow or apartment in a respectable neighborhood. The rest of the time it was* Hey, Milo, *or* Moose, *or* Guy, can you make me up a corned-beef-and-rye real quick? A fried egg on white?*

He remembers one morning in particular after a long night, when he found himself under the hood of the Big Shot's Caddie, a maroon seven-ton tank with steel chassis and bulletproof windows, his eyes like cinders

*in his head, his whole body numb with fatigue: installing a new carbu-
retor and set of plugs and adjusting the idle while Machine Gun Jack
McGurn breathed down his neck, telling him every few minutes how the
Boss needed his rig at a quarter-to-noon sharp, and with every clipped
reminder his fingers got slower and thicker while his eyes sizzled and
blurred, and he was just pulling back from under the long gleam of the
hood and wiping those fingers on a rag while the Caddie purred like a
pussy when here came a clatter of footsteps down the rampway beneath
the Metropole, and it was the Big Shot himself—Capone—swaggering
surrounded by his bodyguards: Albert Anselmi in loose-fitting double-
breasted gabardine with professional bulge to the jacket; Anselmi who
never spoke to him but whose left eye, cocked like an out-of-whack head-
lamp, grazed over him with deadly precision, marking him, measuring
him against some future contingency. And John Scalise, and a much
younger guy he knew only as Joe Batters. And he stepping backwards
quickly and tripping over the edge of his sled and Capone himself catching him with a suddenly outflung, sustaining arm. Capone in maroon
suit to match the Caddie only with wide pinstripes, yellow shirt, yellow-
and-black four-in-hand, and soft white fedora with broad black band.
And then all the others suddenly there, too, surrounding him, and he
staring up close at that adipose face with the livid scars down the left side
that Capone tried to mask with makeup, hating his tabloid nickname
Scarface, though he liked to be called Snorky by his associates. The lips
were strangely vulnerable-looking in this intimacy, red and rubbery as a
comic Cupid's, asking for affection, for friendship, and if not these, then
fealty, but the eyes gray and hard and without depth. The eyes that, even
now when the face smiled down at Herman Weiss, said, Beware, O Beware. He was so close now, closer than practically anyone was allowed to
get except Mae, the Missus, that Herman could smell him, a mixture of
cigar and bay rum and the appliqué of talcum powder over the jowls
that was already beginning to congeal along the shining grooves of the
scars it was meant to mask. "Hey, kid, you wanna watchit, ya know?*

Man could get hurt bad your line of work." And the others laughing now that it was safe to laugh and he trying to smile and Capone reaching into his vest pocket and pulling out the barrel of a long black Havana and sticking it in the breast pocket of his mattress-ticking coverall as if it had been a battlefield decoration, then winking at him as he turned and climbed into the Caddie's back seat with Machine Gun Jack McGurn so close behind that if Capone had stopped short, Jack's nose would have been brown to the bridge. And Anselmi and Scalise going around to the other side with Joe Batters to ride shotgun and the heavy doors clicking closed with the reassuring greased tumble of heavy-gauge steel, tongue-into-slot. And then Tommy Cuiringione asking him about the carb and plugs before climbing up behind the wheel, and then they're off in a roar and a cloud, climbing the ramp onto the street where two escort cars would take up positions, front and rear.

He recalls his mingled sense of relief and deep weariness then, fingering the cigar the Big Shot conferred on him, standing solitary in the underground garage with only the dissolving puff of blue-gray exhaust for company. Capone, who ran so much of the city, now out into it to do his daily business, and he, Herman Weiss, had helped send him on his way.

No false pride in that, though: the parts of the Outfit's machine were so obviously interchangeable, like those he'd just replaced in the Caddie. No ambitious notions, either, especially when Cuiringione turned up missing not very long afterwards, and then two weeks later a couple of kids doubled up on a mare out in the Palos Park woods reported that when they'd reined her in to give her a drink at a cistern she'd reared back in fright, lower jaw pulled into neck, haunches aquiver, and they'd dismounted and looked into the cistern and there a white, blobby something floated just beneath the dark surface of the water with what at one quick, scared glance appeared to be strings or tentacles reaching upward toward the light. The boys led police back there and the bluecoats themselves sent for help and finally a local farmer hooked it and hauled it up over the cistern's curb, and it flopped out onto the ground like some yet-unclassified sea monster that had somehow wiggled in there through a series of subterranean chambers, and the boys saw it was a man—or had been—naked to the waist and with its feet and hands bound with wire already rusting and the bulbous, prune-wrinkled torso covered with yellowed markings that on subsequent inspection proved to be cigarette burns. And when they flipped it over they found it didn't have any back to its head, that it had been blown away, and that the strings the boys had glimpsed were brain matter trailing up through the fouled water the mare had refused and shedding along the way whatever stored filaments of memory and guile Tommy Cuiringione might have accumulated in a short, haunted life. And so then he, Herman Weiss, began to regret that very close encounter with Capone there in the garage beneath the Metropole, whereas before he'd been pleased he had come to the Boss's attention in a positive way. Because now he began to worry that Capone or Machine Gun Jack or Greasy Thumb might tap him as Tommy's replacement. And while he was willing to accept certain risks involved in driving booze trucks and sometimes in the early mornings driving gangsters around the Loop and down into Cicero and Chicago Heights, he had no aspirations to Tommy Cuiringione's old job and not only because of what the boys had found out in Palos Park but also because Tommy's predecessor, Sylvestor Barton, was still in the hospital with bullet wounds. He was tough all right, as handy with his dukes or a club if it came to that as with his mechanic's tools, but he hadn't found any reason yet to kill someone. To chauffeur for Capone you had to have that, had to know at any instant—a sudden confrontation at some intersection where you saw who was in the other car—that you'd kill if called upon. And still less was he prepared to kill to protect his load. He carried a Smith & Wesson .32 strapped under his seat when he made his runs but he'd never used it. After Hellie had gotten him on the Outfit's payroll he'd told her that if he were hijacked, they could have the stuff. He wasn't going to shoot it out with Moran's boys—who'd doubtless done Tommy—for a load of watered sauce, not even for the three a week and the flop at the Calvert. Moran could have the load and Guzik could shove the job if they didn't like it. It wasn't worth his life. And after he'd said all this Hellie had merely looked at him slantwise because she knew—even as he already knew himself—you didn't just resign from the outfit: you stayed in until they said it was okay to get out, and most got out feet first and at a young age. He wonders what the average life span of all of them was— Capone, Anselmi, Killer Burke, the rest—and thinks maybe only Jake Guzik and Joe Batters made it to fifty. He knows Machine Gun Jack never got there.

A stinging itch on the back of one hand brings him back to the ceme-tery where the fireflies have been joined by mosquitoes singing their wordless blues about his head. Rising slowly, deliberately as an old heron, he wonders if mosquitoes sang in a musical key humans could comprehend or one all their own. Without looking at the keyboard Bix could call every note struck in a piano chord, used to do it for money. Moving toward his car parked in the oval, Henry Wise remembers the first time he saw him do it, during that summer of '26 when the kids came out in droves from Chicago and South Bend to the Blue Lantern, crowding up around him on the little bandstand with its painted back-drop of harvest moon sailing over lake waters. That was where it all be-gan, he thinks, reaching the car now, climbing in and turning the motor over so that he could run the air-conditioning: the legend and the huge phenomenon that has grown out of it: the annual festival and the Bix Seven race with its international field of distance runners. Fan clubs from Davenport to Osaka and their endless observances, carrying the worshippers through the year like a liturgical calendar—birthday, first recording date, last recording, death. Bumper stickers, CDs. Fea-ture films and documentaries. Wordy panel discussions of Bix's fingering techniques, unique use of intervals, piano compositions. The veneration of the Bach cornet and its black corduroy case. He was there a few years back when they reunited the Bach with the mouthpiece long enshrined elsewhere. A perfectly competent trumpet player had been entertaining the crowd with his bright renditions of Bix's numbers, yet when he played them again with the Bach and the mouthpiece he sounded so utterly, so eerily different the crowd didn't quite know whether to laugh or cry or clap—or run away—it was so uncanny.

Down the lengthening decades since that morning in New York when he'd finally been forced to turn and face the fact of Bix's death he's been stubbornly telling himself he doesn't believe in ghosts. He leaves that crap, he tells himself, to others caught up in the Bix phenomenon, like the piano player who claims that when he plays Bix's Cloudy he can feel Bix standing behind him, guiding his fingers among the keys. Yet now, sitting here in his car and staring towards a grave he can no longer even see, he's obliged to admit to some kind of haunting: why else would he be here? What else but some obscure force would have brought him down to Rock Island to live within the penumbral embrace of the legend, carrying within him memories that refused to die: Bix and his sound that had cut so strangely, so directly, like a ray, from the bell of the horn straight into Herman Weiss's clamped heart, opening it in a way he had neither desired nor ever understood. Someone—he now forgets who—once said that hearing just four notes from that horn was enough to change your life forever. When he'd heard that, he'd dismissed it as simply more of the legend. But wasn't it true of him? Hadn't his life been changed forever by hearing Bix out at the old Blue Lantern?

That awful night in Cleveland he hadn't said goodbye to Bix. This night, sitting in Oakdale Memorial Gardens, he knows more than ever that he's never said goodbye.

He lights a cigarette, removes the John Deere cap, and leans his hard old head against the headrest. Surrendering now, he sees, more real than this blanketing darkness, a disembodied pair of cracked men's patent leather shoes planted in the hot yellow dust of Hudson Lake while he, Herman Weiss, lies on his back beneath one of the Big Shot's booze trucks, his bag of tools spread carefully on an oil cloth next to him and a round-trip to Chicago still ahead.

❧✦❧

Summer and the heat's on. Has been since an April night when Capone's rivals, Klondike and Myles O'Donnell, decided to give the Big Shot a very public middle finger and went drinking with some cronies in his Cicero clubs. Before they'd finished their first round the word had gotten back to the Hawthorn Inn where Capone sat over dinner, plotting. Here was a provocation too dangerous to overlook—and Capone didn't—and when the O'Donnell party lurched at last out of Harry Madigan's Pony Inn on West Roosevelt, Snorky and the boys were waiting for them with a sub-machine gun, rifles, and pistols: fifty shots pumped into three of the invaders, though Klondike and Myles somehow escaped with only grievous wounds. Missing them was bad enough; killing one of the others was worse because he turned out to be Billy McSwiggin, the young assistant state's attorney who'd sworn to indict Capone for a previous murder. Hue and cry. Scare headlines: GANGSTERS TURN MACHINE GUN ON STATE'S ATTY! BOOZE FEUD BACK ON! Wringing of deeply soiled political mitts: "This is an assault on the very foundations of civilized life." "An outrage too great to be borne." "Shall we live by the laws of the jungle in our fair city?" Etc.

But the problem created by killing Billy is real enough, and the Big Shot has to go underground while he tries to figure out what to do. The inside word is that this has all been a big mistake. Sure, Snorky meant to kill those mick fucks and is sorry they got away, but he had no idea who they'd been drinking with that night. Billy ought to have known better than that. The same word has Snorky

himself behind the Thompson sub, testing its utility as a new business machine. Meanwhile, everybody in the Outfit's hunkered
down, waiting to see what gives, and business is brought to a
standstill with protection for the trade in booze, whores, slots suddenly impossible at every level, from City Hall down to the most
venal copper on the beat. Finally, with nothing happening, Snorky
decides it's simply too hot here in town and so secretly skips up to
Lansing where he moves in with an Italian family, taking with him
a tight band of battle-tested bravos including Machine Gun Jack
and Killer Burke. He's betting that ultimately McSwiggin's suspi-
cious choice in drinking companions will take a lot of the heat off,
but this could take awhile. Meantime, out at clubs like the Blue
Lantern there are thirsty young dancers who'll go elsewhere if
Capone can't deliver. They'll flock to clubs serviced by the O'Donnell boys or Hymie Weiss or Bugs Moran. It's a simple matter of
supply and demand, and in America, 1926, there's nothing wrong
with the demand.

Shortly after dawn on a late-June morning the wall phone in
Herman's room at the Calvert gives its alarming rattle, and he's like
a diver coming up from way under, lying there in his sheets, distantly hearing something but not comprehending what it is. But
whoever it is keeps ringing until he gets over there on wooden legs
and hears a voice he knows telling him that Jake wants him to get
out to the Blue Lantern right away. "We had a breakdown out there
last night," the voice says. "Guy couldn't get the truck started. He
thinks it might be ignition or points maybe. Twenty-four Ford.
Anyway, we can't have the place dry for the weekend." What, Herman wants to know, is the problem some local mechanic couldn't
handle. "We tried that," the voice says. "Our guy went right into
Hudson and rousted a mechanic, but when they get back an the
guy gets a load of the deal, he runs away. Rube fuck." "Well, what
about South Bend?" Herman begins. "Must be—" but he's cut off,

quick. "Now listen, Weiss," the voice says, all its edges honed, "Jake woudna tol me to call ya if it coulda been done another way. Now you get your stuff together, you get your ass down to La Salle Street Station an make that eight-o-eight. An when you get it started, then you call the Drexel number, an then you run it back here, take it down to Taylor, load it up, an run it back out there before the band plays their first note. After that, I don't give a shit what you do with the rest of your day." *Click-off.*

Which is how he happens to find himself underneath that '24 Ford in the sandy lot beside the barnlike club jutting out into the summer-still lake, hearing now another disembodied voice, this one belonging to the cracked patent leathers he can see standing beside the truck in the sunlight. "Gee," the voice says, clear, clean, uninflected, "must be darned hot under there." "Be a damn lot hotter if I can't get this bugger in gear and rolling to Chi and back pretty quick," Herman mutters, teeth and jaw set with effort and concentration. "Wish I could help you out," the young voice comes back, "but I don't know anything about autos—or trucks." "I'll get 'er," Herman says, tapping the starter gently once more with the wrench handle. "Matter of when." And soon enough he does get 'er, and when he's slid out from under and is sitting on the Ford's rubber-ribbed running board, wiping hands and face, the kid belonging to the voice and shoes comes out of the Blue Lantern with a tall glass of iced lemonade, and Herman nods a sweaty thanks and drinks it down. And when the kid asks if he can ride on the roundtrip Chi run, Herman shoots him a glance and visualizes him behind the wheel for the return trip, the sun sinking behind them and he taking a delicious snooze in the passenger's seat while the kid takes them around the bottom of the lake with its brownish curve and the dunes a burnt yellow and the grasses wind-waving and shiny. He draws a rough sleeve across his lip, hearing the rasp of the tough bristles. "Can you drive?" he asks.

"I'm leavin soon's I take a leak and make a phone call." And the kid says, "Sure," bright, ready. And when Herman's had his leak and called the Drexel number, he comes out to find the kid already parked in the passenger's seat and wonders, briefly, as he clambers up behind the high wheel, bored or what? But he has no time to wonder more about this, and the kid's just sitting over there, smiling at him, with a stained oatmeal sweater in his lap and under it the battered spine of a book peeping out and the one word *Revolt* showing in yellow lettering. Herman revs the engine into a preliminary roar as if it's clearing its oily throat, and then they wheel sharply up out of the sandy lot onto the dirt road, over the tracks of the South Shore Line, and then Herman presses the long metal slab into the wooden floorboards, and they head west with the sun high up behind them and the Big Town waiting ahead, simmering on the other side of the dunes and the lake's penile droop and the kid quiet beside him, the stained sweater and battered book bouncing and still with that mild smile, just enjoying a summer's excursion. Beyond Michigan City the kid finally breaks the silence, gesturing briefly towards the line of trees flashing by on their right. "We're going to play over here a few times this summer," he volunteers. "There's a bathing pavilion back in there someplace." He glances over at the driver and sees a big-shouldered guy a few years older than he, wide jaw, long upper lip blue under a day's growth of beard. The driver shrugs those big shoulders. His head is dead-on Chicago like a pointer, and all he says now is, "I figured you for the band. I don't listen to music much." The kid nods, pleasant, unoffended, and that's it for a spell. Then, abreast of Portage, Herman looks over at his passenger, hesitates a moment, then asks, "Kid, you got any idea what we're up to here?" And the kid says his name is Bix and that he figures the truck hauls sauce and that's why Herman has to get to Chicago and back before the big weekend begins. Herman nods. "Okay," he says, "but along through here things can get a little hairy." He points to a side road between the dunes. "There's where somebody might be layin for us." They come abreast of the road and roll past it at a wide-open fifty, but the road's empty with only the blue of the sky visible above it. Then Herman adds, "But they aint. If we get past Gary, we're clear." The kid looks over at him and nods, still with that mild, pleasant expression that makes Herman wonder if he might be a little simple, if there is anything at all behind it. "But even if they are out here somewheres, it oughta be okay," Herman says, "because we're empty, as maybe you can tell. Sometimes we come this way bringin' loads down from Canada, but this here's a deadhead, so, like I say, if they're layin for us, shouldn't be a problem—unless they're in an ugly mood or there's been trouble. Then they might take your truck or torch it. Never happened to me, but this aint my regular run. But if it does, you should still be okay. You just sit tight and don't give 'em any chin music: some of these guys are touchy, unpredictable. I'll tell 'em you're a hitchhiker."

Bix shrugs like it's not a big deal, this prospect of being hijacked by armed men with hair-trigger tempers and the truck torched out here in the middle of nowhere. He knows his friend Mezz Mezzrow's playing at the Club Martinique somewhere near here. Mezz is a tough guy and resourceful and would probably come to their rescue. But he doesn't tell Herman this or that the band had already heard that Capone had an interest in the Blue Lantern. Nor does he feel the need to add that just about anybody playing the clubs these days has to do business with gangsters. Hell, one New Year's Eve outside Cinci his Wolverines got orders from the manager to play China Boy over and over for two hours while rival gangs slugged it out on the floor of the Stockton Club. By the time it was over with there wasn't a bottle or chair intact in the whole place, and their sax player said he never wanted to hear China Boy as long as he lived. In fact, as long as George Johnson was with the

Wolverines he refused to play that number. Of course, in Chicago they didn't fool around with bottles and chairs but got right down to it with knives and guns, and everyone knew about Eddie Tancl, a real friend to musicians, who ran a club in Capone's territory but wouldn't play ball with him and ended up dead on the sidewalk. He doesn't tell Herman about this, either—what would be the point, seeing as Herman has to know all about how things work?

Nor does he tell him about the time he sat in with Armstrong at another Capone spot on the South Side where everything looked so scary at first, beginning with the bouncer who went a good three hundred, to the ringside tables filled with racketeers in ultra-sharp suits with their dames dripping jewels and little cocaine spoons dangling from necklaces and some of the help looking just as scared as he was and falling all over themselves to be of service. Armstrong had seen how scared he was, had been trying to soothe his nerves, but his lips were stiff, and he was still hitting some real clams when a truly tough-looking guy whose teeth even looked dangerous disengaged himself from his girl and the gloom and barged up to Armstrong to say, "Hey, boy, what's wid dis little punk ya got up here wid ya, blowin all this bum stuff an spoilin our night? Ya was goin okay on that joint (pointing to Armstrong's cornet) til he gets up here." And Armstrong—who one day would joke with presidents and princes but was still so deferential to whites that when some of the Austin High kids invited him home and he discovered he was the only Negro there he wouldn't come out of the kitchen—: Armstrong mopped his streaming face and smiled his whitest smile. "Boss," he said, "this here a country boy from way out in the tall *cawn,* and maybe he aint used to Chicago style yet—might take him a few numbers, y'know." And the fanged, sharp-suited tough guy had leaned over Bix, making a closer inspection of this exotic, and then had clapped him on the back in a manner meant to be reassuring. But the blow was so forceful it rattled all his teeth and popped the false one, but it had taken a good hop and landed right on his shoetop, and he'd snatched it up and reinserted it while the tough guy was telling him, "Kid, ya got nothing ta worry about: aint a guy in here'll hurt ya unless he's paid to."

They're past Gary now, and nothing's happened, and the Ford's steady roar and the clear road are relaxing Herman enough so that he can feel how tight he's been holding himself, feel his fatigue, and his mind skips ahead just a moment to the return trip when maybe he could turn the wheel over to this kid once they clear the city, but then he snaps back because that's a long way off, and now the road begins to swing north, and they're up around Whiting and passing Wolf Lake when they see some cars parked ahead and Herman tenses instantly but then sees more and more of them, on both sides of the road, stretching into the heat-shimmering distance. In fields of weeds trampled to dust there are hundreds of cars, parked at random angles, black, baking, flashing their glass and metal under the sun and people mixed in among them and off in the distance blurred by the raised dust and sun and mashed vegetation an encampment of canvas tents gray-white against the fields and oak groves. Herman, slowing for the parked cars that narrow the road and for a group just beginning to cross towards the tents, remembers reading in yesterday's papers about some sort of religious gathering and at the same instant calculates the risk of honking and barreling through and decides it's not worth it and brakes to a halt while the group straggles across, their eyes fixed on their destination. There are women under broad summer brims, white faces shadowed, long dresses down to black lace-up shoes. Children held tightly in hand. One or two thin-necked young men. In the middle of the road a boy's marble bag slips from his fingers, drops, and a single shooter rolls off the road's crown into the weeds on the other side, and the boy in his short pants and Buster Browns breaks from his mother and races to retrieve it, and, holding it up, a glass-imprisoned egg yolk, looks back in triumph towards the truck and the young man in the passenger seat, their glances meeting, something flashing between them, the boy's look saying, I got it. Then the road's clear again, and Herman jams the black, high-knobbed stick into first, and they're out of it, racing onward until they reach the outskirts of the city and are into the South Side where everything is the same hue: black of the soot-soaked bricks and boards of the tenements; black of the cindered alleys and zigzagged fire escapes and stairways leading up from them; black of the stones and creosote ties of the railbeds. Black too the faces that don't register their rush as Herman negotiates the Black Belt, cutting west through it, then north again, into Cicero, the Big Shot's turf, where in the 1600 block of Austin he suddenly swings tightly into an alley behind a yellow brick fortress, a building whose long, exposed wall is utterly blank, windowless, and whose front on the much narrower side street shows only double-thick windows so high up you'd have to lean out to make yourself a target from below. In the alley there's a five-car garage to the building, and Herman pulls up there and is out of the Ford almost before he sets the brake, and as he turns the garage's corner he shoots a glance back, and there's the kid, Bix, just sitting there, smiling at him reassuringly, as if telling him, I'll be fine here; I've got my book. Then Herman's bounding up the back steps, where Joe Batters is waiting for him at the partly opened back door and handing him a package neatly done up in heavy brown paper and twine, delivering it with a ceremonial deliberateness like a process server. "Jack wants this to go up to the Edgewater Beach today," he tells Herman, and Herman stands there, his whole body and mind still spinning from the road, staring stupidly at the package in his hands and its block-lettered address, MISS LULU ROLFE, EDGEWATER BEACH HOTEL. And finally collects himself to ask Joe Batters, "Well, how'm I supposed to deliver this up there and load up and get it back to the lake?" And Joe Batters looks at him out of hooded, oven-lidded eyes, and all he'll say is that this is what Jack wants done. Herman thinks then of the kid out in the truck, doing nothing, and even if he is maybe a little goofy, surely he can deliver a package and so asks Joe Batters for carfare for the kid up to the North Side. Joe Batters gives him a shrug that says, As-long-as-it-gets-done, and fishes for his wallet.

Two hours later, Herman's back at the fortress on Austin, the Ford gassed and loaded with beer in the heavy wooden cases that are corner-splintered with hard usage and with two cases of gin and another two of the bonded whiskey that is made up in the Taylor Street neighborhood by black alky cookers who fill the bottles, then slap official red seals across the tops before packing them for shipment. And there's the strange kid, sitting atop a trashcan with his book and sweater and a paper sack that Herman knows right off has a pint of something inside it. And the kid's smile of greeting is about the same—shy, a touch remote, maybe a bit blurred about the edges so that Herman knows also he's been into that sack. Gin: inside the cab Herman smells that too-sweet berry with the dagger buried within and that always sends a wide, involuntary shudder down his spine and does so now, too, as he backs out, the wheels grinding on the crushed cinders. When they hit Cicero Avenue heading southward Bix swings the sack his way, but Herman shakes his heavy head. "I hate that shit," he tells Bix. "Makes me want to puke just smelling it." Bix cocks his head toward Herman, saying wordlessly, to each his own, and then tilts the sack up, taking a generous hit.

The Black Belt once more, only now with more people in the streets coming home from work: washerwomen and maids in their worn dresses and turbans, their blue uniforms left on hangers in the basements of the homes they toil in. Hairdressers and cooks,

I mean, you get your orders, you better follow 'em. Now, if he was operatin' on his own, that's something else, I guess." "He was fighting for the British, yeah," Bix tells him, "but what *are* the orders, really? He was way out there, by himself. Seems to me, a lot of times they tell you what they want done, but then they don't tell you how to do it, you know? So then, you've just got to . . ." he pauses, hands lifting slightly from the book, "make it up as you go along." He flings one hand outward, toward the windshield, speckled and flecked with the winged life that has smashed against its heavy glass: "They probably gave you your orders today—right?— but they couldn't tell you how to get this truck going—or any of the other stuff you had to do. Probably all they really cared about was getting this stuff"—jerking his thumb back to the heavy load of lashed bottles behind them in the bed—"back out to the club. So, you did what you found out you had to do." He smiles over at Herman as though asking him to forgive so long a speech. "It's like Lawrence says—that's the fellow in the book—nothing's written."

Herman doesn't know about this Lawrence guy, running around in the desert making it all up. Might be a sunstroke case. But he does know that with the Big Shot up in Michigan with Jack and the others the structure of the world he has to operate in down here has become a lot more ramshackly than he's used to, and there's a lot that isn't spelled out—though nothing he's aware of has ever been written down, and the telephone's become a great business tool for people concerned with potentially incriminating documents. Before this afternoon he's never taken an order from Joe Batters, a seldom-spoken hood who less than a year ago was driving delivery just like he is now. All of a sudden, though, the guy is wearing a suit and seems to show up in a lot of strategic spots. It makes Herman wonder what the chain of command is and where Greasy Thumb is keeping himself these days. If he too is up there with the Big Shot, then who's left down here to run hung around, curious to see whether this kid Bix can make the date, or whether he's some kind of on-the-loose freelancer like his hero Lawrence who goes around breaking all the rules. So, he's there in the crowd in the Blue Lantern a little before eight, leaning against the wall when the bandsmen enter in their white dinner jackets with cloth heliotrope boutonnieres, climbing the two short steps to the little bandstand with its painted backdrop of moon and water and palms and they begin to set up stands and charts, snap open black instrument cases, chatting, chuckling among themselves. They're all young and for the moment in their careless athleticism, the way they take possession of the special boundaries of their space, they resemble some sort of sports team or maybe a circus troupe—Fuzzy, Sonny, Doc, Pee Wee, Itzy, Don, and Tram, who's clearly in charge. And Bix is there, too, and Tram's talking earnestly to him while evening up the ends of Bix's bow tie, straightening it while Bix holds still like a schoolboy before his father. The hall is filling and the lot's humming with cars, and couples are standing on the dock behind the club, under an indigo sky; or walking down the road through the dust and sand to a house whose front door is barred and bolted, windows shuttered, but which has a wide-open back door where the colored guy they know as Webb sells them the gin and the newly bonded whiskey and the beer so recently delivered some of it's not well-iced yet. There are colored lights strung up the whole hundred-yard length of the hall, though they're not lit, and couples are visiting among the tables that line the sides, the tabletops filled with glasses and ice buckets and the ginger ale and soda they can buy up front, while the young men on the stand are tuning and tootling and fingering their instruments. Itzy takes a couple of quick, tinkling runs along the piano as Tram moves among them, talking to each in turn while they flip the pages of their charts. All of them except Bix who isn't looking at his charts but instead out at the long, window-lined room that is almost crowded now, the expectant noise building, spreading. He sits there quietly, legs crossed at the ankles, hands cradling his cornet, the fingers motionless on the valves. Tram is now in a last-minute fuss, arms moving at the elbows in the suggestion of a conductor, until suddenly, to some invisible, interior signal, they come to attention, all the tootling and page flippings ended and the youthful faces, as yet unscarred by life though not exactly innocent of experience, trained on Tram who hoists his gleaming sax, slim, white-jacketed back to the room, and then counts off: A-one/two, one/two, one and Five Foot Two. And on the first notes the young men reach for the girls in their summer dresses and strands of imitation pearls and the rolled-down hose the song sings of, and they whirl away from the tables, light young arms encircling slender waists, bodies fronting each other, adjusting to their mutual curvings, finding the rhythm, rising on their toes to it, and there's a scattering of applause because Five Foot Two's a very popular number this summer, a kind of passing anthem for these flappers and their sheiks. The colored lights come up, and on these first notes Herman is amazed because two hours ago the cornet player was out cold in the Ford's front seat and didn't move when he and Webb began hauling out the cases, Webb talking loudly all the while, about Capone up there in Michigan and Webb thought it was Flint, though others said Lansing, and did he think Bugs Moran might make a move, and the kid sleeping right through all this until finally Herman had jostled him. Then Bix had opened his eyes very slowly and for a few moments had only stared blankly at the speckled windshield, then moved a hand to restore the strayed strand of hair and looked at Herman and smiled again that shy, removed smile and reached for sweater and book and then made a lurching swing out of the cab. For just a moment Herman got the feeling he was going to shake himself like a dog after a plunge, but he only reached back inside the cab, pulled out the sack with its empty pint, and shook it upside down. "Well, that's lighter," he said to Herman, "and I kinda feel that way myself. Stick around for the dance, and I'll buy you one." Then he'd walked off down the road towards the club, a bit off-kilter and with one arm of the sweater dragging. Yet now that Tram has counted off and the band has jumped into the melody, there's Bix, right out in front, hitting his notes a hair ahead of the beat and pulling the whole band along with him so that they sound tight, together. Hearing him, you'd have thought he'd done nothing else this day but rehearse and take some sun on the dock.

Herman can't remember when jazz wasn't somewhere in the background of his life. Hellie and her friends loved to dance to it, just like these youngsters now whirling on the big floor. First, at Dreamland, under the El tracks at Paulina and Van Buren, where the mechanics and stenos, the errand boys and bus drivers, chocolate dippers, ticket takers, bell hops, ushers, manicurists and machinists got together after a quick wash-up, a perfuming and pomading, washing the grit out of their faces, the grime from the cracks of their hands. Then Hellie and her crowd had moved up, to the Casino at White City, and then she sometimes let him tag along, her friends teasing him about girls and dancing, neither of which he yet aspired to, nor even the music itself which to him was only the noise that went with the spectacle. He remembers Hellie grouped with her girlfriends, standing in the clackety roar of the Flash, the park's famous roller coaster, their made-up faces transformed into dead-white-and-purple by the outdoor lighting and the June bugs popping against those lights and falling around them, the girls eyeing the tough guys cruising past, some still in uniform—Hey, toots, winya a kewpie doll. In the Casino the jazz bands socked it out, and it was close dancing there, closer than at Dreamland, the girls with their arms clasped behind the necks of their partners, hips thrusting to the beat. And then, still later, they'd migrated to Midway Gardens where the music was hotter yet and there was plenty of real grinding on the floor while the bands jazzed the popular tunes. Jazz as Herman has come to it is part of the big come-on. Get 'em in and get 'em loaded. Get 'em loaded and get 'em laid. Get 'em laid and get 'em out. And all the while the band made noise, laid down the beat. When you got laid, you jazzed your girl, but you didn't want to hit the street with jazz still on your pants. He remembers well the merciless ridiculing of a kid named Angelo who joined a gang of them one late afternoon on the corner and they quickly detected the jazz on his pants leg, faint, white, like lakeshore foam. And Angelo, who'd just returned from his girlfriend's building, indignantly protesting it wasn't what they thought, that he'd merely been petting a dog when it had thrown up in his lap. And someone had said, "Hey, Angie, don talk about your girl that way. She aint no bitch." And Angelo had wanted to bust him, but they'd all been laughing so hard it was tough to just go for him, and, what the hell, jazz is jazz, and, smiling ruefully, Angelo had taken out his pocket comb and scraped it away.

Yet with these first burnished notes from Bix, Herman knows this is different. Same setup, same tunes, same dancers. And still it's different in a way he can't identify, and even if he wanted to there isn't time, because for the moment there is something inside him that instinctively rushes towards what's coming out of that horn and that is leading everybody through Dinah, Washboard Blues, On The Road To Mandalay, Singin The Blues, with the colored lights making more of a difference with every number and the dance floor and the tables, too, completely filled and the temperature going up and up, the faces of the dancers shining with sweat and excitement. Because they've surrendered as well, all of them, the booze beginning to take hold, its toxic contents roaring through veins, mounting into heads topped with brilliantined hair or bobbed, the girls' cheeks flushed like rose petals and the flush creeping down their swanlike necks, past the strings of paste that for tonight are agreed to be the real thing. And the music too seems to be the real thing, for now, instead of what it still may prove to be, the background and pretext for something further. And Herman stands there in his amazement, hearing the music itself for the first time, his thick hands held tensely at his sides, as if waiting for something terrifically important that is already happening, that will keep on happening, only you couldn't predict or anticipate exactly how it will happen next.

At intermission the bandsmen step down into the crowd, and some dancers are reaching over shoulders and backs, trying to touch Bix, but they can't touch him, can't even see him in their thronging midst, only a flash of the remote smile, pleasant in its impersonality, and maybe a word or two moving through, and then he's gone, out into the night with his colleagues. Back up there twenty minutes later, Bix's bow tie's come crooked again, but Tram doesn't bother with it because they're all a little crooked now—except for Tram—and away they go: Jig Walk, Play That Thing, To-Night's My Night With Baby. And by this time there are nearly as many crowded up close to the bandstand as there are out on the floor, and they're hollering for Bix, more Bix. And he just sits there, right leg crossed over left, and the left foot in its cracked and dusty patent leather shoe patting softly, the tarnished bell of the hard-worn little cornet pointed at some mysterious place somewhere out in front of him, his eyes on nothing. He seems oblivious to the fierce noise boiling up around him, the chant of his name. When he finishes a solo and takes down he sits there, apparently considering the notes he's just played, only once in a while a word exchanged with a player sitting next to him. After he blazes through Tiger Rag and the din is ferocious Herman can see Tram talking to him, and Herman thinks they might have to do something and do it pretty quick, too, before these kids begin to take the place apart, and then Tram's holding his hands high and you can see the dark moons in the pits of his dinner jacket, and he's trying to say something, but Tiger Rag has them roaring, and you had to wonder whether they could shout any louder for Valentino or the Babe out at the ballpark. And maybe it's the booze, and maybe it's the lights and a summer night out on the lake and the dark allure of what may afterwards come in those shiny, moveable boudoirs that can be driven anywhere, parked anywhere, and the young hands that here merely press against the girls' backs can find their ways into all sorts of other regions and the pastel summer dresses can be sheathed up past the turned-down hose, and maybe the string of paste pearls will be snapped in the dark heat and scattered like moondrops on seat and floorboards. Say even it's still the Great War and those terrible things that happened and that nobody should have had to learn about; or the cynicism and hedonism that came out of it like a cloud of gas they can't issue masks for: the older pundits and the prudes are saying this. Say it's all these things. Still, for this particular moment, frozen in time like the bandstand's painted backdrop of moon sailing in place over static waves, there's something about this guy they've just got to have. And so when Tram does get it quiet enough he announces that Bix will play a special request on piano, a composition by Mr. Eastwood Lane from Mr. Lane's world-renowned Adirondack Sketches: The Legend of Lonesome Lake. Which is maybe not what they wanted from him, but then maybe just about anything he does will do. Itzy gets off the bench, and Bix slides in, cracking his knuckles in a way his first and only piano teacher had warned him would infallibly ruin his hands for serious music, looking at the keyboard, bass to treble, as if making sure all eighty-eight are there—as on this battered box they might not be. And when he puts his hands on the keys you could hear ice cubes settling in glasses and the building's boards stretch and sag under the crowd's stilled and suddenly stationary weight, wavelets on the shore, ducks out on the dark lake calling in their sleep. And

Bix seems asleep also, only with his eyes open, moving his hands among the keys in an act of sortilege that quickly drops a mantle of outrageous romanticism over the crowd that moments ago had been roaring with the Tiger: where was it, his notes seem to ask each of them, they had been meaning to go, what those half-remembered resolutions of only last summer? Surely, they were destined for something far finer, something that lay just ahead. . . .

Despite himself, Herman too is drifting on the notes, recalling a picture he used to study in childhood. It hung in a west-side tavern frequented by his old man: sawdust floors, plenty of spittoons, high-powered Bohemian beer, tables sticky with ancient suds and the greasy rags dragged hastily across them. And there on the back wall the picture of a gently sloping, leaf-littered path between stately columns of trees, the composition leading your eye inward to a pair of elk that craned their necks towards you as if asking what you were doing in their Enchanted Wood. And he, waiting there for his father, would lose himself in the picture—it was an ad for a Canadian whiskey—and not mind so much that the man at the bar among his capped and suspendered cronies, puffing his immigrant's pipe with its leisurely incurve, its silver rim tar-blackened, would linger long there, much longer than promised. Nor mind really that when at last they left the smoky-sweet place the man's demeanor would instantly alter on the street as though the indifferent outside air soured something in him. Then he'd have to watch out on the way home, careful to keep at least an arm's length away—but not behind—and to pick up his feet, avoiding an attention-drawing stumble.

Then it's over up on the stand, and Herman finds himself embarrassed by this gauzy seduction. But he's got company, because while Bix sits there a moment, looking down on the yellowed keys, the crowd is silent, motionless, before breaking into a clatter-clapping tribute that slowly builds and is still building with Bix back in his can't get inside the mayor's office where Decent Dever is keeping the heat turned up high. Soon, the iron wall of Capone's protection begins to buckle. One of his Cicero whorehouses goes up in smoke and then another one, and while the oily smoke bubbles up into the hot sky and bits of wood and the sad simulations of seduction settle slowly as soot into parking lots and rooftops, on porches and stoops, a crew of firemen stands at ease beside their truck with its coiled pythons of unused hose. "Why don't you do something?" someone asks a fireman in his tall helmet. "Can't spare the water just now," he answers with a smile, watching the whorehouse burn to its footings.

After the second fire Snorky orders Greasy Thumb to put on more muscle at the other Cicero riding academies and at the clubs as well. Greasy Thumb keeps working the newspaper contacts, and when the grand jury's impaneled and the names and photos of the twelve true men are published in the papers Guzik gets going on them through the ward heelers, loan officers, creditors, landlords, business associates, relatives—seeking the soft spot, the pressure point: that unpaid loan or long-overdue account that can be squared; that wayward son who hung out some hot paper awhile back and would love to be able to come back from Canada; the daughter who needs to get herself fixed. Greasy Thumb gets rid of a few of the Outfit's weaker soldiers who are wilting under the heat, including one of the Cicero whoremasters who's suspected of setting the fire at the behest of Bugs Moran. He puts the reliable Herman Weiss permanently on the Hudson Lake run. Buys four Thompson subs in anticipation of bigger trouble, whether from the Klondikes or Bugs. Up in Lansing, Snorky plays gin with Jack and Frank Nitti and Killer Burke. Plays Gangster Golf on a course near Round Lake. Plays his beloved opera recordings. Reads *The Mark of Zorro*. Waits. In nearby Detroit, Henry Ford startles the world with the announcement that he will shortly introduce the eight-hour, five-day work week, and his workers begin to wonder what they'll do with all that free time, while their women are worrying about the same thing. Snorky has his own ideas, if only he can get out of this Michigan limbo and back into business.

Machine Gun Jack is even more antsy up in Michigan than his boss. Snorky harbors some stray affection for nature and has even said he'd like to retire early, live on a farm. Not Jack. Jack's strictly bright lights. He misses them, misses his girlfriend, stashed in a suite at the Edgewater Beach where she has little to do except go to an occasional matinee movie with her girlfriends. No bright lights this summer for Jack and his Lulu, only the whitecaps rolling in off the big lake that separates them. Jack is a compact, hard-muscled guy who walks like he has steel springs in the balls of his feet. Superb athlete, too: can do standing-still somersaults, back-flips, walk two city blocks on his hands. Plays scratch golf and bowls in the 180s. Jack was once a welterweight boxer under the name Vincenzo Gebaldi, and Capone's mentor, Johnny Torrio, had a good piece of him and thought Gebaldi might make a main event guy. But when Gebaldi's old man was whacked outside his Little Italy grocery, life changed abruptly for the only son who saw Angelo Gebaldi lying there on the sidewalk in the brittle January sunlight, clutching a nickel. Vincenzo used his Torrio contacts to find those responsible and then murdered the four men, implacably, brutally, one by one, leaving a nickel in the stiffening hand of each. Johnny Torrio thought that was too much talent to waste in the ring, and thus began Jack McGurn's life in the rackets. Capone loves Jack's style almost as much as he values his services as a gunman: gives the Outfit class. Jack dresses like a movie star, his loud suits tailored to him like a glove, his spats immaculate, every brilliantined hair in place like a smooth and shining helmet. When he encountered Lulu she was Helen Louise Rolfe, wife of a minor-league thug and doubling as a cashier and rudimentary bookkeeper at a State Street movie palace. One look and Jack saw she was bored as hell and not just with her work. Jack made quick inquiries and found her husband was getting around on her, more interested in flashing his fake rings to hat check chippies and muscling immigrant shoe cobblers than paying any attention to his wife. Then Jack took Helen Louise away from Tommie Rolfe by the simple expedient of offering him a choice between moving to Brooklyn where Jack had contacts or a beating he promised would leave Tommie maimed. And right away, Helen Louise had to love Jack's style, too, his brassy attentions. But she wanted him to know, right off, that she was no pushover for anybody. She'd been reading in the magazines about the new woman, the emancipated woman, and she'd seen movie versions of these creatures. She thinks the flapper role suits her to a T. "Sure," Jack smiled. "Sure." Jack began calling her Lulu, taught her to dress like he did, got her to a dentist for the first time in her life. Now Lulu looks terrific.

But she misses those bright lights like Jack does, which is mostly what has him so antsy up in Michigan. Because he's seen the smooth quickness, the avidity with which Lulu has taken to the bright lights. She loves to dance to the jazz bands, loves to be taken to the clubs where Jack is known and feared, where they can count on a ringside table, where people stare when they take the floor. And the ideas Lulu has gotten from those goofy magazines make Jack very uneasy now that she has only occasional matinees to occupy her or the facials she gets down at the hotel beauty parlor beneath the lobby. Some nights she tries to break the boredom by going down to the hotel's Black Cat Room to listen to the very sedate Oriole Orchestra play waltzes and fox trots from behind the potted palms and ferns of the bandstand. She simply sits there, half-listening, sipping on White Rock soda water, though occasionally she'll spike it with a hit of Snorky's best Canadian from a garter flask. Not too much of the sauce, though: bad for the facial tone and gives you that sallow, saggy look she's seen on some of the other girls living this life. No one asks her to dance because they know who she is: "That's Machine Gun Jack's girl. Steer clear, brother!" But one night a boisterous bunch of boys from Northwestern barges into the Black Cat and a big, ruddy-faced kid sizes her up right away and asks her if she'd like to take a spin out on the floor, and Lulu's feeling especially stranded this night, wondering where all this is leading and if the new woman is ever bored like this, and so she says, sure, and out they go. And he's not Jack out there, not by a long shot, but he's not real bad, and he's lean and fit, and she likes the feeling of that big young body close to her, radiating a kind of innocent, animal heat. Likes the reflection of herself she sees in his admiring hazel eyes. They dance to I Cried For You and I'll See You In My Dreams and I'll Say She Does. He tells her about a new dance they're doing out in New York, the Black Bottom, and she wants to learn it so she can show Jack, and Joe College's big arms are tightening around her, and she's getting a pretty good tingle down below herself, and so she says to him, "Kiddo, this is trouble for the both of us," and excuses herself and goes up to her room. She takes a long, lukewarm bath to cool down and dries herself slowly, languorously passing the heavyweight terrycloth towel over her adolescent-looking breasts, dragging it down below her navel, passing it lovingly back and forth between her legs. By the time she's drifted into sleep she's brought herself four times, twice thinking of Jack who likes to give it to her very rough, the only way she's ever known.

When Jack phones the next morning he already knows part of this, and she tells him the rest. Lulu makes no secret of her appetites and found early on she could excite Jack with her artfully drawn-out descriptions of how she brings herself. "Yeah, well," Jack says hoarsely from the other side of the big lake, "I catch that kid near you again, I'll tie his dick inna knot and hang him wid it." Lulu laughs, a metallic cachinnation that maddens and excites Jack on the other end. He pictures her up there in the balmy suite his money provides, thin negligee, platinum hair, huge blue eyes. "O, Jack," she breathes at last, "you got no *cle-ass*. Tell you what, though. Your spies can't tail me everywhere, and, well, you know how it is when a girl's all by her lonesome in a big, hot city. If I were you, babe, I'd make it back here pretty quick before your honey finds something besides her finger for a friend." Jack sputters into the receiver, tied into a knot himself by her taunting talk and the indefinite helplessness of his situation. What can he do about it? Snorky wants him there at Round Lake, and there's absolutely no sign that anything is about to change. He fantasizes picking off the mayor from a speeding car—one shot to the head, and it's done. Imagines ambushing Sergeant McSwiggin out behind his West Washington Street apartment and blowing a line of holes up the old man's backbone. But these are only temporary pleasures after all.

And in fact, soon enough Lulu begins to make good on her promise to find her pleasures where she can. When Herman tells her about Bix and the band out at the Blue Lantern she rides out there with him a couple of times. But she can't dance out there, either, because Jack's got the place completely cased. So, she just listens, sitting by herself or with Herman at a table off to the side of the bandstand. And she has to agree with Herman's gruff assessment: the cornet player's got something special, all right, something in his sound that gets into her in a way that's unexpected and maybe even unwanted as well, since what she wants from jazz is just the beat of a good time, and this isn't just that—not when he solos, anyway. She tries to put this strange sound together with the slightly messy kid who rapped on her hotel room door a while back and handed her a package from Jack—and can't. But in her increasing boredom she thinks it might be fun to find out how these things go together, and on her third trip to Hudson Lake she offers

Bix some of Snorky's best out of a silver flask that looks like a miniature canteen. Some musicians from the Martinique near Michigan City have come over to jam after the dancing's done, but when Lulu gives Bix a hit of this smoky stuff out in the lot his eyes widen in surprised delight. "I'll tell the boys to wait a few," he tells her, and she leans back against somebody's shiny new Olds while he talks briefly with Mezz and Miff and Herman does some business with Webb. Then he rejoins her, and they walk down the sloping lot with the club high above them, bone-white in the darkness, out to the end of the dock where they sit with the lake lapping gently against the piles. Lulu unscrews the cap of the flask, the cap on its delicate chain clinking down against the body, and hands it to Bix, but he smiles whitely in the gloom and stops her. "Ladies first," he says softly. Lulu drinks demurely, and he takes it from her then, their fingers briefly brushing, and tilts. "Boy!" he explains, wiping his lips with the same motion he uses up on the stand. "Boy! That's the real juice, all right. Where'd you get it?" He makes a gesture as if to hand it back, but this time it's she who stops him, and he has another hit, the chained cap clinking down as he finishes. Fireflies are winking around them in the swiftly waning night, and fluttering moths and mosquitoes flare in the lights from the club and the darting swords made by the headlamps of the cars backing and turning in the lot. He brings out a pack of Camels and lights up, and Lulu reaches over and takes the cigarette from his lips and drags on it. He tells her briefly about the corn liquor they've been drinking out here this summer, put up by two sisters over in Rolling Prairie who hide their goods in a cornfield. "Pee Wee and I bought a used Buick so we could get over there," he tells her, "but on the way back from the dealer Pee Wee revved it too hard, and she threw a rod." He shrugs, smiles, drags on the Camel. "May I?" And up goes the little canteen. Beneath the mingled odors of the cigarette and the whiskey she can smell him, his drying sweat and older sweat as well, a stale, musky base. She watches his Adam's apple bob above the crooked bow tie.

"You know, you're really good." Her voice sounds tinny to her, high up in her throat. "What's next?" He shrugs again, letting out a long, hot exhale of the whiskey. "What's next?" he says, repeating her question, looking out at the black lake. "In this racket you never know." He laughs briefly, softly. "That's a joke," he explains. "I mean, this is jazz, so you're not supposed to know that, just—*go*, you know. Of course, you do—or they do, anyway, Tram and them. They're all much better musicians than me—I can't read the charts that well." He shrugs again, the shoulders of his tux jacket coming up almost to his small, protuberant ears as he hunches over the end of the dock, cradling the flask. "But say," he resumes after a silence, "have you heard Armstrong? That's the real stuff there." "You mean that little nigger with bangs at the Dreamland?" Lulu asks. "He's too rough to dance to." "You should listen to what he's doing," Bix says, though maybe now he isn't really speaking to the girl sitting beside him. "It's not just that he's hot—he's hot, all right. But his ideas—." He pulls up, appearing to recollect her presence. "Aw, you don't want to hear all this. Besides, what's the good of talking about it when you can hear it?" He glances at the flask he holds, then back to the girl, considering something. "Maybe some time you'd like to go down to the South Side, and we could listen to what he's doing. Oliver, too—he's another one." "I don't know about that," Lulu comes back. "I'm more of a dancer, I guess." She holds her hand up, palm out, as he moves the flask her way. "Go ahead and finish it, if you want." And he does, draining it, screwing its cap back on, then handing it to her with an ineffable, gentlemanly courtesy that is strange to her. He lights up another Camel and leaves it in the corner of his mouth. Sounds from the lot above are borne to them on the light beams: doors slamming, motors cranking over, the roar of exhaust through primitive mufflers, a stray, loose laugh, a call. Somebody drops a bottle, empty. The club lights high above go out like the eyelids of night closing down. He looks over at her, the cigarette jutting from his face.

"Well," he says, quiet, slow, "I guess we better get back up there. Herman—is he really your brother?"

"Sure he is."

"He'll be looking for you, and the guys'll be waiting for me to jam."

"Do me a favor," she says then, leaning across the little distance between them and taking the Camel from his mouth. She leans her face into his, her eyes wide, then holds up just short of his lips. Then kisses them, lightly, feeling their lax warmth that isn't so much surprise or surrender as it is a sort of passive acceptance, tasting the cigarette and behind it the whiskey's concentrated fire and behind that the metal of the cornet's mouthpiece, reaching in then with her tongue, past the unsurprised and unresisting lips that yet don't quite cooperate with her own, across the threshold of where he lives, where that sound comes from that is like a ray of pure gold.

Twinned chrome yellow beams point down at them, insect life flaring black and white through their cut. She draws back, her eyes on his, and maybe it's the lights but she can't read anything in his eyes, at least not anything having to do with her or with them or this situation. He seems not to be there at all. She feels suddenly the cigarette's stub burning down toward her thumb and forefinger and shakes the thing loose, and it loops out into the lake and disappears with a little hiss. He smiles now, and they arise and walk up to the lot where Herman sits in the truck, waiting. He says nothing to Bix who quickly walks across the road toward the cottage where he can hear two clarinets—Pee Wee and Mezz—noodling. Then Herman takes the truck up onto the sandy road and across the South Shore tracks and glances quickly at his passenger who is already settling herself for the jolting ride into dawn. "You better watch out, Hellie," he mutters. "I do what I want," she answers. "Jack don't own me." Herman only looks at her in contradicting silence. "Besides," she adds, a whisper of sleep already there in her voice, quoting from somewhere, a movie caption maybe, "'it's just a boy and a girl on a summer's night. Oldest story there is.'"

⚜

Snorky assesses the situation in Lansing and concludes something's got to be done. Spell of rainy weather. Cabin fever setting in. Jack and Killer going bugs up here. Last week, playing another round of Gangster Golf out at Round Lake, Jack catches Killer improving his lie, which is just part of the game, and beats the shit out of him right there on the ninth with the clubhouse in full view and the caddies standing around with dropped jaws. When Jack slugs him, Killer grabs his mashie and takes a couple of swipes at Jack, but Jack dodges and comes in low and drops Killer again and takes his weapon away and when it's over they all end up making a sedan chair with arms and hands and carrying the old Killer to the clubhouse like some savage headman from the field of honor, and then everybody settles down to drinks and a couple of rubbers of gin. The clubhouse boys mop up the trail of big, dark drops that rain from Killer's cuts to form perfect medallions on the parquet and in front of his locker. They take his plus fours and soak them in cold water and rub the spots with seltzer and salt. A colored woman in the laundry irons them out while Killer plays gin in a heavy terrycloth robe, holding a raw beefsteak to his eye, and it's all made up. But Snorky knows it's not good to have that stuff out in the open. Gives people the wrong impression.

Jack claims he's got a dandy set of lover's nuts because his blonde bombshell's back in Chi gouging herself silly in bed every night and he's not getting anything on the side up here. He's walking around the cabin with his legs held apart like he's been riding after Pancho Villa through the Mexican bush with Black Jack Pershing's cavalry. Then two days ago Angela Anselmi called to say that little Sammy had been shot with a metal-tipped arrow in a game of cowboys and Indians, and if it hadn't hit a shoulder blade it would have been a serious thing, and what is Alberto going to do about it? So now Anselmi starts muttering spells under his breath and boils up some bullets in onion water and garlic, which is what he and Scalise do when they're getting ready to go to war: they figure what the wounds won't do the infection will. But what is Anselmi going to do about it up here?

But the thing that tips Snorky to how bad things have become is that this morning the eight-year-old son of his hosts—the kid he likes to take swimming out at the lake where they play a game they call The Wind Blew My Hat—picks up a Caruso platter from *Rigoletto* and drops it, and for just a minute there Snorky literally can't focus on anything he's so mad. Everything kind of spins and the light gets kind of grayish-green like when lightning flashes into a darkened bedroom, and the next thing he knows he's standing almost on top of the kid with his fists high above his head and the room's utterly silent, and he looks up to find the frozen faces of the parents in the doorway of their living room and then the record on the floor with this missing piece like a scimitar. Then, at last, he brings out, "S'okay, kid. I know ya din mean it." Sick smiles all around. But Snorky knows this is trouble, and he doesn't even see Anselmi shoot Frank Nitti a look.

Snorky decides to buy a little time. "We'll have a party," he tells the boys, "get some girls from Lansing and a hot band and some good Canadian sauce. Have ourselves a regular wing-ding. Take our minds off stuff." He swings into action, which makes him feel better right away, lining up the girls and the booze and talking with Greasy Thumb who tells him Mondays are the band's night off down at the Blue Lantern. They could easily enough drive up to Lansing. Or they have another outfit at Island Lake. Jack says the Blue Lantern group is hot. He's heard them over WSBT. Jack wants Lulu to come up with the band, and Greasy Thumb tells Capone that Lulu's brother Herman now does the Blue Lantern run. So Capone says, have him bring her up with the band. So that's how it happens out at the Club Roma.

The Roma's a good-time place, re-fitted since the Volstead business to be a dance hall. Sometimes Capone goes there with Anselmi and Nitti when he wants to get out of the house. Carlo Ruggiere runs it and does a little business with Capone, and the atmosphere's good: some dames there that like to laugh, including a cute seventeen-year-old number who visits Capone at the cabin Jack shares with Nitti. When that happens Jack and Frank take the launch out fishing. Carlo has the Roma done up nicely. It's one of those pine-log places, the logs peeled to a harvest moon yellow under heavy coats of spar varnish and the tables and chairs and bar all pine, too. Big nickel-plated slots. Deer and moose heads staring out from the walls. Trophy bass behind glass cases. Huge muskie mounted over the bar. Lynx on a shelf. All very rustic, and Carlo has hung little Italian flags from the rafters and a much larger one behind the bandstand that sits catercorner to the bar. Mrs. Ruggiere does a freshwater version of brodetto that Capone finds appealing, plus he appreciates the effort. The Ruggieres have a buxom, darkly glowing daughter who waits tables, but Jack starts in on that and Carlo gets very upset, and for a week it's a problem, and so after that Jack stays back at the cabin and Anselmi goes to the Roma with Snorky and Frank. Which solves *that* problem but makes Jack that much more bugs, and so it's a relief to everybody

when the bus from the Blue Lantern rolls in Monday near supper-
time. Lulu and the band boil out of it like kids on a field trip. Not
everybody's pleased with this, though. Snorky wants a good party,
sure, but these guys look like they might be too juiced to play. And
Jack's pissed because Lulu's half in the bag herself and is arms-
around with the cornet player whose eyes are like floating clams.

Carlo's instantly worried by the looks of things. Carlo can
handle himself; in this business you have to have that ability. But
it's one thing to spin a guy around, grab his belt, and give him the
rush, or to come out quickly from behind the bar with the short
thick pin Carlo keeps there and bonk some joker who's already
been tossed once. But this is the *iron,* here. There is a moment
when everything seems to come to a standstill, the players just
clearing the bus, Lulu and Bix in the lead, Jack at the foot of the
steps, and Capone on the porch next to Carlo who is watching this
thing happening under a gunmetal sky with the clouds rumbling
away towards Flint and a sickly smear of yellow underneath them
like an old hematoma. Jack's rocking on the balls of his feet and
glaring at the cornet player who's rocking a bit himself and carelessly carrying his horn by the bell, shirttail half out, tie loosened, a
mild, oblivious grin. Pee Wee's the last out of the bus, talking with
thick-necked Herman, but Herman's not listening because he too
can appreciate the grave possibilities. The party on the way up certainly wasn't his idea and none of his business, either. He doesn't
see any heat out in the open yet but knows it's got to be there
somewhere on Jack and Frank and Anselmi. So, he stands next to
the bus, looking toward the Roma and maybe getting ready to take
a dive if something should happen.

Carlo's never seen Snorky mad and doesn't want to. He watches
him out of the corner of an eye and sees him trundle heavily down
the steps. He looks at that huge back and shoulders and then sees
with a flood of relief that they aren't hunched in menace. The big

head is up, and now the burly arms stretch out from the trunk, fingers spread. It's a greeting. And Capone strides, kinglike, into the midst of his liegemen. "Hi'ya, Lulu. Howsa kid?" And then he hugs her, which is like releasing a mechanism, and life moves onward, Lulu looking at Jack out of Snorky's bear hug, Tram approaching Capone, hand out to shake, Pee Wee making a wide swing around the grill of the bus and catching up with Bix, throwing an arm around him. "We're gonna shake Abe Lincoln's logs tonight, Bix," he yelps. Behind Carlo in the Roma's doorway, there are smiles from Margaret Ruggiere, the darkly glowing daughter, Mary Ann, and two young waiters, one of them Carlo's kinsman. And just inside the room, the local talent, waiting to do their stuff—eight women, including Capone's teenaged friend. Carlo begins waving the band inside like a traffic cop, "Come on in! Come on in! Welcome to the Roma." The sinking sun hits the undersmear of bruise-yellow and rosies it while the sullen clouds roll on towards Flint and nightfall.

When the band has set up on the stand under the red, white, and green flag and Tram has imposed a semblance of order he turns to the party sitting at their tables with their White Rock and ginger ale and beer and Canadian whiskey, and he smiles, holding up his hands for a moment of silence. He's looking at Capone when he says, "It's our great pleasure to be here tonight, to entertain you." His long, leathery face already shows what will be the creases of age. "If you have fun, we'll all have fun together." He grins even more deeply at Capone, sitting with Jack and Lulu and the teenager who certainly seems poised enough, considering the company she's keeping. "You know, Mr. Capone has given us our orders: we're supposed to toot to kill, so now we'll just get right to it." And then they're off, alternating between hot numbers and slower sentimental ones, Tiger Rag balancing Valencia, I've Found A New Baby paired with Idolizing, Davenport Blues against I'd big eight-burner stove. Under the unhoused lights of the pantry there are three tall brown bottles and some glasses and setups on the scarred table, and the band crowds in, tired and thirsty too now that they've burned off the booze they had on the way up. "Hey, Herman!" Pee Wee says, pouring, "undo your collar, man, and have a belt, why don't you?" "Herman doesn't indulge," Bix says in the upper-class British accent he's been affecting all week, consequence of reading P. G. Wodehouse. He winks at Herman, smiles, his glass held up under the lights, amber, dense: a toast. Then takes it straight down. "Wow! This is the berries, boys!" "And maybe the bee's knees, too," somebody adds. They're all at it now, the anemic lights showering down on their young heads and faces, gleaming along the sinews of their lithe arms with the sleeves rolled back. Blue shadows pool beneath chins and shoulders and arms, then shift and disappear in the constant, fidgeting movements of young men who've been working hard and are trying to relax quickly, knowing that soon they're going back up there again. They hear the heavy hollowness of pots being rolled in the suds-filled galvanized sinks, and Don is prompted to wonder aloud if there's any of that fish soup back there or maybe even just some bread, and he and Tram head into the kitchen, and presently Mary Ann, blushing beautifully, comes into the pantry with a tureen and ladle and sets it down and gets out of there quickly and right behind her another woman with bowls and sliced bread on a tray. Bix whips down his second and Tram looks over at him from the other side of the table, at his face, which is a bit fuller than when they played the Arcadia in St. Louis this spring, but Tram knows this can't be because Bix is putting on weight, because as far as he can tell Bix rarely eats a normal meal. Yesterday Don told him that Bix and Pee Wee had talked him into driving them over to the sisters' for a jug, and on the way back they'd stopped at a store at Rolling Prairie where Bix bought a sack of chocolate chip cookies and ate them between hits on the jug and that when they got back to the lake both sack and jug were done. Tram has begun to worry a bit. He tries to stay out of Bix's business, and part of the time it's easy enough because he has his own life with Mitzi, there in their cottage down the road past the speak. But from the road it's easy enough to see the disheveled life within the yellow cottage Bix shares with Pee Wee and Itzy and Don, the screen door half-torn from its hinges and still hanging aslant, the straggling ranks of milk bottles along the little porch, soured in the sun and with their cardboard caps unopened, and into the dawn hours or even into full morning the sounds of the men within, drinking, laughing, jamming. And sometimes even after that Mitzi, out for a walk around the lake's lower end, hears the old square piano chording softly, then breaking off. Then it begins again—a note, a single, suspended note like the sun, poised on summer's gauzy horizon. Then Mitzi walks on, leaving the cottage behind her, and hears the unseen player begin again with a cluster of dissonant notes, as if searching among them for something. Probably Stravinsky, Tram tells her, Bix's latest love. And if the guy doesn't eat or sleep, how in hell does he live? So now Tram reaches across the table and hands Bix a slice of bread, and Bix says, "Thanks," and eats it absently while he keeps after that authentic Canadian sauce.

Yes We Have No Bananas and Who's Sorry Now under the flag that Mussolini's making Italians proud of again. Lulu and Jack are back on the floor and, standing at the entrance to the kitchen and pantry, Herman catches her eye as she breezes past but he can't read anything there but thinks again of that quote she produced from somewhere, "Just a boy and a girl on a summer's night." Then he hears Bix call for Lulu's Back In Town where Frank Di Prima does the vocal, and they swing into it. But Jack hears Bix's call, too, and drops his hands, leaving Lulu stranded amidst the others—Burke, Nitti, Scalise who's picked the toughest of the local girls and is shoving her around the floor. Jack stands there, his face working, hands slightly cupped and held away from his taut body. But Bix isn't looking—never does—just plays to that invisible spot in front of him, and Lulu, looking at Jack now, says, "O, fer Christ's sake, Jack! Leave it alone, willya?" Capone's had a snootful and isn't noticing. He's leaning over Miss Round Lake, hand on her smooth and supple knee and talking above the music, which isn't his. But Jack can't let it go and strides to the stand where he shouts into the bell of Tram's C-melody sax, "Cut that shit out!" Behind his instrument Tram's eyebrows rise, widening his dark eyes, asking with them, Say what? "I said, cut that shit out! Play something else!" Tram swings around towards the others and takes down and motions them to do likewise, and the band toot-tootles to a stop, Bix the last of them, his gaze finally focusing on a pair of highly polished two-toned shoes planted in the middle of that spot he plays to, and he looks up into that working face with its cap of brilliantined hair. He looks over at Tram. "Man here wants us to get off that and play something else," Tram says, with an affable shrug. "I'll See You In My Dreams? You like that one?" Jack doesn't do anything for a few seconds, just stands there in front of Bix. Then they hear his voice as though struggling through long disused and rusted pipes. "That'll be fine." Bix wipes his lips with the back of his free hand and works the cornet's valves, and then the band takes up Dreams, Tram supplying the smooth, vibratoless intro. Carlo, who's turned from wiping off a table to see what's happening, turns back to it, an extra towel draped over his shoulder. Capone, deep into Miss Round Lake, looks up to see what's happened to the music, and when it starts again, goes back to the girl. Above the polished bar the little Italian flags hang like fringe from the rafters, and the five-foot effigy of the muskellunge (actually hooked, then mounted, over in Wisconsin years before) disregards all of it, its head artfully twisted up and sideways, its

them has ever seen him move, and his eyes are popped out of his
head so far it looks like they might arrive before he does. Herman
knows right away something big must be up and is already standing
when Webb heaves up like an old fire horse. "Gotta call," Webb
pants, and Herman can see the big artery in Webb's neck jumping
against the café-au-lait skin. "Jack—from Lansing—Said you aint to
go nowheres—till you hear from him—Best you come back with
me." And an hour later Don, fishing by himself on the dock,
watches as a midnight blue roadster tears over the tracks and past the
club and cottage, and then Herman and Webb see it too as it rocks
savagely to a stop in front of the storehouse, a little cloud of hot yellow dust pluming up around it, and out jumps Machine Gun Jack.
He's in his city clothes, though not completely assembled, his collar
off and his vest and suit coat neatly draped over the passenger seat.
And this is how Herman learns that the Big Shot will surrender this
afternoon so he can clear his name in the McSwiggin thing, handing
himself over right on Herman's route back to the city. "An he don
want nothin to queer the deal there," Jack snarls, "like some dumb
sonofabitch Dutchman comin through just at the wrong time.
Which means you and me are gonna sit tight until we hear it's all
done." He pokes Herman in the chest with his first two fingers, a
hard emphasis. Plainly, Jack's unhappy. He's wound pretty tight anyway, but in this situation is doubly dangerous. His face is working
hard, and for the first time Herman notices some slight disarray in
the glossy helmet of his hair, and so Herman's glad when Jack goes
out to pace in front of the house. But it's too hot for much of that,
and pretty soon Jack's back inside, whipping the sandy dust from his
spats and shoes with a rag and ordering Webb to get him a glass of
beer with plenty of ice in it. Then he goes back into the cooler where
they stash the beer, and Webb brings him a chair, and that's where
Jack waits until Joe Batters calls near sundown with the word that
the Big Shot has surrendered and will appear in Criminal Court

tomorrow before Judge Tooman—bad news there, because they've never been able to get to Judge Tooman.

And Capone does appear before the judge, all right, denying everything, and afterwards talks to a horde of news hawks on the courthouse steps, flashbulbs going off like little bombs and their white smoke hanging like clouds around the crown of his hat while he tries to turn his scars away from the cameras, only he can't because this time they've got him surrounded. "Why would I want to do Billy?" he asks rhetorically. "I liked the kid—we had drinks together." He lights up a huge cigar, rolls it along those liver lips to the corner of his mouth, giving the reporters time to scribble, and one of them asks if McSwiggin was on the take, as some have been saying. "I paid McSwiggin, sure," Capone admits. "I paid him plenty, and I got my money's worth, so I got no reason to kill him. That's stupid business."

Then everybody in the Outfit has to sit tight and follow developments in the papers and wait for the phone to ring. Herman doesn't like to call Hellie with Jack around, and she doesn't call him. So he simply sits there in his room at the Calvert and waits. Waits like all the rest of them, the other drivers and mechanics, the front men and mistresses, the bartenders and bouncers, gunmen, alky cookers, club managers, horn players, piano ticklers—the whole noncommissioned army stationed throughout the city and beyond it who march to the beat of the Big Shot's baton. Nights, he goes out for hamburgers or chop suey. Pays a solemn visit to Bev, one of Hellie's old girlfriends, who can tolerate an on-and-off thing. Sees Fairbanks in *The Black Pirate* three times. On a Sunday afternoon, the phone silent and dead and nothing in the papers, he sits at the wide-open window of his room while a west-blowing wind rattles the scattered, spread pages of the paper and the sash, bringing a fine-grained load of grit into the room—coal cinders and long-desiccated horse shit from the streets and dirt from the unseen fields and prairies beyond the city's limits, out there in Iowa and Nebraska and Wyoming where they only read about this terrible metropolis of murder and mayhem, if they even do that.

Shooting another glance at the dead-silent, baked-rubber receiver stuck to the wall it comes to him that he's been living like this, on the edge of danger, for almost as long as he can remember, all the way back to when his mother died in the epidemic and the old man began a restless, destinationless journey from one west side flat to another, and with each move young Herman would face a new set of dangers. Hanging out on the corner of the new neighborhood, he knew he'd have to fight, if not this day, then the next and the day after that as well, until he'd established himself. Then another move, and it would all begin over again. For Hellie, too, though she was three years older and already beginning to run with a fast crowd that wasn't so confined to any neighborhood. And back then there'd been a morning when he'd come back from his dawn paper route, tired, cold, grimy, knowing he wouldn't go to school this day, either, and that no one would notice that he didn't, to find Hellie with her big eyes red with recent tears and a good-sized welt under the left one, and her nose red, too. And while he ate his second-day bun the baker gave him each day and drank his mug of coffee, the two of them sat in silence with the only sounds those within the building: doors opening and shutting, schoolchildren bound out, a man saying something in a foreign tongue to his wife as he stood with his hand on the blackened copper of the doorknob. He drank his mug down, waiting for her to say something, but she never did, and from that day on it was different in the three-room flat—edgy, tense with something the boy couldn't identify, the old man gone more and more and when home mostly silent, he and his daughter rarely speaking, avoiding each other. Herman made himself scarce, pumping gas at the filling station, working his paper route, hanging out with his pals. And one day the old man went silently off to his work at the Yards and never came back, leaving them, leaving behind also his coat and the grease-stained brogans and the old grip that sagged in the closet.

That was the beginning of his life with Hellie and with a new set of dangers as they struggled to keep their little household together, moving to a two-room flat with the toilet downstairs. He sold papers in the mornings at a corner stand, then worked in a garage while Hellie doubled as a chocolate dipper and movie theatre cashier. He was fifteen. Times were tough all over, and even with Debs running for president from a federal penitentiary his ideas about what was wrong with the system fell on a lot of sympathetic ears.

Four days before the election it was plain Debs would stay right where he was and that Harding would stomp Cox. But the Chicago papers were as full of the Black Sox thing as with national politics. Entering the drab gloom of their apartment at evening, he found Hellie's door closed and figured she might be entertaining Tommie Rolfe who'd been coming around a lot. He dropped his cap on the table and the papers next to it with their headlines about Shoeless Joe and sluiced his face at the kitchen tap, wiping it on the sleeve of his mackinaw. In the battered saucepan that had stubbornly survived successive moves he found enough of this morning's coffee for another cup and rasped a match across the tabletop, then heard Hellie's voice from behind the door. "Ya in there?" he called, hearing her again, her voice muffled as if under the covers or half asleep. "Come see me," she answered, and when he had his cup filled he did that.

She was in her bed, which was more cot than that, under a faded pink coverlet with a raveled silk border that had once belonged to their mother. Tacked to the wall above the bed hung a tire company calendar he'd brought her from the garage: a pretty, rosy-cheeked girl, bending forward to peer through the oval of a truck tire: Rolling Right Along On Royal. She struggled up into the pillow, making a diagonal of her body so that he could sit on the bed. It was dim enough in there so that he couldn't be certain, but he thought she might have been crying. "Howsa kid?" she asked, trying for some brightness and failing. "Can't kick. Eagle flew today." He reached into the mackinaw's pocket for the pitiful show of his weekly pay. "That's nice." He looked at her quizzically then: "That's nice" wasn't Hellie any more than her being in bed at this hour. "What's it with you?" he asked, bending for a closer inspection, "in bed like this on a Friday night. Sick or something?" No, she wasn't sick, she told him with a shake of her head. Maybe it was the chocolate dipping job that was getting to her— all that chocolate all the time. Or maybe it was that her friend Muriel had missed her monthly and was going to marry the guy, just out of the navy and no job. It all was making her feel old, she said with a deep sigh, like life was leaving her behind. And then Tommie—well, Tommie was nice enough, good dancer and all, but she wasn't stuck on Tommie. "I don't know what the hell it is, kid," she said suddenly, tossing aside this sad little litany, "except sometimes at the end of the week, everybody talkin about Saturday night, dancin, the new hot band they got somewhere, and all, and I get to thinkin 'What's the big deal, anyway?' Saturday night. Sunday. Monday, ya start all over again, and I'm wonderin what's it all add up to, ya know? Ya work your fanny off, and then ya die, like Ma." She brought her hand from beneath the coverlet and reached up, flipping the pages of the hanging calendar. "Sometimes even this gives me the blues, just to look at it." "I think you're tired, is all," he'd said. "Why not have yourself a nap. I'll hang around; I aint read the afternoon paper. Then, if you're not doin something with Tommie or whoever, maybe we could split a chop suey at Sam's." She shook her head. "S'okay, kid. You go get your kicks. I'll be okay here."

But he'd stayed, reading the paper in the other room by the light of the stinking kerosene lantern they used to economize. Russians bashing the Poles. Funeral of the Greek king, bitten by his pet monkey. Harding and Cox. The Black Sox scandal—Chick, the Swede, Eddie, now Shoeless Joe. The gloom had gathered around the lantern's little pool of light when he heard what he took to be something between a sob and a sigh, and picking up the lantern, he went in, holding it high, the light finding her wide, glistening eyes there in the bed, and, as he brought it closer, throwing monstrous shadows against the wall. "Hey," he said bending over, "Hey." The coverlet was tucked high under her chin, its raveled edge like a badly stitched scar. She started to say something but it wouldn't come out, and in annoyance with her weakness she tossed her head on the pillow and tried again. "Could you," she began. "Could you . . . ." He put the lantern on the tiny nightstand. "What," he said, wanting to understand but feeling out of his depth here with her. "Could you just . . . *hold* me a minute?" she asked. "I got such blues somehow, kid." She made room again, and he lay down on his side, feet hanging off at an angle, covering her with his rough-sleeved arm as she turned her head into the crook of his neck and shoulder. And he could feel her there against him, warm and slight and shivery. Later, he couldn't remember how long it was they'd been like that or how it was that the thing had happened, whether it had begun with something so simple as a shift in positions or a sigh or a hand blindly reaching, a finger brushing his temple, a glimpse he caught of her huge eyes staring at him in the lantern's yellow-white waver. And then the sour pink coverlet being folded aside with a ceremonial slowness and the lantern light falling on Hellie's face, which is where he fought to keep his eyes: her wide, generous mouth, the eyes with their light lashes, and then the mouth curving at the corners into the first approaches to a smile but a smile such as he'd never seen before, so serious and solemn and seeming to come to him from somewhere so far off. And then his eyes fell from her face, down to the tiny breasts with their aureoles like black diamonds stabbing into him, the glossy, hairless thighs whose lines and curves traveled with the resistless force of gravity itself into that valley that also was almost hairless. And then his own voice grown furred, husky, saying, "Jesus, Hellie," and she saying, "Come on, kid," and his manhood up and his pants down, leaning over her, leaning into her, her hands on him, placing him, and he gliding within as though this was something he'd always known. Afterwards, when he'd tried to disengage, Hellie had held him to her, and they lay there in the lantern light, brother and sister, lost and abandoned, an unstoried Hansel and Gretel in the lawless jungle of the great city. They never did get out for Sam's chop suey.

Hellie's call to the Calvert comes only minutes after Herman has finished talking with Bix and Tram who are in town making plans for the fall. She doesn't know anything new except that something must be up because Jack and all the rest are over at the Metropole, and maybe it might not be too bad an idea if he drifted over there. "If you do find out anything," she laughs harshly, "let me in on it, willya. Jack never tells me nothin." "I been doin some thinkin about this whole deal," he tells her in response. "I been thinkin about maybe gettin out of this." There's a pause, and he can hear her breathing, waiting. "See, I got this possibility now—nothing definite—but Bix and the whole band from Detroit are gonna tour the East. Jean Goldkette's band, you remember. And they might need a driver, someone who knows cars, motors—tote gear, make sure everybody's aboard—like that." She's still waiting, and so he goes on. "I been thinkin I'm not cut out for this deal, Hellie. I thought I was. And I appreciate you gettin me included—money's great, free room. But I wouldn't mind a change, something—O, restful like—see a bit of the country maybe."

What he doesn't have to say is that he wouldn't mind living a few more years, and the way things are looking there might be some real fireworks pretty soon if Bugs or Hymie think Capone's vulnerable just now. And if they should come for him, then Greasy Thumb would certainly have orders to roll out the heavy artillery. He'd be sure to see action of one kind or another. "They'll think I'm chickenshit if I tried to quit now," he says to her, "but what about you?" "I'll miss ya, kid, miss ya like hell, but I can hardly blame ya. Could be real hot for a while here. But if ya want, I can square ya with Jack. No problem there." She gives another harsh chuckle. "I wouldn't mind gettin outta town with the band myself for a few weeks. But restful? Maybe not."

The Metropole is like a besieged fortress; if they had a portcullis, it would have been rung down. Just to get into the underground garage where they all know his face takes Herman some talking: guys posted everywhere, on corners, in parked cars up on the street, and some of them he's never seen before. Hat brims snapped down, hands in jacket pockets, hard looks. When Gillespie, the mechanic who now keeps the Caddy in shape, sees him coming he raises his eyebrows, and all he'll reply to Herman's questions is, "Lotsa muscle out." Gillespie nods in the direction of Joe Batters, leaning against a big Chrysler, smoking, no hands, blowing big blue clouds that don't go anywhere, just hang in front of his face. Joe Batters watches Herman walking his way and doesn't move a muscle, and his slightly Oriental eyes don't blink in the smoke or register anything when Herman tells him he'd appreciate the opportunity to have a word with Jake. Nobody allowed up there just now. Important meeting. But he'll pass the message along, and what was it about? "Private business," Herman tells him, and Joe Batters shrugs, and so then there's nothing left for Herman to do but to walk out of there just the way he came in, empty, past all the hard-eyed men who watch his back until he's out of sight, walking eastward, towards the lake, and from there a long walk up through Burnham Park. And after a sullen supper and a visit to Bev that doesn't go that well he's back at the Calvert and beginning to loathe his room when Greasy Thumb surprises him with a call, and Herman finds himself telling him he's got this job with the band if he wants it. Jake gets quickly to the point. "You think this is right for you, son, you should take it. We might have to lay off some people anyway. Season's about done out there at the lake." The rumpled little man pauses, and Herman can hear papers being shuffled, other voices in the background. This is small potatoes to Greasy Thumb, something to be handled while his mind wrestles with weightier matters. "Now, I want to tell you, son," Jake continues, "you did very satisfactory work for us, and I know Al appreciates that. Also, that you're a man who keeps his own counsel, if you follow me." Herman signifies that he does, and then Jake is conveying his best wishes and telling him to drop by the Metropole so that Joe Batters can give him his last pay when there's some small commotion on the other end, someone speaking to Jake in a loud, harsh voice Herman knows. "Jack would like a word," Jake says, and then there's the other voice on the line. "Listen," Jack says, "it's good you're goin on the road. This here's too hot for you, pal, and listen, you take that fairy horn player wid ya and that other guy, too—that clarinet guy, who don play worth a shit. I don wanta lay eyes on either one of em for a while. Ya got that? Well, *fine!* Tell em for me that Jack says you little fucks better make yourself scarce: I don wanta find either one botherin Lulu: she don't appreciate it." The phone goes *thunk* as Jack slams home the receiver, and that's the end of that for Herman, all but collecting the last bunch of bills from Joe Batters.

✥

They're all out there at the Hawthorne track on their last day in Chi before barnstorming east to Boston and New York, the hard drinkers in the Goldkette band—Bix, Dorsey, Howdy, and Don Murray, whose attentions to Lulu at another Club Roma party angered Jack. Tram is back in the city taking care of last-minute details, and Jean Goldkette has sent Herman on to Boston to lease the bus they'll use in New England.

Don has the word from the Big Shot himself that they're to look up Capone's man out here, the Camel. The Camel will fix them up with a nice little day. Don and Bix go up into the high-priced boxes to find him, Don chortling away to Bix: "This will be a *gasser,* Bixie! Found money! I just *love* gangsters, don't you?" They've both had a couple on the way out, and Bix is telling Don they'd better pace themselves since it's only the second race when they spot the Camel sitting two seats in from the aisle: smoked glasses, binoculars, beautifully cut blue suit. The Camel takes a lot of sun, and with the blue suit and white-on-white shirt and tie, he's very sharp. The Camel's men see them coming and stand up around him, but the Camel's right at ease in his chair, no form sheet, no pencil, just the binoculars, and the program on the slender table of the box. Down below, beyond the cavernous overhang of the roof, lie the washed brown of the track, the white railing, the emerald infield with a pond on which some ducks slowly scud. Flags riffle in the light westerly breeze: mellow for a Midwestern mid-September day and a pretty nice weekday crowd on hand. The horses for the Second are just now coming onto the track, throwing giraffe-like shadows.

"Been expecting you boys," the Camel says with a polished smile. "Al told me you'd be along, and a pip of a day you picked for it, too. Now, which is Don?" Murray, his square face ruddy with sun and sauce, reaches out to shake with the Camel, but the Camel doesn't shake, merely nods with that polished smile, and Murray pulls back his hand. "I'm Don," Murray says, "and this here is Bix." "Ah, yes," the Camel says, assessing Bix who looks to him like a college boy in his shirtsleeves and bow tie. "I've heard about you, young man." Behind them the Camel's men stand at the ready, not blending in too well with the sporting crowd. The Camel hands Don the program. "This is all you'll need today, boys," he tells them, his voice soft, conversational. "You follow the tips in here, you'll have a good day—better than most of these." He gestures dismissively to the crowd below in the sun, a sea of yellow-white straw boaters with here and there the vivid color of some woman's dress or corsage. "Most of these guys can't afford to be here; they're buying on margin, mortgages, time payments— everything. But out here"—he taps the table with his index finger—"they pay cash at the window. You can bet on that, too."

Back with the others down at the rail, Don opens the Camel's gift and points to the small, neat check marks next to certain entries for the Second, Seventh, and Eighth. "The fix is in, fellas!" he laughs, stabbing the program with his forefinger. "The fix is in for these races." "What isn't fixed?" Tommy Dorsey asks. He's had a few as well and the sun's making him slightly cranky. "They fixed the Series, right? And Teapot Dome. The Sacco–Vanzetti thing's rigged, poor bastards. It wouldn't surprise me if the Dempsey– Tunney thing's fixed." He shrugs. "They can't get to Jack," Howdy says. The indicated entry for this race is Eight, The Bristol Road, and they look up now at the horses prancing past the grandstand, and here comes Eight, a bright sorrel with blinkers and bandaged legs, stepping high. "What're we waiting for, fellas?" Don exclaims. "Let's get some bets down on him!" They race up the grandstand steps towards the windows, but there are long lines in front of all of them, except the hundred-dollar window, and the big clock shows only two minutes to post time. "I say we pool and go for the bundle on Eight," Don says quickly. "We can't lose on this." And they crowd toward the hundred-dollar window, arriving at the same moment as a heavyset elderly gent in three-piece white suit, boater, wife in tow under a picture hat. Don shoots in front of him and leans into the wicket while the others fish for bills. "I say," White Suit says, tapping Don's shoulder. "I say, you're being very rude, sir." Don looks over his shoulder, then turns back to the teller. "Give us a hundred on Eight, on the nose," he says. "I say," the old man begins again.

"Beat it, Pops, or wait your turn," Don snarls, not even looking back this time.

Bix puts a hand softly on Don who turns to see who it is. The teller is waiting. "Don't do this, Don," Bix says. "They were here first." He smiles at the couple. "O, for Christ's sake, Bix," Don says, "cut it out!" But Bix reaches out now to pull Don out of the way. Don squares around and glares at him, squeezing the priceless program, face scarlet and eyes blazing. The others hang back. "I'm awful sorry, folks," Bix apologizes to the couple. "Just a misunderstanding—here—you go right ahead." White Suit slides into position and puts down two bills on Seven, another on Three to show. The clock ticks down to post time, and Don's hollering in Bix's face and Dorsey moves up to intercede. "But I don't want to fight, Donnie," Bix is saying now. "You know that wasn't the right thing to do: those people are old enough to be our grandparents. Look," he says, smiling a little, hands relaxed and gesturing with them at his sides, "we have all these other races covered, so why not be polite?" White Suit completes his transaction and moves off without a glance, looking instead at his tickets to make certain of them while the Missus looks over her shoulder at the knot of young men, the well-knit one in the crooked bow tie smiling a little and talking in conciliatory tones to his enraged friend. The last thing she sees is the one in the bow tie pat his hip pocket and say something about "having one," and then they're lost in the crowd moving out into the September sun and the westerly breeze to watch as The Bristol Road comes from far back to score an upset.

⚘

Pulling out of La Salle Street station, the boys in the Goldkette band settle in for the hop to Toledo, where they'll play two dates, then Pittsburgh, Wilkes-Barre, Scranton, and finally Massachusetts, where Herman will meet the train at Southboro. They play cards and witless pranks on each other, drink, wrestle, read two-day-old newspapers. The day some of them were out at Hawthorne getting rich with what Bix calls gangsters' gold the papers carried a story of a would-be assassin in Rome who threw a bomb at Mussolini's car, but the rig was even more heavily armored than Capone's, a veritable tank, and the device bounced harmlessly off and blew up in the street. The Premier has now survived five attempts on his life, including one when he was shot in the face by a deranged Englishwoman. Today's paper has Mussolini threatening the French who, he claims, tolerate dangerous radicals on their southern border. The French respond that they would be delighted if all the Italians in the south of France would go back where they belong, taking their knives and pistols and piano wire with them.

In Toledo the papers give the band good notices and one paper carries a related item, the report of a heated exchange between the American King of Jazz, Paul Whiteman, and British music critic Ernest Newman. Don Murray reads it aloud to the whoops of the assembled. "'Goaded into a *frenzy* by recent remarks of Paul Whiteman, archpriest of jazz, defining that *exotic* product and disparaging the *classics,* Mr. Newman devoted hundreds of red-hot words expressing his utmost *contempt* for Mr. Whiteman, his arguments, and all connected with the ultra-modern cult of the great god *jazz.*' Well, I *must* say," Don says, affecting Bix's best Jeeves. He reads on: "'Your typical jazz composer or jazz enthusiast is merely a musical *illiterate* who is absurdly pleased with little things because he does not know how little they are.'" He pauses and scans ahead. "Oh, get *this!* 'The brains of the whole lot of them would not fill the lining of Johann Strauss's hat!'" The young men in the car laugh and holler and slap each other on backs and shoulders, and the train rocks along toward Pittsburgh, clacking rhythmically over the crossties, windows open, car doors sliding heavily back and forth, soot and cinders eddying in.

As Don finishes and tosses the newspaper aside Howdy lurches into the aisle, his shirt stuffed with his dirty laundry and newspapers, transformed into a bulbous, waddling figure. "I, sir, am Paul Whiteman, King of Jazz! You cannot, sir, so insult me without I have my . . . *satisfaction,*" giving a broad leer that excites the others to more laughter. "I demand it, sir." Don Murray stands, imperiously offended. "Where do you want it, Paul," he asks, "ear or anus?" "I'll see the color of your insides, you pompous English asshole," Howdy hollers. "That you shall and speedily," Don says, dropping his drawers, and turning around. Then he turns around again, hauls his pants up, and they fight a Fairbanks duel with the rolled newspapers, back and forth the length of the car, like a jerking pendulum. The car's in an uproar and even Tram, who's in charge here, is convulsed, his long, mournful face red and white with exertion. "Die, you fat archpriest of nigger music!" Don puffs, lunging forward and crumpling his sword into Howdy's slipping girth, the old news delivering a death-blow. Howdy goes down in a dusty, crinkled heap. "Ahhh, fuck," he gasps, expiring. "I'll drink to that!" shouts Dorsey.

And the train rocks on toward Youngstown, flashing past oak groves and green swatches of winter wheat and cornfields that have mostly been harvested except for the field corn, the residue

stalks lying in ranks like soldiers mowed down by machine guns
or poison gas in the Great War every one of these rollickers is too
young to have seen. Dorsey produces a bottle of clear lightning he
scored in Toledo, gift of an Ohio State kid who came both nights
with a swarm of alligators, as the press now styles jazz fans. The
bassist Steve Brown produces another out of his satchel, and
somebody else has several bottles of Coca-Cola. Don gets Dixie
cups from the dispenser attached to the water cooler, and they
settle down to catch their breaths and mix, stirring with index fingers. Somebody gets a cup for Bix, but Bix is looking for something along the aisle—Don's newspaper sword, battered, its print
twisted into a greasy smear, and some portions of it detached and
scattering in the little wind that blows along the floor. He stoops
for these, but they flutter and dodge and he has to get on hands
and knees to catch and corral them. "Hey, Bix! Whatcha doing?"
they call. "Hey, Bix! They got niggers who'll do that for ya." "Hey,
porter! You got competition here." "*This* is the guy we had to
throw in the lake he was so dirty?" But Bix pays no attention: he's
matching the detached tatters with the twisted sword he holds in
one hand. The bottles go around. Tram fills his Dixie with Coke,
watching Bix out of one eye. Dorsey begins to tell about the cop-
per-haired coed who came last night with the Ohio State kid.
"And let me tell you, if the rest of the tour is as good as the start,
I'm not gonna be able to *walk* when we get done: *beaucoup*
broads!" They scoff, but they did see Tommy leave with the girl,
and Itzy, who shares a room with him, knows Tommy didn't show
until twenty minutes to check-out.

   The train rocks and sways onward, outracing the September sun
that falls ever farther behind on its own journey, arcing across
Toledo and Chicago and the waving prairies with the grasses throwing spears of shadow and the Rockies all but shorn of their white
crowns, out toward the Pacific, while their train, the Limited,

rushes towards darkness, the groves getting denser to the eye, the farm buildings more starkly white, the standing stock in the fields more immense in bulk until at last they become indistinguishable from their browse, and the lights go on in the houses and the towns they clack past, the crossing bells ding-donging into the distance. And the bottles go around, the Dixie cups begin to melt and more are fetched until the last of the liquor is emptied into the handy cups, and now the lights come on in the car, and the world outside is gone. Bix sits at the window, the story pieced and read, looking out into something he can only hear as a dark rush.

"Hey!" Howdy hollers. "Let's jam."

⌖

The band wants a picture taken: history is about to be made. They're just off the train and feeling that liberation, high-spirited as hell, and on their way to the Southboro Hotel where they'll practice and then take all of New England by storm. Howdy shows Herman how to work the camera, and Herman braces there on the rural road and squeezes off the shot: twelve grinning young men in suits sitting on the roof of the bus, a fringe of fall foliage visible behind them and a banner taped to the bus's body: JEAN GOLDKETTE ORCHESTRA NEW ENGLAND TOUR. Steve Brown sits on the hood, brandishing Herman's Smith & Wesson, sole souvenir of his days with the Outfit, and at the very rear of the roof, almost falling off it, the band's newest addition, Bill Challis, an arranger from Wilkes-Barre. In another shot Herman takes they've gotten down from the bus and are holding out an even more grandiose banner: *BATTLE OF MUSIC WITH JEAN GOLDKETTE* AND HIS WORLD FAMOUS VICTOR RECORD ORCHESTRA THE *PAUL WHITEMAN* OF THE WEST THE GREATEST AND

MOST SENSATIONAL BATTLE OF MUSIC EVER HELD ANYWHERE IN NEW ENGLAND. Goldkette has designed this one and Herman has seen it through the print shop in Boston.

Their hotel's a big, rambling barn of a place with a sure-enough barn out back where you can still smell horses and hay, though it's been some years since the stock made way for the auto. Herman shares a room with Bix—first of many—and there's an attic they use as a practice room, going over the hot new arrangements Challis has worked out for them, Blue Room and Baby Face, and working with his suggestions for some of their old numbers like My Pretty Girl and Dinah. Challis wants to play reeds with the band, and has arrived with an armload of instrument cases, but Tram talks to him with Bix listening in. "Listen, Bill," he says earnestly, carefully, "this band can be great, but we've got problems because Jean had us split in two groups for the summer and we're not really together yet—you've heard that, I know. What we need are more good, tight arrangements like Baby Face, and we don't have that much time." Tram smiles when he tells Challis that reed players are a dime a dozen. "What we need, Bill, is arrangements that show us off. We go into the Roseland down in New York on the sixth, opposite Fletcher Henderson, and those black boys are gonna kick our fannies unless we can pull this thing together up here." Bix says nothing, only nibbles away on a ragged fingernail, looking up occasionally at Tram and Bill.

That evening they get going again up in the practice room, a good, hard session until almost midnight. Two more the next day, and now Bix is working on piano with Challis, adding in his own suggestions: "Gee, Bill, I love this, but don't you think the brass has to play a few more notes here?" "What if we gave Steve the window here, Bill?" No practice that night, though, because they're all gathered in the parlor around the big new RCA radio shaped like a chapel to listen to Graham McNamee announce the Dempsey–Tunney fight from Philly. Bix is taking the bets of everybody who likes the champ, and then they listen, incredulous, as the Fighting Marine in his Galahad white trunks punches the champ dizzy in a driving downpour, until at fight's end Dempsey's face is the color and texture of an overripe plum. Dorsey says it was fixed, but Bix pockets fifty—only briefly though because he owes Tram and Don.

The next day they cram in two more long sessions, and then the band boards the bus for Nutting's-on-the-Charles. Nutting's is a huge old wooden dancehall built out over the river where college kids and the younger set—some of them even arriving by canoe—come to dance the fox trot, one-step, Charleston, Black Bottom, shimmy. Five years ago dancing seemed like a youth fad, one of the manifestations of post-war pent-up emotions. Surely, it would go away. While it lasted though, volunteer policemen and -women patrolled the dancehalls, trying to save American girlhood from syncopated copulation. The Albuquerque YWCA warned that social diseases could be contracted through jazz dancing; that jazz itself was as demoralizing as bobbed hair and smoking; that seventy percent of New York's prostitutes were brought to ruin by jazz dancing. If you must dance, a Cleveland municipal notice read, then dance only from the waist up. In Oshkosh, close enough to Chicago to know what's what, an ordinance still forbids men and women from making eye contact while dancing. All in vain. America is dancing more than ever. And now, it is admitted, the whole country is so nervous it just has to dance, and the pace of life is quickening, quickening, like some god-awful machine that is out of control, its gears and wheels spinning towards some terrible crack-up. We might not know where we're going, a prominent pundit writes, but for better or worse, we're going, going, going, and the dance fad of Flaming Youth has persisted and spread like a rash that makes even matrons and stockbrokers and ad men itch. So the Shribmann brothers, Kenneth and Clyde, have capitalized on it, like others, and run a string of dancehalls all over the northeast. Here at Nutting's-on-the-Charles when the dancers crowd the floor the whole joint sways so noticeably it would be alarming—if anyone cared.

Despite Goldkette's banners, Kenneth Shribmann's not sold. He has listened to the records Goldkette brought out from Detroit, but he doesn't quite get it. "Sure, they're good," he tells Goldkette, "but maybe too advanced? These kids, they want that dance beat, y'know—*dat-dat-datta.*" He beats his meaty fist into the palm of his other hand. "If it don't have that, you can skip it." Musicianship to Kenneth and Clyde is of no consequence. Goldkette is a precise, French-born guy who behind his spectacles looks like a concertmaster. He never appears with his bands but is a savvy promoter and now he tells Shribmann that the band he's bringing into Nutting's-on-the-Charles is different from what's on the earlier records. "We have now this fellow Beiderbecke," Goldkette tells him. "He is wonderful. He cannot read well at all, and so he must play the third trumpet part. But when we spot him he makes us very hot. The college kids out west made him their hero. You'll see."

Kenneth remains doubtful. He hasn't heard the new band with its hot cornetist so he hires two additional bands for opening night. If the western hotshots fizzle, he's covered. Mal Hallett's orchestra goes on first. They play smooth dance music interspersed with comedy routines. All in fun. Then Barney Rapp's band, which follows the same formula. By the time Rapp is wrapping up his set the crowd is warm and ready to hear from the western hotshots who wait in the wings, all of them smiling ever more broadly, though not at the comedy stuff. They know now they have both bands carved. "Boys," says Tram as they're about to go on, "is there any doubt?" They laugh. No doubt anywhere. They'll open with My Pretty Girl and Clementine and Ostrich Walk; close with Blue Room and Baby Face.

Up on the stand Bix takes another long pull at the needle beer he and Don are working on, wipes his lips, slots in, and Tram counts off for Pretty Girl, a very fast one-step. And they're just a few bars into the verse when there's a loud *Whoop!* from out on the floor that tells them they've hit a vein. After the verse Spiegle Willcox plays sonorous melody on trombone while Don weaves in and around him, and there's Steve Brown slapping the string bass—still something of a novelty—while the brass belts it out, and it's not just hot, it's *on,* it's like nothing they've heard around here, the beat so solid, the section work tight, Don's solo more intricate than any jazz they know of in Boston. The applause is huge and Tram stands in the midst of it, boiled tux shirt sparkling, smiling, blinking into the hands that spank themselves ruddy. "Folks," he announces, "you ain't heard nothin yet," and counts off for Clementine, which is a bit slower, but not much, and there again is that big, beautiful beat they love, but this time they can hear the golden ray from the back row, Bix, triple-tonguing through the verse, and in the midst of their own turns and pivots, faces close or touching, moving away and nearing again, eyes locked—heedless of warnings—in the midst of all this they hear that horn and turn towards him, looking for that marvelous sound.

And where is he, the golden-toned guy? They can't pick him out until after a reeds passage when a single horn makes a sort of reprise of the melody, a nod in its direction, as if the player were saying, "Thanks for the melody, but now, listen to this": a suspended note that veers away from the melody and into regions of blue invention, speaking of worlds only dimly suspected here on the Charles: dim-lit corridors with all the doors closed, piano keys yellow with age and dirty fingers, a cypress wharf running between tall reeds, a guitar chording in another room. They don't understand much if any of this, and maybe the player himself doesn't understand all of it, either, but somehow he *knows* it. Then he pulls back from the blue regions, smoothly, superbly, rejoining all of them and gets into that *dat-dat-datta* they all have to count on. But they've found him by now— way in back, third chair—kind of a handsome guy, playing at the floor. And Herman, watching from the back of the hall, sees it all happening again, just like it had at the Blue Lantern—the same surprise, same seduction and surrender—and it's almost like watching a movie that's slipping on the reel where the same sequence gets run again and again, except here the notes are different because Bix is inventing anew, though there's no way for these dancers to know that.

Now the applause is so thunderous Nutting's vibrates, and the old square-head nails leap in their holes while long-sleeping scrolls left from the carpenters' planes are jostled from the high joists and find flight, downward, settling on shoulders and bobbed hair, on tabletops and instrument cases, on the sad, sallow breast of a wallflower, dragged here by her popular younger sister. Kenneth Shribmann looks around with mingling emotions. Goldkette was right about the band and this kid who obviously has something the dancers go for. So who needs Hallett and Rapp? Here's a big expense he and Clyde could have spared themselves if they'd known. He pulls up his pocket watch, and of course it's too late to change anything, but he can't help thinking, fleetingly, that maybe he could get Barney to take a powder and call it a night but knows he can't get away with it, not if he wants Barney back here and Hallett, too. He walks back into the dim, sawdust-flavored office to call Clyde and tell him, "Clyde, cancel these triplicate bookings in Waltham and Salem. The Goldkette group'll fill the place, no problem there." And when they finish talking business Clyde wants Kenneth to have a word with his teenaged son Arthur who has begun to neglect his studies to listen to jazz recordings on the home Vic, and while he's doing that duty there's a perfunctory knock at the already-ajar office door, and it swings inward and here's Ruth, his secretary from Blue Hill, and she's already removing her glasses as he watches her come towards him swinging her ass. He finishes quickly with his nephew, reminding him that a boy who neglects his studies may well end up like these lost young men who have to live out of their instrument cases and are paid so poorly, which is just what Arthur wants most to hear, and maybe Arthur hears also on the other end of that marvelous wire stretching from Nutting's to Roxbury the band ending a number and the crowd's raucous response. Surely, surely they can't *all* be lost.

Herman, making his way back towards the office to check on the Salem date, hears something else going on inside that room where the door is left heedlessly ajar, hears a muffled moan, another sort of suspended note, a rustle of clothing, something light—fountain pen?—hit the floor and roll briefly. And so turns back and walks quickly into the hall where he comes upon the Hallett bunch, and they're telling Mal they won't go back up there after what the Goldkette band's just done. "Hell with that." "We aren't gonna touch that, brother." "Mal, we go back on, those kids'll kill us—murder, brother." And so Hallett has a mutiny on his hands, and who can blame the boys for not wanting to put their heads in a meat grinder, and where in hell did they get these arrangements, anyway? Moving forward behind his best professional smile, running the gauntlet through the rhythmic, building handclapping, Hallett catches Tram at the edge of the stand: "You see how it is: you want to take another?" And Tram says, "Certainly," and Hallett climbs up to face what his boys don't want to, the rhythmic clapping laced with whistles now and a few boos, but not many, because these are well-behaved youngsters out here at Nutting's. Only, they know what they want, and it isn't Mal Hallett, who now must hold up his hands in polite supplication, asking for a moment to speak, which shortly they grant him. And Mal puts the best face on it and says brightly, "Who can follow that?" Turns, waves at the Goldkette band, and then gets off to a swell of good-natured cheers, heading for the office where Kenneth is trying to get his bookkeeper to do something she knows is unnatural and that she is pretty sure only Negroes and Portagee do. Mal is thinking about his strategy, how he'll approach Kenneth, who is going to try to skin him for the difference between one set and four, and thinking that he might have to make up the difference out of his own pocket to pay his boys if he can't talk Kenneth out of this. And like everybody else he knows, including Kenneth Shribmann, he's overextended and has just signed on for that new Alaska refrigerator his wife has been campaigning for: white enameled exterior, seventy-pound ice capacity, thirty inches deep, and twenty dollars down.

When the band finally breaks for intermission there's a flock around the stand and most of it around Bix. Often he stays up there between sets to work out on the piano, trying to graft bits of Stravinsky, Gershwin, Delius, Eastwood Lane, Debussy, or Ravel onto slender thematic stems he's had running through his brain since long before this summer at the Blue Lantern. But tonight there'll be no piano because they've got him surrounded, and he has to sit there, listening to their youthful gushes, their sweaty enthusiasm, bearing the hands that keep reaching out to touch him. Some of the girls try to catch his eye, but it's tough because he looks mostly at his shoes, only peeking up now and again just to be polite, an abashed smile around his mouth. He's there because he has to be, and that's all. Standing just below the stage, Herman watches while a pint-sized youngster with short-cut black hair waits his turn, then says something to Bix, who nods, appearing to consider it, then nods again but says nothing, and so the little guy has to falter on, and to Herman it's a toss-up as to which is the more bashful. But when Herman hears the kid invite Bix to a

Braves game tomorrow Bix's head comes up, and he says, "Sounds fine to me" and tells the kid they're staying out at the Hillcrest.

Next day at noon they're just wrapping up practice when the kid rolls in driving a Model-T. Sitting outside in the mellowness of early autumn, Herman sees no reason why the kid shouldn't go up to the practice room, especially since he's got a cornet with him and tells Herman that Bix is his absolute idol. He wants Bix to write out a transcription of his Blue Room solo, but Bix has no idea what it is, and anyway he can't write that well. He turns to Challis for help: "Bill, Maxie here wants the chart for Blue Room where I take that spot. Can you help him out?" And Challis does, but the chart of course is blank just where Maxie most wants it full of Bix.

They roll off in the Model-T toward Braves Field on the Charles, Maxie sitting on a cushion behind the wheel to give himself a better look at the road. He's worried he won't be able to sustain a conversation with Bix, but it's okay. Bix is completely preoccupied with his own thoughts and simply looks out the window as they chug through Natick and Newton. Once in a while Maxie can hear a snatch of some song he's humming under the Ford's throaty rumble, but mostly it's silence in there until they get stalled in traffic right outside the park where a milk cart has gotten fouled up with some parked trucks and the horse is in a fright, jerking back and forth in the shafts, its neck lathered and the driver shouting at horse, drivers, pedestrians, everybody at once. Now Maxie hears Bix humming something from a Bessie Smith recording. "The whole song's right there in that one phrase," Bix says, looking over at Maxie but not seeing him. "Right there in that phrase—hear it?"

II

Astoría

Sat.

Dec. 28, 1928

Dearest Dad & Mother

You must be pretty fed up with me for not writing when I told Burnie I would but it's been hell since Pops switched to Columbia. Victor kind of held him hostage when he said he was leaving and so they wanted to get the vaults filled with as much of the orchestra as they could. And Columbia wanted us to lay down a lot of wax to compete with the new Victors so it's been tough. We did about two weeks @ Leiderkrans, 2 sessions in the a.m. another 2 in the p.m. Then we had the shows @ night. Then we had the tour as you know. It was pretty much of a grind I guess Burnie must have told you about that.

Not all bad though. Saw Sis in Atlanta and what a grand time we had @ her home. She really put on the dog for us & I know the boys appreciated it. She made Jack Fulton sing That's My Weakness Now so many times he had a sore throat! She looks great! Saw my old heroes Mares and Nick LaRocca in N.O. & it sure was nice of them to show. Poor Rap is in the assylum & they don't think he's getting much better. Had a quick escursion out to west La. which I'll tell you about when I'm home next time. Don't know now just when that will be.

Well Folks that's about it from here. Were all tired out from the tour even Pops got sick for a bit & now we have the busy holiday. But this is the life & this is the best "damn" orchestra in the country! Wish you could have come over to Clinton.

Lovingly,

L B Beiderbecke

P.S. Not gloomy about work—just tired.

PPs. Highlights of the year have to be playing for Sis & the kids & meeting Ravel.

Am sending pkg. of last records we made for Victor—think youll get a kick out of some—Parade of the Wooden Soldiers that Ferdi Grofe arr. Ole Man River, My Heart Stood Still, Poor Butterfly (I'm not on this)—Wait til you get a load of the new Col. label—Wow!

This doesn't quite bring them up to date because Bix himself is a bit behind. Up on the stand his sense of time is faultless as ever. Earlier, with the Wolverines and Goldkette he was in fact the timekeeper, rushing the beat a bit because he had to make them swing. But the Whiteman orchestra always knows right where it is, even in the midst of the most overstuffed arrangement—twenty-six guys, singers, chimes, whistles, bells. And Pops Whiteman himself is the timekeeper, up there on the podium waving that white stick at them, all three hundred pounds of him, his dimpled knee knocking back and forth like a girlish metronome. So he can't do anything about the time except try to keep track of it, of where they are in the number and if he has a four-bar spot coming up.

But other kinds of time begin to slip away from him more than ever, as if he were falling ever farther astern of life itself. Sometimes, late—or is it early?—dawn light filtering through into his hotel room because he's forgotten to lower the shade, he finds himself thinking back to those old paddle wheelers churning out from the wharf at Davenport, the caramel waters fanning away from the stern, lapsing, licking the pilings, the Illinois shore dark against the summer's shimmer, remembering how desperately then he wanted to be *on time,* catch that boat and so be up-to-the-minute, like the song said, instead of left behind, stuck there in Davenport. How much he wished himself up there on the sweltering deck where the steam calliope was, and you practically had to stomp on its metal keys to raise a sound, but he could do it, hammering those infernal keys, the sound shooting up into the riverfront air, lifting, rising—Smiles That She Gives To Me—hooting out over the riverfront town surrounded by all that corn, over the waterfront streets, up toward the gingerbread stolidities of the homes of the German families, monuments to order, tradition, that looked sternly down on the great river. And three ranks back, on Grand, 1934, there would be Bismark, Agatha, Burnie, Mary Louise, sitting at the laden oak table and his place empty, waiting, and the heavy cut-glass water pitcher in the center. And they would hear then that calliope, hooting, winking at time with its syncopated notes, the Iowa air compelled to listen, too, and then the next phrase, catching up, hurrying on, fooling really with time, and Mary Louise laying a consoling hand on Agatha's arm: "Mom, at least we know where he is." Once, he'd written his high school girl Vera about wanting to beat Fate's time and be up-to-the-minute with her. Now time's fate begins to confuse him some, and the letter he dates as the end of 1928 is really written in the first days of the new year he has yet to recognize, written from a hospital bed in Astoria where Whiteman has placed him to recuperate from the walking pneumonia he's had for more than a month.

But maybe there's more to it than that. Sometimes, when they get off the train or the bus it looks as if he can hardly put one foot in front of the other. As he tells the folks, the schedule's a killer. Carelessly, the boys play their customary broad jokes on him, and it's so simple because they all know that most of the time he's off somewhere, hearing harmonies they don't, thinking back over a recent solo, trying to imagine a conclusion to a theme he's had in his head since '25. Once, while he's asleep on a train—and he's a deep sleeper now, when he does sleep—they paint his face like a clown, dotted cheeks, red nose, bumper lips—and since he never looks in a mirror except when shaving he stumbles off the train (was it Little Rock or Altoona?) and into the amazed sniggers of station personnel and passengers and then the cabbie too. Bix barks at him, "Hey! You don't look so hot yourself, pal!" Only when he catches a fleeting flash of his face in the hotel's revolving door does he tumble to what the laugh's all about, and then nobody laughs harder than Bix. Another time they spy his outsized Gladstone unattended on the station's brick platform and put a busted-off part of a brake shoe beneath his shirts and socks and a Sinclair Lewis book he's reading and watch covertly as he comes back to it with a sack of peanuts and then hoists it with a puzzled look. It's days later when he remarks to someone, "Jeez, you know, I must be getting weak or something because I can hardly lift this thing."

A few—Herman, Tram, pianist Roy Bargy—don't find these pranks that funny anymore, if they ever were. But the rest do. Hell, they're young, they're loose, and they live on the run, and a strange tribal culture develops that survives changes in personnel and is complete with lingo, sayings, humor only they can appreciate, so that one, asking aloud if anybody has some razor blades to spare, might be answered, "No, but I gotta take a crap pretty quick, if that'll help you out any." Time is an issue for all of them as well, though in different ways, because there is never enough of it, never enough time for a decent meal, a good night's sleep. Even when they're in New York, where the orchestra is based. For there,

when they do get to bed it's at the end of an eighteen-hour day—
rehearsals, the studio, a radio shot, three shows. They all show the
strain. Whiteman tells Tram that Bix is drinking too much, but,
hell, they all drink too much, and you almost *have* to drink to do
this kind of work. Even Pops will get a skinfull when the studio
session's over or the air shot. "You should talk to him, Tram,"
Whiteman says. But Tram, who worked out the deal that brought
them into the orchestra, and Herman along with them, has his
own problems, his own family to worry about. "Bix is a big boy
now," he tells Whiteman and shrugs. And Herman, who shares a
suite with Bix in the 44th Street Hotel, can't do more than venture
an occasional sidelong admonition. "Jesus, Bix"—after another all-
nighter with the college crowd egging him on—"why not slow
down a bit and let em catch up with you?" And Bix: just a laugh.
Maybe an ambiguous head shake. Now when Herman comes into
Bix's bedroom to wake him for rehearsal he sees him reach for the
jug before he swings that first foot out onto the floor. "*Ooooh-
whee!*" says Bix, and shakes and shivers like a dog as the High and
Dry gin hits bottom and his darkening eyes pinball around.

Suite 202 at the 44th has the two bedrooms, bath and kitchen.
The lights are always on except when the maid turns them off. Bix
has a Chickering upright squeezed into his room, and if he isn't
on it, somebody else is, and so gradually the rooms on this floor
are taken over by other musicians and night owls while the respectable others have moved elsewhere. When the piano is silent,
there's the Vic in the kitchen, its velvet turntable spinning with
the latest recordings of Armstrong, Oliver, Ellington, or the
Enigma Variations.

When the orchestra's in town 202 is always overflowing at night,
though Herman has been able to insist they stay the hell out of his
room, even when he isn't using it. There are, first and always, the alligators, the college kids, most of them from Princeton where a

stocky trumpet player named Dickie Tanner has grappled onto Bix as the absolute greatest. Dickie knows where every baby grand is located on the upper east side and midtown; knows every penthouse where bottles of expensive booze can be had, and if somebody else doesn't claim Bix after the last show, Dickie's got him, and off Bix goes. Or they'll end up in 202, a boisterous bunch, faces red and smooth as a baby's ass, raccoon coats as soon as the weather permits, the girls dressed in the John Held fashion down to the last detail. They want to be able to say they were up in Bix's room, and: man, even way in the bag that guy plays more piano than anyone sober and Tom puked his guts and I had to clean up Bix's bathroom and Tom, too, and we didn't get back here till this morning, but what a gas! Also, the boys from the white bands: Jimmy McPartland who replaced Bix with the Wolverines; Jack Teagarden—Big T from Texas; Miff Mole; Don Murray; Benny Goodman, fresh from Chicago, who said when he first heard Bix, "Wow! What *planet* did this guy come from, anyway?" One morning out in the hallway a violinist boozily leans against Herman and confides, "You know, Herm, before Bix got here all these trumpet players sounded just alike. I close my eyes, I can't tell one from the other—O, except maybe for some goofy little lick. But then there's Bix, and those *bee-yoot-i-ful* notes of his, they just fell all over Broadway. Just *bee-yoot-i-ful!* Like stardust over all of us. And so now, see, all of 'em try to play like him—and they can't do it! Now, us violinists—we don't even try to copy him, and that's good, that's good. But, what I want to know is—where do those notes come from?" Herman's nodding, yes, yes, and turning the violinist around and giving him a quick nudge towards the elevator at the end of the hall, watching the man teeter off towards the bronze doors of the Otis, hands stuffed in tux pockets, still murmuring to himself about stardust.

A lot of the players are less articulate, but it's clear they feel something here, feel they're in the presence of a talent that showers light on them, and from what planet is it, anyway? Bix hardly knows most of them, and only a very few by name, but still they get the impression that he kind of understands why they're up in 202, and what he has up here is theirs: electricity, juice, setups, ice, the Vic, and the Chickering. All this and the diffident, wordless gift of his company, of the knockout chords he'll drift into on the Chickering when talk has run down like a watch and the sensible or the half-sober will have thought hazily about the hazards of the morrow. When they jam up in the suite Herman often finds himself sleeping on the sofa in Jack Fulton's room. Fulton's a tall, placid man who plays trombone and sings in the falsetto style that's as popular these days as the sobbing sax. He keeps regular hours. Or else Herman uses Crosby's bed because most nights Bing's down there whooping it up with Bix. Crosby's no musician: during production numbers like Rhapsody in Blue, Whiteman gives him a violin with rubber strings just to look like he's doing something on stage. But Bing's no fool, either, and like the others he knows he's around something special, and he's picking up tricks of phrasing and intonation from his friend, and the two of them are true heavyweights in the gin department.

So are McPartland and Mickey Walker, though both are physically middleweights. Jimmy likes to spar and so does Bix, and the two of them take to going up to Stillman's to hit the bag, jump rope, spar a little, though careful of their chops. They shadow box, and when they work up a sweat you can smell those juniper berries blooming suddenly among the resident smells of ancient sweat, leather, rosin, the secret unguents dabbed into bloody slits. It's up there they run into Walker who then begins dropping by 202. Walker's the middleweight champ, a body banger who's easy to hit, impossible to stop. His face at twenty-six looks it: thickening ridges over pig-eyes, lips stitched with scars, jaw like a bulldog. Still, Walker's no punchy palooka, is in fact mentally quick, despite the thousands of punches he's willing to take to get in on his man. While he hangs around it isn't clear to Herman or Jimmy whether Walker actually gets Bix, what he's doing—but how many do? Anyway, Bix doesn't care. Walker is clearly drawn to characters and to the high life, and in the bat-eared Davenport boy he's found both. He and Jimmy start calling themselves Bix's Boys, pretending they're his bodyguards who'll protect him from any imagined menace. They count Herman as one of them, but Herman has plenty else on his mind besides this postadolescent foolishness.

Walker's really in the chips these days, fighting regularly for big purses and knocking his opponents stiff, though occasionally his mob-connected manager, Doc Kearns, will insist he carry some stumblebum the distance. So it's no surprise when Walker turns up one night with three large, garish badges he's had made up: fourteen-K in the shape of a boxing glove and the legend, slantwise across, "Bix's Boys" and pins them on Jimmy and Herman. Then they're off to Harlem and Small's Paradise where Jimmy and Bix sit in. Bix insists on playing under Jimmy's lead, and since Jimmy is so much in Bix's style it sounds like Bix is playing duets with himself. Jimmy Archey's leading the house band this night, and so Bix gets that hard-hitting drive all around him for once, the rhythm section pushing the soloists to come up to *their* time, and Walker's pounding the table with his mallet fists, and the glasses are jumping and spilling but no one cares. Herman's glance keeps locking with that of a cocoa-colored girl in boa and skimpy skirt. She's with a party, but he can't tell if she has an escort or not, but he doesn't dance well at all and at Small's everybody out on the floor can really cut it, and so when he finally leaves with Bix and Jimmy and Mickey, they're still just lock-eyes, and the opportunity, whatever it was, is past him.

Now he follows the others into the dawn-blued streets—Bix with his cornet in its black corduroy case; Jimmy casually holding the Conn Bix has bought him, fingers wrapped in its valves. Herman's searching his pockets for the keys to the big Chrysler. On the corner at West 135th three guys are slouched against a building, hats low, hands in jacket pockets, clothes dark and baggy, eyes searching out from under those broad brims, catching the glint of Jimmy's cornet and making a swift, succinct assessment and pushing off from the wall with back feet to intersect quickly, lithely with the tipsy tread of Bix and his Boys. One reaches for Jimmy's horn with an arm that's like a wire cable in its sleeve, another spins Bix about and makes a grab for the black corduroy case, and the third squares up to Walker. Herman has never seen Jimmy work up at Stillman's, but now he understands that this is not just some tough-talking guy from Chi, for Jimmy instantly lets loose of the cornet, and the bandit stumbles back with his easy prize, but Jimmy's inside, quick, and *bam!* the guy's down, and the Conn goes *clatter-clank.* But Bix clutches the black cloth case to him—but only with his left—and his right is coming over the top in a clubbing, chopping swing with maximum torque, and Herman knows Bix has connected because he can hear the squish of flesh mashed against bone and see the man loose his grip on the cloth case at the same time Bix lets it go, too, and Bix digs a left in there somewhere, but it's probably superfluous because the guy's going, *"Unnnh"* on his way down. And then there's Walker, the Toy Bulldog as the writers call him, taking his man's best shot high on the forehead, enough to raise what proves to be a nice welt, then wading in, chin hooked into the padded shoulder of his powder-blue pinstripe suit coat, and it's too late for flight, and Walker paralyzes the guy anyway with a short left to the kidney, a pile-driver right high in the chest, and another right, a hook, that hits the guy's throat and his hat flies off and sails high in the dawn-blued air and rolls on its brim neatly around the corner into Seventh Avenue as if on an errand of its own. Jimmy's man is out. Bix's is trying to find out where his knees went. Walker's is stretched and making a bad gurgle. "Well," says Jimmy, theatrically dusting his hands, then stooping to pick up and inspect his horn. "Well, *that* was fun!" Walker grins at him and kicks at his man's upturned shoe. He opens his suit coat and pulls at his shirt, the silly, gaudy badge reflecting dully in the dawn. "We earned these, boys!" He looks over at Bix who's holding the corduroy case and looking from one to another of the sprawled figures. "I gotta say, kid," the Toy Bulldog says, "you can *hit!*" A couple of windows are going up across the street, and Bix says, musingly, still peering down, "I wonder what they wanted with these?" gesturing with his case. "Who gives a shit," Walker says, still grinning with pleasure and admiration. "They didn't get 'em." "I think we better get in the car," Herman says. "That guy doesn't sound too good." They move off toward the big Chrysler, and it isn't until well into the day that their hands begin to hurt.

That cinches it for Walker: he can't get enough of Bix. He begins bringing Doc Kearns up to 202, and Kearns is nothing but trouble with a mouth on him that begins to work overtime after a few belts. Then he thinks he can do anything better than anybody in the room—fight, sing, play the piano. He's well connected and up to a point entertaining. He and Walker like to take Bix over to Texas Guinan's speak where she gives them the big, brassy treatment: "Hell-o, sucker!" She sets them up with good whiskey at twenty-five a bottle. Texas is backed by the mob, of course, which ensures that steady flow of quality sauce, and one night Walker takes Bix down to Jersey to see just where she gets the stuff, watching the blinking running lights of the fishing smacks that have off-loaded, and then the cases lined up on the beach at Seabright. There the truckers take over, hauling the stuff up to Red Bank where there's plenty of police protection. When Bix tells Herman he's been on this run Herman only grunts and says, "Y'know, Bix, you're nuts." Bix just grins and shrugs. "What the hell, why not try it once?" he asks, and Herman wonders where the limits are for this guy, especially after Bix tells him one night that he's tried smoke, a denatured alcohol drink that has killed hundreds already.

When Walker's set to sail to London to defend the title against Tommy Milligan, Texas wants to give him a sure-enough Broadway send-off and gets Bix, Jimmy, Jack Teagarden, and three others to join a parade down to the Cunard Line pier. She lines up a dozen phaetons, stocks them with her showgirls and tubs of iced champagne. Then the gamblers, touts, Broadway sports, and newspaper guys get aboard—Ed Sullivan's there with Bugs Baer—and off they roll at eight on a fine May morning and nobody's been to bed yet. Manhattan's north–south streets are still shrouded in shadow, but the sun's shooting through the crosstown ones, and as the parade comes tootling along, heading down to the piers, it's like descending through a long shuttered hall of sun and shadow. Bix and Big T are standing to blow and there's a girl holding on to Bix by the belt so he won't fall out. Office workers and ad men and delivery guys stand on the sidewalks with open mouths so that the parade wails through a line of gaping faces, and Texas has to pull over every few blocks when a particularly incredulous one comes in view and hand out a bottle or three, and so it goes, down to the docks where they rumble to a halt under the booming black prow of the *Berengaria* that will take Walker and Doc across. The band spills out of their phaeton and falls loosely into ranks and they play Maryland My Maryland in honor of Walker who's slumped against Kearns's natty shoulder like a boy. Walker's from Elizabeth, but Maryland's close enough this morning, and there is more confusion than that down here just now because Sir Ramsay MacDonald, former and future British prime minister, is coming down the plank of the *Berengaria,* which has brought him to America for a goodwill tour. In his derby and morning coat and severely striped tie he looks down at his American welcoming committee and sees five lopsided bandsmen and a flock of high-kicking chorines and a blonde woman all in white and decked with pearls and jewelry standing on the hood of a phaeton and directing. The dock workers freeze—baggage handlers, stevedores—and the gulls are screaming at the brass and the

high-kicking chorines, and the suddenly insignificant official welcoming committee is frozen, too, looking up at Sir Ramsay and
then at the paraders. Until at last one of the committee hurries over
to Texas, standing on the hood of the phaeton and denting its dark
green hood with her heels, and hollers up at her, "Say, what's the
meaning of this?" Texas puts a hand to her ear, signaling that she
can't hear the question, what with the band, the gulls, the boat
horns. "What's the meaning . . ." The rest of the repeated question
is lost in the hoopla, and now the band's blasting Margie. "Meaning? *Meaning?*" Texas repeats now, turning to assess her splendid
creation, her heels biting into the hood. She pauses just a phrase—
"You are my inspiration, Margie"—then spreads wide her spangled
arms towards the city, its squared shoulders backlit by spring's sun.
"Why, Pops, there is no meaning!"

⋰⋰✦⋰⋰

But life with Whiteman's orchestra is no picnic—or parade,
either—and Bix's tardy letter to his folks hardly captures the pace
and pressure. Day after day they're in the studio where the orchestra does its last recordings for Victor, then has to turn right around
and compete against these for its new label, Columbia. Day after
day in the dead-air confines of Liederkranz Hall, feverishly laying
down what seems to all of them an unending cascade of forgettable
tunes, leavened only once in a while with some genuine material—
a medley from Showboat, Coquette, Victor Herbert's Suite Of Ser-
enades, A Study In Blue. And it's doubly tough on Bix because he
has so little to do on most of the arrangements. He waits back
there, lost in the brass, engulfed by the tuba, trying to stay alert for
the few hot bars Bill Challis has been able to give him. A bottle
stashed back in the can, beneath his chair, behind a curtain or an
instrument case. Time hangs.

On March eighth they have a night off and Bix goes to Carnegie
Hall with pianist Roy Bargy and Ferde Grofé, Whiteman's heavyweight arranger, to hear Ravel conduct a program of his own
works. Two days later he turns twenty-five and has forgotten the
occasion until reminded of it by Sis's cheery message, left at
the front desk. The next day the city's paralyzed by a late, heavy
snow, and there's no work. But the day after that the orchestra is
back at Liederkranz, slogging through When and I'm Winging
Home and Down In Old Havana Town, which they can't get right,
and by the third take the mood is sour, dispirited. Whiteman
drops the stick disgustedly on the podium and runs his hands
through his thinning hair. He calls up to Bix in the brass, "Take a
few on piano," and says to the others, "We'll break for fifteen." Bix
comes down to the bench, and Roy Bargy slides off, and Bix tries
to soothe things with an unfinished sketch from his midwestern
days, Crosby and a couple of others hanging over the piano and
one of them sticking a lighted cigarette in Bix's mouth as he chords
into something he's calling Cloudy. When Whiteman rumbles
back down the aisle he's got a tiny guy in tow in starchy suit and
collar, big head of white hair, aristocratic beak, darting eyes taking
in everything. Bix doesn't look up, continues to work through
Cloudy until Whiteman raps his stick. "Boys," he calls out, "I
want you to say hello to Monsieur Maurice Ravel." Bix almost falls
down getting away from the bench and back up to the brass. But
Ravel's presence gets them all up on their toes and they finally get
Havana Town right, Bix and Tram executing a pretty good chase
chorus through the last of it, and that's it for another day.

A line forms to shake Ravel's hand, and after all the others have
done so it's Bix's turn and he steps hesitantly forward with a sheet of
manuscript paper he asks Ravel to sign. Ravel's hand feels cold and
bony in his, but his smile is warm enough when he places the sheet
on the piano, signing it in a slanting, jerky fashion, and then it's just

the three of them left in the hall, Whiteman pulling on his suit coat
and asking the composer if he can drop him somewhere, back at his
hotel perhaps? But Ravel is evidently in no hurry to go anywhere
and cocks his great white head at Whiteman, still smiling warmly.
"Ah, you Americans," he says, slowly, "always rushing somewhere.
Such fantastic energy—California, Texas," his voice trailing off, his
hands gesturing to indicate the size of the country and its energies,
which he adds have quite exhausted him. "Everywhere I have been
so generously treated," he goes on, his gaze swinging from the massive Whiteman to Bix and back to Whiteman. "Such hospitality,
everywhere. Yet, I wonder." He pauses, still with his head cocked in
that quizzical, questioning attitude. "I wonder whether it would be
terribly impolite if I were to voice a small sort of complaint, *une pe-
tite plainte.*" Whiteman spreads wide his hands as if saying, "Anything we can do." "I wonder," Ravel says, "if there might be
anywhere here in your great city where I might have a quiet glass of
wine. Champagne I have had everywhere. Whiskey, which does not
agree with an old man's digestion. Gin. Yet a simple Pomerol—even
a Gigondas—that I cannot seem to get. It would be most agreeable." Whiteman looks at Bix who asks if Ravel can wait while he
makes a phone call, then sprints up to the lobby phone to call the
special number Mr. Big has given him. Mr. Big is the gambler
Arnold Rothstein who admires Bix's playing and told him so when
they met at Lindy's where Rothstein makes his deals late at night.
So now Bix reaches Charlie Lucky who runs booze and other things
for Mr. Big, and Charlie says it's no trouble at all if he wants to
swing by for some of the authentic French stuff, and how many
bottles does Bix need?

Outside, it's overcast and blustery, yesterday's snow in smutty
heaps against curbs and corners where the emergency force—eight
thousand jobless men, the papers say—has shoveled it. Bix hails a
cab cruising for rush hour fares, and he and Ravel head for a down-

town address where Bix pays for a brace of fancy-labeled bottles and wonders whether they really are the French stuff. Back in the cab and with the cabbie asking, "Where now, gentlemen?" Ravel says he suspects there may be people waiting for him at his hotel and would rather not see them just now, and so Bix tells the cabbie to drop them at his place. On the way up he can't think of anything to say, just sits on the edge of the seat, clutching the sack with its dubious contents. But the tiny Frenchman seems at ease with the silence, watching Manhattan rushing toward evening: hurrying men in hats and heavy topcoats; white-gloved traffic cops high on gleaming horses; movie marquees winking and a long line already in front of one advertising a show called "Wings"; long-hooded automobiles at every angle; a forest of flagpoles leaning out from the stair-stepped skyscrapers that are the modern city's last acknowledgment of its small-scale Dutch origins.

The maid's been in 202, and the place looks pretty good, the dishes washed and racked, beds made and folded cleanly back. The only bit of realism is the hunk of meat greasily reposing on top of the Vic's turntable, unaccountably overlooked—or maybe the maid thinks these young savages want it left there for some strange later purpose. Bix doesn't notice it, but Ravel does, drawn to the Vic to see what might be on it. When he sees what's there, he turns quickly to inspect a shelf where Bix has flung some books, taking down one called *John Brown's Body* and flipping its pages while his host fumbles with a corkscrew. Ravel takes a seat at the kitchen table with its hundreds of intersecting ring marks and the long, dark snakes of forgotten, dying cigarettes, and tries to put his host more at ease, speaking to his back of his American tour, so long postponed. Everything about America fascinates and amazes him, it seems: the gigantic cities; the skyscrapers; loco-motives like great fire-belching beasts; roads racing off into unimaginable distances and towards destinations with impossible, unpronounceable names—Ogallala, Waxahachie—; endless skies without dimension; the crushing roar of the falls at Niagara; the Grand Canyon. And California! In California, Ravel says to Bix's back, he felt the nearness of the Orient lying unseen over the blazing Pacific there on the beach at Santa Monica where Mr. Fairbanks and Miss Pickford held so touching a soirée in his honor—tall, flaming torches plunged into sand soft as sugar and an orchestra playing for the dancers on a platform surrounded with potted palms. And here in New York, too—so much of everything: the photographers and movie people clustering about him, the telephone ringing in his room, admiring bouquets piling up so that some must simply be placed outside in the corridor. Fantastic, all this. Ravel recalls his friend Delius who found such inspiration here, and thinks the problem wouldn't be any lack of sources but rather how to filter the staggering barrage of stimuli and find in it what you could truly use. Otherwise, it might be like the great falls—deafening.

In his nervousness Bix has broken off the cork and has to chip out the rest of it with an ice pick, but now he hands Ravel a tumbler, and Ravel notes the corkage floating on top but says nothing, nods gracefully, and takes a small sip. From the south-facing window he sees the darkening clouds hanging low over the stony skyline. "Ah," he says, delicately extracting a crumb of corkage with a forefinger's tip. "A good Burgundy at last. Nuits-St.-Georges, perhaps?" Bix mutely hands him the bottle, so relieved it's the real McCoy he doesn't notice the flotsam he's served with it. Ravel looks at the label, drawing down the corners of his mouth in approval. "Twenty-five," he says, looking up with a smile. "And at last a quiet place to enjoy it. I am grateful." He takes another small swallow. The young man at the sink strikes an odd, responsive chord in him and he wonders where it could come from. The nearest approximation is one of those wild young men in Paris at the turn of the century, *Les*

Apaches, but even making the association he knows it's gross because this fellow is so radically of this strange New World: earnest, eager, gifted in a special, narrow way; lost in this national stew of ferocious novelty and unharnessed energy. The profound precariousness of his situation, trying to express that special, untutored talent here, puts him oddly in mind of the movie actor who hung high above a vertiginous, concrete chasm from the hands of a giant clock. It makes Ravel want to reach out to him, to give him something, anything. And so he finds himself speaking of personal matters in a way he could never do in France. The tune he heard during the rehearsal, Down In Old Havana Town, prompts him to speak of the Spanish tinge in his own background, *Chere Maman's* gift from her Basque background. Someday, he remarks musingly, he means to make more of it than he yet has. Perhaps it might be possible to somehow write the Spanish sun itself into a composition. An amusing idea, at least. He speaks feelingly of his early teacher, Gédalge, who stressed always the importance of the melodic line. "That," he says, focusing on his eager host, "is what I find so agreeable in your own playing. *Vous êtes toujours, ah, dans le voisinage de la mélodie.*" He breaks off with an apologetic smile and translates himself: "You seem always to be there—in the vicinity, so to say, of the melody."

Bix smiles back, telling him his grandfather was always very strict about that sort of thing. "He hated what he used to call the 'chassers,'" Bix says with an ingratiating smile of explanation. "'Chassers'—that's how he said 'jazzers'—guys like me." Ravel nods, sympathetic. Sometimes, it seems, it is hardest for the older family members to understand our aspirations. It isn't quite clear to him what Bix's aspirations are, but he is certain that he's heard no one over here who sounds quite like him. He goes on to tell Bix he's been agreeably surprised by the quality of American orchestras. "You have many accomplished players," he says, "quite surprising, if I may say so, until it became evident to me that many of them were of the German background." He nods at Bix. "Like yourself. I think that purity of tone is so often German, though it is, to be sure, quite curious at that." He looks into his replenished tumbler, still with a few flecks bobbing on its silky surface. "I say 'curious' because I saw the Great War, and one would not have believed such a people capable of such bright, clear intonation on the brass instruments." He glances out the window into the bejeweled nightscape. "Life," he continues with a small sigh, "is full of such mysteries. You have it too." He looks up at Bix, cocking his head into that same quizzical angle he'd assumed at the hall when he wanted to ask for the wine. "Would you be so kind as to play for me?"

Bix is aghast, as he was earlier at Liederkranz when he discovered Ravel listening to him chording for the boys. A visceral feeling of naked shame instantly suffuses him and with it come indelible images of his audition at the Davenport Musicians Union back in '20 before starchy old Roy Kautz. He'd been in there with the other kids in Buckley's Novelty Orchestra. The others had all passed muster when old Kautz commanded him to sight-read a difficult and unfamiliar trumpet part and halfway through had rapped his stick on the piano and waved him off. He'd failed, miserably. And then Kautz had told him to go home and practice— *for two years!*—and come back to try it again. He'd sat there, useless instrument in his hands, eyes filling with hot tears of humiliation and remorse, and all the others looking at him. He'd let them down: without him, as they all knew, Buckley's Novelty was nothing but an amateur joke. Now, here he was again, about to be exposed as the faker, the imposter, the jazzer he is—only this time it's in front of one of his heroes, the great Ravel. He glares wildly around the silent rooms as if hoping to find help there, some of the boys, maybe, left over from last night—Mezz, Pee Wee—. Or even a gang of those faceless, nameless, evanescent moochers and goodtimers who crowded in here at all hours. Where the hell were they when he needed them? But there is only the courtly, courteous gentleman at the table, smiling expectantly at him, awaiting what has to be his gracious assent. "O, sure," he hears himself saying from far off. "What would you like to hear?" And then, "The thing's in here," walking woodenly into his bedroom and the suddenly spectral Chickering. He sits at keyboard, condemned, and glances helplessly up to find a Bellows print hanging crookedly and wonders how long it's been that way, and instantly his naked shame is joined by an angry bafflement as he wonders why he finds himself in this awful predicament. *Why* is his life so slovenly, disorganized, what were the lazy meanders that brought him to this moment, panicked and unprepared? Botched childhood piano lessons, compositions unfinished because he isn't competent to finish them, flunked classes, dismissals, dirty laundry piled like shameful secrets behind a hundred closet doors, socks floating in the sink until Herman raised the windows and finished washing them himself because he'd forgotten; the silly, shrunken tux he'd worn through the late summer of '26 until Goldkette made him buy a new one before they went into Roseland; the electric blue bowtie Hoagy had lent him and that he'd lost until he discovered it beneath a tangle of filthy shirts, one end of it stiff with ancient vomit, and he couldn't remember if it was his or that of some girl who'd snuggled up against him in a taxi, woozily asking for something. He looks at his hands, paralyzed above the keys, and wonders how long he's been sitting this way with his heroic guest waiting patiently, politely in the next room. He plunges abruptly into the opening parallel phrases of one of his unfinished compositions and then the third phrase that extends these, moving with uncertain tempo further into the piece, approaching that passage beyond which he hasn't been able to go. When he reaches it, he segues into Cloudy, trying to make it seem like a medley, if not a suite. But too soon he's finished, there's nothing more to play, and he dreads the return to the waiting Ravel.

Ravel has had his own struggle with Debussy, whose early influence on him was so strong that he'd had to live down the talk that he was merely derivative. "Ah, yes," he says now as the young man comes into the kitchen, cracking his knuckles. But he doesn't say, "Ah, yes, the great Debussy." He only says, "Ah, yes, I recall one of those from the rehearsal. Quite pretty. I think it might easily enough be extended." There's a pause, and then Ravel says, "But what I had hoped was that you would play something for me—on your cornet. You see, your tone intrigued me so." For an instant Bix has the hope he's left it at the hall, as lately he's begun doing, but, no, the damned thing is right there on the counter, cozily next to the sack with the wine. He steps to it, snakes it out of its case, regards its gleaming length, the suddenly arcane twists of its tubing, wondering whether he can possibly raise a sound out of it. He fumbles in his pocket for the mouthpiece, finds it, and turns his back on Ravel, reaching quickly into the cupboard for the bottle of High and Dry, pouring a slug, and whipping it down. Then he spins about on a worn heel, pointing the bell of the Vincent Bach directly at Ravel before lowering it a little, and Ravel's slightly surprised to hear a foot begin to pat the floor on the other side of the table: *pat, pat, pat-pat-pat*: the first two beats the more emphatic. And then the young man begins, and Ravel who has been so oddly drawn to him understands why. For into the room with its worn, rented appurtenances—sink, two-burner stove with nickel handles, ochre walls with music store calendar punched onto a nail and three months behind—into this anonymous and terrifically unpromising setting intrudes Wonder on a tone as mellow and pure as the big-bellied moon he used to see shining on the bay waters at St.-Jean-de-Luz when as a boy he sat up late with his beloved mother. Perhaps the tune is trivial. Ravel doesn't care

because for the moment he's gripped by what the player is doing
with it, weaving a marvelous pattern the Frenchman is instantly
certain is an immeasurable improvement on the original score—if
indeed one exists. The player attacks each note with the precision
of a Prussian bandmaster, hitting it squarely, definitively. You
might, Ravel thinks, almost march to it. But then, right behind
that precision, there's the mellowness, the moon-glow, and at the
ends of the notes just the slightest waver, as if the player wasn't
quite certain this was the right, the very best possible sound he
might have made there. So in the act of weaving the moon-glow
pattern there appears a kind of provisionality that saves it from
sentimentality and safety as well. It puts him in mind of his own,
half-forgotten diatonic improvisations, played so long ago for the
equally improvisational dancing of the dangerous young American, Mademoiselle Duncan, who frightened them all with her
wildness and who came to so sad an end just last year.

Ravel is fascinated to discover that the young man's fingering
appears to be completely wrong. He looks more closely and can't
figure out the relationship between the movements the fingers
make on the valves and the notes produced. Everything seems
backwards to him, or as if the player had heard in his head the
sound he wanted, then hunted along the valves and dark interiors
of his instrument's contours for the passageway that would give
him that sound, like a sort of miner, deep in the earth, picking towards some rich and undiscovered vein. At last, the player executes
a filigreed coda Ravel is sure has never been played before—it's too
fresh, too full of surprise—and then it's over. Ravel claps softly
three times while the young man wipes the back of his hand across
his lips with their scattered-looking moustache, staring at the floor
and not at his listener, and then with a soft deliberateness disengages the mouthpiece and puts the horn away. Only now does he
turn and smile boyishly at Ravel. "You see, Monsieur Ravel, we

don't play the real jazz with Paul. For that, you've got to go up to Harlem."

Ravel says quickly he'd like nothing better, that he's already asked to be taken up there to hear real Negro jazz, but no one has yet been willing. He tells Bix that some years ago he'd been so intrigued by a Negro musician in Paris that he'd written a blues movement into his Sonata for Violin and Piano. "It was just after the war," Ravel remembers, ". . . so very many Americans in the city just then. But this fellow played the woodwinds in an extraordinary fashion." Bix asks if he remembers the name. "*Bien sur,* yes, of course," Ravel smiles. "I shall never forget it; it was French: Bechet. But he could not read a note." Bix's face lights up and his shyness falls away. "Yes! Yes!" he exclaims. "We know Bechet! He's terrific. *That's* the real thing, Monsieur Ravel. If you liked him, you'll like what Ellington's doing up at the Cotton Club, for sure."

Later, as they're climbing into a cab for the ride up to Harlem, Bix spots Herman about to enter the hotel, leaps out, and talks him into coming with them to the Cotton Club. Ravel thinks he makes the young cornetist so nervous he needs company. The burly newcomer reminds the Frenchman of some trusted Alsatian functionary, the maitre d' at a brasserie, perhaps, and Ravel's pretty sure he has little idea who he is, and that's fine, too: Ravel is weary now of the ferocious lionizing of these Americans—though that may be what he came for. In any case, there's only sporadic, stilted talk as the cab leaves Manhattan's glitter behind, speeding up into regions where the lights are fewer and dimmer, but as they draw nearer their destination Bix begins to speak about Ellington and his band. Ravel thinks once again of what a strange country of violent contrasts America is—the blazing blue of the Pacific, the baked landscape of Texas, this huge metropolis, so divided by color you began looking now for border guards. And meanwhile this white musician here beside him, speaking with such enthusiasm and even affection about the Negro ones, when what Ravel recalls of the cherubic-looking Bechet is a growling, buzzing wail of profound suffering that could only come out of this very chasmic divide they now negotiated so swiftly, the cab heedlessly, effortlessly entering the black heart of Harlem.

The Cotton Club was originally Jack Johnson's idea and so was the choice of Ellington as the house band. But Johnson's been muscled out by the white gangsters Owney Madden, Big Frenchy DeMange, and their bunch and now serves principally as a greeter, standing at the door in a heavy-cut suit and the British bowler he loves to affect, massive, black as basalt, his gold-capped teeth glittering in the marquee lights that shower on his shoulders like powder. The old champ's perfect for the spectacle inside. He's knocked men senseless, fixed fights, done time for illicit activities with white women. He's dangerous, damaged, debonair, and so it's a thrill for mid-towners, out-of-towners, visiting firemen and their wives when Champion Jack doffs that bowler at the doorway and offers you the great, pink-palmed mitt that once crashed against the jaw of Jim Jeffries, settling the hash of the Great White Hope. It's just right for the Cotton Club, because inside the door Johnson holds open for you, you get the same heady mixture of color, crime, and high style. There's Big Frenchy himself in a conspicuously loud suit, sitting at a table just below the bandstand. And over there is the speakeasy owner Mexico Gomez, who once served as a machine gunner for Black Jack Pershing. And there's the gyrating dancer, Snake Hips Tucker. And Duke, too—he's part of the whole, artful package: brilliantly handsome, lacquered hair, moustache so perfect it looks like somebody drew it on his lip; French vanilla–colored cutaway; smile as ordered and white as the piano he plays with flashy hand flourishes. And up behind him and his sharp-suited band, Sonny Greer and his spectacular pile of percussive instruments—traps, bass drum, tom-toms, chimes, wood blocks, cymbals, Chinese gongs. Owney Madden bought him these, and so now every bootlegger with big American dreams wants to back a band with a drummer setup just like Sonny. And who knows? the way new clubs keep opening all over the country, there may still be room at the top with Owney and Scarface, Dutch and Bugs.

Ravel's been taken into a number of high-class clubs over here, but still he's astonished that there should be so huge and glittering a display as this, right out in the open—and in the Negro quarter, too. The place seats seven hundred on two horseshoe tiers, and everything in it has a high, uniform polish, from the greeter's gold teeth to the sound of the showers of the silver dollars flung at the feet of the waiter who sings at your table between sets, his tray balanced on palm, ceremonial napkin draped over his arm like a flag of state. The theme is jungle. Palms everywhere. Potted palms around the edges of the vast room. Palms painted on the stage curtains, on the cover of the program they hand you when Champion Jack shows you in. Also on that cover, in front of the palms, depictions of jungle men pounding out savage rhythms on tom-toms bigger than kettle drums, white-fanged mouths ecstatically agape. Savage women there as well, with ripe, bared breasts.

Duke plays along with all this, and his band formerly booked as the Washingtonians is now popularly called the Jungle Band. They play Jungle Blues, Jungle Jamboree, Jungle Nights In Harlem. But what fascinates Ravel, once he's adjusted to the visual assault of the place, is how the band talks through their instruments. Even listening to Bechet in Paris hasn't prepared him for such a full-throated, communal conversation. The players laugh, cry, worry, argue, scoff, banter, gossip, explain, wonder, grieve. He hardly notices Snake Hips Tucker and the long-limbed chorus girls who are all the same light bronze color as if issued by a machine. He feels he's listening to a tribal council and tries to figure out how this effect is produced, what its essence is, and the more he listens, the more he finds it isn't the leader himself, whose playing he finds colorful and stylish but ultimately ordinary. Nor is it the drummer, high in his shining, thundering authority. Instead the heart of the band is one of the trumpet players with his vocalized style, his growls and shouts, interjections and *wa-was*. He's where that unique sound comes from, flipping his mute back and forth so deftly he seems to the listening composer more magician or conjurer than musician. He asks about him, and Bix says that's Bubber Miley. When Miley isn't waving that mute, producing those growls and *wa-was*, he wears a diffident, even haughty expression, eyebrows slightly lifted, as though the disparities and contradictions of his situation are nightly impressed upon him as he surveys the black waiters, black dancers, white patrons scattering their silver over the floor. Ravel wants to know more about him, whether such an extensive, dexterous use of mutes is common in jazz music, and Bix tells him that very few can use them the way Bubber does. Most of the time, he says, players use them to disguise inferior tone. Only King Oliver comes to mind as Bubber's equal. But he stops there, deciding not to go on about the King, down there years ago at Lincoln Gardens on the South Side, the place stinking of urine and spilled beer, and the King with the plunger over his horn on the deep blues: on those numbers he could get down so low, so quiet, you could hear the dancers' feet gliding through the dust, through the dry, burnt husks of discarded cigarettes. Instead, he merely asks if Ravel wants a refill of the seltzer he's drinking, and when Ravel says yes, Bix signals the waiter and orders also two more of Madden's Number One Beer—vile stuff that Herman says Capone would never sell even in his crummiest dive. Bix only shrugs what-the-hell.

It's well after one when Ravel signals with raised brows that he's had enough, and Bix, watching for this and amazed at the old man's stamina and level of interest, springs up and asks Herman if he'll wait with Ravel while he sees about a cab. When he gets back to the booth, there's Herman talking with Big Frenchy. At a distance Big Frenchy has a kind of Teddy Bear look until you're close enough to see the merciless eyes set deep beneath Paleolithic eyebrows that would meet over his crooked pug nose except that Big Frenchy in some obscure gesture of vanity shaves the intervening space; and maybe it's for the best because with the eyebrows joined he wouldn't look merely colorful to Mort and Mabel from Minneapolis. He'd look positively terrifying. So this is a cosmetic compromise, like many other things in the Cotton Club.

"I made you right off," Big Frenchy's saying to Herman with Ravel still sitting in the booth, looking up at these American behemoths, fingers poised on his thin lips. "I made you from Chi, musta been, what, two years ago." Herman nods. He remembers Big Frenchy, too, from a big gangster get-together at the Metropole, but he doesn't say so. In this world it's often best not to admit you remember a man's face. So he merely nods and when Big Frenchy asks what he's up to these days, Herman tells him he's band manager for Whiteman. "And this," he says, turning to Bix, "is Bix—he's with Whiteman, too." Big Frenchy looks down at Bix, and a slight, sardonic smile comes on his face. "Whiteman and that guy with the French name who writes his stuff—they come up here, musta been five, six nights in a row. Sat right over there," gesturing toward a table right under the bandstand where a comedian is doing a number with a dog and a girl assistant. "Looking, listening, trying to figure out how Duke does it. O, I seen em. Did everything except take notes." Bix smiles up at Big Frenchy, open, disarming, spreading his hands slowly from his sides in wordless assent. "But you can't get down what Duke does," Big Frenchy goes on, the smile now shading into one of satisfaction. "That's stuff you and Whiteman can't heist. Can't be done."

He turns back to Herman, and Bix, beginning to get anxious about the waiting Ravel and the cab idling out front, looks to Herman to somehow wind this up and sees Herman looking easy enough, standing clear of the booth, and Bix can see too that his long upper lip is quite dry under the blue glaze of its heavy beard. "How's it suit ya, this band stuff?" Big Frenchy asks, "Okay?" "Okay," Herman comes back. "Okay. Still workin with cars, motors, still haulin. Long nights, short sleeps." "Yeah, well," Big Frenchy says, dubious, raising his voice through a laugh the comedian's gotten with the doggie and the girl, "you ever want to change your shoes, you found me here." The laugh begins to die. "You'd be surprised," Big Frenchy says, "good's the money is, how hard it is finding reliable people. Steady. I heard about you in Chi." Herman nods again in acknowledgment, and Big Frenchy sticks out his hand, and Herman, hesitating something less than a beat, extends his, and they meet in a clasp that regains something of its ancient signification: no weapons here. Then Herman says he appreciates the idea, and Big Frenchy turns away, presenting his wide back, bulging under its suit coat, and begins working a few tables on his way to his own table, right next to the stage, where he'll sit until closing. And then, while everything's being packed up and the mops and brooms come out, he'll play whist and pinochle with Duke and the boys until breakfast is served with the sun.

On the ride back down to Ravel's hotel the little Frenchman is huddled and silent, as though suddenly exhausted by the long night's dark dazzle, and neither Bix nor Herman wants to intrude with so much as a stray word. At the hotel Bix hops out to escort Ravel to the door where a sleepy doorman, slumped within his heavy braid coat, makes only a perfunctory gesture at his job. And then Herman watches an exchange between the composer and Bix, Ravel speaking earnestly and Bix nodding quickly, three times, and then Bix almost running back to the cab, and Herman's already told the cabbie the next stop's the 44th Street Hotel. But then Herman finds Bix almost glaring at him in the white, flittering lights, and saying, "Herman! Hey, Herman! Let's live a little!" And Herman, looking at that now-drawn, white-and-black face, feels something between a profound weariness with it all and a disgust with it, too, and says, "Aw, Christ, Bix, why not let it alone."

❧

Finally, in June, they're sprung from the studio for the summer tour, and at least it'll be a change of scenery and routine for them, even if it won't be much of a letup, because the summer tour's tough and the fall one lined up right behind it is a killer. Bix claims to the folks that this is the best damned orchestra in the country— a popular perception—and Whiteman intends to keep it that way by getting them maximum exposure. He's figured out that a yearly work schedule of around three hundred and thirty days is near the limit of what his boys can take, and that's what he's got them booked for this year. When they leave New York and Columbia behind, they play Minneapolis and then a long engagement in Chicago before they get a break, their only one this year. Then Pennsylvania. New England. Back into the studio. A couple of big New York performances to advertise the fall tour. And then they're off again on what the boys are calling the Monster, heading into the South, to New Orleans, and from there all the way into the West Texas dirt country before they begin a long loop back that will have them out until the middle of December. Four and five shows daily plus the radio shots.

At first, Bix can handle it. At the Chicago Theatre he's brilliant in the midst of the big, buttery sound Whiteman wants, and after a matinee there Armstrong surprises him backstage, and they leap into each other's arms, laughing. Armstrong's packed some weight on his short frame since Bix last saw him, and they laugh some more about that, Armstrong patting his growing bay window with both hands, reminding Bix that when they'd first met back in Davenport they'd both been teenagers, just growing boys, and Fate Marable, who ran that band on the *Capitol* steamer, worked his boys so hard you couldn't put on any weight and had to feed like a horse just to stay even. But Armstrong's a star now, out from under King Oliver's bulky shadow, and playing so hard every night Bix can see the chewed flesh on his upper lip beneath the sheen of the heavy salve Armstrong's been using. "From Monday On!" Armstrong shouts in his gravelly voice. "That number *killed* me! Your first chorus, man—so sharp. And the brass section, you leadin there!" He leans back from Bix, chins braced, teeth clenched in pleasure. "And that 1812—they ringin them bells, shootin off guns, si-*reens*, everything—but I can hear my man back there, just cuttin through—beautiful. Gets me here, man," he says, his face suddenly serious and poking his chest. "You really can hear me on that?" Bix asks, surprised. "Like a bell, daddy." They make a date to jam down at the Sunset after Bix is through up here, and it's well past midnight when he gets down to 35th and Calumet with a few of the boys, including Bing whose scatting delights Armstrong.

Armstrong's Stompers are in full cry before a packed house of the after-theatre crowd, a few black couples scattered about like stray grains of pepper. Armstrong's told the Sunset manager to expect Bix, but Joe Glaser isn't prepared for the five others Bix arrives with, and his hard, hooded eyes kindle briefly with resentment, but he gives them the best available table. Glaser's a pimp who's working his way up the ladder of the Outfit, and part of his job here is to do what he can to keep Armstrong happy because he's really packing them in and Greasy Thumb is making good reports to the Big Shot on how Glaser's doing with the Sunset. So he shows Bix and his pals quickly to the table, then gets back to his command post, because he's got a lot more on his mind than a few boozy bandsmen: the heat is on once again for the Big Shot, though this time it's coming from rivals, not coppers. Yesterday in Brooklyn four guys in a Buick hit Frankie Yale, Capone's longtime rival, while he was out for a Sunday spin, lacing him up and down with sub slugs, and when Yale's car careened over a stoop, one of the killers jumped out and made sure of him at pointblank range, then flung the sub into the face of the corpse. Naturally, suspicion's swung to Capone, but Capone's been conspicuously in Florida for some days, shedding bucks on the ponies at Hialeah and at Miami restaurants where he's all smiles and handshakes and lavish tips for everyone, cigar bobbing in those rubbery lips as he makes jokes, stuffing rolls of bills in the bodices of cigarette girls and singers. Nobody's seen Machine Gun Jack or the Killer for more than a week, though, or Scalise and Anselmi, either, and so maybe Snorky's sent them on an errand someplace. A siege mentality has once again clanged down over the empire here; nobody's moving or talking. When Herman tries Hellie's number at the Drake, where Jack has her now, there's never an answer. Joe Glaser and all the other soldiers are braced for trouble, and so it's a relief to Glaser when the last set's done here and nothing has happened, not so much as a drunk to toss. Now he can relax a little. He doesn't drink. His relaxation is to call for the cashier's count while the doors are bolted, a street watch is set, and the stacking and mopping begin.

The Stompers shed coats and collars and bottles are brought out. Armstrong's pianist, Earl Hines, drags over some chairs for the Whiteman boys while Armstrong rolls up a stogie-sized cigarette of what he tells Bix is his special New Orleans gold leaf, and when he blows out that first deep hit he grins at Bix and extends the thing in his direction. But his friend shakes his head and holds up a newly filled glass of gin. "Hoagy smokes that stuff," he tells Armstrong, grinning back. "He can play all night on it. Not me." "To each his own, man," Armstrong laughs. And then while the hooded-eyed ex-pimp checks the till against receipts, hunched at his table and oblivious to all else, the black scrubbers and sweepers and stackers move about their tasks, pausing often, wooden handles held in work-hardened hands, to watch these young men playing purely for each other, laughing joyously between solos, at the ends of numbers, shaking their heads in admiration at some high flight— Armstrong's pyrotechnic brilliance balanced by Bix's melodic mellowness—oblivious to the hood in the corner making the count, to the whole hooded empire of which this is a part, of which they themselves are the interchangeable, easily disposable parts.

How long this goes on, nobody knows and nobody cares either until Roy Bargy hauls up his watch and reminds the Whiteman bunch they have a ten a.m. show at the Chicago, and though no least sliver of sunshine is ever allowed to steal into the Stygian Sunset, they all know the sun's got to be up, and so Armstrong mops his streaming face and asks Bix what he wants to do for a last number, and he says, "Well, what about the old Tiger?" And off they go into Tiger Rag.

When his turn comes he thinks as he always does of Nick LaRocca's once-famous solo on the Original Dixieland Jass Band recording Burnie brought home after the war. Theirs had been a most musical household, sure—Opah, his mom, Agatha, on the piano—but nothing remotely like this stuff that spun off Burnie's record. And at first Burnie'd get sore because he played it so often: "Gee, Bixie, you're gonna wear the darned thing out. What's the big deal about it?" He couldn't answer Burnie because he didn't know, and shortly Burnie forgot about it anyway: he had a lot of catching up to do—girls, cars—and so let the kid wear it out if he had to. All Bix knew was that he needed to learn right away how to play LaRocca's Tiger Rag solo and so bought Fritz Putzier's beat-up little cornet and set about the task, sitting there in front of the parlor wind-up, the cornet tilted at the rug, playing the record over and over at slow speed, figuring out through trial and error how to approximate those sounds LaRocca made, paying no attention to how at slowed speed the cornet's notes wobbled off into comic distortion. Never heard, either, how stilted LaRocca really was and, amidst all the band's musical hijinks, how much more comical they were than they had ever intended. What he heard instead was what he thought the player was aiming at—a something apparently utterly novel, a music never played before, an approach to the unknown. Later, of course, he'd learned how derivative LaRocca and the rest of the ODJB were, how much they'd aped Oliver and King Keppard and the others who'd come out of New Orleans. Still later, when he'd been flunking out of prep school north of Chicago, he'd been exposed to another, much hotter, white band at the Friar's Inn, the New Orleans Rhythm Kings. "Forget LaRocca!" his friends shouted at him. "Forget the ODJB! You've got to hear Paul Mares and these guys! They play just like niggers, honest!" And they did, too. But he didn't forget LaRocca, would never, and so now, surrounded by real niggers who sound nothing like the ODJB or the Rhythm Kings, either, he begins his solo with a loving quote from LaRocca and doesn't care if his tribute sounds corny in this dark, racing context.

LaRocca means nothing to Armstrong. His models are Buddy Bolden, Keppard, King Oliver, and by now he's gone so far beyond any of them he's off there all by himself—as he is now as he follows Bix with thirty blistering choruses, spearing those high Cs, unwilling to let loose of the old Tiger, tearing it up, so that those grouped around him can only look at each other in wonderment. Bix doesn't know whether it takes a nigger to do this. He just knows nobody else has ever done it.

He doesn't sleep that day. Or the next, either, and the day after that Pops gives the band a week off, and he stumbles back to Davenport where he doesn't do much of anything. Plays some golf, a little calliope on the boat shuttling over to Rock Island. Goes to the movies where there's an air of disappointment now because they have talkies in New York, and suddenly the silents with their white-lettered captions look creaky, cumbersome, making folks feel rustic out here in the cornfields, and who knows how long it'll be before talkies get to them and they can actually hear Fairbanks and Vilma Banky and Clara Bow? He's not at all impatient for the talkies though, because he's always been more interested in what the pit band's doing—or even just the piano player, if that's all they have—than whatever's up on the screen. When his friend Les Swanson plays piano, Bix goes, regardless of the feature, because he likes what Les does, down there in the pit with just that little light to play by so he won't be a distraction to the audience. Les isn't anxious for the talkies, either. "This thing's going to put me out of business," he tells Bix with a shake of his long head, "me and a thousand other ticklers. But you can't stop progress, they say." The rest of the time he sleeps late, catches up on the news, reading the local paper and the *Des Moines Register* in the shade of the wrap-around verandah with the big oaks overhead, rustling lightly in the wind and making dancing dapples on the lawn. The Kellogg–Briand plan forever outlawing war is endorsed by Mussolini and Germany's Streseman. Somebody sets a new speed record for getting around the globe. In the most expensive presidential campaign in history Hoover and Al Smith are heading for a showdown with Norman Thomas as the dark horse. Bismark Beiderbecke rhetorically asks Bix and Agatha how anyone could take this Socialist crackpot seriously. Bismark keeps his collar and tie on at the dinner table, though as a concession to summer will leave his coat in the parlor. He reminds them of the foreign Socialist radicals of '19 and still subscribes to the policy promulgated then, S.O.S.: Ship or Shoot. "Thomas is a dangerous man," he tells them. "Times are good, and folks want to keep them that way.

Hoover will continue the president's policies, and that's good enough for us." Another day the paper says, "Federal Authorities Padlock Twenty-Three New York Speak-Easies," and Bismark reads the item aloud, then looks at his son over the top of the newspaper. "Is that all they do there?" he asks, "drink and dance?" Bix shrugs and smiles. "Seems like it, Dad, the way it comes out in the papers."

On his last day home he comes in off the golf course to find that a woman giving her name only as Lulu has called from Chicago. No return number. Will call back. Leaving, he promises to write often.

And he does write, finally, sitting in the enforced quiet of the hospital in Astoria where he's allowed to sit up an hour a day in a chair by the window. The sill's too high for a view, and so he looks at the sky a lot, making a game of guessing the time by the light: he's lost his wristwatch long ago, and here there are no clocks. His roommate, lying unseen behind the curtain dividing their lives, sometimes awakens and hoarsely calls out into the hallway, asking the hour, and sometimes gets an answer. He has some visitors, but they won't allow him many, and in any case the boys hardly have the time to get out here. Still, some make flying visits of a few minutes: Bing, Herman, Jack Fulton. Big T drops by with a flask, but he turns it down, and Big T laughs and says, "Another time, podnuh." Once, Whiteman himself shows up for a ten-minute visit, and Bix knows it's sincere and also that Pops wants him back up there in the obscurity of that third trumpet chair where he gives the orchestra a lift they're missing with him out here in his bathrobe. One day, no visitors, the building as still as if abandoned, he writes that letter he promised the folks long ago, describing in a few laconic lines that fall tour, the Monster, in the latter stages of which they might have caught him in Clinton, thirty miles from home, but only Burnie had come out, and maybe it was just as well, he tells himself, because by then he was pretty run down and not playing very well, and Pops, who'd been leaning on him heavily through the South, was now giving others his spots or else telling Bill Challis to write around him. Sitting there, his pen poised over the page at that point where he wants to tell them something about the tour, he tries to put it all back together and can't. Not all of it, not consecutively. But remembers how it began, anyway, there in Jimmy Plunkett's speak on West Fifty-third. . . .

❧❖❧

They've been in the studio all day, one of the terribly few days they have in town between tours, and at dusk he's drinking with Crosby who looks at him now with blue eyes glazed and says, "You know, my good fellow," gesturing with his glass, "you almost have to do this to stand it." They laugh, partly because they know it's true for them. And they have company: just down the bar Dorsey's knocking them back with some of the rhythm section. Around town the ads are out for the greatest Whiteman tour ever: two months, twenty-one states, plus Canada. It exhausts him just looking at these posters, their mindless, machine-made description of the coming ordeal. The kickoff's a Sunday concert at Carnegie Hall, and while Crosby talks about a number he'll do with the Rhythm Boys, his mind is on the fact that Pops has talked him into playing one of his piano compositions. But Bing rattles right along; he never seems to get nervous and certainly isn't cowed by the prospect of performing at Carnegie Hall.

By Sunday morning he's jumpy enough to be out on the streets with those going to ten o'clock services, slightly hunched, coat collar up, cigarette in the corner of his mouth. His eyes bore briefly into the faces of the circumspect churchgoers, as if searching for someone, then flick away: there's no one he can talk to about how

drained he's feeling, how much he's dreading tonight's performance and all the hundreds of others after it. Not Tram or Crosby
or Herman. He thinks about giving Don Murray a call out in Los
Angeles, but they've kind of drifted apart, and, anyway, what can
Don do for him? What can anyone do? He's alone with this. But
he knows Armstrong had seen how he was feeling in Chicago,
looking suddenly, acutely into his eyes as they stood there, holding
each other, saying their goodbyes in the morning sun outside the
Sunset, saying to him, "Why'nt you go home, man, get yourself a
shower. Get yourself some fresh clothes. Get some rest."

But it was already too late. Too late.

He finds himself standing outside Carnegie Hall, looking up at
the posters plastered across its broad, brown façade, fluttering in the
morning's chill, the stylized portrait of Whiteman with his ringmas-
ter's moustache and below the mouth the single upcurving line suggesting the signature chins that proclaim, "These are *good* times!
High times!" And he knows they are good times, that he's one of
the merrymakers who helps make them so. But staring up at the
fluttering posters of Pops that make the image seem to move its lips,
saying something incomprehensible, he feels a sense of Time that is
neither good nor high, just due, as if some spectral Meter Reader
were on his way to collect a bill, to tell him how much time and
youth and juice he's used up. And standing there outside this hall,
the seat of musical achievement in America, he thinks once again of
that moment when time ran out for him, and the bill came due for
all his excesses and shortcomings and he'd had to play the piano
for Ravel. Now he must do it again—same piece—before hundreds
in there. Whiteman's going to spot him after intermission, and he
wonders now with dulled amazement how it was he let himself get
talked into this insane exposure. When Whiteman had first come
to him with the proposition he'd asked for time to think it over, and
then when Whiteman came to him again he'd said he'd rather not.

"Nonsense, Bix," Whiteman said. "Nonsense. They'll love it, coming from you—a surprise, change of pace." Big smile of paternal reassurance, arm flung around his shoulders. "Tell you what," Whiteman went on, the showman thinking aloud, "if you're that nervous about it, we'll get Roy and Lennie to accompany you. You know, that might be a nice touch: three concert grands out there in front of the band." He gestured with his free hand, out toward the newly glimpsed future he had just created. "We'll set it up with Steinway," he said, giving Bix a hearty back-clap, moving off to other business.

And so he had: yesterday he'd gone with Roy Bargy and Lennie Hayton over to the Steinway Company, only a few blocks from here, to pick out the pianos they wanted to play. In the huge storage space, the instruments glowing darkly in the carefully muted light, they'd walked around, reading the cards atop each one announcing which artists had played it. While Roy and Lennie talked casually his fear lay coiled in his stomach like a giant anaconda. Finally, he'd settled on one Gershwin had played and sat down to riffle carelessly through a few phrases and then softly asked the others if they could once again go through the routine they'd worked out at a club over in Jersey. Bill Challis had helped him settle on a provisional ending to the piece he's now calling In A Mist, and with Roy and Lennie filling discreetly you didn't notice that provisionality.

A voice is speaking to him, and his eyes swing slowly from the posters to the sidewalk where a man his age is standing a few feet away while his cocker spaniel humps its body in the effort of evacuation. "Aren't you Bix Beiderbecke?" the man asks smilingly, ignoring the inconvenience of being attached by a length of leather to an animal from whose stub-tailed rear end a couple of magenta-colored turds roll silently onto the pavement. "I saw you a couple of times last spring up in Harlem, and, say, you were just swell! You sure don't have to take your hat off to any of those darkies." The dog has finished its business, and the man starts forward to shake hands, but Bix mumbles, "Well, right now I'm taking a walk," and turns abruptly away, leaving the man behind, staring after him and the cocker staring up at its master, asking what's up.

It's a sellout that evening, and Whiteman gives them what they've come for, a thoroughly pleasing pastiche of popular music that never asks too much of the audience and caters to their well-toned sense of themselves as sophisticated participants in these good times. The opening numbers are designed to warm everybody up and to reaffirm Whiteman's title as the "King of Jazz." Before the heavy curtains are scrolled upwards and the house lights dimmed to the tiny twinkles of far-off stars, jungle drums are heard, beating like blood. It's the beginning of a big production number, Yes, Jazz Is Savage, that takes the black-tie-white-gloved audience on a rapid tour of jazz from its primitive origins to its creamy domestication with the Whiteman orchestra and ends with a Dixieland spot where Bix has a hot chorus. Then Bix and Tram chase each other through Sugar, and then the hot unit does Tiger Rag, and by now Whiteman has them just where he wants them, where he can work with them, taking them through his orchestra's grand repertoire, constantly changing the pace, something for everybody and not too much of any one flavor: Gershwin's Concerto in F, My Melancholy Baby, Valse Inspiration, Gypsy, Ferde Grofé's symphony-style tone poem, Metropolis. After the break— cigarettes and cigars in the lobby and the gayer blades racing out for a nip at the nearest blind tiger—Whiteman features Willie Hall in a number he calls Free Air: Variations On Noises From A Garage. Hall is an eccentric genius, part acrobat, contortionist, musical inventor. Plain-spoken and retiring off-stage, in the spotlight he's a musical marvel, and on this number plays a fiddle behind his back and standing on his head; then Stars and Stripes on a bicycle pump; and finally Nola, played so fast on a slide trombone you'd swear he was using a valved version. The crowd's still laughing when they roll the concert grands out, and when the last chuckle has died in the grand hall and the new spectacle of the three pianos has begun to register, then Whiteman steps to the microphone and tells them in confidential tones that he's arranged a special treat for them tonight. He pauses for dramatic effect, turns slowly, and looks up at Bix. "You all know him as the incomparable hot cornetist he is," Whiteman rolls out, "the boy who lights the fire in our orchestra, who makes our tiger roar." He smiles, making reference to the earlier rendition of Tiger Rag. "But what you may not realize is that this young man is also a very gifted pianist and composer who's absolutely thrilled us so many times in rehearsal rooms and studios with his marvelous inventions. So I thought, why not share this thrill with you, our fans and well-wishers?" He turns once more to the brass. "Bix!" he calls, cupping hand to mouth, "Come on down here, boy, and share something of this with these good people!" And so now he has to rise to his cue and carefully pick his way down the tiers, telling himself through gritted teeth not to make a misstep, not hearing the boys cheering him on his way down—"Go get em, Bix!"

He remembers little of his actual performance. Remembers thinking on the way to the piano of something Ravel said to him as they said goodbye at the hotel entrance; remembers, when it's over, Jack Fulton's red, laughing face, his arm outstretched and blocking his attempted retreat back to his chair and Jack's mouth saying something. Remembers at last understanding that he can't go back to his chair, that he has to turn around. And there's Whiteman standing with one hand on the piano he's just played and waving him back with the other. And beyond that there's nothing but blackness, and he can feel the steady pressure of Jack Fulton's hand on his back, prodding him onward towards that nothing, and so he advances toward Whiteman who in white tie and tails suddenly assumes the aspect of a funeral director. Then Whiteman enfolds him in his bearish embrace, and he can see a little way beyond the footlights, can see the house on its feet, the white-starched shirt fronts, dark gowns, jewels, white-gloved hands. Those hands are moving, waving, but still he can't put it together that all this is acclaim, and he looks to Whiteman for directions but Pops is laughing, and there's a roaring around him, in his head, so that he only dimly hears as from somewhere high above and far off Whiteman's voice, "Bix! Bix Beiderbecke, ladies and gentlemen!" And then, just as Whiteman lets him go, his glance finds like a dowser's wand the great Rachmaninoff himself, there in the first row beyond the lights, looking up at him with an inscrutable fixedness. Back at last in the grateful obscurity of the brass, he lets Harry Goldfield turn the pages of his book to the next number, Rhapsody In Blue, where, mercifully, he has almost nothing to do, and then it's over, and then next thing he can remember is Herman down at Grand Central Station, giving him a hand up and he swinging up onto the car's corrugated metal platform and Herman down below, signing to him that he's got the cornet. A few minutes later the poker game's organized, the money's out on the suitcase that serves as a table, and they all feel the train's first spasmodic backward jolt, and they're off on the Monster.

Norfolk, Lynchburg, Greensboro, Greenville. Chapel Hill and a raucous college crowd, and Pops has to turn Bix loose here, with Tram and Bill Rank, because the kids are stamping and shaking the balcony and beginning to sail programs, hollering, "We want Bix!" And so after the break Pops gives them quite a bit of Bix, and he takes it and goes with it, plays well, and gives the balcony shakers and stampers a couple of upper register rips, and after the second of these Harry Goldfield says, "Where the hell did *that* come from?" But he only smiles and shrugs, and the balcony shakes even harder.

Winston-Salem, Charlotte, Ashville, Columbia, Augusta. Sunday
in Macon's an off-day, and that's a blessing because a number of
them were out all Saturday night and on this warm, overcast day
there are some queasy young men lying around the hotel. Atlanta's
next, and Herman's reading the *Constitution* aloud to an irritable
Bix who lies on his bed, pushing back his cuticles and feeling his
whole body—veins, organs, nerve endings—contracting in dry
deprivation. He needs to be stony sober when they play the City
Auditorium tonight and afterwards as well when Sis will host a
party at her home on the edge of the Georgia Tech campus. Herman reads to him about the rally yesterday in Madison Square Garden where more than twenty thousand cheered themselves hoarse
for Hoover and prosperity, and the candidate himself denounced
Alcohol Al Smith's prescriptions for the problems of Prohibition
and the farmers. When Herman rattles the pages Bix is about to
snap at him, but Herman unwittingly preempts this by exclaiming,
"Christ! I *know* this guy!" He reads about a federal Prohibition
agent shot in the back in a Chicago courtroom while waiting to testify. "He was on our payroll," Herman says, lowering the paper.
"Must've been getting ready to try the old double-cross. But, Jesus,
in the *courtroom!*" "That'll teach him," Bix says, dry, sardonic.
"What's bad for business is bad for America. You'd think he'd know
that much."

Chattanooga, Nashville, and the longer they're down here, the
more Dixie flavor Whiteman wants, and he has Challis adding more
spots for Bix and Tram and the hot unit. In Memphis Hoppy Evans
shows up at the Peabody where they're staying. Hoppy played banjo
in Dickie Tanner's Princeton band and wants his bride Nan and her
brother to meet the fabulous Bix, but Bix telephones down to the
lobby that he's too tired. His disappointed visitors are just leaving
the vast, ornate lobby with its central fountain where ducks circle
endlessly when here's Bix after all, with a test pressing of Margie, a

small band side he's cut with some of the old Wolverines gang. Good old Bix—never lets you down. But he looks worse than he'd claimed on the house phone: face puffy, color like green putty, breath bad. But they scout out a record player in the hotel and give the platter a couple of spins. Bix listens in silence, a sheen of sweat on his temples. When Hoppy's bride tells Bix how neat she thinks Margie sounds he looks at the record, stilled on the little felt turntable and cryptically replies, "Well, it goes around and around, anyway." And that's it. Later that night, after a supper of scrambled eggs only slightly scorched, Nan says to Hoppy, "Gee, honey, I don't think your friend is very healthy—or very polite, if you ask me." Hoppy waves it off: just run down, is all. "Hon, that's not Bix. We'll catch him at the winter house parties and you'll see what I mean: dynamite!"

Tram sees how the tour is wearing on Bix, but in Macon when he says something about taking better care of himself, Bix snaps at him: "Frank, if I'd wanted Agatha along, I'da sent her a ticket." And Tram would let it alone, except Pops keeps calling for more of their popular chase sequences, and these Southern crowds keep lapping them up. But he's finding he can't rely on Bix to play his parts the right way. Tram likes to sound jazzy, all right, and it was that sound Pops wanted when he came after him and Bix when the Goldkette band was falling apart. He wanted those hot spots to punctuate some of his heavily upholstered arrangements. But Tram has never been very comfortable with improvisation. His beautifully clear solos are all carefully worked out in hours of practice, and the chase sequences—Tram/Bix, Tram/Bix, a contrapuntal conversation coming to a logically satisfying conclusion in the melodic reprise—are things they've worked out over the years, the two of them in hundreds of hotel rooms, rooming houses, empty clubs, parlor cars, trying various triggering phrases that each will use to keep the conversation flowing, artfully disguised bits of a musical semiology. Down here, though, Bix isn't talking to Tram in any prearranged fashion, won't answer Tram's call or question, and when Tram shoots him a look above his horn's mouthpiece—where are we going with this?—Bix won't look back. Later: "What the hell, Bix? I thought we had this worked out." "Well, hell, Tram, I didn't feel that way tonight." Never any apologies, either, because Bix doesn't feel like apologies. He has so little space in this huge outfit, and if he can't keep even that. . . .

But Bix is enlivened by New Orleans, even the train's slow crawl into Union Station and the backs of the buildings along South Rampart, because this to him is like the Valley of the Kings in Egypt, home to the kings of the trumpet, Bolden, Oliver, Keppard, Armstrong, and his white heroes as well, LaRocca and Paul Mares. The very bricks of the station platform hum with music under his feet, and he has to drop his bags and stand there, head lifted, as if he's listening for blue notes on the slightly sooty afternoon wind.

The night before they open at the St. Charles the Godchaux family throws a lavish party for the whole orchestra at their home in the Garden District and Missy Godchaux's cousin Linda is visiting from St. Louis where she heard Bix several times and is utterly thrilled to find him here in the very house where she's staying. She pursues him about the living room, corners him, tries to peer into the long-lashed eyes he keeps lowered, his head nodding to her breathless gushes, smiling remotely, offering nothing, finally excusing himself to make a beeline for the sunroom where there's a bar amidst the lush and almost threatening greenery spilling from pots and planters around the ends of the room. "Hey, Bix," Harry Goldfield says, "what's with you leaving that cutie-pie back there? Some of us would like to have a little of what you're throwing away." Bix doesn't even look at Harry, only says over his shoulder as he steps to the bar, "Looks like Peaches Browning." "So what's wrong with that, I'd like to know?" Harry says to Bix's back.

The man behind the bar is a small hatchet-faced guy who answers to Snoozer and is a marvelously dexterous mixologist, as the boys like to style any bartender. He's also very funny and getting funnier by the minute as he introduces the boys to the wonders of the local drink, the sazerac. After a while, hearing the whoops of laughter followed by anecdotal hushes and missing more and more of his special guests, Austin Godchaux comes back to the sunroom and instantly understands the scene. "Edwin," he says simply, smiling indulgently at his bartender. "Ah might have known. Ah was saving Edwin for an after-dinner surprise," he tells the group, "but Ah see he has anticipated me. Well then, Edwin, suppose you favor our guests here with a song or two." Snoozer's hatchet face takes on a sharper edge as he grins, coming quickly around the edge of the little zinc bar to fetch a guitar from behind a potted palm. And it turns out Snoozer can play the hell out of that thing—blues, jazz, country dance tunes—and can sing a bit too and by the time he's done, Whiteman, who has several of Snoozer's sazeracs under his belt, absolutely must have him and offers him a job on the spot. That's okay with Snoozer who isn't doing that much these days except tending a little bar for the upper crust and hopping bells down at the Roosevelt.

By evening's end when Linda from St. Louis has definitely gotten the picture, Bix and Snoozer are chummy, and Bix says he'd love to hear some of the real hot Negro jazz. But Snoozer tells him most of the really hot players have gone north, to Chicago, to New York, a few to the West Coast. "Rest of 'em," Snoozer says, "have gone out with the shows, I guess—y'know, them little vaudeville things—medicine shows, circuses." He stops and thinks a moment, then adds, "Now, they *is* a hell of a band way out there in the western parishes—around Crowley, Rayne, in there. Now, that's a band y'all should hear. Kid Casimir, cornet player like yourself, he leads that group and that man can play above the staff higher'n a clarinet. I mean, he can play a whole god-danged *tune* that-a-way, 'cause I heard him do it once during Mardi Gras at a nigger joint over on South Rampart. See, I knew the clarinet player with him, fella named Lewis, and he tipped me about the Kid, and I went over. That's a rough place, the Astoria, but I had Lewis's name and I got in. But he would be worth your while." "Sounds like he's another Armstrong the way you talk about him," Bix says. "Listen, brother, he's better than Armstrong!" "There's nobody," Bix says soberly, "better than Armstrong." "The Kid is," Snoozer says. "Then I gotta hear him," Bix says.

Snoozer finds out where the band's playing and makes the arrangements: his older brother Tom will drive them out to Rayne after the St. Charles date and then on to Beaumont the day after where they'll rejoin the orchestra.

That night backstage at the St. Charles he's filled with the prospect of catching Kid Casimir but makes a big mistake with LaRocca and Mares who've come to see the boy they remember from Chicago days when he'd show up on the lam from school, his battered little cornet in a paper sack, politely but persistently asking them if he could sit in. Now here he is in tux and boiled shirt, a featured member of the Whiteman orchestra. They're delighted and he's thrilled, and it's skittles and beer until he asks LaRocca about this Kid Casimir, and LaRocca leans into him and asks, "Who?" and he repeats that name and compounds what he doesn't yet recognize as a mistake by adding that a friend claims the Kid's better even than Armstrong. Mares drops out here, stepping back in the little cubicle Bix shares with Min and Rank and Tram and sets his eyes on LaRocca who's in a three-piece suit with pearl stick-pin and looks a lot more like a solid businessman than the musical revolutionary who touched off a national craze. "Who did you say? *Armstrong!*" he spits out, "that nigguh!" And now of course too late, Bix sees the mistake and it can't be taken back, retracted: it's out there where LaRocca can savage it with the wormwood of his scorn, and it's nigguh this and nigguh that and the nigguhs who stole the ODJB's material and aped his hot licks. Nigguhs who couldn't play real jazz but get all the credit for it up North where all the nigguh-lovers live, and if they're so almighty happy with all the nigguhs from down here who went up there, that's jake with him. They can keep 'em and raise their half-nigguh children and listen to all that mongrel music made by monkeys and baboons. And Bix must simply stand there in front of his old hero, listening, and once he looks over LaRocca's shoulder at Mares, and Mares just looks back at him out of that pudding-plain face, and he knows there's no help there, but then he finds in the very midst of this spittle-flying solo of LaRocca's that he's more determined than before to get out to Rayne tonight to hear the Kid and while thinking this finds LaRocca almost out of nigguhs and concluding, "Nevah hoid of him—the nigguh."

Then he's in the blackness of the speeding coupe that slides a little when Tom takes it into a gravel curve with the dust pluming white and unseen behind it and Snoozer passing the bottle of clear liquid back to him, saying, "We like to be the only white folks in this hall, y'understand. But I know Lewis and it'll be fine. They'll look at us funny-like and this late there might be a buck or two that'll look ugly, but it'll be fine and you won't believe this Casimir. Lip must be iron." Tom isn't saying much, is concentrating on the wheel and the loose roadbed under the Ford that he hasn't paid off just yet but soon will because now he's a fishing and hunting guide for the wealthy of New Orleans and Baton Rouge, and there seem to be more and more such folks these days and more and more spare money around and already within this past year he's raised his rates higher than he would ever have dared before, and still nobody has said no, and soon enough, maybe by year's end, he'll have this snazzy rig totally paid for. And so he wants to watch it on this run to Rayne and only once in a while takes a hit of what brother Snoozer is passing around. Later, when they get out to Rayne, he intends to unbutton his collar and have himself a few good ones while listening to this guy his brother is so ginned up about. Tom appreciates musicianship even if the man is a nigger and was once a fair country picker himself until he caught two fingers of his right hand in a trap eleven years back. He sees a sign that flits past in the yellow glare. "Broussard," he says over his shoulder. "Be there within the hourah."

But in Rayne they can't find the hall despite the directions Snoozer's gotten from Lewis the clarinetist. Everything is wrapped in an impenetrable shroud of obscurity. A midnight fog lies on the low fields of cane and corn and rice. No street lights in town, no shop lights left burning, very few lights showing in the huddled, dark-wood houses. Nosing blindly about the dusty streets, they see the intense yellow-white glow of a kerosene lamp, but when Snoozer gets out at the house to ask directions he hears a low growl from inside and something heavy flings itself at the door, and Snoozer decides from now on he'll ask his directions from the safety of the Ford. The only thing they hear in the streets is the sound of their own tires rolling slowly through the dust. Here might almost be a city of the dead, the inhabitants smothered by some unnamable blanket of pestilence. Then their headlamps pick out dim forms down at the end of a street and they see a few cars and trucks, some carts with tethered mules and then a huddle of figures that seem spectral, animate condensations of the fog and dust and deep night, drifting about in the road before a long low hall from the windows and open door of which light spills weakly and is quickly swallowed, blotted. Caps, straw hats, mattress-ticking coveralls and denim ones, some held up with a single strap, flannel shirts, singlets, the bright print of a woman's dress flung defiantly against the enveloping gloom. "We're too late," Bix says as they get out and approach the figures.

"It's over." "Can't be," Snoozer comes back. "These guys go till the rooster crows."

Intruders, they walk through the slowly parting figures to the low gallery of the dance hall. A few murmurs: Cap'n, Boss. But nothing else and when they see the instruments on the empty stand—cornet upright on a chair, trumpet brown with tarnish and age, Lewis's clarinet—they get the picture, and then Snoozer spots Lewis himself coming from across the road and he's coming fast and sees the three white men but barely pauses as he comes past them and into the long narrow hall with its unhoused bulbs burning overhead and then stops abruptly and faces about, looking not at the white men but back into the blackness across the road, the spidery figures of one hand raised to his lower lip, poised, listening for something, until Snoozer speaks to him and he swings his gaze over them, not seeing them, but muttering, "Trouble. This is trouble." "What is?" Snoozer asks. "I don't want no part of this," Lewis says in answer and his eyes are wide behind his rimless spectacles and he turns from them toward the bandstand and walks quickly to it and climbs up and picks up his instrument and sits down as if defending a position. Then here come the others, and standing just at the door Bix gets his first look at Kid Casimir who wears a rusty box-back coat such as has not been seen in New Orleans in twenty years and a collarless shirt and high-buttoned shoes. The Kid's very dark, a powerfully built man with a bullet head and sloping shoulders that fill out the box-back coat. Maybe he's thirty-five but it's hard to tell and he looks worried too—they all do, the other horn players talking in quick, tense cadences into the Kid's ear as they mount the stand and grab their instruments. The piano player is last up and sits down quickly in his chair and rolls his eyes at the horn players while the dancers surge back into the hall behind them, blinking under the white bulbs with their mysterious wire guts plainly visible.

The crowd gives the white men a wide berth as though they too were incandescent and Bix, standing at the door, is thinking they should get out of the way, move back against a wall when there's an explosion of noise and two shouts from just outside on the gallery and then a man is flung backwards into the hall, falling among the dancers, and another man, the one who has flung him, is in the hall, striding down its middle, dead-on toward the stand, but instead of mounting its side steps as the players have just done he vaults with feral agility onto the stand and Kid Casimir sees him coming and starts to rise from his chair, cornet in one hand, but he isn't quite quick enough, and the man's hand shoots out like a cobra striking, grabbing the throat in the collarless shirt, jerking the Kid upright while the other hand swings across in a short, brutal backhand chop, and the Kid's saying something that sounds like Gilbey or Gilkey—something like that. But whatever it is he doesn't get it out because the backhand blow cuts it off and the Kid might have fallen back, except the man has him in his grip though the Kid's chair spins away like a top and the others are already lunging out of the way. And now the man's free hand dives into his waistband and comes out with a long deer-handled dirk, and seeing it suspended above him, its long gleam caught and held by the lights as if it might be forever, the Kid spins out of the man's grasp and leaps from the stand, but he's still not quick enough, though by now it's clear this is a mortal matter and the man leaps almost with him, grappling onto the box-back coat, slipping off onto the floor, then like a jack-in-the-box instantly upright again and racing through the sea of parted and astonished dancers to catch the Kid just short of the door. And then the right hand arcs high in its fatal geometry and the dirk swings down, slicing through the yellow air, slamming into the rusty box-back coat with the sound of a hammer hitting something hollow. And now the Kid looks into the eyes of the white man standing just there at the doorway, the white man's moustached mouth parted in silent exclamation, and the white man looks back, sees in that flashing instant something enter those dark eyes that was never meant to be there, and the Kid says softly, almost meditatively, "O my!" and makes it out onto the gallery, grabs a post and swings all the way around it so that he's coming back towards his assailant. But the man's unarmed now because his dirk is buried in the Kid's back, and he runs right past the Kid without touching him, back across the road and into the impenetrable obscurity. And the Kid runs too, first as if to follow his assailant, then like a football player in a broken field, veering off down the road towards where the white men have parked the Ford. Bix hears Snoozer at his elbow, "Run! Run! This is bad!" And he does run, and so do all the others in the hall. Shouts. A woman's high wail. And then the clustered herd of footfalls hitting the road's deep dust, and he's separated from the brothers, on his own in the midst of dark and fleeing forms and quickly loses direction, running down a side street, then into an alley of sheds and stables where he hears the occasional slow stamp of hoof, feels the heat of invisible horses, mules; smells the warm, blanketing scent of alfalfa, the sharp sourness of grease from an emptied crank case. A dog darts out at his leg, white ruff, white eye, and he breaks stride to evade it, becoming in that instant one with that other runner, cornet player, who several blocks away dodges nothing, running brokenly until he sees dimly whited railings and porch posts and heaves himself up a few steps to flop face forward on the dark boards and lie there breathing deeply, thinking it was lucky Gilbey somehow missed him with that pig stabber because he feels nothing now, only the sort of enveloping sweet numbness he's known after sex and within this thinks of his horn back there in the hall and wishes he'd thought to grab it. Maybe one of the others would bring it to him. . . .

And if any of the startled occupants of this house on the porch of which the Kid now lies drifting into dream had dared to look out to see what had so shaken them out of their own dreams, they could have seen little more in the lightless night than a dark shape heaving on the porch boards. For it is so dark they could not even have seen the dirk standing straight up nor the even darker substance seeping slowly over the boards as if it too might be a dream. And tomorrow, after the police have hauled the stiff off to the morgue in the horse-drawn wagon, they will find on those boards a broad stain oddly resembling a photographic negative of a human torso and find also that they cannot efface it, not with soap and hot water, not with lye, not with anything, so that no one can sit there in the fall's last twilight hours sipping a cooling drink, fanning; no kids play their games of jacks and tops. And the porch inhabited by this nameless stain will become a waste spot, until with a weary dread they rip up that portion of it and lay down a section of new pine.

And across the town, in the alley, the other runner, Bix, is heaving too and seeking rest on some porch and so at last blunders through the gate of a picket fence and into the backyard of a house where he totters past a little brick smokehouse and then around the corner of the house itself to fling himself, panting and wet to the waist, on the silent, shadowy steps, hearing the thunder of pulse in his ears and then the distant clanging bell of the police wagon and a few confused, muffled shouts. Then even these die away and the pulsing pounding in his ears fades like drums moving off into the dark distance. Lying there unreckoned minutes he begins to consider how he might rendezvous with Snoozer and Tom and get away from this place of death.

There is the creak of heavy rope on metal. His head snaps up. He sees the blurred, partial outline of a figure sitting above him in a porch swing. It wears a broad-brimmed hat and a heavy coat or maybe a blanket over its shoulders but he can't be sure which. He stumbles backwards, away from the steps, hands held out imploringly toward the figure. "Sorry. Sorry." Breathing heavily again, the new sweat of fright popping out all over him. But neither sound nor further movement from the figure in the swing. He is about to turn and run back the way he's come when a voice asks, "What do you want?" "Just had to get my breath," he brings out. "Sorry." "Everybody needs breath," the voice low, velvet-lined, a woman's. Then a long silence in which he stands irresolute. The swing makes a slight creaking movement. "Come closer," the voice says and hesitating he takes a couple of tentative steps back towards the porch. "Come closer." At the bottom of the steps and staring up into the denser darkness of the porch's overhang he stops, then moves up the first two steps hearing them moan under his weight. "Give me your hand," the words measured out with intervals, the voice even, velvety, calm in its cadence. He makes no move. "Hold out your hand," the voice says again, but he can't make himself do so, his hands locked at his sides, staring bug-eyed at the unmoving shape in the broad-brimmed hat only one half of which he can truly distinguish. Then he says, "Sorry," once again, turns about and in shuffling half-trot goes back through the yard with its smokehouse and into the alley, slowing to a walk now though he feels he ought to run but can't, looking anywhere for light and finally after a sequence of dark gropings sees some lights and finds himself at the Rayne train station with its freight wagons and empty waiting room and the ticket window so barred and final-looking it seems it had never been opened: no passage out.

In morning's swimming autumnal light this is where Snoozer and Tom finally find him, stretched out along the rough planks of the waiting room's table—its single piece of furniture—hands tucked under his armpits for warmth, for comfort. And not a block away in another sort of waiting room lies the Kid on an equally rough bier, mouth slightly ajar, hands rigid along the seams of his twill pants, slugs weighting his eyelids. When the brothers jostle Bix awake he can't place the faces that lean over him, wavering, billowing as though he were a diver looking up from the deep.

Later, in Texas, where he rejoins the orchestra, he decides after some days of thought that he needs to tell somebody about this and picks Crosby. But before he's well launched into the narrative he sees a shawl of incomprehension come down over Bing's smooth face, those mild blue eyes retracting slightly and at the same time hears his own voice, distant, rambling, inconsecutive. It's all come out wrong somehow, like a solo that begins in the wrong key, but he can't figure out how to fix it and so stammers finally to a stop. Bing pours out a drink for him and tries to frame a question that will seem both polite and interested. "Let me get this straight," Bing says. "You say there was a woman who *wanted to hold your hand?* What the hell." "Forget it," Bix says shortly. "Forget it. Doesn't make sense the way I tell it." Later, after he's swung up into his berth and the train is swaying on through the night, he tries to put it all together, tries to find out where, at what precise point, his telling of it all took a wrong course. He decides his motive in speaking of it has been to distinguish between dream and real life but he can't. Somehow this seems to him terribly important. Of course, there is no point in asking Snoozer.

Houston after Beaumont. San Antonio. Abilene and Hardin-Simmons, the beginning of a ten-day bat that starts when the Jazz Hounds, the tiny campus jazz club, surprises him, disarms him, serenading his steps from the little brick hotel on the main drag as he comes out with the others to go over to the auditorium. They've rumbled up in a couple of convertibles with hand-lettered banners proclaiming their undying allegiance to him and across the hard-packed dirt street they're lined up playing Jazz Me Blues and a pimple-faced kid takes his solo note-for-note, eyes big behind the bobbing bell, face purple with exertion, over-blowing in admiration. How then can he refuse to jam with them after hours and one of the group—they all know his habits—is tight with the local bootlegger and has on board a couple of bottles of serviceable corn and tasting it, he's whirled back to the two sisters and their buried bottles in the cornfield back of Hudson Lake in '26 and one of the kids says to him with a leer and a wink, "Once you get by the smell, you got 'er licked." Ha, ha. So that he ends up playing horn with them until his lip is numb and then switches to piano, soloing a little but mostly comping behind their solos. And they play until morning when he jauntily steps out onto the dry late-fall grass of the quadrangle (even if he's hardly feeling so jaunty inside), tux jacket casually draped over arm, corduroy case in hand, and bids them a soft, polite goodbye so that he can catch the 6:43 to Waco where they'll play the Cotton Palace and Pops will spot him once again on In A Mist; leaving behind in Abilene a fragment of the legend-to-be: "Listen, I *knew* Bix, *played* with him." "Bullshitter!" "No, it's really true. Nineteen-twenty-eight: he came through here with Paul Whiteman and stayed up all night with us and caught the train out next morning. Honest."

Dallas. He can't recall Dallas nor Wichita Falls that much. Wichita Falls is Election Day and none of them can vote from here but Crosby has had the foresight to lay in a couple of pints of gin because, so he tells Bix, Edgar Allan Poe got drunked up on Election Day some years before, voted twice, and so forever spoiled what otherwise would be a perfectly good holiday. Bix has never voted but mumbles that Al Smith has his vote. But the papers that day are as much filled with stories of gangsters and the roaring stock market as they are about Hoover and the Happy Warrior: a member of the Birger Gang in downstate Illinois pleads guilty to killing a policeman; rival gangs shoot it out in broad daylight in

South Philly; Arnold Rothstein, who once took a shine to Bix, lies near death in New York, shot in the belly at the Park Central but refusing to name his assailant. "I'll take care of it myself," the papers have him saying. And the market, sensing a Hoover victory, is poised for a stampede of the bulls with crude oil leading the way.

Oklahoma City where indeed oil is king. Norman and the college crowd again, though this time Pops is ready for their boisterous demands and gives them Bix in the opening number. And he's up to it too, sensing them dimly out there, their adulation, rising for the sixteen bars of That's My Weakness Now that Harry Goldfield's been taking since Abilene. Tulsa. Tulsa provides all of them two years of laughs because the next morning he's jostled by Herman who has his hands full of responsibilities, has to collect the fleet of cabs that will deliver them to the station, pay the hotel bill, see to the luggage and the instruments. Herman doesn't have the time to nanny him down to the station; best he can do is what he does: wake him, get him on his feet, find the horn and see to it.

They're all down there in the chilly dawn, standing slump-shouldered, bleary-eyed on the soot-blackened bricks of the platform, the train making up, Herman standing by a high-wheeled baggage cart talking to the black men who will push it, one of them already behind the long iron-heavy tongue; Whiteman not looking too good himself this morning; Herman glancing around, wondering, where the hell is he, and, I can't manage this band and him too and beginning to think he might ask Jack Fulton if he's seen Bix since Jack has kind of been taking on that duty lately. Then here comes a cab, smartly braking, rocking back on its haunches, and Bix rolls out and hands the hackie something without waiting for change and Gladstone in hand marches with long, uncertain stride toward the train, not looking at any of them and though Roy Bargy calls, "Hey, Bix!" he doesn't so much as glance over and the porter hasn't even got the footstool down yet when he grabs the hand-smoothed iron of the handle and climbs the four steep steps and disappears into the interior, and Bargy finds Herman's eye and they sign their relief. And inside he's walking with that same stiff-legged stride through car after car, eventually walking out over black bumpers and into open air and on into another car and its compartment of startled porters with their brass-bound caps off and waiters and cooks with their mess jackets unbuttoned, and when they see who it is the alarm and irritation quickly die out of their eyes because this is after all a white man carrying a grip. And he walks on until he feels he must have come far enough and slides the Gladstone under a seat and with grateful sigh sinks down and awaits that premonitory jerk which when it comes he doesn't feel, this train separating from the one he's just walked all the way through, pulling away, heading southeast toward Muskogee and Sallisaw while the other train, the one with the band aboard it, gets ready to haul northwest for Ponca City.

At Highland Park the conductor shakes him, asking for his ticket, but all he mumbles is, "They have it—the band." "Mister," the conductor says again, shaking him, "Mister, there ain't no band on this train. I gotta have that ticket now or you gotta get off." He pushes his fedora off his nose, rubs his face angrily, unable to get it straight: *why* isn't the band aboard if this train's heading for Ponca City? And it's then that the conductor is able to assemble it for him, that he's walked all the way through that Ponca City train and taken a seat on the Muskogee/Sallisaw one and the next stop is Broken Arrow and, "Mister, I have no idea how you can get to Ponca City this afternoon." He's still asking that plaintive, hopeless question, asking it with increasing urgency of the railroad personnel and the loungers at the Broken Arrow station, a rumpled city slicker, hat cockeyed. Until finally one of the loungers takes a crusty kind of pity and says that if he could find Buddy Harlowe, maybe Buddy could fly him up to Ponca, because he has a Curtiss

Jenny, and there are some sniggers at this because Buddy's a half-
Osage and a full drunk, though he does indeed own a plane,
bought with money he got when oil was discovered on his family's
allotment. But where in hell would you likely find Buddy this time
of day? But they do find him, since by now this has become an ad-
venture and several of the loungers have taken a kind of liking to
the young man who seems so desperate to get to Ponca, and most
of them have heard of Paul Whiteman and are intrigued that there
should be amidst them an actual corporeal emissary from that fabulous invisible world the sounds of which are brought to them all
the way from New York City. So while Bix shyly answers their shy
questions about what goes on in a radio studio they drive him the
eight miles out to the Harlowe place—cabin, outbuildings, corrals,
some grazing horses that don't lift their heads as the car boils up
and the plane off by itself in a cleared space. Mrs. Harlowe might
be full-blood with braids and a bit of vermilion showing, tall and
slim in flannel shirt and jeans, bending over a huge smoking kettle
out by the corrals. She simply looks at them a long moment when
they pile out, then waves them toward the cabin, and inside it they
finally excavate Buddy from beneath a pile of blankets and burlap
sacking and when they dig him out and set him upright, red of
face, nose flanges shining with grease or sweat, and explain their
errand he scratches through his black hair cut white man's style,
and says, yes, he'll do 'er—for forty bucks. And when Bix says,
okay, the others look at each other and think maybe it might not
be that bad to be an Indin—if you've got an oil well under your
house and an aeroplane in the pasture next to it. And at least one
of them thinks, and not for the first time either, that it might be
kind of fun to saddle up Buddy's missus and watch them braids
bounce a bit.

   This morning both Buddy and Bix could badly use some hair of
the dog and providentially Buddy has some on hand. And so out

on the strip with the wind lashing the red grasses Bix sits on one of
the rough chocks Buddy's kicked away from the plane's wheels,
drinking carefully enough from Buddy's bottle while Buddy checks
the engine. Then Buddy motions him to the plane and he clambers
up on the wing through the maze of piano wires and into the little
seat in front of the open cockpit and Buddy sets the spark, then
grabs the wooden propeller and gives it a mighty downward yank
and it catches right away and he runs back to kick the other chocks
away and by now the plane's skittering slightly like a nervous horse
on a tight rein and Bix, who's never flown before, begins to wonder
whether his first flight is going to be a solo. But Buddy is quick and
agile and is up in the cockpit now and working the levers and then
is taxiing over the rough stubble and turning so the wind's behind
them. He waits a moment, feeling the wind lift the tail, then guns it
in a long, teeth-rattling rush back down the strip and then the
ground falls steeply away and Bix can see the plane's shadow de-
taching itself from the ground and Buddy has the nose up and then
makes a tight turn and they sail over the cabin and corrals and
horses, and Mrs. Harlowe looks up, shading her eyes, and Buddy
wiggles the wings and they're off to Ponca. Just short of there the
bottle's about done, and Buddy has the last gurgle and flings it
through the air. Watching it flash downward with the sun catching
its spinning sides, Bix wonders if it might conk one of the cows
they can see in the dry pasture beneath them but guesses he'll never
know because they've already flown beyond the bottle's trajectory,
and ahead of them lies the Ponca City airstrip—wind sock, plane,
parked cars. Buddy makes ready to set the plane down, comes in
low, expertly, the fixed wheels skipping high but only twice and
then they're rolling through dust and chaff with the harvested cornfields flying by on either side until finally the plane slows to a stop,
and Buddy cuts the motor and it coughs out into what is to Bix a
sudden and immense silence. He sits there stunned, his head burn-

ing and the wind blowing hard and the sun a grayish yellow behind thin overcast with the dust already billowing away toward the parked cars. He climbs down on legs that are stiff and shaky, but, hell that was a wonderful ride! And, "Buddy!" he calls up to the man in the cockpit, "you've got to be the best damn pilot in America!" And Buddy just might be because when he climbs down off the wing he falls face-first into the dust and stubble and lies there motionless until Bix turns him over to find his vacant grin and a sharp little puncture beginning to bleed on his cheek, so the flight and its expert landing have both been accomplished blind.

While Buddy hangs around the Whiteman band that day and night he stays drunk like that and the last they see of him is slouched on the bench at the Ponca station, waving goodbye with both hands, the cut on his cheek dried to a dime-sized black blister.

Lawrence, Kansas. Joplin, Warrensburg, Kansas City, Salina, Hays. Omaha, where the Boy's Town band greets them at the station and Whiteman gives them ten dollars for soda pop. Sioux City, Sioux Falls, St. Paul, Cedar Rapids, and then Clinton near Bix's hometown. Dozens of Davenporters make the trip to hear him, and Whiteman spots him on Limehouse Blues, That's-A-Plenty, and Sweet Sue. Afterwards, Bix talks with Burnie but it's brief and strained because they must skirt the thing that lies so large and silent between them: why Dad and Mother didn't show. Burnie thinks his kid brother looks very bad—pale, sweaty, deep cough—but Bix is sober, the one thing Agatha wants a report on. "You can tell me," Burnie says, as they shake hands backstage at the Clinton amidst the sounds of departure—cases snapping shut, trunks slamming, stage hands stacking chairs—: "You can tell me, Bixie. How are you really? You don't look that hot to me," looking at Bix with what he wants to be brotherly sympathy. Bix claps Burnie on his broad shoulders with both hands. "I'm okay. Really. It's just this darned cold I can't shake. But we only have a week to go and then I'll be able to rest up in New York." He gives his head a rueful wag and smiles. "The road's tough, Burnie, no getting around that. Tough on everybody, Pops included. But I can make it another week, that's for sure: Don't worry about the kid here." He taps his chest, lightly. "I'll make it back to New York and get my rest there." He thinks a moment, then decides he has to add this: "You can tell Dad and Mother that. Tell them not to worry."

But he's wrong about the rest of the road. It is longer than a week and there is no rest waiting at the end of it anyway: Peoria, Chicago, Lafayette in Indiana. Ypsilanti. Akron. Down to West Virginia for a date at Charleston High School. Back up to Cleveland. Cincinnati, Detroit, Athens and back to Cincinnati. And by now it's December. The King of England has pneumonia. Al Smith, the defeated Happy Warrior, is preparing for the odious task of handing over his party leadership to New York's newly elected governor, Franklin Roosevelt, whom Smith despises. Massey Hall in Toronto. Buffalo and Auburn, New York, and from here the boys can begin to smell the barn. Symphony Hall in Boston and then, finally, New York—and the next day into the recording studio for Columbia.

He finds the local papers still full of the Rothstein case that evidently no one in City Hall or the police department wants solved and wishes would somehow go away. But Rothstein, who died silent and unrepentant, is still too big in death, and the case stays above ground like a rotting corpse. A sacrificial head must be had, and on the thirteenth the police commissioner sends his resignation to Jimmy Walker, the Night Mayor, who himself knows far too much about Rothstein. That same day Bix reads of a ship with fifteen hundred cases of rum seized off Rockaway Inlet: this must mean Rothstein's once-impregnable protection has vanished along with his killer.

That night he drags himself to Carnegie Hall with Lennie Hayton for the premier of Gershwin's An American In Paris. Jazz laced all through it, but he finds himself unbearably depressed by this because it's clear the composer has taken only what he needs of jazz to build something far finer, something that sounds grand and racy and futuristic all at once. Afterward, outside the hall in a harsh wind he pulls his coat collar around his neck, shoulders hunched, and looks bleakly at Hayton. "What are we doing, Lennie?" he asks finally. Hayton's having trouble getting his cigarette lighted in the wind. "Well," Hayton says, "you want to go for coffee?" "No, I mean what are we doing, really—in the band? We're not really doing anything is what. Did you hear that?" He nods in the direction of the now almost-empty hall. "Gershwin's so far out ahead of what we're doing it's silly, and every time we do Rhapsody again we get farther behind." He pauses, looking toward the hall and its windows that have begun to go dark. "Even Gershwin's behind. Have you heard Copland's Piano Concerto, Lennie?" And Lennie, who knows how Bix has to struggle with some of the tougher parts already in the Whiteman book, looks at him carefully and after a moment says quietly, "Bix, let's go back to the hotel. You need to get to bed." Bix shrugs and they turn away from the hall. At the corner newsstand by the hotel Bix stops to scan the stacked papers, the front page lifting and riffling under the rock that holds the pile in place. King Still Sick. Rothstein Case Fugitive Trailed To Havana. Colonel Lawrence denies he's a spy for the British against Bolshevist intrigues in the north of India.

The next day Whiteman sends him to the hospital in Astoria.

III

Hollywood

The train rocks and sways, down past Erie, about to cut sharply south on its way to Cincinnati, and he's in the club car with a few of the others, the ones who don't play cards, or occupy themselves with magazines, newspapers, or who simply stare out at the snow-flecked countryside sliding past the pitted, green-glass windows in the late afternoon light. The poker players have a rule now: Bix can't play. Jack Fulton made it up, and the others were quick to agree. Jack loves him—they all do—but Jack's tired of losing money to him. He'd slide into a warm seat somebody had just vacated, pick up his hand, and study it a long time, never looking up at the others. Then he'd make his moves, and before very long he'd cleaned the table. Then Fulton and the others, the card sharps, the students of the game who would play on iron asses through three states and two days without turning up into their bunks, would throw down their cards and glare at his departing back and wordlessly ask each other, how does this guy do it when he hardly seems to know where he is? So, Bix can't play.

And so sits in the club car with Bing and Snoozer who has his banjo across his lap and picks at it, quietly, the notes single, suspended, and Snoozer's playing of that minstrel instrument almost meditative in the afternoon's graying flitters. A few civilians are camped up in the front of the car, away from these young men with their paper sacks and glasses of gin swaying with the train, Snoozer with his gaunt, pocked face and shirt collar splayed over suit coat lapel, plucking that banjo—*plink-plinka-plunk*—, and the train hitting the creosote crossties in time. And Bix has been hitting it, too, regular as the wheels, ever since he got out of the hospital. Yet now he sits, staring silently at the floor and not going for his glass like Bing and Snoozer are. Bing has been talking with him, but that was forty miles back, and this silence is deeper now than his friend's customary reticence, so that Bing begins to feel a trifle self-conscious about the sound of his own voice and so pats the man huddled in a blue overcoat. "Hey, there, Bix, m'boy. What's up with you?" Bix just shakes his head, still staring down, and then after maybe twenty crosstie clacks says, "Got the blues." This gives Bing something at least to work with. "Ah-ah-ah," he cheerfully chides, "can't have that. Must leave the blues to Louie and his Stompers. Our business, m'boy, is *brightness*, symphonic swing, airs that are debonair. Here, take a little toddy for the body, and we'll 'chase those blues a-wa-ay!'" quoting the lyrics of From Monday On that Armstrong had so loved last summer in Chicago. But when Bing hands him his glass Bix isn't buying. "Doesn't taste good," is all he says. Bing draws back in mock horror, hand histrionically spread on chest. "*What?!* My good fellow, I secured three bottles of this silvery substance from our esteemed friend, Mr. Lucky, late of Italy—and at ruinous personal expense, I might add—just to get us to Cinci."

"You know what that—." Bix stops, shakes his head, and begins again, still looking downward at the floor with its humus of dirt, cinders, the flayed residue of rubbed-out cigarettes. "Do you know what Mr.—what Ravel said to me?" "Ravel?" Bing asks, "*The* Ravel?" still genial, still in that slightly arch, convivial mode they so often slip into in these situations. But it isn't working, and Bing doesn't quite see this yet, humming something that isn't Ravel. "Well, what, m'boy? I had no *ideahh*." In the clackety silence of the car Snoozer sounds the deepest note his high-wired instrument can give. "He said it was already too late for me," Bix says softly, grimly. Clickety-clack, clickety-clack. Bing tries to work up through the gin towards something he senses is serious. "He told me I was already what I was meant to be." "And what was that?" Bing asks, still less than attuned. "What are you meant to be?" Bix is exasperated now with his crony's persistent obtuseness and raises his voice, looking up at him. "Don't you see? Don't you get it?" "Can't say I do," Bing says, swinging his gaze to Snoozer across the way, but Snoozer's only looking at his banjo and is no help. "He's telling me it's too late to change," Bix says. "He's *sentencing* me, don't you see." Bing looks back at him out of those mild blue eyes and shakes his head. "Bix, m'boy, you're leaving your old dad a bit behind here." Bix shrugs deeper into the blue overcoat. "He . . . told . . . me," he says, hitting these words like he sometimes hits the first notes of his solos, definitively, "that I was a 'gifted improviser,' and that it would be a mistake to try to become anything else." "Well, you *are*, you know!" Bing cries, jovial, reprieved by the apparent splendor of the famed composer's compliment. "You are: gifted and an improviser, *par excellence!*" He bears down theatrically on the foreign phrase.

A great flame of anger flares from the moody man as if his friend had carelessly dropped a lighted match down a sleeping oil well, and he bolts out of the seat to stand, feet spread, torso hunched in fury, glaring down into Bing's face with eyes popped and blazing. "Goddammit! God-*dammit!* I don't want to hear this from you!" His voice is suddenly close enough to a screech that the others in the car turn to stare and Snoozer's fingers are staid on the strings. Bing starts to say something, but Bix backhands the unsaid syllables out of the smoky, fetid air.

"You think I want to spend the rest of my career—my goddamned *life*, for Christ's sake—thinking up different ways to play In My Merry Oldsmobile? Felix The Cat? Dolly Dimples? Too Much Banjo? By The Waters Of The Minnetoka, for God's sake!

Baby Face? Five Foot Two? Makin' Whoopie? They call for this crap night after night, and it's getting worse. We play stuff now we wouldn't have touched when Tram and I came on. Japanese Mammy! Krazy Kat!—*Krazy Kat!* You think I want to end up a forty-year-old geezer with bad teeth playing sophomore sock-hops for a bunch of brainless, beaver-coated, pimple-pussed college kids? 'O, come on, Bix!'" He mimics the college crowd's high excitement, waving his blue-coated arms, simulating their acclaim. "'Come on, Bix! Davenport Blues, Bix, old sport! Wolverine Blues! Sweet Sue! Come on, Bix! We want Bix! O Play That Thing!'" His face that before had been a grayish white in the winter afternoon and the fogged lights of the club car now is transformed by a choking rage into ghastly heliotrope, and his arms continue to flail but now without sound as he descends into a silent, paralyzing coughing that sucks air and sound and everything else out of him like a man drowning and seeing that succession of trivial tune titles flashing before his despairing eyes. And whatever Crosby's feelings might have been about Bix's sudden verbal assault, his strange refusal to be comforted by compliment, he now rises and enfolds the choking, flailing man in his arms and signals to Snoozer and together they help Bix back into his seat, and Snoozer eye-motions toward Charlie Lucky's gin but Bing shakes his head and now they have Bix back down and Snoozer shoves over his banjo case to prop Bix's feet while Bing tries to reach into the blue overcoat to loosen Bix's collar, but Bix, feeble, pushes his hand away. There is foam flecked in the corners of his white mouth, at the edges of the sparse moustache that persistently fails to be stylish, and while they hover the eyes roll down out of the skull like lemons into the windows of a one-armed bandit. The mouth opens some, dark, silent, but then begins to move, and they lean into it, trying to catch what lips and tongue are trying to articulate. And then they hear that ultimate objurgation, the last bit of the harangue against history and fame and fate, the tenor of these times he's ridden to some strange sort of summit—the final joke in a title, whispered, rattling, breathy: "Yes . . . Jazz Is Savage," he whispers, the whisper transforming itself into a silent laugh, his eyes closing as tears drool from their corners and slide down the smooth cheeks. "Yes, jazz is . . . "

"Son-of-a-gun, Bix!" Bing exclaims softly. "Son-of-a-gun."

"Say there," a voice says behind them, and they turn from Bix, shielding him with their bodies. "What's the trouble with your friend there," the speaker asks, leaning around them, trying to get a look at the man in the blue overcoat half-lying across the seat with his mouth open in something like a mocking simulation of a laugh—or is it a scream? "Well, sir," Snoozer says smiling, "he's just dandy right now. Had him a bit of a coughing fit a minute ago, but we got him settled, sure-nuff." The man, rubicund, mustard-brown fedora shoved back on shining forehead, looks dubious. "He don't look dandy to me," he says, drawing out the last word. "The missus and I are having a little something down there," jerking his thumb over his shoulder, "and here comes all this ruckus. Upset her, y'know." "Well," Bing says now, baby-blue-eyed smile back in place and patting the stranger's shoulder in friendly reassurance, "he's just fine now. A bit of a spell is all." He pauses, then lowers that marvelous instrument of his, that smooth baritone voice. "We're musicians," he confides, "and you know how musicians are." Winks.

⚜

In Cleveland he's on the wagon and has been since the episode on the train and so irritable everybody steers clear. He paces the floor of his room, chain-smoking. Tries sitting in the lobby like some of the others, hoping to be diverted by the show at the reception desk, the news counter where they dispense cigarettes, cigars, sen-sen, chewing gum, fountain pens and fingernail clippers: top-coated men whisking up, plunking their coins down on the scarred glass, then moving off to tear off a cellophane wrapper or snap open the *Plain Dealer.* Women in hats, with veils and gloves primly held, wait for their male companions, trying to appear self-possessed and occupied at once. He tries walking the streets, hunched in the blue overcoat, fedora jammed down on the batlike ears, but the city strikes him as foreign, a hostile, gray place where everything is like a knife, its edge always towards him, especially the wind sweeping off the ice-choked lake. Walking along the river's no better with its speakeasies that lure and wink, and when he passes one as its door swings wide he gets a warm, beckoning blast. At a corner a huddled streetwalker mumbles, "Dream face," through her cigarette as he slouches past in the ceaseless and searching wind.

At the theatre he stands backstage, chilled, avoided, while the sign circulates like electricity—ten minutes till curtain—and searches with unfeeling fingers for his mouthpiece in the pockets of his tux jacket. Pulling it out, he fumbles it, grabs for it, misses, and it falls to the floor. He has it on one hop, like an infielder scooping up a hot grounder, and in one motion flings it across the space and it hits again, takes a long, skating slide, then fetches up hard against a pile of cases. The others, eyeing him, watch this bit of business and stand there not knowing what to do until Herman retrieves the mouthpiece, looks it over, and brings it back to its owner. Bix has turned away, but when Herman says something he turns quickly around to find the mouthpiece being handed him. His eyes look up, locking with Herman's, and his lips curl away from his teeth in what might be a kind of smile but isn't, is a snarl instead. "Well," he says in mock surprise, "here's my *mouthpiece.* Brought it back, did you? And here all this time I thought your name was Herman. And it's—now don't tell me!—it's Fido, am I right? Or is it Rover." He reaches for the mouthpiece but Herman yanks it back. And Herman, who has been living with the frantic man's sarcasm for days, leans in close to Bix, so close the watchers can't hear him, and says, "Bix, take this thing and put it in your horn, and then you take that horn out on the stand and put it in your mouth, where it belongs, because if anything else comes out of there tonight, I'll put your ass in a sling so quick you won't have time to tell me you didn't mean it. And I don't give a shit if it does cost me this job."

Somehow he gets through that concert and back to his room at the Cleveland where he orders up ginger ale and plenty of ice, watching the hand that holds the phone begin to tremble so violently he can't get the thing back onto its cradle and drops it, hearing the line buzz and buzz and then mechanical glottal sounds on the other end like a monster trying to swallow something and the operator's peevish questioning, "Sir, sir, are you there?" "Where else would I be," he snarls through clenched teeth, yanking the cloth-covered cord from the wall. The ginger ale's no help and tastes to him like scalding piss. He sits on the edge of the chair, glass in hands, then shifts over to the divan, searching for any sort of comfort, his whole body now in mutiny and his skull feeling as if it's been shrunk by the Wild Man of Borneo. He tries to get his mind off how he's feeling by thinking back to tonight's concert at the Palace, but it's only another form of torture because he knows how bad he was. Before, on so many other nights, he could feel the eyes of the others swing to him after he'd ripped off some brilliant little invention on a clichéd number they'd played uncounted times, something that quickened their spirits and made them believe for a moment in what they were playing. Tonight, though, he felt their eyes on him because they'd heard that sad timorousness, the sudden, shocking absence of that old cavalier assurance, no least chance taken when, before, he'd have attacked any passage boldly, then let the spaces pile in until you were sure he couldn't catch the next beat—but he always did. At intermission they'd left him to himself in the drab little backstage cubicle he shared with four others, smoking half of one Camel after another. When it was time again Harry Goldfield had poked his head in and started to say something, then, seeing Bix's face had stopped. "I know," Bix heard himself saying, "I know, I sound like crap." "Time, Bix," Goldie had said.

He burrows into the divan, trying to ride out the deep internal waves surging through him, holding himself with both arms, the ginger ale slopping out of the glass and running in fizzy beads over the striped fabric. He tries to focus on the wall in front of him, but it won't hold steady, keeps jumping, moving, the vertically patterned wallpaper crawling sinuously toward the ceiling. A framed portrait of a man in a cravat, heavy of face, full moustache, hangs amidst this crawling jungle, and he tries hard to remember who it is, because it seems that earlier he did know that face, and his mind races frantically after the coattails of that recognition—something to hang onto. But something's badly interfering with this effort, a rapping-rapping that's getting louder by the second. The radiator. It must be the radiator. He looks around for it, fails to recognize it under its ornamental casing. What kind of a crappy, Christ-awful fleabag has Pops stashed him in now where the goddamned radiator raps so loudly a man can't think straight? And then, eyes starting as he swings his gaze back to the portrait, he has a flash of recognition. *It's Roy Kautz!* It's Roy Kautz back at the Davenport musician's union audition. And the rapping is old Kautz, hitting his stick on the piano top—"Young man! Young man! Don't play the piano part. Play the trumpet part." "You son-of-a-bitch," he whistles through his teeth. "You moldy-assed, high-collared son-of-a-bitch, sneaking in here like this." He swings his gaze around the room, looking for Whiteman. "Pops!" he cries out, "you did this! How could you *do* this, putting this old son-of-a-bitch in here with me? You know what he did to me!" From the frame Whiteman looks out at him, fat-faced, moustache curled into an oily smirk. "You did this to yourself, Leon," he says. "*I* did this? *I* did this?!" Whiteman's refusal to confess his treachery is monstrous, hideous, the ultimate betrayal because Pops truly has become Pops to him, the understanding paternal presence he's never had—and now clearly never will. To sneak, smuggle, insinuate old Kautz in here, and then to blame it all on him. In enraged disbelief his arms, weightless, fall from his sides, the ice-choked glass dropping heedlessly to the floor, its contents spreading across the carpet while he glares at the portrait that even as he fastens on it with boiling eyes assumes its final transmogrification into Carl Beiderbecke: Opa, Oompah, Oompah-Papa, with black button eyes and heavy moustache, silently, contemptuously articulating a single, two-note word that his grandson strains fearfully to understand, though already, when the mustachioed mouth first began to wriggle into the word, he knew what it was going to be. "What. *What?*" he whistles, his body leaving off its shaking, beginning now to jerk in time to the unceasing, incessant tapping that is coalescing into a drumming roar while the vertical pattern like a nest of vipers loosed crawls past Opa's face, which as a boy he'd always feared, remembering how in his turreted, balconied second-story bedroom on Grand, Opa would come in dreams to stand, spectral, at the foot of the bed, pronouncing failure on him. Opa, who led the church Maennerchor with relentless exactitude, the leaden Lutheran hymns lining out of the long room that always felt cold to him even in the depths of summer when, outside, the locusts whirred their wings in prophecy of six weeks more of crushing, corn-growing heat. And still he hangs now, trembling, on that single, two-note word that Opa mouths in the jungle of the rioting wallpaper.

"Chasser."

"Chasser? *Chasser?* I'll show you a chasser!" The green, heavy-barreled ginger ale bottle flies across the room on a low, deadly trajectory, magnetically finding the framed portrait of Caruso, and on the other side of the wall where Goldfield and Matty Malneck and Bill Rank sit over cigarettes and cards and nightcaps it's an explosion, and Rank, trying to leap from his chair, gets tangled in it and falls sideways to the floor, and in the momentary, ensuing silence looks up into the frozen faces of the others, asking, "Jesus! What was *that?*" Though by the time his words are out they're beginning to hear the rest of "that," a staggered series of smashes, and they rush from their room to find the door of 607 locked. "Bix!" Rank hollers above the invisible mayhem within. "Bix!" The answer is a high, long-held cry in which a rage almost joyous in its release streams along atop something else that none of them wants to name, and Rank, who's known Bix since Davenport days, suddenly wonders whether it really is Bix in there—but who the hell else could it be? "Herman!" Goldie calls out. "Herman, are you in there with him?" But they know this can't be, and there's another smash, another scream that makes their flesh crawl, and Rank looks at the others and says, "Frank. Go get Tram!"

And finally they get to Tram who listens to them and throws on robe and slippers, and they race up two flights and find Rank kneeling outside the locked door, trying to talk through the keyhole to whoever it is—or whatever—and all along the corridor other doors are opening and frowsy-faced men are beginning to emerge, tying the sashes of their bathrobes, and Tram stands above Bill Rank, listening a moment, then goes into the next room and gets the house dick on the line and tells him to get up to 607 in a hurry and bring a pass key. But it's awhile before the man arrives, and by this time the smashing sounds have ceased, and they can hear only a low sobbing, broken by deep coughs. But when the house dick's pass key turns in the lock they find the brass chain of the upper lock still barring them, and so the final bit of destruction is when Tram and the dick together slam their shoulders into the door, and the chain gives way in a splintering of wood and plaster and they tumble over the threshold, and quickly Tram turns back towards the others, trying to shoo them away. "Okay, fellows, go on now. We've got this taken care of," not wanting them to see Bix like this. And there in the wild disarray of what had been the sitting room and over which a little cloud of plaster dust is still settling, the man himself, slumped on the floor, surrounded by a shipwreck of smashed furniture and broken glass, his tux shirt in tatters, a long cut on a hairless, bone-white forearm, head hanging, and out of it long strings of saliva and snot and tears. And he doesn't even look up at the splintering sound of their forced entry, and so for a moment there's only silence and the settling plaster dust, and then the house dick whistles low and says, "I gotta report this." At the sound of that raspy, cigarette-roughened voice the man amidst the wreckage lifts his glistening face and finds Tram and raises one hand in which he holds a cup mute. "Look, Frank," the voice says. And Tram now has the same eerie impression Bill Rank did outside the locked door, that this isn't really Bix but someone or some thing that has gotten inside his skin and is impersonating him, though the voice is only an approximation. But in that same instant it comes to Tram that it's been awhile since he truly knew who this man is: back at least to '27 when the Goldkette band broke up and he and Bix briefly joined a band in New York at a club run by racketeers. That man who seemed so instantly at ease when Arnold Rothstein and others dropped by rehearsals wasn't the guy he'd known out in St. Louis or Hudson Lake, the one he'd dearly loved and whose incandescent talent had so awed him. That wonderful guy had vanished somewhere along the way, wandering off into strange passageways where dark figures like Rothstein waited with supplies. Still, *this*. . . .

He moves forward through the wreckage, uncertain of what to do first. "Look, Frank," the man in the wreckage says again, holding up the mute. "This is all I have now, just this." "O, for Lord's sake," Tram says, kneeling by the man's side and taking the mute from him. "O, for Lord's sake, Bix. You need a doctor." "I don't need a doctor," Bix says, looking dully away through the wreckage. "I need a drink." But Tram hardly hears that and is already rising and darting from the room to try the phone next door, but then, finding the house dick using it, riding down to the lobby to tell them to get a doctor up to 607. By the time he gets back up there others are in the room, trying to set the place somewhat to rights. Bix sits on the divan, a large tumbler of whiskey in both hands and a pint bottle at his feet. He looks past the men cleaning up after him and makes an effort at a smile. "Feel better," he manages. "Who in hell gave him that?" Tram demands, angry, incredulous. Nobody answers or even looks at him, continuing their silent stacking of broken furniture, gingerly dumping the larger pieces of glass into the wastebasket. And looking at Bix, Tram has to admit that in some ghastly, bizarre way he does look better, the unearthly pallor replaced by a faint flush around the gills, the sobbing and coughing gone, and somebody—maybe the same misguided Samaritan who supplied the bottle—has cleaned up his face and gotten him out of the rags of the tux shirt and into the blue overcoat. "O, hell—!" he starts, then breaks off. "I have a doctor coming up, Bix," he says trying to steady his voice. Bix holds up the tumbler, both hands, like a well-coached child with a full glass of milk. "Just what he ordered," he croaks, and Tram turns away, thinking, "This isn't my scene any more. This is Paul's or Herman's or Agatha's—somebody else's." On his way back down the corridor he finds the doors of the curious closed again, the salesmen and executives back beneath their warm blankets, dreaming of yet another upward bump on the big board, of all of life's new necessities they will buy and sell on time, of this new year, 1929, that will prove to be the most stupendous yet in human history. And then he spots Herman coming out of the elevator, broad-shouldered, beetle-browed, blue-jawed

Herman, and Tram can tell by the way he's hurrying that he's heard something. "He's in there," Tram says as they come abreast, barely breaking stride. "He's busted up the room." A look passes between two men moving in opposite directions, the look of those powerless to do more than merely witness a mystery they cannot penetrate but must simply live with.

⚶

Yet as soon as Herman had entered that room he saw, understood, that he couldn't live with this any longer: it was too terrible to watch. If Tram and Crosby and the others wanted to hang around—or if they had to because they were musicians—he didn't. He'd stood there look-ing at the wreckage, the smashed picture frame dangling on its raveled wire, and Bix on the divan staring at him with an expression he couldn't read, and his first thought was, I gotta get out of here; and right behind it, I'm gonna call up Big Frenchy.

    He's never been one to reflect much on life, his own or anybody else's. There had always been too much to do *without piling on the burden of reflection. So until this moment, sprawled in the cockpit of his car in Oakdale Memorial Gardens, he has never asked himself why it was that in that first instant in the wrecked room he'd known that he must get out of it and out of the wreckage of a life, forever. Now he thinks it might have been simple anger. Anger at having to watch—and to watch up close, too, closer than anyone else—what was happening. And even if he's never understood why he should have cared that much if the guy wrecked himself, he feels certain he has a lot of company here. Why, after all these years, were these crowds of latecomers milling around Davenport and trampling the grasses of the grave when all they had to base their adulation on were a few old recordings? Hell, the records never got much more than a whisper of what made the guy so special, how he spoke so directly to you. And the ones he'd made with*

Whiteman were actually painful to listen to: you waited through three minutes of crap for four seconds of Bix, and much of the time it wasn't worth the wait. So, what was it about for these latecomers? Why did they care so much? As for himself, he finds himself remembering now an earlier festival at which Bill Challis had been the guest of honor. He'd stayed away from that one, knowing Challis might recognize him. Afterwards, though, in the Society's newsletter he'd read what Challis had said at a panel discussion. "You can't really understand genius," Challis said, "and I don't think the genius can understand it himself. He just endures it, if he's lucky. Bix wasn't lucky that way." Maybe then it wasn't lucky to be close to a genius who couldn't endure his condition; he'd never thought of it this way before.

Still, that moment in Cleveland won't release him yet. It keeps him pinned down amidst its awful wreckage, and he feels suddenly breathless, sweaty, and so quickly hits the buttons, rolling down all the windows, letting the night in, taking deep breaths, trying to quickly force away the ancient images he's forbidden himself all these years: the sight of that well-loved face, boozy, beseeching, looking up at him from the bed to which Herman had half-carried him, Bix mumbling wild things he didn't want to hear; then himself, trembling badly, closing the door on Bix and waiting in the outer room until the doctor arrived with his black-snapped bag and the sedatives that would silence these ravings. And early that morning, his suitcase already packed, he'd phoned Whiteman and said he was quitting and Whiteman, at first irritable, then surprised and a trifle hurt, had asked him to stay with the orchestra at least until he could line up a replacement back in New York. He'd agreed; he owed that much to Paul. But he'd agreed only after Whiteman explained that the band would be leaving Bix behind here with a nurse who had explicit instructions to take him back to Davenport as soon as he was strong enough to travel. But he never said goodbye to Bix, had only peeked in at him once, finding him asleep, his face smoothed by sedatives and looking boyish once again, as if

Time had gently, silently been repealed. And then the band had gone on, to Detroit, where Whiteman picked up cornetist Andy Secrest from Goldkette's reorganized band, and by the time they hit New York again Whiteman had Herman's replacement lined up, and he had himself a new job with Big Frenchy.

The work with Big Frenchy was the same as he'd once done so reliably and steadily for Capone and Greasy Thumb out in Chicago—at least in its larger aspects—some mechanical repair work, some pickup and delivery, some chauffeuring. Occasionally, he carried a pistol, but things were different here than just a few years ago in Chicago, and he was glad of that. There was still rough stuff involved, and the threat of violence was the gas that made the rackets run. And now narcotics were involved, too, though Owney Madden and Big Frenchy and his bunch didn't really understand the vast potential of this new product line like Mr. Big had or his lieutenant, Charlie Lucky. This involved a new set of dangers. But everybody in New York had learned something important from Rothstein: that you could actually run the rackets in a more orderly and civilized and lucrative fashion than even old Johnny Torrio had imagined. To get things done you didn't have to barge around town, blasting away like a bunch of crazy gorillas. Business went better and the police and politicians were more comfortable if you had a little polish.

Of course, there were still lunatics around, guys like Dutch Schultz and a younger guy appropriately called Bugsy, and he thinks now of a face-off out at Montauk in '30 with some of the Dutchman's boys, himself and four others against eight of the Schultz bunch and every man with a gun out, only his group had two Thompsons, and so they'd just stood their ground, all of them afraid to move a muscle, the hardware getting heavier by the minute, and no single word exchanged after the initial, blundering encounter. Then, after what seemed like several hours but wasn't, a single smear of puce dawn had shown over the solid surface of the sea, and somebody on the other side said something like,

"We're all gonna end up in Dannemora if we don't call this off quick."
And that had broken it, and everybody backed stiffly away and jumped
into their trucks and roared off. It was only when they'd gotten as far as
West Babylon that he'd started to shake, and he was still shaking,
quicker now, when he stopped at an Uptown speak and made directly
for the can where he unloaded at both ends and when he finally felt up
to it walked uncertainly to the bar where he had three boilermakers in
quick succession.

For the most part, though, he found his duties peaceful enough. Big
Frenchy hadn't hired him as muscle, and the money was good. "This is
appreciated," he'd told Big Frenchy, adopting the passive voice, the
gangsters' odd grammatical effort to avoid responsibility. Once in a rare
while he'd run into guys from the Whiteman band, and on one such occasion, soon after he'd begun working with Big Frenchy, he heard something about Bix, how, shortly after the band had gone on to Detroit,
Bix had given his nurse the slip and made his way back to New York,
not Davenport. And then they'd discovered him up in 202 of the 44th,
in terrible shape. Herman hadn't wanted to stay around and listen to
any more of this, and was trying to figure out an exit when the boys
added that Bix had been wounded in a bar fight, slashed somewhere
below the belt. Then, when he did manage to get away from this talk,
he could still hear them behind him, arguing about the location of the
wound. And a couple of days after that, making a delivery, he bumped
into Tommy Dorsey who told him Bix had finally been sent back to
Davenport where Whiteman was keeping him on full salary with orders
to stay there until he was healthy and sober and ready to play. "But,
hell, Herman," Dorsey had said, punching his arm playfully, "he could
come back tomorrow, if it was just a matter of being ready to play.
When wasn't he ready to play—you know what I mean?" O, he knew
what Dorsey meant, all right.

Machine Gun Jack has been itching to kill the Gusenberg brothers, Pete and Frank, for what feels to him like forever. But he can't
get Snorky's approval for the action until he sweetens the deal by
telling him he's figured a way to take out the Gusenbergs and their
boss as well, the hated Bugs. This does get Snorky's attention,
though he knows right off that Jack's motives here are mixed. Early
last year the Gusenbergs set Jack up, luring him into a phone
booth outside the Lexington: a strange caller had told Jack that if
he were to go to the booth at a specified hour, he'd hear something
interesting about Lulu. Jack bit, going out to the booth and waiting beside it until the phone rang and he stepped inside to answer.
There was the strange voice again, laughing this time, then saying
simply, "She's a cunt." By which time the Gusenbergs were already
closing in on the booth. They hit Jack with a sub and a .38—twice
in the ass, once in the calf, once more in the lower back. Jack lived,
minus a kidney and restricted in his movements, tough on so acrobatic a guy. Snorky figures this is just the breaks and more or less
disregards Jack's talk about the Gusenbergs until he adds in Bugs,
because Bugs has tried more than once for Snorky, and the idea of
wiping him out along with his top layer has an appeal that's a nice
mixture of the personal and the strictly commercial. But the scale
of Jack's planning is also a problem because such a massacre would
certainly bring on all the heat the city could summon, and for a
while business would suffer like it did following the McSwiggin
mistake. On the other hand, if Jack actually could pull off such an
action, wiping out Bugs, the Gusenbergs, and the other lieutenants
all at once, business was bound to improve over the long haul. And
there would also be the undeniable satisfaction of seeing Bugs join
Dion O'Bannion out at what Capone calls Mick Acres, the cemetery. "Lemme think about this," he finally says to Jack one night
when they're all down at the Green Mill where Joe E. Lewis is
cracking wise on stage. "Plus you haven't convinced me you can

get inside. Widdout that, it's no go." Jack starts to tell him again about the inside man, Nick Kick, but Snorky holds up a fat, jeweled hand. "I wanna listen to Lewis," he says, and so what can Jack do but shut up? Jack himself hates Lewis, and it's mutual because a couple of years back Lewis took a shine to Lulu who thought he was just terribly funny. So, it was beautiful when Lewis crossed Capone in a contract dispute and the Boss ordered the comic seen to. He sent Joe Batters and two other goons up to Lewis's room at the Commonwealth and they stabbed him a few times, then scalped him. Somehow, Lewis survived all that, but now he works where Snorky says, though, as Jack is happy to point out to Lulu, he looks like warmed-over shit. But for the moment—a long time for so impatient a man—Jack has to sit there and listen to this kike's crap, because Snorky finds Lewis funny, too, plus it gives him a satisfaction to see Lewis up there, working for him, with his mug and neck looking like they've been under a spot-welder's torch. Free advertising.

Finally, Snorky lets Jack know he's ready to talk about Jack's big plan. Up in his office at the Metropole the Boss wants to hear right away about the inside man, and so Jack tells him more about Nick Kick, who for a sufficient inducement will set up Bugs and the rest over at the North Clark garage Moran uses as a distribution center. Outlining the plan, an odd little smile comes and goes like a moving shadow about Jack's small, tight mouth. He's particularly dapper this afternoon, dazzling almost in a bold-checked, three-piece suit with a carnation in the lapel. Capone hasn't seen him looking so vital since the Gusenbergs caught him in the phone booth, and looking at the shadowy play of that little smile, Capone thinks how truly dangerous Jack is and how maybe after this caper is over with he might have to have Jack himself seen to. But right now he's listening to Jack tell him about Nick Kick, a burly, sullen, monosyllabic Greek Capone remembers from Blue Island: a hijacker and sometime strong-arm robbery guy with no love for the Capone bunch because he's married to a relative of the Klondike clan.

"It's beautiful, Snorky," Jack says, placing his wide, big-knuckled boxer's hands on Capone's crowded desk, palms flat, "really beautiful. We give Nick five cases of the Log Cabin. He sells em to Bugs at sixty a pop and says he can get hold of another five at the same price. At sixty you know that greedy fuck's gonna bite, especially if he thinks Nick is underselling us." He hunches up in his chair, withdrawing his hands. "We pick the date for the second buy. We set up surveillance on North Clark. And then I get this like *brainstorm.*" He smacks his forehead with open palm. "We got our guys in place, right? But we got em wearin *police* outfits, monkey suits. An we got a paddy wagon ready to roll. So when we see Bugs and the boys arrive for the buy, then we pile our guys into the wagon an go clangin up there like it's a fuckin raid. We line em up in there an wipe em out, an then off we go in the wagon. The guys take it back to the garage, put the monkey suits in suitcases—and blow." Jack lifts his hands, fingers spread, like a magician completing some legerdemain, and sits back in his chair, eyes on his boss, awaiting approval.

"How much for the Greek?" Capone asks, rubbing his chin. Jack tells him twenty-five hundred, plus Nick wants to go down to St. Louis to work. "Can be done," Capone says, still rubbing his chin reflectively and thinking again that if this homicidal fucker can control himself enough to work this big, he probably does need to be seen to. He twists the huge diamond ring on his thickening finger and smiles at Jack. "I like it," he says at last. "I like it. Who ya gonna use?" "Killer. Killer'd come up from St. Loo," Jack says, feeling expansive now that he's put this over with Snorky. "You know nobody's better on the typewriter than the old Killer." Capone nods, eyes heavy-lidded with murderous satisfaction. "Anselmi and Scalise, that's three. Then I got Joe Lolordo from Detroit. That's four, an that's all we need: good, tight squad, not too big." Capone wants to know about the wagon and uniforms, and when Jack tells him everything's ready to roll, Capone's face breaks into a big grin, the scars getting deeply involved as it spreads. "This is good," he says, "gonna work out good." He thinks a moment, then says, "Jack, I'm gonna give you ten big ones for this. But from now on, you deal strictly with Jake on this, because this is the last I wanna hear about it, just this here," tapping his desktop with its ash trays and pens and inkwell and the clustered collection of family photos of Teresina and Mae, Sonny, Frank, Mitzi, Rose, and the rest. "This is it for me. I'm gonna be in Florida for this, take Teresina and Mae and Sonny down there, get em outta this stinkin cold. Teresina, she likes the flowers—sea grapes an all—. Good for her, too. Good for her joints." He leans forward in the high-backed leather chair, puts his elbows on his desk and clasps those thickening hands that bear the baubles of an outrageous success, that look so innocently vulgar, that have done murder. He looks up from under his battered brows at his lethal liegeman, a smile breaking again, scars dimpling, and says in a voice softening with lust, "I gotta broad down there, works one of the clubs. Oughta see her. Sixteen. Great tits. Ass like two boulders. I'm gonna fuck her cross-eyed resta this winter while you're up here freezing your cajones off." The red liver lips are stretched, shining, and he rubs a hand over them, over his chops, and Jack can hear the whiskers rasping under the soft palm. And Jack can see also the gray, depthless eyes that aren't smiling, that don't have anything to do with the leering lower portion of the face, that aren't joining the lascivious levity, that tell Jack, Watch out, pal. "Sounds beautiful, Snorky," Jack says, careful.

Back at the Lexington Jack gets to work on the lobby phones, lining up his ducks, and by the middle of February they're all in a row. Then he announces to Lulu that she's got two hours to pack because they're going over to the Stevens for a few days. Lulu's used to these sudden moves and only asks if they'll be going out nights. Jack says no, but he wants her looking extra good for the check-in where he makes a flourish, talking loud, ordering the bellboys around. Up in the suite, it's different, Jack tense, angry, coiled like a spring mechanism. Unpacking, watching him out of the corner of an eye, Lulu knows this won't be one of their old-time sex-fests when, purely for the thrill of the strange, Jack would take her to some new hotel and keep her in bed all weekend with his insatiable demands, his acrobatics. Now Jack doesn't even glance her way while she unpacks her lingerie, hangs dresses. He paces near the sitting room phone, smoking. Things have been going pretty much this way since the Gusenbergs tattooed him, something for which he blames her. "If I din hafta chase around to find out who you was bangin," he tells her often, "I would never have gone out to take that fuckin call. A moron could smell that for a setup."

Anyway, Jack can't do it like he used to, and these days all he wants her for is to suck him off, not exactly a romantic routine for her, despite the dresses and jewels Jack drapes her with, the show the two still make at the clubs and in hotel lobbies. Muriel Finch who she used to go dancing with out at White City once told her that swallowing too much of that gunk wasn't good for your guts. Well, now Muriel would know for sure, because after Charlie the Fish had had enough of her he sent her to work in one of the Cicero whorehouses. Poor Muriel—Lulu pushes the thought away because that kind of thing happens often enough, and so the only thing a girl can do is try her best to keep her man happy, not an easy thing these days with Jack the way he is. A lot of the time now when he does say something to her he's mean and sarcastic, calling her the Mexican Hairless because she has so little pubic hair, or Tee-Tee, short for Tiny Tits. But there's a lot of silence these days, and Lulu knows that whatever's up today, it's something big and she'll be pretty much on her own up here. The only thing he's said since they got into the suite was that he doesn't want to hear the fuckin radio, that it makes him nervous with all that yackety-yack and those crummy jazz bands she likes. Lulu has three movie magazines she picked up in the lobby, and after picking at a room service supper she gets in bed with these, leafs through them, and settles on a story about the Talmadge sisters and the powerful mother who engineered their routes to stardom.

In the morning-gray room the phone rings, awakening her, and she looks through into the sitting room at Jack clad in pants and undershirt, listening to the caller's lengthy recitation of something. Then he says he'll hang on. She goes into the bathroom, snaps the switch, and two dozen little lights come on around the edges of the mirror, a beautiful movie star touch that delights her. She gives herself a close inspection in the slightly tinted mirror. She doesn't have the class you can see in every line and contour of Norma Talmadge's face, but she's still not bad, she's thinking. Still not bad. There are a few faint lines radiating from the corners of her eyes, so faint you have to stare as fixedly as she's doing now to find them; also two faint lines curving around either side of her wide, generous mouth. But the teeth are good. She bares them into the rose-tinted mirror like a tigress, resolving to stay away from tea, which is very bad, and to cut back on the coffee. Maybe Jack will let her have a facial today, even if it's only up here in the room where they usually don't do as good a job as down in the beauty parlor. Coming out into the sitting room in her white-on-white kimono with its fake blue fox ruff, she finds Jack still on the line, waiting. He doesn't look over at her, and she can feel the heat, the coiled tension from where she sits, see the muscles in his bare forearms racing beneath the taut skin like boas underground. She sees the intruding edge of the morning newspaper under the door and crosses to pull it in. Alderman Haffa, convicted in the operation of a multi-million-dollar bootlegging ring, will leave tomorrow for a two-year stretch in Leavenworth. Colonel Lindbergh still won't speak to the press about his engagement to Miss Anne Morrow. General Pershing has the grippe. She turns to the movie pages to read Louella Parsons. Everything these days is about the talkies, and Jolson's Singing Fool is playing all over town. She flips back through the pages, coming again to the front page where she notices the date, the fourteenth. Hey, she thinks, that's Valentine's. "Do it!" Jack says into the phone, dropping it with a feral finality into its cradle.

He gives a brusque no to the facial, won't even let the maids in to clean. He doesn't look at the *Herald-Examiner* which lies spread where Lulu's left it, only sits close to the phone, smoking. This must really be some big deal, she thinks, whatever it is. More than an hour passes this way, Lulu going through her movie magazines, Jack coiled, and the slate-hard light of the bitter day invading the room and giving everything a sharper edge—furniture, drapes, their faces that avoid each other. Then the phone rings, just once, and not again, and Jack doesn't reach for it, just sits there, looking at it, and after a few minutes lets out a deep breath. Lulu ventures a quick glance and sees his face, haggard, unshaven, old-looking in the pitiless light. She knows from the lie of the bedclothes he never came to bed last night and doubts he slept much, if at all, on the couch. Jack moves now to the couch, lowers himself carefully onto it and runs his hands through his hair. He leans back into the cushions, sighing again, imagining vividly Bugs sprawled now in the North Clark garage and beginning to stick to the cement, and next to him, at awful angles as if flung from impossible heights, the Gusenberg brothers. The next time Lulu shoots a glance over there he's deeply asleep with the corners of his mouth slightly curled like he's dreaming of something good.

And is still sleeping when the afternoon paper is shoved under the door. Lulu's gone through all her magazines by now, and even the Talmadge sisters are looking a little stale, so in the bedroom she flicks through the paper, glancing at the stories: the suicide of an editor who flung himself out of a window on Madison; the electoral college certifying the victory of the Hoover–Curtis ticket; the arrival of Trotsky in Constantinople. Then she hears Jack's voice on the other side of the partially closed door, ordering maid service. And this is how the very latest news—too late to make the afternoon editions—is brought to the suite at the Stevens, because while the two maids are dusting and emptying ashtrays and running the carpet sweeper Lulu hears them chattering about the awful thing on North Clark and how the gangsters are just going to kill everybody who gets in their way, and the younger one says her mom will be after her more than ever to come back to Duluth before they murder her, too. Lulu looks at Jack who's oblivious to the maids and their talk and is standing, spread-legged and blowing a luxurious lungful of smoke against the windows, and now she knows what they're doing over here at the Stevens.

Something like panic grabs her throat, and she brushes quickly past the maids, into the bathroom where she locks the door, turns on the faucets to the tub, and sits down on the covered toilet, trying to think what to do. And of course there's nothing to do; it's already been done. She's never wanted to know what Jack actually does for Snorky, but she'd have to be a real dope not to get the general idea. That was another thing she'd learned from poor Muriel: that it was a lot healthier all around if you made it your business not to know anybody else's. Never to ask anything, never to snoop, or look into pants pockets or read anything that might be scrawled on the back of a hat check. Jack was a tough guy who worked for Al Capone, period. Only now it wasn't "period." Now she knew and was trapped by that knowledge. Now she understood the full import of Jack's two words on the phone this morning; understood too that one, fatal, signaling ring this afternoon: it had been done,

done on Jack's orders. She doesn't want the maids to leave, casts wildly about for some pretext to keep them in the suite. There isn't any, and now she hears the door of the suite clanging shut, and silence descends like lead. She hears Jack coming into the bedroom and fleetingly remembers the childhood story about the man who told his bride never to look in the basement of his castle, only she couldn't help herself. I wouldn't have done it, she thinks, panting, never.

"Ya dead in there or what?" Jack says just outside the locked door. What if she really was dead in here? Who would care—a gangster's moll. Had it coming. Made her bed, etc. An image comes to her, of her dead on the floor, blood spattered across the bunting-blue, scoop-necked gown she wears. Or herself underwater in the tub, staring sightlessly up into Nothing, her makeup still in place. She fights these images away, rising quickly from the toilet and looking into the rose-tinted mirror. "Hey!" Jack calls, his hand trying the handle. "Hey, yourself!" she comes back, unlocking the door and defiantly yanking it open. "What about living a little tonight, huh, Jack?" she says, getting the drop on him, bright, metallic, bravado flushing her cheeks. "That's my gal," Jack answers with a bleak smile. "Let's do it."

⌖

Bix sits in his old room of the house on Grand, an unfinished letter to Tram lying aslant on the jackknife-whittled, ink-stained desk of his boyhood. He'd begun it yesterday but hasn't gotten very far, and now, trying to compose the next line, he glances away through the window to the grade school across the street and can see some bright kids' decorations lining the long windows of the classrooms. In past years he'd sat just so, trifling with his lessons, daydreaming of escape, of baseball or tennis or music, anything but the subject at hand. He'd done poorly over there and even more poorly at the high school down the hill where he'd finally fallen so far behind Dad and Mother had deported him to that prep school outside Chicago. Now he's been deported once again, back here from New York. "Davenported," as he puts it to Tram. He tells Tram he's on the mend, though still having some trouble walking because the pneumonia seems to have settled in his knees, making no mention of the deep gash he somehow got in his groin. Mostly, he says, he's not doing too much of anything, which is just what Pops had ordered when he put him on the train in New York: sleeping late, reading the papers, going to the movies where his friend Les plays piano for the weekend shows. But the clock is ticking down for good old Les because the theatre's being wired for sound, and they're saying they'll have talkies in there by July at the latest.

"This a.m. is pretty much like the others," he continues, "—or was until I went down to the kitchen for a cup of coffee and looked at the *Register* and there's this picture on the front page of the gal they're calling the 'Blonde Alibi.' Who do you think? *Lulu Rolfe!!* is who! Remember Herman's sister that rode with us up to Mich. when we played that party for you-know-who. They say she's the girlfriend of one of the guys involved in that Valentine's massacre, and is his alibi because she says he was with her at the Stevens. Didn't we play the Stevens once—'26 or so?

"Anyway, Tram, my friend—." He breaks off, poised now on the verge of the business portion of the letter and looking through the window's wavy glass at the small half-circle of the balcony and the wind-drift of last autumn's oak leaves brown and curled on the weathered boards. "—somehow I got into a hole back there in Ohio and lost my money. I could get some out of the bank if I was there. Or I could tell my broker to sell some stock except everybody's saying you should be putting everything you've got in the market not taking it out. But what I'm wondering about is if you could see your way clear to sending a 100 to your old friend. Could ask Dad but you know how it is. I can pay you back as soon as I get back to N-Y which will be pretty soon.

"Could you ask Herman to ship me my Bach? That way I can practice some. Well, Frank, that wraps it up from out here in the tall corn, my friend. Tell all the boys I'm strictly gleaming above them all—on the 'Wagon'. When I get back we'll make some *hot* sides for Okeh."

And signs it with a hearty flourish, "Bix."

He's about to hunt up Agatha to ask her for an envelope and stamp when he remembers he hasn't washed or shaved or brushed his teeth yet and goes into the bathroom to clean up for Mother. Rinsing the lather from his chin and cheeks he inspects his moustache in the mirror and thinks again about shaving it off; it's never come in quite right. Not today, anyway. When he reaches for a face towel on the nickel rack and finds none he remembers it's the maid's day off and limps down the hall with dripping face and hands to the hall closet where such supplies are stored. But there's something else in the closet besides the towels and washcloths, sheets and pillowcases, blankets and coverlets, the box of camphor and another one of Fels-Naptha soap. Something else underneath the neat, fluffy stacks, and when he sees the edges of the packages he knows right away what they are and simultaneously knows that he doesn't want to know but watches volitionless as his hand reaches in and lifts aside the terry cloth and percale and cotton folds to find what isn't really a discovery; since somewhere, in some cobwebby cranny of his mind, he has always known, feared, this knowledge: a stack of parcels, still with their tape seals intact and on their covers the ink-waved postal markings that announce "Used": St. Louis, Detroit, New York: all those places from which he'd sent home his recordings, his pressed sounds, his breaths preserved in wax like a winged creature caught in ancient amber or sap: silent, silenced, unopened, unheard, and, surely, never to be heard. In this immense moment that crushingly gathers together all the years of his life he hears now a sound behind him, footsteps ascending the back stairs and so hurriedly slides the heavy parcels back into their fluffy coffin and turns around to Agatha heaving heavily into the hall. "Did you eat your breakfast, son? I saw the milk bottle left out. . . ." And he must apologize for that and stumble back, disguising the limp as best he can, motioning with the clean face towel, into the bathroom, locking the door behind him. He sits on the toilet's closed lid, digging the towel into his eyes, trying to blot out the sight of those dead gifts that lie beneath the massed artifacts of that most essential aspect of Beiderbecke family life—hygiene. While beyond the locked door he listens to the heavy tread as it pauses in its sentinel round; can almost hear too the maternal mind grinding toward some intrusive question that, voiced, would be like a skeleton key, unlocking the door and exposing the son who sits, frozen in anguish and dread, on the toilet. He holds his breath, thinking, Please, O, Please. And then the heavy tread creaks on, and he can carefully let out his breath, can breathe, fast, shallow, thinking of those other breaths again, the ones he wanted them to hear, the wind of his very soul, entombed.

❧❖❧

Wearing the white-on-white kimono with its fake blue fox collar and cuffs, Lulu crosses the room to the RCA set and snaps it on, watching the dial light up and all its little numbers and markings become outlined against a theatrical yellow background. She twirls the dial to the setting she wants, sits on the sofa, legs stretched, and waits. Soft April evening, windows opened and the sheer curtains bellying gently inward. Seven floors down traffic swishes past and a few of the vehicles, cabs mostly, have turned on headlamps the size of dinner plates that give off a mellow glow matching that of the radio dial.

Ever since she emerged as the Blonde Alibi in what the papers keep calling the St. Valentine's Day Massacre Jack has kept her under wraps: no visits to friends or lunches out; beauty parlor appointments only in the Lexington; damned few nights out and those way down in the protected zone of the South Side. Jack lets her go to the movies but only at night; he figures no one will spot her in the darkened crowd. Partly all this is because he doesn't want the news hawks to get a chance at her where she might say something dumb and incriminating. But partly too it's because she has some notoriety now, and while Jack has always wanted to show her off, at the same time he's always glared at anyone who gives her a real look, and nowadays that happens whenever they're out, so he goes around mad all the time. But when they're alone together he's sullen and mostly silent except when he's thinking out loud about his situation.

Right after the thing on North Clark he insisted they get married as a precaution against the possibility that she might be called to testify against him. She'd laughed bitterly about this with one of her friends over the phone, telling her it was about time Jack made an honest woman of her. But the real source of the bitterness lies in irony: now that at last they're married Jack has no interest in her. So, she thinks more and more these days of poor Muriel who told her so many of the facts of life for girls taken up by guys in the rackets. When Charlie the Fish began staying away from home nights Muriel had said to Lulu, "They all get it on the side, all of em. And if Jack aint now, he will be. You'll know when it happens, and when it happens"—she shrugged her padded, fur-draped shoulders—"what can you do but wait and hope he comes around?" But for Lulu there's more to this than just Jack seeing Another Party, if that's what he's doing when he's away so much: there's this thing on North Clark that's come between them like some shapeless monster that's moved in and takes up so much space there's no room for anything else. And for the first time she's actually afraid of Jack, and he can smell it on her the way dogs can or horses. There was always a whiff of menace about him, right from the start, and he was rough on her, especially in bed. But since this was the way she'd begun when Pop smacked her around when she'd tried to fight him off, she figured this was just the way things were supposed to be. And she has to admit she felt a certain thrill, being in bed with such a tough guy, a boxer, a guy who maybe might have done some pretty bad things to other guys. But this North Clark thing's different—for both of them—and over the last few months she's had plenty of opportunities to be reminded of those seven bodies strewn about the floor of the garage, the black rivers of blood snaking out from them and running erratically down to the drain that was used to empty crankcases. And there is absolutely no one she can talk to about this; even if Herman was still with the Outfit, she doubts she could really open up to him. There's no one she can tell about her fears, about the awful dreams that come to her, especially that recurrent one where suddenly, out of nowhere she finds dark, heavy things being flung at her, one on another, until she's draped with them, smothering beneath them, and they're soaked with blood that begins to flood into her mouth. She struggles to free herself but is drowning when she wakes up, gasping for breath. She's taken to staying up late, walking the floor, smoking, afraid of getting into bed next to Jack, afraid of sleep and this murderous image. But this new habit only makes a greater gulf between them because she gets on his nerves with her pacings. "Fer Chrissake!" he yells at her out of the darkness of the bedroom, "Willya cut out that fuckin *walkin!* It's drivin me bugs!"

Despite the endemic precariousness of her situation—being a "moll"—Lulu has never thought about another kind of life, lived elsewhere. Until lately. She knows she doesn't want to go back to taking tickets or dipping chocolates. Just the thought of Muriel makes her shudder. But this thing with Jack has gotten bad enough that she's begun entertaining stray notions of fleeing to somewhere and trying to make some kind of new start. California comes often to mind. And it does again tonight as Ted Husing's familiar voice flows from the set's speaker, announcing ABC's coast-to-coast weekly broadcast of the Paul Whiteman Orchestra, America's King of Jazz. "And as you know, ladies and gentlemen," Ted Husing says, extending his vocal embrace to the invisible tens of thousands gathered around their sets just like Lulu, making them for an enchanted moment one grand family of fans, "the Whiteman Orchestra will soon be entraining for Hollywood, California, to make the first-ever all-talkie musical. How appropriate then for the maestro to begin tonight's broadcast with a medley of tunes from that fabulous, fair-favored clime of fruit trees, sun, and sea! California, Here I Come!" After the California medley the orchestra plays Jericho, Ramona, and Charmaine, and by now Lulu's dancing, gliding across the sitting room floor and feeling the night breeze tug gently at the hem and sleeves of the kimono. She's certain she hears Bix on An Eyeful of You—sixteen golden bars—and by the time that's done she finds herself thinking that she wouldn't mind very much an eyeful of him right about now, even as she remembers how odd and remote he was at that club over in Indiana when just for the hell of it she'd kissed him at the end of the dark dock, felt the strange and resistless texture of his lips, and wondered what it was about this guy, what made him tick. While Bing Crosby croons Castle In Spain she relives the funny ride they took with Herman up to that wop joint outside Lansing, how tight they got, and how sore Jack was about Bix; also, how he'd slugged her that night at Snorky's cabin, chipping her tooth. Well, they'd fixed that, anyway, gotten it filed down and capped so you couldn't tell, though Jack probably wouldn't care now if you could. They'd patched up the quarrel when she'd convinced him there really wasn't anything going on between her and Bix—"that fairy horn player" as Jack called him. Then Bix had moved on, and they'd moved on as well, to other squabbles, other slaps, other imagined boyfriends, and she thinks it unlikely Jack would even remember who Bix was, unless he happened to run into him somewhere. Then Jack would put it together because he never forgot a face. It was important, he said often, never to forget where you'd seen somebody. You had to place them. You had to stay alert.

These days Jack's always on the alert when they're out. Up here he's lost in moody thought or else talking out loud, trying to assess his position in the Outfit. Jack thinks that since the North Clark thing Snorky's been acting funny towards him. Lulu thinks Snorky's been acting a little strange towards everybody ever since he got back from Florida. Around her anyway, he's always been a polite guy, kind of quiet really, but the last two times they were out with him he was irritable, distracted, abrupt. When she mentioned this to Jack he dismissed it: dumb broad, what would she know about business? Jack thinks the problem is Snorky blames him because they missed Bugs at the garage, but, shit, the lookouts, the Keywell brothers, were supposed to know Moran, and they had him going in there at 10:30. They had it wrong; Moran never went in. The way Jack dopes it out Snorky thinks it isn't worth the heat they're taking if they didn't get Bugs. Snorky wanted Bugs so bad, Jack thinks, that he's forgotten they did the Gusenbergs and the rest. Plus, there's this: the other outfits, especially the slick bastards out east, are looking at the Capone bunch like they're outlaws, real wild men, bad for business. Jack doesn't get any of this directly from Snorky who has yet to say a word to him about Bugs or North Clark, any of it. He has to get it from the guy who drives for Joe Batters. And he's glad to get the information; it helps explain some stuff at least. But if he has to hear it from Joe Batters's driver, where does that leave him? This is what has him worried these days and talking to himself, not the investigation of the action on North Clark. With the Blonde Alibi in his corner the screws aren't going to lay a glove on him.

Jack's no drinker. In a certain tunneled sort of way he knows his capacities, knows he's wound too tight to add in the sauce. Years ago he had an experience that's stayed with him: Johnny Torrio assigned him a shakedown, but by the time he arrived at the business—a Greek guy's linen place—he was full of beer and fight. The result was that when the owner put up some resistance Jack kicked the crap out of him and left him for dead, precisely what Johnny Torrio didn't want. What Johnny wanted was Mr. Pelikidos's cooperation, not a defunct business with an unsolved murder hanging over it like sewer gas. Jack learned his lesson from that and now drinks sparingly, yet three nights ago up here Jack surprised Lulu by mixing up a pitcher of Manhattans with Snorky's best Canadian. He gave her one, and then they drank in silence, Lulu wondering what the occasion might be. "Lotta oil in this for Canadian," Jack said at last, holding his glass into the light from the sitting room windows and frowning. He rose with a slight, telltale slowness, already set for a refill. "You want?" Lulu shook her head, but Jack was already turning away from her. She watched his back as he poured himself another, then began talking to himself, pacing the room, sipping the Manhattan.

"Tough to figure," Jack said, his tone somewhere between conversational and conspiratorial, "real tough. Ya work for a guy alla these years, ya figure ya got it down. Then comes a big job for him, ya pull it off." He paused, slightly hunched forward, focusing on his line of thought, the glass held a bit in front of him. "An maybe that's it. Maybe . . . that's what the guy wanted ya for all along, just that one big thing. An now ya done it, maybe you're like finished there. Maybe." He stepped to the sideboard and the pitcher, pouring himself another. "Anyways," he continued, moving back to the windows to stand, spread-legged, a thumb hooked into the armhole of his blue vest, "if that's it—if that's really it—then ya gotta be careful." Listening to this, Lulu had seen a suddenly revealed parallel between her own situation here and Jack's: maybe they'd both arrived at the end of their usefulness, only his situation might be even more dangerous than hers because he had to watch out for everybody whereas he was her main concern. Who could he trust? Jack was just now wondering this aloud, then asking himself what the most dangerous situations might be for a knock-off and how these could be avoided without giving suspicion. He went through a muttering inventory of those he might make veiled inquiries of, and talking over Fischetti—no, yes, maybe—he finished off the pitcher and set it carefully—but not cleanly—back on the sideboard. He turned around, looking for the Dumb Dora he knew he had stashed somewhere around here and spotted her in the corner chair with her manicuring kit open on her lap. He stared at her a long moment, his face thick with drink, eyes slow, then said hoarsely, "Hey, Tee-Tee, come over here and do me." And Lulu had looked up from her nails, eyes steady, appraising, and calculated there was little risk of reprisal, swacked as Jack was. "Jack, honey," she said softly, "you do yourself," and folded up her kit and swept past him into the bedroom.

There'd been no nightmares that night. Or the next, and tonight Whiteman's got her in a good mood with his sophisticated swing, his sentimental tunes, his songs of sunny California where she once went with Jack on Snorky's business. And it was the thrill of a lifetime when over dinner a big-time producer had pinched her under the table and over it had said that if she ever wanted to be in pictures, she should call him. While Ted Husing slides into his sign-off she thinks of Hollywood, all sun and flash, the land of the silver screen, as they always put it. The Whiteman Orchestra's still playing in the background, as if they just went on that way all night and it was only this portion of their performance that's on the air. Then it's over and she snaps the set off and settles into the chair before the windows with their bellying curtains, gazing out over the dark cityscape with its thousands of twinkling yellow lights. Spring: it comes to her on the wind, light, seductive. She lights a cigarette, inhales, blows the smoke sideways to watch the breeze take it across the room, seeing the flapper in the Chesterfield ad who says to her rosy-cheeked boyfriend as he lights up, "Blow some my way," thinking the breeze, the night, and the music have put her in a mood as close to happy as she's known for what seems like forever—and maybe as close to it as she's likely to get. As for Jack, she doubts that whatever it is he's really up to tonight it'll improve his mood. Getting dressed for it, he was clearly nervous, though all he'd say was that he was going to a banquet Snorky was throwing.

⚜

In fact, that's all Jack himself knows, except of course for the location: over in Hammond, across the line. And that isn't a good sign to Jack because if Snorky wants somebody taken for a one-way spin, that's where they go, and a couple of times Jack's been sent down there to dump a stiff. Which is why he'd been edgy, dressing for the date, strapping on the shoulder holster, checking the chambers of the blued .38, and sliding it into the holster, knowing as he did that it would be useless to him tonight if his number was up. Then he'd slipped into his lightweight, silk-lined suit coat and faced the mirror, looking at his blunted boxer's features staring back, checking to make certain his eyes had that blank, slightly dulled, professional inscrutability. "Mrs. Gebaldi's boy, Vincenzo," he mouthed, so close to the mirror his breath had stuck fleetingly to the shiny surface, then vanished.

Yet down in Indiana at the Calumet Athletic Association everything looks straight up to him, the big bare-bones hall filled, tables set for what must be close to a hundred. Pretty odd setting for a knock-off, Jack's thinking, but then his first glimpse of the Boss isn't very reassuring because Capone looks tight as a drum and brushes right past him without so much as a glance, striding quickly to the head table where he stands only a moment, then abruptly sits as if worked by puppet strings. Then after the others have followed his lead and a sort of loaded quiet has begun to spread through the hall, the voices trailing away and all the chairs squared up to the long tables, Capone rises with heavy effort and glances over them for a few seconds while a thin smile comes to his face, though to Jack, watching cautiously, even this looks like some special sort of effort. Then Capone announces that the banquet's being given in honor of his valued friend, Joseph Guinta of the Unione Sicilione. Polite applause scatter-claps through the room though it's not long sustained because it's clear Capone has something more to say. Capone nods over the applause, still wearing that sickly sort of smile, and Jack thinks fleetingly of Lulu's observation, that since he's been back from Florida Snorky's been acting kind of strange towards everybody and wonders whether maybe she could actually be right. But what the hell could have happened down there with only his family? "So Hop Toad," Capone's saying, lifting his wine glass and swinging it in Guinta's direction, "here's to you, pal. Health—it's precious." And he takes a sip, and that's all he says and what had looked like a speech turns out to be nothing more than these very few, terse words that are certainly short of celebratory.

As the wine is poured and the platters of pasta and chops are passed down the tables Jack looks around. Everybody's here: Jake

Guzik, Joe Batters, the Camel, the Fischettis, Frankie Rio, Frank Nitti, Scalise and next to him Albert Anselmi. Jack lets them pour his glass full but he takes only a ceremonial sip, and he doesn't eat much either, and some guy he barely knows kids him about watching his weight, and Jack mutters something back. Across the hall Hop Toad Guinta seems to be enjoying himself, his thick, mocha-colored features often creased into a grin, his hands gesturing in wide generosity of spirit. Meantime, the big clock high on the stuccoed wall above the double-doored entrance to the kitchen inches up to and around past midnight and then begins its inexorable descent towards dawn, and still the wine goes around but now too with mineral water and coffee, but none of this has improved the Big Shot's mood, has instead appeared to darken it. He seems to be withdrawing into himself with every downward tick of the minute hand, has stopped speaking to those nearest him, gone into an ominous silence, and the more silent and withdrawn he gets the bigger he looks to Jack, mountainous there in his dark blue suit still with its sheen of store newness on it. So that it looks to Jack like he's filling up with something and must soon let it out or else explode. Jack doesn't know if the others are noticing what he thinks he is, but he decides it might be best to go to the can where he can check the pistol, freshen up, think over what he might do if Capone does do something out there to break up the party. The guy at the urinal next to him doesn't seem to be worried about anything, but he's stewed and unsteady on his feet, and when Jack steps back into the hall he knows instantly this is a different room than the one he left a few minutes before. Capone is up, speaking, leaning forward on his knuckles, arms stiff, like one of the gorillas in the Brookfield Zoo. Jack stands at the door to the can, listening while Capone talks about the Outfit, about how it's like a big family, and how they've worked, worked hard for what they've got.

"We got the best of everythin," he reminds them, "the tops: booze, broads, slots, protection, you name it. Plenty for everybody." He pauses, looks down at the table between his fists, clears his throat a couple of times, seems to be having some kind of trouble making his point, unusual for a guy who's known for being decisive and quick in conversation. "Which is why it hurts to find out some guys can't get enough. 'Why is this?' I ask myself. 'Why should this be?'" His voice takes on a heavy whine. "I'm down in Florida with Mae, Teresina, Sonny, and I gotta hear this kinda stuff from up here. I gotta hear how some guys can't get enough, how they're actually workin to wreck the family, all we built. That they want the whole thing." His huge head swings slowly around the room, looking at them all, then swings in the direction of his valued friend, Joseph Guinta, the Hop Toad. "This is hard for me to believe," he says slowly. "I treat everybody square. Not a man here tonight can say I don't." He looks away from Guinta to the hall, getting the affirmative nods and murmurs he wants. "So I come up, leavin my family down there, to see about this thing myself, because, like I say, I can't hardly believe it, an I listen, an I listen. An I hear more an more of the same thing. So, I make a plan, an I set up a meetin with some of my family what have been telling me all this, these things that hurt me very much. An I say to one of them at this meetin, my valued friend over there who you all know, Frankie Rio." He gestures with one hand towards Rio who's sitting directly across from the Hop Toad. "'Frankie,' I say, 'Frankie, there's this thing I gotta find out an I want you to help me. I don wanna find it out; I wisht to Christ I din havta find it out. But I gotta.' An Frankie here, who's a friend, loyal, says to me, 'Sure, Snorky, what we gonna do?' An I say this: I say, 'We'll set up a lunch with some individuals I have in mind, that I keep hearin about, an you an me, we'll get into a beef about somethin, an we'll get real hot about it, an at some point—I don wanta know just when—make it more realistic like—you're gonna haul off an sock me one ona kisser. Anen you blow an we wait to see what happens.' An Frankie here, he says, 'But I don wanna smack you Snorky—can't do it. We're like family.' But I tell im, 'Ya gotta. Ya gotta cause I havta find this thing out an this is the best way I can figure.' So Frankie here, because he's *loyal* (Capone bearing down a bit on the word), says 'Okay, Snorky. If that's what you want. But what's the deal?'"

Capone turns now once more to look at the Hop Toad, a long steady look, the look of a predator fixing its prey just before the strike, and the prey, the Hop Toad, knows, has known ever since the introduction of Frankie Rio's name into the narrative, that he's been had, and so he turtles down, pulling his head into his shoulders while across from him Frankie Rio comes up with a black .44 and covers him while elsewhere about the big, hushed hall there is strategic movement, a deadly choreography afoot, men sliding into position while Capone completes the spare story, every motif of which, like some ancient myth they all know in their bones, points inevitably to treachery and its fatal conclusion. How after that staged luncheon argument where Frankie Rio dared to slap the Boss while the others stared aghast, Albert Anselmi had leaped to his feet and said, "Boss, I can take out that Guinea fucker before he makes his car even." And Scalise too. But Capone had said, No, it was okay, that he wanted to handle the matter himself. And how after that Frankie had waited, but he didn't have to wait very long, and then Scalise had gotten in touch late that same day and said he and Anselmi would like to have a meeting to discuss some things, but Frankie had played hard to get. Then Scalise had called again, and this time Frankie had agreed to a meeting in a car parked just off Halsted where Scalise had confided that he and Alberto had already made themselves a sweet deal with the Hop Toad and would Frankie want to come along? Capone was all done, they said, and the incident at lunch had merely confirmed suspicions they'd had for a while. "You know yourself, Frankie," Anselmi had said, "six months ago, would you have raised your voice even to Capone? No. But now you can even slap him an get away with it."

When Capone finishes this part of the narrative, he lowers his head, and a great, tragic sigh is called up from the profoundest depths of his being—the great king betrayed by the venality of his trusted vassals—the sigh making horizontal creases across the massive, blue-suited back. "Frankie tells em, yeah, yeah," he says, voice lowered in resignation, but then, instantly, it flames upward and the towering rage Capone's been repressing all evening is there in his scream. "*YEAH! YEAH! O, YEAH!!*" His head shoots up while the major vein in the bull neck bulges into the wilted broadcloth collar. "Yeah, *you!*" He stabs his forefinger at the Hop Toad. "Yeah, *you!*" Then he wheels around towards Scalise and Anselmi on the other side of the hall and points them out as well, the diners around them shrinking back suddenly as if from a contagion. "*An you! An you!*" There are men in place now behind Scalise and Anselmi, swiftly, deftly binding them to their chairs with black wire, and Anselmi, his out-of-whack right eye glowing with the ferocity of a cornered creature, tries briefly to rise, then sees the whole hopelessness of everything and sinks back, waiting like Scalise next to him and the Hop Toad across the hall. Capone has disappeared into the kitchen, but now the double doors are flung back, cracking against the wall, and Capone, coatless, sleeves furled over the fine-haired forearms and great sweat stains in the armpits of his shirt, strides into the hall with a gleaming brown, thick-barreled baseball bat. He stops, switches it in short vicious arcs like a batter preparing to step in against a pitcher. "Riggs Stephenson!" he cries out to no one in particular, apparently identifying the model of the bat he holds. "The Old Hoss himself! Gonna be a great year for the Cubs!" Then he moves with a pantherlike grace over behind Anselmi who tries to turn in his chair to face the Big Shot and say something to him, but Capone won't let him. "Don you turn your face to me, you betrayin son-of-a-whore!" Capone's voice is a scream. "This is what we do to the likes of you!" And with this he takes a home run cut with the Riggs Stephenson, the barrel of the bat crashing into the side of Anselmi's neck with a broad, wet sound and sending his head sideways like a broken doll's. "*This* is how we take care of traitors!" Capone screams as another hit catches Anselmi's right arm, shattering it. "An *this!* An *this!* An *this!*" With each scream there's another belt with the bat, and by now Anselmi has toppled unconscious to the cement floor, still bound to his chair, and his boss stands astraddle him, raining down blows like a man driving posts into hard ground and the sweat raining down too on the victim whose face is unrecognizable, and the baleful wayward eye has been slugged so far up into the skull that only the blood-flooded white remains visible.

And then, without breaking rhythm, Capone switches his assault to the horrified Scalise whose mouth is opened in a silent O, and that's right where Capone catches him with a long, looping swing, and the false uppers fly out like yellow bats from a cave. Frank Nitti braces the chair to give Capone a better angle, and Capone gives Scalise one in the chest, one in the temple that crosses his eyes, and another in the throat that produces the victim's tongue as mechanically as a coin produces a selection at the automat. A backhanded swing doesn't do much damage because Capone's beginning to lose steam now, his clenched-teeth grunts almost as loud as the thumps when the bloodied bat barrel slams home. When Scalise lies dead or dying on the floor Capone raises high his savage scepter and brings it down with all his remaining strength and it hits the canted arm of Scalise's chair and a big splinter of it whangs off into the crowd that has been standing witness to this. Capone staggers back from the bodies, flinging the shattered bat from him. His eyes are like garnets on fire when they light on Machine Gun Jack standing there just outside the door to the can, and in three leaps Capone's there, grabbing Jack's arm and yanking him into so close an embrace Jack gets a blast of Capone's breath that is like a copper smelter. "*You!*" Capone hollers, breathless, hoarse. "You! Shoot em! Shoot the guts outta them! *DO IT!*" And Jack, somewhat numbed, now goes into action, not wanting to be told twice, whipping out the .38 that feels hot to his hand, and running to the bleeding lumps, firing down into them, the entry holes making powder burns in shoulder, ribs, neck. And then Joe Batters takes over with a sawed-off shotgun he's produced from somewhere handy, a barrel for each. And still there's the Hop Toad, the honored guest on whose behalf all this has been done, still in his chair and Frankie Rio sitting opposite him, comfortable, waiting, the black barrel of the .44 steady through the mayhem. But now Capone releases Rio into action with another hoarse scream. "*Kill that fucker! Kill him!*" And Rio does so, coolly, professionally, and without altering position, pumping three quick shots into the Hop Toad's chest, then rising, leaning across the glasses and cutlery and crumb-strewn plates to fire a final, disfiguring round into those mocha-gray features, and the body topples backward onto the floor. For a moment it looks like Capone wants to do some shooting over there himself because he trots breathlessly around to where the Hop Toad lies with a big black hole under his eye, but he only kicks the head once, then turns away, his shirt and vest clinging to his trunk as though he's been standing under a shower faucet. He moves drunkenly towards the double doors to the kitchen, his arms held out from his sides as if for balance, his guests scattering from his lurching path, some with their hands held out to help, though none dares touch him. Capone stops just short of the doors where Joe Batters stands, the sawed-off breeched and cradled. Capone leans into Joe Batters, says something, and then the doors swing inward to him, and he lunges through them, disappearing.

The crowd in the Calumet Athletic Association stands stunned by the sustained ferocity of what they've just witnessed. Not a man there, many of them with old blood ground deeply into the whorls of their fingertips, has ever seen the like. Jake Guzik whose hands are unbloodied and only greasy from thumbing through stacks of dirty money, is sick, and two men help him outside where he vomits helplessly into spring's budding bushes. But it's dangerous to be sick now, even momentarily helpless: there's blood in the air and blood and teeth on the floor; there's a hall full of killers, many with drawn weapons; there's gun smoke and the odor of burned cloth hanging low over the messy tables; and everyone is a witness. For a few electric moments nobody seems safe, and Machine Gun Jack reloads as quickly and inconspicuously as possible, his back to the wall. Then everyone's talking at once in the loud room, about those fuckin rats, about the betrayals by Anselmi and Scalise, so close to Snorky all these years, about the sanctity of honor in a family operation like theirs. Joe Batters makes his way towards Jack who watches him coming, feeling the pistol beneath his armpit, and when Joe Batters gets close he says quietly, his oven-lidded eyes opaque, "Snorky says for you to load these things into Hop Toad's car and take it out to that place we use at Wolf Lake. Frankie'll follow you an bring you back."

By the time this chore gets done and Frankie drops Jack back at the Lexington it's morning. They haven't said a word since they stood in the field at Wolf Lake and Jack had casually tossed a lighted match through the opened door of the Hop Toad's Buick. They were almost to the road when they heard the muffled *whump* of the explosion behind them. Now Jack alights from Frankie's car, still without a word, and stands there on the sidewalk in front of the Lexington, hat shoved back, face slick with old sweat, dazed and deeply tired and only dimly grateful that he's lived to see another day, which is already well up on the City of the Big Shoulders, a mild sun mellowing the upper portions of the stony façades, sky like a baby's new blue blanket. Out in the lake innocent whitecaps fleck the gently dipping length of a trawler making its way down to Whiting. The doorman is looking funny at Jack, but Jack's far too tired to work up a flare of anger, even to think, fuck him, as he makes his way across the lobby to the elevators. Within five minutes he's in his suite and has shucked his clothes and fallen into the big bed across from the sleeping Lulu who's barricaded by pillows and piled blankets.

When she awakens she's glad to find it's nearly ten and looks across to see Jack asleep and is tiptoeing out of the room to call room service when she stumbles over the clothes flung across the floor—very unlike Jack who is obsessively neat about his clothes and person. Yet here they are underfoot—suit coat, vest, collar, shirt, pants in a tangle, and the shoes and spats strung out behind like he'd been running out of them and had just made it into the sheets. Lulu sees the shoes are heavily caked with mud and that the spats are spotted with what she instantly knows isn't muddy water but is blood. She stands there, half-bent in the room's shrouded light, looking at the spats and then over her shoulder at the sprawled form swathed in the sheets and coverlet. And for some seconds now an interior voice has been telling her with a mounting shrillness to get out of the bedroom, not to inspect any of this. But still she can't stop herself from bending further and cautiously pulling aside the suit coat to look at the pants and to find there on the one cuff she dares examine more blood. And something else, too, some partially dried matter that might be food but that she knows—again—isn't: a small whitish thing with a fleck of red through it and shaped vaguely like the continent of South America. And now the interior voice is shrieking at her, "*Don't! Don't!*" But her fearful forefinger is drawn, mothlike, towards the whitish flame of this bit of something, tremblingly descending, until it touches it.

It's slippery-smooth with a certain softness to it, and she knows that whatever it is now, it was once, and not long ago, either, a part of something alive that can't do without this piece of itself, this integument, not and have its life. And moth-like, her finger, singed, darts back and is clasped by sister fingers and thumb—but not comforted—and then in the front room she sits on the sofa, clasping her hands while beneath the kimono's silky folds her limbs jerk and twitch, and she can't call up room service because she can't handle the phone, and they couldn't bring her anything she really needs anyway, and so she must simply sit, twitching while the light slides down the stone walls of the city. And is still sitting so when the telephone's rattle shoots through her like an electric bolt, and before she knows what she's doing she's answering it, hearing Joe Batters saying, "Hullo, Lulu. I gotta speak wid Jack." Jack is still sleeping and from what she can tell hasn't moved since he hit the sack. The bedside Westclock says three-twenty, and she thinks this can't be right but shakes his shoulder gently, and he looks up at her, wild for an instant, the sheet covering his face from just below the eyes like the bandits in the movies. "Joe Batters on the horn," Lulu says, stepping back while Jack tries to work on this.

When she comes out of the bathroom Jack's in the front room sitting at the opened windows, smoking in his undershirt, and when he turns his head she sees he's smiling. "Snorky wants me to go with him to New York day after tomorrow," he says. "Big meetin there." He shakes his head, drags deeply on the cigarette. "Ya never know, do ya," Lulu manages, trying for nonchalance while a thought, forbidden, fatal, flashes through her mind of what she's going to do the minute Jack leaves town, and almost visibly she has to yank herself away from it, has to train her attention on this murderous man by the window. "Ya gotta know," Jack says. "Ya gotta." The smile's still there when he adds almost playfully, "But sometimes ya don't."

Two days later it's Lulu at the same windows, craning her head
to look the seven stories down, watching as Jack throws his grip
into the backseat of a cab and then climbs carefully in himself.
Lulu watches the cab pull smoothly into the stream of midmorning traffic, watches until she can't see it anymore, then turns with
an almost military determination and crosses to the sofa where she
grabs a movie magazine, sits down with it, and checks her watch.
She's got to sit here forty full minutes, she's told herself, beginning
now distractedly to flip the pages, the famous faces flitting in front
of her eyes like the movies themselves that, so she's read, are really
made up of thousands of static images run quickly together in sequences. In forty minutes if Jack hasn't returned for some reason,
he'll have gone to Dearborn Station to catch the train to New York
and that big meeting he's so proud and relieved to be attending.
And at the end of those forty purgatorial minutes, when Jack really
is gone, then she'll jump from her chair and fly into action, flinging gowns and jewels and hats into suitcases. Because Lulu also has
a train to catch and a ticket for it, too. Yesterday, while Jack was at
the Metropole, she'd gone down to Union Station, loitering there
in the great, echoing stone lobby with its high windows from
which poured dusty shafts of sunlight, checking every few minutes
from beneath the brim of her hat to see if she'd been followed. And
when finally she'd satisfied herself she hadn't been, then she'd
stepped away from the newsstand and with thumping breast and
constricted throat approached the wicket and boldly booked passage. Now that ticket lies secreted beneath the carpet's edge near
the door to the suite. She wants desperately to go over there and
peel the carpet back and take the precious thing in hand, scan once
more its tiny, lettered legend. But she doesn't. "Helen Louise," she
says aloud through clenched teeth, "you keep your ass right where
it is. Forty minutes—thirty-seven, actually." But she does at least
permit herself the all but unbelievable relief of imagining the

hidden ticket while she sits there, flipping the glossy pages. It's one-way. To Los Angeles.

⤳❖⤝

Rube Goldberg makes almost two hundred grand a year with his intricate cartoons and his wacky answers to John Q. Public's dumb questions. He's unquestionably the funniest man in print, a comic genius on a par with Chaplin and Will Rogers. Goldberg doesn't mind spending this fortune freely, and so today, a balmy, breezy April one, he's pulling out all the stops for his brother-in-law Billy's marriage to the actress Phyllis Haver. His Honor himself, Jimmy Walker, will officiate at Goldberg's mansion at Seventy-fifth and Riverside, and then the whole shebang will motor out for a party at the country estate Goldberg rents at Great Neck. Because Billy and Phyllis are jazz hounds, Goldberg's hired a ten-piece unit from the Whiteman Orchestra, featuring Bix, a special favorite of the wedding couple. A while ago Phyllis fixed Bix up with her friend (and bridesmaid) Ruby Keeler, and they double-dated a couple of times, not that it turned out that well: Ruby told Phyllis she found Bix so remote and shy she wondered if he knew he was in New York City with her or off in some other world all by his lonesome. Really, Ruby said, it was almost insulting, though Bix was certainly polite enough. Phyllis and Billy had laughed: that was Bix, all right. You just had to know him. He didn't mean anything by it, and he was a true, if odd, gentleman. Bix himself isn't wild about playing the date—the ceremony's at ten in the morning—but he likes Billy and Phyllis. Pops Whiteman isn't wild about it either. The orchestra's schedule is bulging dangerously, players are dropping out because of it, and Whiteman has his hands full preparing for the Hollywood trip. Snoozer has had enough and has gone back to New Orleans, replaced by Eddie Lang. Matty Malneck's had a breakdown and is recuperating in Denver where the band will pick him up on the way west; Whiteman's replaced him with Joe Venuti who plays hot violin. Pops is also having problems with Crosby and the Rhythm Boys because they want to book dates on their own, but the orchestra's schedule is too heavy to permit this, and the issue is festering. Bix isn't all the way back, either, and Whiteman's worried he won't be up to the demands of making this movie. So, he's kept Andy Secrest on to help out and play some of Bix's spots, something Secrest can do because he's studied his idol's style so assiduously he can do a fairly convincing imitation of him. But Andy's no Bix, and for today Goldberg's told Whiteman it's got to be Bix. No substitutes for Billy and Phyllis.

The ceremony calls for the Whiteman unit to set up on the sidewalk outside the mansion, ready to play the Wedding March. But what emerges at the appointed moment isn't the glowing couple but instead the florist, feet first and dead drunk. But it's only a momentary letdown and kind of in keeping with the spirit of these wacky times. Maybe Rube even planned it, somebody laughs. Anyway, finally everything goes off the right way, the mayor's in top form, and afterwards they all pile into the caravan of cars and drive out to Great Neck. There on the Italian stone terrace with its low balustrade and the lawn flowing immaculately down to the tree-fringed Sound Bix plays well in the cut-down unit, and at a break the band is drinking Veuve Clicquot when Whiteman looms up and claps Bix on the shoulder. "You know, Bix," he says after a moment or two, gazing at the crowd on the terrace and spilled out on the blue lawn, "this Hollywood thing can make you an even bigger star than you are already." Bix shrugs, looks down into his gently fizzing glass, shy smile with something else shadowing it these days. Lately his popularity has begun to seem like a chimerical thing to him, something out of a bygone age, and he almost ghostly at times to himself. "Well, Pops, I don't know about that," he says quietly.

But Whiteman insists, his great medicine-ball head glistening with perspiration in what has turned into a warm afternoon, and Bix listens politely while Whiteman goes on to describe with a champagne-fueled animation the epochal nature of this first full-length, all-talkie, Technicolor musical, the fictionalized biography of the King of Jazz. Pops takes another giant swig of the Veuve Clicquot so that the hovering waiter with napkin-draped arm can supply a refill and then launches into a description of the plans sketched out by Universal's Carl Laemmle and Laemmle's nephew, Julius Bernstein. "I'm telling you, Bix," Whiteman says, "this thing's going to revolutionize the whole damn country—the world, really!—the way the Victrola did. Why, do you realize what's been happening here just since the end of last year? Thousands and *thousands* of theatres all over the country have been wired for sound, even in small towns. It's absolutely phenomenal! There are now"—he breaks off, sips, stops. "Well, hell, I don't have the figures here. But here's the point: by the end of this year everybody'll be hooked into this thing, and the ones that aren't, why, they'll just be out of business like the guy with the horse and cart. And this time next year, what'll they be going to see?" He spreads his arms, his white jacket flanging out over the expanse of his chest and belly. "Not Chaplin!" Whiteman claims. "Not Fairbanks! Not America's Sweetheart!" He pokes Bix in the lapel with the hand that holds his glass, and a little of the champagne slops out, hitting the pitted terrace like raindrops, but Whiteman takes no notice. "No! They'll want an honest-to-God musical spectacle—'The King of Jazz'—that'll make 'The Jazz Singer' look like Wilbur and Orville out at Kitty Hawk."

Bix has to chuckle. He's never seen Pops so excited, and maybe it's the Veuve Clicquot and the warm bath of the April afternoon, but whatever it is, it communicates itself to him a little as Pops rolls on about Universal's plans for the film that will dramatize his career from his Denver boyhood beginnings to his current pinnacle and how Julius Bernstein has said the scriptwriters wanted to focus on a couple of band members to chart the stages of the Jazz King's saga. Whiteman says he'd immediately thought of Ferde who'd been with him almost from the start, but Bernstein had said that for maximum dramatic effect the band guys probably had to be horn players, and so right away Whiteman had thought of Bix. "They'll have an actor playing you," Whiteman tells him, "though I don't know if they can get Rin-Tin-Tin," poking Bix with a ponderous playfulness, though this time no champagne spills. "But they can put your sound on the film—I don't know how they do that—but it'll be you in all those theatres, even the little ones out there in Po-dunk and Paducah. Why, man, you'll be reaching audiences you could never have reached, even by radio and records." Bix shakes his head, smilingly, about to make some demurrer, but Whiteman cuts him off. "No, no, no," he says, again poking Bix with a fore-finger. "Listen to me now, Bix. I know what I'm talking about here. This is big. *Big.* But you've got to get yourself in shape for it: they tell me this movie stuff is hard work, very demanding, and Laemmle has a hell of a lot of dough invested in this project." He flashes a conspiratorial smile down at Bix and moves his glass to clink with Bix's in a toast. "You know," he says, "I love this stuff myself. Look at the way I'm lapping up Rube's best. But business is business, Bix, and this"—nodding at his glass—"and that"—a side-ways head wag towards the gay crowd with their picture hats and boutonnieres—"don't mix. Anyway, not the way you've been mix-ing them lately. You've got to take hold now. I mean it." Bix nods, asking how he sounds today. "Better than anybody who ever played that thing," Whiteman tells him. There's a pause, laughter filtering in, the sound of other glasses clinking. "But you're not the old Bix yet. You know that." Bix nods, looking into his glass and taking a small, reflective sip. Champagne really isn't his drink. "Yeah," he says at long last, breaking a silence between them that has begun to feel uncomfortable, looking away from the looming Pops, across the lawn's aqua flow to the trees with their new-flung leaves shining in the afternoon sun like a thousand banners. "Yeah. I don't feel really strong yet. My legs don't work right." "You'll get it back, m'boy," Whiteman says, clapping him on the back, beaming down on him. "You'll get it back, and we'll make history together out there!" "I'll get it back, yeah," Bix says.

Yet out on the Great Plains, aboard the gaudy, gold-lettered Old Gold Special, he's still feeling far from strong on the long California crawl, and the combination of onboard hijinks and dismal weather is hardly helping. Nothing to do but read at a Sinclair Lewis novel he can't get into (Gopher Prairie being like places he knows too well) or visit the club car, strategically positioned between the four passenger cars and the four cars of baggage, where he finds himself outside the roughhousing, wrestling matches, four-part harmony singing, the gag shots taken of disheveled men imitating Strangler Lewis, the daily drinking that starts just short of eleven and continues until they stop for concerts in Indianapolis, St. Louis (an old girlfriend for him to handle there), Kansas City. And then it begins all over again as soon as the porter swings up that heavy platform step with a final *thunk* and the steam hisses out beneath the cars and the giant wheels that are silver with wear grind down the shining tracks and the train—OLD GOLD SPECIAL THE PAUL WHITEMAN ORCHESTRA—wheels westward once more. But the lettering's looking pretty drab out on the Great Plains because the nation's midsection is soaked with the rains that have been sheeting down for weeks, and the famously fecund soil can take no more, and so when he looks up from the Sinclair Lewis novel or the battered newspapers passed around since the last stop he sees only the interminable rain filling further the new-made lakes, the sodden hillocks on which stranded livestock stand submissive, the bleak prospect of leaden, dimensionless skies stretching on and on. In some places the railbed itself is submerged, and the Special must creep along, tie-by-tie, its fixed cyclopean searchlight peering blindly into the gloom and the steadily falling rain.

In Lincoln, Nebraska, the weather relents long enough for them to be mobbed by five thousand gathered at the Burlington Station. Bix, standing on the car's platform and smoking his Camels, assesses the situation as they pull in and ducks back inside. But eventually they all have to climb down and are instantly engulfed, surrounded, cut off. He immediately loses the cane he's been using, but he doesn't fall because he can't, held upright by the feverish press of bodies smelling of damp wool, gabardine, felt, rubber, as more and more of them are trying to touch the players, grab them, reach over intervening shoulders and backs with pencils and fountain pens and slips of paper, envelopes, timetables snatched up from the station's waiting room. Whiteman's stuck far from his men, his vast bulk immobilized like some ocean liner run aground, his coat torn and all its buttons missing. Finally, he's able to break free and get the band, or most of it, up on the platform where they play Diga Diga Doo and China Boy, but when they get into the opening of the age's newest anthem, Runnin Wild ("always goin, don't know where"), the surge begins to build once more like some monstrous wave that has begun to gather far out in the ocean and that will destroy the first thing it reaches. The crowd begins to climb up among the players, and Whiteman drops his stick in mid-tune and hollers, "That's it, boys!" and they break for the train, each man for himself.

They're glad to get off the Special in Denver where at last they see the sun again, yellow as a daisy's heart in a new-scrubbed sky, and that first night they're the guests of Pops's parents. The venerable Wilberforce J. Whiteman is Denver's Mr. Music because of his long and loving service to the city's school kids, and the Whitemans have their son's entire entourage—players, managers, technicians—

out to their big home on the edge of town for a fried chicken supper. The next day they're all driven up into the mountains along
rocky switchbacks to the grave of Buffalo Bill where they pile out
like schoolboys and are momentarily awed by western immensities:
the high air, the long sweep of the wind across the peaks and
through the pines, the blue distances. And there in the foreground,
the cairnlike grave of the old sharpshooter and showman. Joe
Venuti, their new hot violinist, begins to strut about the gravesite,
blowing raspberries, broad, farting sounds he produces by curling
his index finger tightly over his thumb and blowing through the
aperture. Venuti can play whole tunes this way, and the boys are
howling with laughter at the incongruity of the situation. Only Bix
isn't amused. He's chilled, and his knees are bothering him, and the
violinist's antics strike him as disrespectful because, as he tells Bill
Challis, he can remember as a small boy seeing Buffalo Bill when
the aged hero played Davenport, can remember the hush descending like twilight when Bill entered the sawdust arena on his stallion
and the spotlight picked out the rider in his high boots and pearl-
handled pistols. Then the thrill of sadness that swept through the
crowd when Bill doffed his Stetson and his wispy hairs gleamed like
strands of silver and every line in the handsome old face was visible
like the topography of the Great West and Bill looked down into
the shadows of Death itself. So, for Venuti to be high-stepping
around the grave, blowing those raspberries—it's not right, Bix says
to Challis. Some of the boys bring out their Brownies, and Bix
stands there at the edge of the rollicking group, tie and hair whipping in the wind, shoulders pinched together in that ineffectual
stance humans assume when cold. When they're back at the Whiteman home that afternoon Mrs. Whiteman notes his chilled, withdrawn behavior, the pallor of that boyish face, and wants instantly
to mother him with some special herbal tea that she brings him
where he stands talking with others on the verandah. And bless her

ample heart, she also has a shawl for him, and so what can he do but graciously accept both tea and shawl while his colleagues draw back and make eyes that say, "Aw, Bixie, lemme fix that shawl for you." But he finds he wants the tea and its medicinal warmth, though when it's safe to do so he takes the shawl from his shoulders and carefully folds it over the railing. But nobody says anything to him then, and by the time they haul for Salt Lake the incident's forgotten. Denver's been good for them, some decent weather, a chance to stretch their legs. Except for Pops, who's the first into the club car when they pull out, glad to be sprung from that straitjacket where the old man is Mr. Music, and he is just the son whose current popularity is merely puzzling to his papa.

In Salt Lake the Mormons are up for a good time in their own way. Their eyes are as clear as the Utah air, and they listen with polite attention as Whiteman takes them through the more patriotic, martial portion of the book, staying away from anything too jazzy. With little to do, Bix tries to peer out at the earnest, honest faces so like those he's known back in Davenport, and, unbidden, a sense of his own strangeness, even his foreignness, comes over him, and he finds himself wondering once again about the Whiteman approach, something for everybody but not too much of any one thing and nothing that would challenge an audience anywhere. You couldn't really fault him for it: the formula's fabulously successful, the level of musicianship consistently high, and he can vividly remember that when Tram had clinched the deal that brought them and Herman, too, into the band, he and Tram had hugged each other and howled with an uncharacteristic glee. Can remember, too, telling his folks with unabashed pride that he was now with the best damn orchestra in the country. It was. And where, in fact, was the audience for a more daring and authentic American music? Certainly not here. Nor in Denver or Detroit, and maybe not even in New York. How could you write music for so vast and various a country as they'd been training across for days and days? He thinks again of Ravel, of his amazed response to all the spectacular and contradictory American realities, and wonders whether the great composer could be equal to them. Next to him Andy Secrest kicks his foot, and he's a trifle late for a section passage, but when that's over with his mind swings back to those few who aspired to write contemporary American music, like his old hero, Eastwood Lane. Who had Lane been writing for? These Mormons? The folks in Davenport and Dubuque? What about the avant-garde guys who went to Paris after the war? Or Gershwin, for that matter? And the other modernists, hidden here and there in unlikely places around the country, composers unheard-of and more daring by half than Lane or Gershwin or Copland—who were they writing for? In St. Louis where they'd played a concert he'd been talking about these things with Lennie Hayton, and Hayton mentioned to him a guy who spent his daylight hours selling insurance but his nights composing. This Ives, Hayton said, had gathered together camp meeting hymns, ragtime, minstrel tunes, all sorts of scraps of popular music, and fused them into symphonic compositions. Hayton had heard a couple of them performed by an informal orchestral group in New York and thought they were so experimental the public would never be ready for them.

Boarding the Old Gold Special after the concert, all this is still running like a millrace through his head, making him even more remote and unreachable to the others, and when he tilts his fedora down over his nose they know he's completely unavailable. So he slumps there, sprawled in seeming sleep but wondering under the shadow of his hat what the essential sound of this country would be like if you could capture it in musical notation. He knows the jazz of the so-called Jazz Age—Ted Lewis's jazz that rhetorically asks, Is Everybody Happy?—expresses nothing more than a current mood. And he has to admit, too, that the jazz of his old heroes, LaRocca and Mares, doesn't reach deep enough. If any jazz could be part of the sound of America, it would be that blue-toned sort that Armstrong and Oliver and Ellington played, and without ever hearing him, he feels now that what had taken him out to that dusty dancehall in western Louisiana was his certainty that Kid Casimir also hit that blue vein. Gershwin obviously understood this, at least in Rhapsody if not so much in American in Paris, and even Ravel with no American background had sensed that blue-toned jazz expressed something essential about the country, even in the midst of its long euphoria: to Ravel, Bechet was better, more American, than Whiteman. He probably was. A mood of disgust with the terrifically ephemeral nature of the Whiteman book begins to overcome him as if he were sliding into some pool of cold grease, and he finds himself thinking it was no wonder his folks hadn't opened those packages he'd sent home: they knew they were essentially empty. He fights off the dreadful image of the packages, entombed in the implements of a virtue right up there with godliness itself, their unviolated tape seals and strings, forcing his mind to contemplate instead the opening notes of a composition he'd begun years ago, back when he was hanging around Bloomington with Hoagy Carmichael, and one afternoon at the fraternity house Hoagy had scribbled some of it down—as much of it anyway, as they could get after all the gin or the needle beer or whatever the hell it was they'd been working on since morning. And Hoagy had fuzzily asked him, "What're you calling it, anyway?" And cloudily he'd answered, "O, I don't know. Cloudy, maybe." Cloudy it remained, unfinished. And he didn't know whether his friend had managed to save that transcription, whether it still existed somewhere, dog-eared, liquor-stained, fragmentary, the penciled notes smudged and fading. Once again he senses the random messiness of his life. So much was unfinished, abandoned.

He feels the first jolt of the Special and the two that follow in swift succession, as the train trundles towards the desert under a million-starred blanket, into a part of America where songs were chanted and drummed by natives who knew nothing of the giddy national mood, nor of jazz or blues or Gershwin either, but who did know what music it took to bring on cloudy weather and rain with it.

❧❦❧

Since dawn they've been stalled in Tonopah, and now the early summer sun has arced across them towards the blue Sierra. It's a goddamned hotbox, somebody says, and they settle for that. What the hell: so many delays on this crawl you'd go nuts if you began to wonder what the latest problem really was. So, it's a god-damned hotbox, and somebody else says he could use a hot box himself right about now. In threes and fours they walk the town's dusty streets, visit the general store—tack, plow line, fencing pliers, barbed wire, chewing tobacco, rock candy—where the weathered loungers regard them with the same steady, undiminishing incredulity they would visitors from another planet. In a corral behind the filling station a man is forcing a gaunt roan to trot around and around the enclosure, hazing it with a rope and a bullwhip. Under the shadow of his Stetson his face is the color of new brick. When the horse slows and wants to stop the man snaps the whip into the dirt and swings the rope, and the roan jumps, then goes into its nervous, unwilling trot again. The roan's withers begin to darken as they watch and still the brick-faced man keeps it moving. "Say," one of the watchers calls out, "how come you keep him going like that? Looks to me like he needs a rest." The brick-faced man doesn't take his eyes from the roan, only swings the long rope in a lazy loop. He has a straw in his mouth and an-swers through clamped jaws. "Needs to work," he says. "Got tan-gled up in some wire over the winter." When the roan works past them again the watchers can see the deep traces of the wire on chest and foreleg. "Gee," one says, "that looks pretty bad." The man doesn't answer.

Up around the engine of the Old Gold Special there's a gaggle of men in greasy mattress ticking coveralls and caps. Every once in a while there's a heavy clank as a spanner is dropped on the rails. After Crosby and Venuti go up there and start horsing around with the repair crew and Crosby offers them a drink Whiteman orders everybody to stay the hell away. Pops is worried. There's a welcome parade scheduled for tomorrow in Los Angeles, the band to be brought from the station in open cars down to City Hall where the mayor will present Whiteman with the ceremonial keys. Laemmle has organized the show as a piece of advertising for his expensive new project. Pops keeps walking back and forth between his car and the repair crew, then standing off in the cinders, looking at his pocket watch.

A few minutes after four the mail truck pulls up at the general store and three copies of the *Nevada Appeal* are dustily dropped on the wooden counter along with a few weary-looking parcels, and one of the boys reaches for one of the papers, but the proprietor puts out his hand and says, "They's all spoken for." But after some dickering the proprietor agrees to sell the store's copy for a quarter more than it costs, and they go out onto the splintered gallery to read the news that isn't quite as fresh out here as it is back in New York, but it's better than nothing. And nothing is what there seems to be plenty of around here, the high desert stretching relentlessly away in every direction they look except to the west, California, where the Sierra rears up, prehistoric and impassable. Then an exclamation from one of the readers, "Well, shit!" But like the endless delays en route they're used to this kind of thing from someone, and what one guy finds remarkable or amazing another will find worthless, and so nobody thinks much about this until Bill Rank drops the paper on the boards and stands and strides off the gallery, and then they gather to read what he's flung aside—a story two days old with a Los Angeles dateline:

LEWIS MUSICIAN DIES OF HEAD INJURY
Los Angeles, June 4—Donald Murray, 25, a clarinetist with the Ted Lewis band, died today at California Hospital here. The Lewis band is in Hollywood making a motion picture. Mr. Murray, well-known in musical circles, fell from an automobile running board Sunday, striking his head on the curbing. He never regained consciousness. Funeral arrangements are at present unknown.

"Well, for Christ's sake," another says, "we gotta show this to Bix." But a third guy says, "You do that, brother, not me." Somebody asks where Tram is.

Bix is back in the club car with Bing. He hasn't been feeling so hot today, but he's starting to feel a little better and he and Bing have mutually agreed to make the transition from beer to gin. Jack Fulton has drawn the short straw, and so it's he who now comes down the aisle towards Bix and Bing, holding the newspaper between thumb and forefinger. Bix looks up. "Hi, Jack. Have a drink?" But Jack stands there above them, tall and slender and says, "No thanks," and hands the paper to Bix like it's the Black Spot. "There's an item here, Bix," he says and turns away up the aisle. Bix looks down at the paper folded open to the item, sees *LEWIS MUSICIAN* and then Don's name leaping out of the agate jumble, and he reads what little is there and hands it to Bing and rises slowly. He pulls his wrinkled vest down, smoothing it reflectively with both hands, and then walks to the end of the car and steps down into the afternoon light that has just begun to take on mauve undertones. Up the track the crew is still gathered around the engine, and as he stands there, thumbs hooked in vest pockets, one of them throws up his hands in a gesture of helplessness or resignation and steps over the rails towards the station. Whiteman, some papers in hand, emerges from his car, glances down at Bix, and turns up towards the repair crew. Bix crosses the tracks and the creosote-and-coal-blackened stones and limps through a patch of goat's head weeds that crackle under his shoes. Then he's surrounded by the usual detritus that collects, magnetlike, next to railbeds: a pile of rust-red rails, some ties, a broken-down freight wagon, a pick leaning on a pile of stones. Clearing the station and its yard, he emerges at last into the desert, still strewn with the inevitable human traces: brown bottles covered with yellow dust and pocked with old raindrops or maybe coyote piss; a bicycle tire; a motorman's glove, its fingers folded into the padded palm as if it had slowly surrendered there. He walks on through the last of the strung-out refuse, out into the creosote bush and yucca and squat little cacti and figures this is as good a spot as any to have a smoke. He searches in his pockets and vest for cigarettes and matches and sends his first blue-gray puff straight into the west-blowing wind, into the huge sun that still hangs a couple of hours above the far peaks.

Donnie. Well, they'd certainly drifted apart since those Chicago days when he was still in prep school and Don had talked Jimmie Caldwell into adding him to the Jazz Jesters for the date at that girls' school, and Don had laid it on old Miss Tremaine, the headmistress, convincing her that their new cornetist came from a solid family, was a nice young man, etc. And Miss Tremaine, tall and spare and white of face and hair had finally agreed the Jazz Jesters could bring the cornetist along. "All right," she'd said at last, "but there is to be none of this . . . *hot* music," pronouncing the word, so Don had told Bix by phone, as if she were really saying, "Fuck," the two of them howling at Don's gloss and Bix doubling over, dropping the receiver on his end and Don on his end hollering at him, "Bix! Goddamn it! Are you there?" And that night at the school there was Miss Tremaine, a head higher than he and looking down that long nose at the nice young man who had arrived in a rather wrinkled Iowa suit instead of a Chicago tux and carrying his instrument wrapped in newspapers. This would never do, she'd said to Don and Jimmie after a full minute's severe inspection, but they'd talked her into letting them hide Bix behind the piano and a potted plant and a fringe of curtain, and Bix had turned that boyish smile on Miss Tremaine, and that had maybe been the clincher. Everything might have gone all right, except he got going after a few numbers, sitting back there in what he recalls as an almost perfect obscurity where all he had to do was play his horn without having to worry about the girls out there dancing with each other in their taffeta gowns and the forbidding Miss Tremaine, seated amidst her withered court. And following his lead, the band had begun to cook as well, getting warmer and looser, until it got dangerously close to that actual hot Miss Tremaine had warned against, and then it was the break, and *he* was hot, hot to talk with Jimmie and Don about what they'd just done, the way they'd been able to work in some of the licks of the New Orleans Rhythm Kings. But Miss Tremaine was in no doubt as to the source of the problem and while he was trying to escape through a side door to meet Don and Jimmie under the fire escape Miss Tremaine had spotted him and called out, "You there! Young man!" and was already at the same moment intercepting Don and Jimmie and telling them, "Your 'nice young man' is exciting my girls! I want you to make him stop!" Jimmie tried to defend Bix, wanting to keep that golden sound that had just made the Jazz Jesters for the first time something more than a joke, but she'd cut him dead. "Do it!" Miss Tremaine said, and that had been the end of Bix for that evening. Afterwards, on their way back to Evanston they'd roared about it in the cold blackness of the unheated car with the lights flitting through the windows, flashing lime-white across their youthful faces. Standing now in the racing sun half a continent and long years away Bix can perfectly picture Don's full-jawed face, the glint of the bottle going up, hear the gurgle and the gasp, and Don's imitation of Miss Tremaine's "Do it!"

Behind him the train hoots and he drags on the stub of the Camel and drops it, blowing out the last lungful followed by the cough he now lives with. Turning back, he sees a white-shirted figure near the station waving his arms like a semaphore and trudges towards it, thinking that maybe it would be all right if the Special did pull out without him. But the figure, which he can now recognize as Jack Fulton, continues to wave and when Bix finally gets there Jack sticks out his hand and says, "Tough, Bix. I know it's tough about Don." Jack doesn't pretend to understand Bix and still less the Bix of recent months who's more mysterious and elusive than ever. Still, when Bix glances at him, then says merely, "Yeah," Jack is quietly shocked: he'd been supposing that Bix was out there in the desert grieving his friend, yet his mild glance and one-word response made it seem he was only out there for a private smoke and maybe thinking it was a bit of a bore being stranded here in Tonopah. But shortly, Jack has reason to revise his thinking yet again.

They're sitting in the club car, maybe ten of them, glad to feel Tonopah receding by the second, some card players and a few others with their instruments out. Maybe they'll noodle a little to get them underway, nothing very strenuous. Eddie Lang plays the lead-in to a B-flat blues just as Bix and Tram enter the car. "C'mon, Bix," Tram says, "let's get our horns." Bix shrugs and they go into the first of the baggage cars where the instrument cases are neatly stashed. When they get back the players are feeling their way into Diga Diga Doo, but there's no enthusiasm for that one, and it dwindles quickly into separate riffs and stray toots, and the boys shift around, making room for the newcomers. Bix sits on the outside of the group, the Bach still in its corduroy case. "What about Tin

Roof?" someone says, and they try that out and play through it, but Tin Roof doesn't go very well, either. But what the hell, they're just noodling, just putting Tonopah behind them. "I like that," Bill Rank says, "Let's try it again." Negative murmurs, other suggestions. "Well, what?" Rank asks. Venuti says, "I gotta crap," and someone asks how that one goes. "Like this, asshole," Venuti says, raising a cheek.

"City Of The Blues," Bix says, so quiet they aren't sure for a moment that he's said anything, but when they turn to look at him he's got the horn out and raised and has already assumed that posture some of them know so well, right leg crossed over left, staring down at nothing. City Of The Blues is based on the chord structure of Careless Love, the old country ballad the early jazzmen appropriated. They all know it, and simply the fact that Bix has called it brings them together now, and they make the thematic statement cleanly enough and then get out of the way because here he comes, right behind. And from his first two phrases, parallel but the second extending the first, they hear a strangely different voice, the tone still pure but the notes not hit with quite the same clean, military precision, the mallet not striking the chime straight on. The antiphonal phrases, call-and-response, tumble into the next phrase, which comments on them, drawing out their inner implications, and then he hits a note three times, really stands on it, before coming up for air. These are not smitten college kids hearing this different voice among them, but stretched and seasoned pros he plays with every night, yet now they're looking at each other with raised brows, and even the card players lower their hands. Tram has heard him in every conceivable situation—St. Louis, Hudson Lake, the New Yorker after hours with Rothstein and his bunch sitting in the shadows behind their richly glowing cigars— and thinks he's heard everything, including the light classical, modernistic piano probings he doesn't understand and doesn't think Bix does either. But he's never heard him play the blues like this, not the real blues he's playing now, the heart's weary road that begins in some situation, some house or rented room, some railway platform where the goose-necked light floods mercilessly down on the dark bench by the midnight tracks; some juke joint or crossroads tavern; some break-of-dawn city street or empty, unkempt bed: and then departs from there on the destinationless journey that, so the repeated phrases tell, is fated to circle back to its beginnings. But Bix is taking them along just that road in a sequence of repeated, reinterpreted phrases, some traditional, some purely his own, and every one of them discarded at last, as if their best reach, deepest aspiration, falls short somehow. Listening to him, accompanying him, the others seem to understand for the first time in this mauve-shadowed, high-desert moment the inmost pathos of the blues: that they can't quite get there, where the pain dwells, but can only point to it, from a distance; as if the soul's cry must finally remain untouched, unassuaged, and the blues must be the sound not of relief but the impossibility of it. On he travels, chorus after chorus, not so much piling effect on effect as exploring the few he's evoked, and as he does their wonderment grows, for surely such mastery of the form must come from somewhere. Where then? Sure, they know he's jammed with Armstrong in Chicago and sat in with McKinney's Cotton Pickers at the Cadillac in Detroit. Sat in a time or two with Duke up in Harlem. But those like Bill Rank who heard him in those settings knew he didn't try to play black with those guys, didn't dirty up his tone, slur his notes, wail or moan. Nor does he now. He's still, inevitably and unmistakably, Bix. But a tougher, bluer Bix than they've ever heard.

Nor would they discover where this outpouring comes from, its long, unsuspected and shadowy foreground, because after he leads them back to the journey's beginning and they restate the theme twice to end it, he takes down, slowly disengages the mouthpiece, and walks away without a word, leaving the Bach lying there on the wicker seat next to the corduroy case, still brilliant in its sudden silence. They look at his retreating back, at the horn, discarded like the blues phrases it has just given voice to, and then at each other. They look at Tram and Bill Rank, but those two look back with the wordless expression that says, Search me.

Later that night, jostled in his dark berth as the Old Gold Special hurtles southward through California, Jack Fulton awakens and thinks back to the sight of Bix limping slowly towards him through the rail yard weeds and tries to find some clue to what Bix had really been doing out there by himself, as if somewhere in that scene there might lie a clue to the man, to what they'd heard in the club car. He doesn't find it. But what he does know is that what they heard had come straight from Bix's soul, which has been indigo, all along.

⚹

Whiteman's excited predictions to Bix about the talkies are right on the money. It is a revolution. But what Whiteman doesn't see yet is that in Hollywood itself no one quite understands the nature of the new, rough beast let loose in their midst. Some awfully big names are convinced the talkies will go away after awhile, when the public tires of the new claptrap, just the way it has tired of mah-jongg and Shipwreck Kelly's flagpole-sitting act. The high gods who created the industry believe this—Griffith, Chaplin, Lloyd, Pickford, and Fairbanks. Yet now the high gods have to reckon with the sensational box-office success of a wretchedly made talkie, *Lights of New York,* a gangster film that has played to s.r.o. all across the country. You could understand, maybe, the novel appeal of *The Jazz Singer,* where Jolson did a few numbers and a bit of dialogue. But *Lights of*

New York?! *Lights* has neither Jolson nor music nor plausible plot. All it has is talk, and apparently that's all it needs. Audiences are clamoring for more and more talkies, and so maybe the high gods are wrong and the pundits and producers right about America's insatiable thirst for novelty, sensation, more of everything: more speed, more fads, more home runs, bootleg booze, noise—jazz, the radio and the roadster's unfiltered roar. And now talking pictures. "FROM NOW ON," shouts a scare-lettered elocutionist's ad in *Photoplay,* "VOICE WILL BE *THE* FACTOR IN PICKING MOVIE STARS!" "If I was a star with a squeaky voice," croaks *Film Spectator,* "I would worry." And there are a lot of worried people in the Hollywood into which the Old Gold Special innocently steams: Slapstick stars like Mack Sennett and Ben Turpin and Larry Semon with their violent sight gags. Stylized flappers whose batting eyelashes and shoulder shrugs now seem obvious: Louise Brooks and Mae Murray and—some dare to say—even the It Girl, Clara Bow. Latin lovers who never had to mouth much of anything, only emote. And European performers whose English is heavily accented: Pola Negri, Emil Jannings, Vilma Banky. Ali Nazimova declares she has no intention of staying on in such a circus; she will give up her mansion, the Garden of Allah, and go back to New York and legitimate theatre. Nobody knows yet whether Garbo can talk.

With the studios rushing talkies into production like autos off Henry Ford's assembly line, Griffith tries to organize a boycott of talkie productions. Chaplin had a sound test a year ago, suffered a severe attack of what's become known as mike fright, and is now declaring he'll never appear in a talkie. Fairbanks says he can't see a future for himself in an industry where action is forfeit to sound, for how can Zorro, Robin Hood, the Black Pirate, D'Artagnan be held hostage to a gadget that must be concealed in a telephone receiver, a flower pot, suspended at the end of a fishing pole? In this new Hollywood that is just shambling towards shape, though, it looks like Fairbanks and all the others will have to play to the mike, bow to the sound experts, rough, boorish men with no movie backgrounds but whose tyranny is as absolute as it is unprecedented. All the contract players, from Clara Bow and John Gilbert and Wallace Beery on down the line must report for sound tests, and as Beery tells a colleague, "Better bring a change of underwear."

In such a setting the Whiteman Orchestra is bound to get a mixed reception. On the one hand, Laemmle has committed a lot of money to their movie. And yet they're fated to be despised by some as interlopers, noisemakers, hired help several cuts below true artists. Universal has built them a clubhouse that symbolizes their anomalous status, a huge, rustic structure containing a rec room–rehearsal hall big enough to play basketball in: grand piano, pool table, locker room, in case the boys get lathered up. But it's situated at the far end of the lot, back there where the vegetation begins to take over and next to the spectral silent sets of Lon Chaney's *Hunchback of Notre Dame* and *Phantom of the Opera*. But from the day of their arrival there's a distinction made between Whiteman himself and his boys. In Hollywood everybody instantly wants Whiteman. And when they have their galas, they want Whiteman's boys as well—but they'll have to come in through the service entrance and wait for their cue. When the dancing's done, Whiteman stays on as a celebrity guest. The boys go out the back way.

Universal wants to keep them happy, though, if it can. It gives them the run of the lot, and the local Ford dealer chimes in with a nice arrangement: a new Model-A (coupé or convertible) for every man in the band who wants one, at a special discount, the price to be deducted from their weekly paychecks. These are racy rigs, too, because Mr. Ford has made a startling concession to the restless tenor of these times and now issues autos in a variety of colors, to which the local Ford dealer has added his own splashy touch: a tan canvas cover for the spare with a caricature of Pops painted on it—double chin, moustache, receding hairline. Bix signs on for a coupé, bright violet.

He has a reputation as the best drunk driver in the band, can work the gears and navigate when his passengers are blind and legless. So when he gets the violet coupé, he and Bing and Boyce Cullen get tanked up and go for a boozy trial spin, west to Santa Monica, then up the coast with the thorny, empty hills on their right, a dusty green in the sun. Past Malibu, he sees a sandy road and turns down it to where it ends on a high bluff above the sea. He stares down at the gentle rollers purling about the edges of huge rocks, changing their colors from blue to milky green to white with concentrated brine. "Gee," murmurs Cullen from the passenger's seat. He hands a bottle across the gearshift but Bix shakes his head. "A swim," Bing finally brings out from his cramped position in the back. "That's what we need, a swim." "We don't have trunks," Bix reminds them, and they sit there in silence, mesmerized by drink and the light and the waves until Bing and Cullen sink into sleep. Bix finishes a cigarette and flips the stub out the window, wondering a little why the Pacific isn't the thrill the Atlantic was when he first saw it on Long Island in '22. He and Doc Hostetter had been up all night with LaRocca and the Original Dixieland Jazz Band, he'd sat in with them, and then somebody had driven them out to a beach where they'd watched the sun come up out of the sea. He remembers thinking at the moment when the huge fireball quickly emerged from the dark, placid waters that now his life was complete: he'd played with his heroes in Manhattan and he'd seen the Big Drink, as the doughboys had called the Atlantic. So, what could go wrong? He wonders what has gone wrong, and can't come up with an answer, sitting there above the flashing sea in his brand

new car with its painted caricature of America's most famous band-
leader stretched over the spare. All that comes to mind is that he's a
long way from Iowa. After a time he wheels the Ford sharply about
and starts back to Hollywood, a thin veneer of sand and dust
dulling the spanking new finish, his friends lolling about unconscious around him. The next day he and Cullen set off for San Juan
Capistrano, which they've heard is scenic, but they give up short of
Laguna, and the day after that Bix flips an amazed Cullen the keys
to the coupé. "Consider it yours," he tells him. "Just give me a lift
when I need one, okay?" So Cullen then joins the others who are
exploring southern California in their new rigs and beginning to
collect sheaves of traffic tickets: within a week every motorcycle cop
in the area is on the lookout for the cars with the fat man's picture
on the spare, and one day in the clubhouse Venuti says he's being
stopped just because of that picture of Pops, and others report the
same. "The hell with that," Venuti says, and they all shuck the telltale covers and are thereafter distinguished only by the recklessness
of their driving.

And really, there isn't anything else they've found to do yet. At
first, they're hot to see how movies are made but quickly discover
that the magic of the screen is made up out of a lot of delays and
retakes and repositionings, which are all distinctly unmagical.
Their freedom of the lot turns out to be the freedom to be bored
and in the way, and after Venuti ruins a few love scenes with loud
off-camera raspberries and there are some skirt-chasing incidents
Laemmle orders his nephew to get rid of these guys. It's the clubhouse or nothing, he instructs Julius Bernstein. Whiteman corrals
them at the clubhouse so the nephew can give them the word.

Bernstein turns out to be about five feet high and spits when he
speaks his German-accented English. Immediately Whiteman
sees big trouble here, but what can he do except introduce Bernstein to the boys, then stand aside? Besides, he's becoming angry

at Universal and its writers who haven't produced a shooting script, and so if there are these disciplinary problems, the studio has itself to blame. He and his boys came out here ready to go to work. When he introduces Bernstein the tiny man tells them that the lot is now off-limits except for the lodge, which should certainly be adequate to their needs. They should rest assured that soon a shooting script will be ready, and then their work will begin in earnest. In the meantime, they must find their amusement elsewhere, "und vee cannot any longer hoff these . . . interruptions." There's a moment or two of silence following this ukase, and then from somewhere near the back of the room there comes a long, slow farting sound, sustained for close to a minute, and then another sound suggesting a load has been dumped. The room is convulsed with laughter and even Pops has to turn away, and they can all see his huge shoulders helplessly heaving. Bernstein is enraged by the insubordination and makes the mistake of staying on to lecture them about the seriousness of this project: two million dollars budgeted for it, "und vee hoff not, I hope, hired clowns, but musicians." The spectacle of the diminutive executive, face purple above his florid ascot, increases the general hilarity. Bernstein looks to Whiteman for help, but Whiteman's back is still turned, and so Bernstein storms out, and somebody hollers after him, "Go take a shit in your hat, pal!" Laemmle never learns just what happened at the clubhouse, but the cutups are off the lot, and that's all he cares about.

But he still has to deal with an increasingly irritable Whiteman who tells him bluntly that further trouble can be expected unless his boys are given something else to do other than to drive around and collect traffic tickets. And so shortly a hasty sketch is given to Whiteman and Ferde Grofé who tries to work out a score for it. Then another script arrives, annulling the first. And then still another. Ferde tells Pops he can't work this way, and Whiteman tells

Laemmle not to have his writers bother Ferde until they have a finished script. So, with nothing to keep them hanging around and no
prospect of a script any time soon, the boys scatter into the hills,
out to the beach at Santa Monica, the flats of Beverly Hills. Their
only regular obligation is a Tuesday morning rehearsal and later
that day a five p.m. Old Gold spot over KMTR. Boyce Cullen
hears about a house for rent high in Laurel Canyon and asks Bix if
he wants to take a look at it. Everybody's tired as hell of hotel
rooms, and the idea of rural privacy is appealing. A steep, winding
dirt road leads up to a Spanish-style bungalow, its white stucco flaking off and lying in scatters around the foundation like the residue
of a very local snowstorm. A few bits of broken roof tile mingle
with the stucco, and the lawn has gone to moss because the shrubs
and trees have choked out the sunlight. Inside, the rooms are
gloomy, but there's a spinet in the parlor and the beds are soft and
spacious. Cullen wants to take it. "What the hell," Bix says, agreeable. "Good as any. Maybe I can get some rest up here." When they
move in he doesn't bother unpacking but lives out of his suitcase.

Some vague notion of health—inspired by the daily sun, palm
trees, California's up-to-the-minute tourist promotions—prompts
him to invest in bathing trunks and a set of dumbbells, and Cullen
hears him around noon, working with the dumbbells in his room,
the panting breaths, the heavy clunk as the pig iron implements are
wearily set down. But after a few days he doesn't hear this any more,
and Bix announces he'd rather take his exercise on the links at the
Lakeside Club with Bing, Al Rinker, and Roy Bargy. "Be better for
me to get out in the sun," he tells Cullen, "work my legs in the fresh
air." But Bing and his buddies are serious golfers, not casual hackers.
Big bets. Eighteen holes in the morning beginning at nine sharp.
Drinks in the clubhouse: gin rickeys. Then another eighteen in the
afternoon. Still, it turns out that Bix can hold his own with them,
for a few days anyway. With some rented sticks he hits a long

straight ball with the woods and mashie. But there's no short game, and they laugh at his efforts on the green with the putter wavering in his hands. "Steady, steady," Crosby croons to his chum. Bing's utterly at home out here on the course and everywhere else in southern California. The whole scene makes a beautiful sort of sense to him, whereas Bix is having trouble making any sense at all out of all this glitter and endless leisure. But to look at Bing in his plus fours, argyle stockings, and four-in-hand tie tucked in like Bobby Jones, you'd think this was where he'd been always. It's certainly where he wants to stay, and without saying anything to Whiteman or the Rhythm Boys he's been quietly making the rounds of the studios, taking sound and screen tests: with all these musicals scheduled for production, Bing knows they're going to need singers, and why shouldn't he be one of them? Bix just smiles at his friend's marvelous adaptability; he's glad for him, though he's already come to intuit that none of this is very good for him, including the golfing scene.

After a few days of the thirty-six holes routine he tells them he'll sit out the afternoon round. His knees are bothering him, he says. That afternoon when they come in from the back nine they find him in the lounge area, just off the locker room, playing the weathered old piano, a tall frosted glass atop it. He's working through a passage of an unfinished sketch he thinks of as Candle-lights, stopping where it doesn't seem right to him, returning to the beginning of the difficulty, oblivious to the men drinking, playing cribbage and backgammon. And while Bing and the others watch from the entrance a heavy-shouldered man, his face reddened by sun and drink, strides up to the piano and slaps a tenner on its top. "Hey, fella," he says, holding his hand on the ten, though it's not in danger of being blown away, "take this and play something else, okay? We can't talk with you practicing, or whatever it is you're up to. What about If I Had A Talking Picture Of You—you know that one?" Bix doesn't look up but shakes his head. His hands keep moving among the keys. "Well, what about Sweet Sue? You know that one?" "Yes, I know that," Bix replies quietly, rising from the chair and walking past the man. "I know that one." And that's the last Lakeside sees of him.

Maybe walking will be the ticket. He announces this one morning, surprising Cullen in the kitchen where the trombonist has just finished squeezing some orange juice. Cullen wonders whether he's seen Bix up before noon out here, except for the brief golfing phase, and decides he hasn't. Cullen has a girl in his bedroom, still asleep in the hammered sheets of last night's lust, someone he picked up at the Montmartre where the Rhythm Boys are appearing with Professor Moore and his orchestra. "Uh, o, hi, Bix," Cullen stammers. "Juice?" Cullen is a few years older than Bix and as Whiteman's lead trombonist is more important than a fourth-chair cornetist, but you'd never know it from the deferential way he acts around Bix, and now he's embarrassed about the girl. But Bix is oblivious, even though the bedroom door's partly opened. He wants to talk to Cullen about a regimen of morning hikes up the canyon. "See, I need exercise," Bix says as Cullen hands him the juice he'd intended for the girl. Bix takes it, looks at it with a strange gleam in his eye, and then offers Cullen a toast. "California, Boyce," Bix says, "sun in your eye." When he's finished it he searches his wilted pants for a cigarette, talking while he does so. "But I need company. I need somebody to get me going. What about it? Every morning we get up with the birds, have a glass of this stuff, and then take a hike up the canyon." "Sure thing, Bix," Cullen says. "Be good for the old lungs, eh?" He pats Bix on the shoulder. "Well, what're we waiting for then?" Bix asks, grinning. "Why put off health a day longer, like they say." "Well, uh," Cullen starts, making an involuntary half-turn towards the partially opened bedroom door, and Bix's eyes follow, and he sees two small feet, heels up and peeking out of the tangled sheets. A crimson flush mounts immediately from the neck of his undershirt. "Gee, Boyce!" he hisses, eyes wide, "why didn't you say something?" He turns quickly towards his room, Cullen following. In the parlor Cullen catches up with his fleeing hero and grabs his arm. "Hey, Bix!" he says, noting the back of Bix's neck is red, too, though Cullen can't say whether this is anger or embarrassment or a protest against the girl's presence here in their bachelors' bungalow. But when at last Bix does stop and turn around Cullen can see it's simply a gentlemanly chagrin at having blundered into an intimate situation. Following him into the shuttered dishevelment of his bedroom, Cullen tries to reassure him that everything's okay, that the girl never heard anything.

And the next morning they set out up the canyon, the two bent against the slant of the slope, moving at first at a manful pace. After a hundred yards they slow down, Bix already drenched in a poisonous-smelling sweat like bathtub booze strained through an old sock, but still limping grimly upward past huge sprawls of agave and precariously leaning eucalyptus, his patent leather pumps gray with dust and white where the dust has collected in the insteps. Cullen has already noticed that he's wearing different-colored socks this morning and is pretty sure he's slept in his shirt. There's no chatting now, and the morning that minutes before had seemed new-made and bright with promise now seems sullen and the hike an ugly chore. But they keep silently at it another ten minutes until Bix reels over to some boulders and collapses against them, his chest heaving under the gray and sweat-stained shirt. His face is gray, too, and in shocking contrast to the red, partly opened mouth. Cullen's worried but can't bring himself to say anything and so busies himself with lighting a cigarette, back turned to Bix, giving him time. When he turns around Bix mutely gestures for the cigarette and Cullen hands it to him. He takes a shallow drag, coughs it out, and keeps coughing, and Cullen turns away once more and hears the coughing turn to choking, and then there's a moment of silence and Cullen hears the spearing cry of a bird and sees a sapphire flash of something, and then there's the awful sound of Bix gagging, but there's no splash of vomit that follows, because there's nothing to come up, only the thin bile of a system protesting its chronic violation. Again there's the cry of the bird, a jay scolding from the branches of a eucalyptus, and Cullen pretends difficulty getting another cigarette started and finds in doing so that the real difficulty is that his hands are shaking. But finally he has to turn around, and there's Bix, seated on the ground, head against a boulder, cigarette in the side of his moustached mouth. His face isn't gray now, it's a dead, calcimine white. But he's affecting a casual air—two-guys-resting-on-a-mountain-hike—and attempts to accompany the illusion by saying hoarsely, "Next time, kid, we'll begin downhill."

≈❖≈

On the advice of his agent Richard Barthelmess sends out invitations to a Fourth of July wingding. Barthelmess has been one of the silents' leading men and has just completed his first talkie, *Weary River,* in which he's heard singing a couple of numbers. But rumors are aloft that it isn't really Barthelmess singing in that footage, that it was done for him by a singer from the Cocoanut Grove in a new process they're calling dubbing. The agent's gotten word that *Photoplay* will shortly run an exposé of the process, using *Weary River* as its chief illustration. "It'll be a good thing if you beat them to the punch, so to say," the agent tells his nervous star. "Why not have a bunch of the big players over, make it a festive event, and then you announce that when your contract's up, no more musicals for you. Strictly dramatic roles. This way, you see, you get the advantage back, so to say. You can't do anything about *Photoplay,* Dick. Believe me, I tried. But this way, you'll be out in the open about sound." He grabs Barthelmess lightly by both shoulders and gives him a steady, reassuring look in the eye. "You've got a good, strong voice, Dick. You can do drama with it." Barthelmess starts to say something about poor John Gilbert and his squeaky voice, but the agent cuts him short with a raised hand, as if to ward off a curse. "Dick, you aren't John Gilbert, thank heavens. You've got a good, manly voice."

So Barthelmess gets to work. He lines up Whiteman and the group Whiteman's begun using for these occasions, a kind of all-star outfit that gives the movie folks the essential flavor of the Whiteman Orchestra, but jazzier: Willie Hall on banjo and bicycle pump; Roy Bargy to do a bit of Rhapsody; the Rhythm Boys; and Bix, Tram, Venuti, Rank and Eddie Lang—the hot unit. On the far shore of his swimming pool Barthelmess has carpenters knock together a stage for the band and over it a broad-striped canopy. The invitations feature the band: JAZZ AND THE CLASSICS UNDER THE STARS—AND FOR THEM. And the stars turn out, many of them because they too are nervous and know that Dick Barthelmess's problem may shortly become their own: Pickford and Fairbanks, filmdom's royal couple; Chaplin, Vilma Banky, Gloria Swanson.

Whiteman's heard the rumors about the *Weary River* dubbing but knows nothing of the strategy that brings him here. He plays into it beautifully, though, by telling Bill Challis and Ferde to work up a number that will shine the spotlight on their host, and they dash off an opener they call Weary River Blues. After it, Barthelmess steps out onto the low board and makes a carefully scripted speech in which he tells his guests he won't be doing any singing tonight—or any time soon again. They all laugh at that, the dangerous rumor thus lightly diffused, the problem acknowledged and made mutual, and when he's finished they give him a hearty hand. Maybe this sound thing will turn out all right after all, if you handle it the right way, the way Dick's handling it tonight. Then the band strikes up again, and the beautiful dancers take to the raised teak floor on the pool's near side. At the ten o'clock break someone in the band goes to the rear gate to let in a party-crasher who joins the band at the bar as if he'd been there all along. Hoagy Carmichael is just one smooth son-of-a-bitch, Joe Venuti observes with an admiring, sardonic grin.

Like a lot of other tune-pluggers, song-and-dance men, one-string musicians, crooners and contraltos, Hoagy's come out here for the gold rush the talkies represent. When Pops first bumped into him in downtown L.A. he asked, surprised, "Well, Hoagy, what in hell are you doing out here?" And Hoagy had smiled that lean, crinkling smile of his, the one that enlivened his slab-sided Irish face, the one you couldn't say no to, and said, "Same thing you are, Paul." And from that moment Hoagy's been an informal adjunct to the band Whiteman brings to these parties. Hollywood hosts and hostesses find in hiring Whiteman's group that they get a baker's dozen, and when Hoagy slides in for Roy Bargy he gives the partygoers some of his own tunes and sings them, too, in a voice as oddly unadorned and homely as the wind across his Indiana flatlands. This is good business for Hoagy, who picks up solo jobs this way, and those who hire him find he's not only a fine cocktail pianist but also carries a constant supply of high-grade marijuana and is generous with it. Hollywood is getting very keen on the viper, though already some like Pickford's brother and Jeanne Eagles have moved on to the heavier stuff. This night Hoagy's already lit up by the time they let him in the back way, and when the dancing begins again he's out there on the floor, his white-jacketed arm gracefully encircling Vilma Banky, and the boys up on the stand are having trouble playing they're so amused by this. Later, they see him with Louise Brooks. And still later, to their barely contained hilarity, they watch as he approaches Mary

Pickford and makes a deep bow, inviting her to the floor. But America's Sweetheart is not especially gregarious under the best of circumstances, and these are not the best of circumstances. She and Doug are in the midst of filming *The Taming of the Shrew* as a talkie, and things aren't going well on the set, Doug chronically late and petulant. Yesterday she'd had to take him aside and tell him he was behaving like a sulky schoolboy, and since then they've barely spoken. So when Hoagy comes out of his exaggerated bow he finds Fairbanks glaring at him out of that impossibly handsome, sun-blackened face and then hears Pickford's cold decline.

An hour later, though, Pickford finds herself almost wishing she'd said Yes to that invitation, but this is after a couple more scotches and the young guy has left the dance floor for the piano bench. They're playing Sweet Sue, last year's slightly saccharine addition to the Twenties' bulging song bag of hymns to bobbed-hair beauties—Sweeet Sue, just yooo—. They don't have the bank of sobbing saxes for this nor the falsetto singer, but still this one reaches her now as she gazes across the pool at the pianist who's accompanying the pop-eyed, cock-eyed cornetist on a solo, and for a minute or two she allows her terrifically disciplined mind to slip its iron harness, submitting to the music, its seductive lilt and flow, the vague images the cornet's bringing her; imagining the light pressure of a partner's arm as he leads you through the delicate diagram of the steps; the scent of another person, so close to you, yet separate; the look in their eyes as they gaze down at you and you see—always—that awe that you alone inspire: I'm actually dancing with *Her!* A cloud of heavy cigarette smoke across her nose breaks this drift—Doug.

When they finish Sweet Sue the band watches the dancers moving back to their tables and Whiteman peeks at his watch and finds they have something less than half an hour left of this engagement. Maybe there's not much more bounce left in this bunch, he thinks, watching the dancers become table-sitters, the cigarettes and cigars lit, the glasses lifting. Barthelmess, half-gassed in relief, is strenuously waving Whiteman to his table, and Pops turns it over to Tram. Somebody has requested Sweet Sue again, and Tram hears the groaning from the ranks. "Let's do it the way we would with Goldkette," Bix says, looking over at Tram. Tram smiles. "They won't get it," he says. Bix smiles back, "What the hell." Tram turns to George Marsh and tells him for this treatment he's really got to *ride* that cymbal, boy! This has got to be that old sock-time! And away they go, Marsh rocking along on the cymbal and the wood blocks but Bix, just beginning to catch fire now at the end of the evening, still pushing Marsh just a little, and after his shimmering twenty-bar burst Tram calls over, "Take one more, Bix!" And he does, but he doesn't stop there, and now Hoagy shoots Tram a glance and shakes his head in astonished admiration, and when they're through with Sweet Sue as she might have sounded in '26, only better, a knot of pure listeners has gathered near the stage and Chaplin's among them, and the band can see his smooth face with his prematurely graying temples and his long, vulpine teeth bared in delight. Chaplin's hardly a jazz hound, has in fact taken little interest in the signature sound of this decade he has practically made his own. Chaplin finds the ricky-ticky sounds of the bands showing up now in Hollywood merely annoying and recently offended some jazz enthusiasts by walking out on Ted Lewis, saying the band made noise, not music. Chaplin has come to regard himself as an artist, a high and solitary calling, and feels more and more alienated from his Hollywood colleagues, even from Doug, his sole close friend. Doug has never thought of himself as an artist or of movies as an art form. He's only Peter Pan with muscles, a perpetual boy just having fun in front of the cameras—or was until this talkies business, anyway. But to Chaplin movies are art, or ought to be, not cheap entertainment, and looking up at the cornet player, listening carefully to his beautiful inventions, he realizes he's in the presence of another like himself, a genuine artist disguised as an entertainer. When they've finished with that version of Sweet Sue, Bix doesn't even wait for another call but says something to Hoagy and begins again on a variation of the theme, with only Hoagy for accompaniment, and in this version the tune's easy sentimentalities are discarded, exchanged somehow for a haunting and irremediable sadness, and little sweet Sue is transmogrified from a Pickfordesque doll into some remote feminine essence, some supernal being, or even an incorporeal entity towards which the artist stretches out his hand but which eludes his grasp—just—and so is lost to him forever. At this level, which the player has attained by himself, the listening Chaplin can feel the skin along his jaws and on the back of his neck tighten and prickle, and then he knows for certain he's in the presence of something rare. Some evenings, in the privacy of his theatre at home, he gets this visceral reaction watching sequences from his own films, and then he sees which portions of them will outlast any fad or new technology. The choral finale to Scriabin's First Symphony had this effect on him the first time he saw it performed—though not since in recorded versions. But what makes this experience so impressive to him is its context: the slight, sentimental air played for dancing and for an audience, he thinks, that could hardly be more heedless. It's like finding the authentically tragicomic elements in the Little Fellow who most assume was made merely for laughs.

When it's finally over and the cornet player has quickly slipped away with the others, out the back gate, Chaplin catches up with the piano player and asks, "Who is that fellow? The trumpet player, I mean." Hoagy looks at his questioner with genuine surprise, then smiles that Irish smile and says simply, "Why, he's Bix! He's the great Bix!"

And surely it must be this that a few nights later brings Chaplin to a brawl at the monstrous pile William Randolph Hearst is rearing for his mistress, Marion Davies, in Santa Monica. Chaplin has come to loathe the vulgar displays of wealth that are Hollywood high-style and has withdrawn more and more from the nightly social swim. So they're surprised to find him out here at the castle-in-the-making, but not surprised to find him distantly polite. He's here for the music, the band. But while Whiteman socializes the band must wait in the pool house and Chaplin must wait as well. He does so with a better grace than Joe Venuti's displaying out in the pool house. "Hey," Venuti says to Eddie Lang, whose real name is Sal Massaro, "they're treatin us like we're dago wops just off the fuckin boat. We're artists, just like they are, those fancy pricks!" Venuti has recently been confirmed in just this opinion—minus the colorful language—by Jascha Heifetz, who is amazed at Venuti's skills and has had him twice to his home. "Why tell us?" George Marsh says. "Tell them." Venuti says he would if he could, and someone hands him the house phone and Venuti roars into it, "Send out fourteen steaks, and make it snappy!" But a few minutes thereafter when the liveried flunky arrives he's empty-handed and has only come to tell them they're on. Chaplin waits patiently through the first numbers for Bix to get warmed up. I'm Referrin' To Her 'N To Me. Song of Siberia. Drigo's Serenade. But the cornetist remains puzzlingly ordinary and plays most of the time into a derby mute. It Goes Like This. Your Mother And Mine. Canoodle Oodle Along does it for Chaplin, and he leaves feeling betrayed. Surely, he could not have been mistaken about this man, but tonight it's as if he'd left his rare gift at home and showed up with only that wretched prop, the derby mute. Perhaps it's another of his disguises? As he climbs into the backseat of his darkly gleaming limo and the chauffeur closes the door behind him the band can be heard playing Out Where the Moonbeams Are Born, and the blue-eyed lead singer is doing his best with the terribly trivial lyrics. Chaplin knows him slightly since only a few days ago he showed up for a screen test at United Artists. But they'd turned young Crosby down because his ears are too big.

The parties and the empty, golden days between them weigh on Bix. Dumbbells, golf, walking—all are over with. Cullen tries to return the keys to the violet Ford but Bix won't take them, and Cullen can't even get him out in it for a spin. They play cards and drink in the afternoons, but Cullen can't keep up with Bix every day. Meanwhile, the word from down at Universal continues to be discouraging. The fools there have written a script casting Whiteman in the romantic lead. Pops is on a drastic diet just now because he's fallen hard for a movie gal; still, at two-seventy he cuts a very portly figure for a movie swain. He bluntly tells Laemmle this latest idea is ludicrous and mutters about taking the orchestra back to New York. Quickly Laemmle pulls Charles MacArthur, one of his best writers, off another talkie project and puts him on "The King of Jazz" and tells Whiteman it might be another week or so, but then MacArthur will have something they can really work with.

One day Bix phones Bill Challis to talk about getting together so that Challis can make transcriptions of some of Bix's piano pieces. Challis is eager to try. He's even more idle than Bix and is worried by the reports he gets of him from Tram and Roy. Twice he drives up Laurel Canyon to the crumbling house, ready to go to work on a collaboration they started talking about in the fall of '26 when the Goldkette band burned Fletcher Henderson at Roseland with Challis's arrangements. The first time, he finds Bix and Cullen sleeping off a drunk, and after trying for half an hour to raise Bix from the sty of his room he gives up and drives back down. The second time Bix is up, all right, and waiting for him in the parlor, but when he sits down at the spinet it's quickly apparent he's in no shape to work. Flushed and bleary-eyed, thick of fingers and tongue, Bix fumbles into In A Mist. Stops. Flexes his fingers. Tries again. No better. "Wait a minute, can you Bill?" Bix asks and goes into the kitchen. Challis follows and stands in the doorway watching the man pull a quart bottle from the cupboard. "Bix," Challis says, his voice sharp with concern and exasperation, "that crap isn't going to help you. That crap's what's bothering you." Bix pours and turns towards him, lifting his chin and speaking down his nose in his P. G. Wodehouse British. "Rot, my man. Sheer rot. Been doing it for years, what?" Challis watches him take it down, both hands on the tumbler. Bix puts the empty tumbler on the sideboard, the residue of the gin drizzling in greasy streaks down its sides like dirty rain. He pounds his chest in a ghastly caricature of a physical-culture freak after a bracing workout. "Let's go to work," he says. But Challis isn't like Cullen or Crosby or all the others who are in awe of Bix and are only too happy to look the other way. Challis is a blunt guy from the Pennsylvania hills. He spins sharply about ahead of Bix, walks through the parlor, pausing only to scoop up his pencils and paper and shove them in his briefcase. "Bix," he says, hand on the loose brass doorknob at the entrance, "don't call me again until you're really ready to go to work." And Bix, standing at the spinet, looks at his friend with what he thinks is an air of casual defiance but that is actually the look of some thing cornered. "Fine, Bill," Bix says. "I'll keep it in mind." The door slams behind Challis, leaving Bix there and no sound in the empty house but the muffled beating of the metronome within his breast.

Andy Secrest calls and wants to come up, and Bix tells him, fine. Andy wants some lessons from his idol, though he doesn't put it that way. What he really wants is for Bix to help him become more than what he is, a thoroughly competent musician who's learned enough of Bix's stylistic mannerisms to take a few of his briefer breaks. But when Secrest does his Bix there's a studious premeditation about it all, and you can almost hear the one player getting ready to try to reproduce the sound of the other—okay for Whiteman's purposes, but Secrest can hear this too and has other aspirations. Maybe if Bix could show him a few things—his fingering technique, how he determines his odd, beautifully effective rhythmic placements—then he could work on these, assimilate them more fully. Maybe he could eventually sound more like a finer Andy Secrest instead of a substitute Bix. But Bix, self-taught, can't explain why he'll use one fingering method to get a note and then in another passage a different method to get that same note. He can't remember distinctly how in the Golden Age of his self-creation there in the living room on Grand he hunted through the mysteries of his instrument, trying to get Nick's notes and how, often, failing to get them one way, he'd figured out how to get them another, like a tennis player lacking a proper backhand might run around a shot to make a forehand return. After working with the earnest Andy for more than an hour on these mysteries all Bix can finally answer to the persistent, polite question, "Why this way?" is, "Well, Andy, I dunno. It just depends on the passage, is all I can tell you." Even at his best he's never been very articulate about technical matters, and these days he's far from his best, is more diffident, less certain that what he has to offer is of any use to his friend, or anyone else. So much has always been feeling, anyway, how *you* feel about something, not somebody else. After a couple of sessions both men are feeling a little funny about it all, Bix because he knows he isn't really helping Secrest and Secrest because the mystery of the man's special sound remains as impenetrable as ever.

And there's something more that's making Secrest very uneasy: Bix's sound, that golden, glorious thing, is only intermittently there these days, like a sudden blaze of pure sun through a leaden overcast, and one afternoon after Bix has been trying to show Secrest something on Jazz Me Blues and it comes out dull and weak, even less than ordinary, Bix pulls the horn away from his mouth with a strange look, as if suddenly stabbed from behind, his eyes wide with what Secrest doesn't want to put a word to but must— fear: Bix is afraid. Bix looks away quickly, into a shadowy part of the parlor, and Secrest can see his face and neck working. And then

Bix turns around, sits down, and slowly begins to take the Bach apart, the disciple watching silently, afraid himself now. When he's finished and what had been an instrument, this conjurer's staff, is now an unarticulated heap of metal parts on the glass-topped table, Bix stands and claps Secrest on the shoulders with both hands. "C'mon, Andy, let's get the jug and sit out back on the terrace." And they do that. An hour passes, silent except for the sounds of the birds in the tangled vegetation and the bottle being set back down. Secrest tries to slow the pace by smoking, excusing himself to go to the toilet. Coming back from it, he sees Bix with his head in his hands, motionless as a statue of despair, and when at last Secrest says he's got to be going Bix barely glances at him. Outside in the stabbing afternoon light, Secrest maneuvers his custard-colored Ford with exaggerated deliberateness, telling himself he's not drunk, only a little tight. He could, he thinks, make the turnaround in the small driveway and head nose-first out into the road, but this would take some doing—a couple of half-turns and correcting reverses, anyway—so he decides to back out, swinging uphill for the downhill run. He rolls out in reverse, craning his neck around, feeling his starched collar pinching his neck, rolling the steering wheel through his hand. But he's not rolling it enough and not quickly enough, either. The Ford jerks across the road at a lazy angle, its driver sensing too late that his turn hasn't been tight enough, the left rear wheel already slipping at the road's friable edge and Secrest now clawing at the wheel, slamming at the brake pedal. And then the car's weight shifts and it tilts, slowly, and topples sideways downhill in a billow of dust and stones and torn branches and slides into a boulder where it completes its destination and turns turtle. Secrest, still gripping the wheel, finds himself looking up at his hands. The motor is still miraculously running, but there's smoke or maybe it's dust inside the cab and the stinging smell of bruised pine, and his feet are frozen against what is now the cab's top. After a minute he slowly pulls them away from the pedals and the motor chokes out, and he collapses into a ball that rolls easily enough through the opened door and out onto a rocky ledge. It feels very cool to him and solid too as he lies across it, watching some large drops of bright blood spangle out, starlike onto the stone, and someone far away is hollering down at him. "Hey!" the tiny voice hollers. "Hey! Are you all right?" Twenty minutes later, having clambered cautiously up the scoured slope, he finds himself in Bix's bathroom, gingerly inspecting his only injury, a shallow scalp wound that bleeds histrionically. But the custard-colored Ford, Andy Secrest's nine-hundred-dollar beauty, is done for and has to be hauled away for junk.

❊

The pale green stucco of the vast mansion makes a queasy contrast with the color of the surrounding hills, but Keaton doesn't care. Color considerations have never been his strong suit, and Natalie Talmadge Keaton's interest in colors and combinations is focused on the huge wardrobe her husband's fame has bought her. What he does with the house and grounds is of less concern to her than her latest gown, though she has privately observed to her sister that after all Buster is a thorough vulgarian. Other stars have fancy names for their estates. Lloyd calls his Greenacres, and Keaton can see the late Valentino's Falcon's Lair from his place. But he calls this The Italian Villa. He isn't drawing down Lloyd's thirty thousand a week, but he makes a lot more than he and Natalie together can possibly get rid of, and the mansion represents his best effort in that direction. Since his obscure first days in Hollywood Keaton has aspired to the kind of outsized opulence once enjoyed by his pal, Roscoe Arbuckle. In those days Roscoe lived in a twenty-room castle, once the home of Theda Bara, with gold-leaf bathtubs, caverns of wine and booze, a six-car garage for his Rolls, his twenty-five-thousand-dollar Pierce Arrow with full bar and fold-away crapper, his three Cadillacs. Roscoe, or Chief, as Keaton still refers to him, liked to keep his place jammed with merrymakers, night and day, including an all-but-resident jazz band. Now Roscoe exists in blackest disgrace in the aftermath of the Virginia Rapp scandal, but his grand style lives on at the home of his loyal friend: the twenty rooms, the six baths, the servants' wing with its staff of six, and out back a sixty-foot staircase winding grandly down to a marble swimming pool surrounded by palms and cypresses, the trees of the ancient gods. Like Chaplin, Keaton's no jazz fan, but since the Chief had jazz, Keaton's got to have it as well, and on this Sunday he's got Whiteman and his boys out to tootle for one of his celebrated barbeques. At these huge affairs Keaton does the grilling himself and will cook double-thick English chops to your individual satisfaction. And so, while the long, raised pits are glowing down to perfect pitch and the staff is bringing on the chops and chicken and steaks and arranging the master's cooking implements, the master himself is showing Bix and a few others in the band some features of his domain. "These palms here cost me fourteen grand," Keaton tells his tour. They all have drinks in hand and group around him like tourists being introduced to the Medicean splendors of the Old World. "They used to be along Wilshire, but I bought em and put em out front. But then I changed my mind and had em moved back here. Gotta landscaper working for me used to work for the goddamned Pope! Can you beat it?"

High above the group the migrant palms clack dryly in a light breeze, casting fleeting shadows on the bent lawn that is like a billiards table. Next to Keaton his Russian wolfhound, Trotsky, stands dripping wet from a refreshing dip in the marble pool. Now Keaton takes them away from the pool and its palms and cypresses, along a winding drive towards some distant outbuildings, and as they come around a blind curve they're almost run down by the Keaton kids, Jimmy and Bobby, out for mayhem on their motorized go-carts. The tourists leap aside, spilling drinks, as the tykes roar past, and Trotsky gives joyous, high-bounding chase. Keaton says nothing, doesn't even give the kids a glance; he's intent on showing the band his newest pet project, a mechanically regulated trout stream that's being entirely rebuilt to his latest specifications. "This part's finished," he informs them from its grassy bank. "I can turn it on and off with a button up at the house." All this is delivered without facial expression, just like in the movies. Up close, the boys find him a handsome, hard-faced man, older-looking than they'd thought, his skin brittle and traced with many fine lines about the mouth and cheeks. He has a childish compulsion to showing them his toys—but no pleasure. Rather, he's like a victim of child abuse for whom all this and more will never be enough. And that in fact is just what Keaton is: the battered survivor of what once was known as the Roughest Act in Vaudeville in which his parents threw little Buster around the stage, bouncing him off the floor, pitching him through papier-mâché walls. They billed him as the Boy Who Can't Be Hurt, though hurt he often was, arriving at an utterly school-less adolescence with the aches of a man three times his years, moving reminders of the folks.

Out at his garage, only a little smaller than Roscoe's and with an apartment above it for the chauffeur and his family, Keaton leads them through a side door and into a full bar with a hand-lettered sign on the wall behind it: REST AREA. He doesn't ask how their drinks are, just starts pouring, gin for this guy, scotch for that one. They drink up in silence, and Keaton appears almost to have forgotten their presence. When he's finished his drink he reaches for the scotch and the wicker-wrapped seltzer bottle and builds himself another. Willie Hall, not much of a drinker, mutters something about having to get back to play for the guests.

"Fuck em," Keaton says evenly. "Nothing happens till I get back." And eventually he does get back, captives in tow, and by now everybody's well-oiled and famished and Whiteman's wondering where in hell his band has got to, and the white-coated servants have to put on another layer of charcoal. Natalie Keaton has long since disappeared in a huff. She was mad to begin with because Buster insisted that Roscoe be invited and Clara Bow as well, and neither of them is received in polite society, though Bow remains among the brightest of stars. When Venuti spots her across the pool he tells Keaton they all want to meet her, and Keaton shrugs as if to say, What's the big deal? But at a break he remembers and brings her over, her hair blazing in the sun, her eyes going over each of them like fingers, giggling as she gives autographs and shakes hands. When it's Bix's turn he has trouble making eye contact because her clinging polka dot dress plunges steeply in front, and you could hardly avoid getting a good gander at some of what makes the It Girl it. She instantly catches on to his embarrassment and tries to make eye contact, moving with exaggerated gestures from side to side, bending down, trying to find his eyes while the boys are howling at her pantomime that is as hilarious as it is wildly provocative. "Pleased ta meetcha," she says finally, "if I did meetcha," shaking his hand and holding it. He nods, dares a glance at her laughing face, then looks away. She's still holding his hand when she says, "They tell me ya play Sweet Sue real nice," and he nods and returns her smile in muted fashion. "That's one of my favorites—like to hear it," she says. "Well," he says, looking back to the others for support, "we do it different ways. Which would you like?" "Whichever one ya have for me, honey," Clara coos, dropping his hand at last and taking her leave, swaying back around the edge of the marble pool. And when the boys break into spontaneous applause she flashes them a smile bright as a klieg light and gives them an extra bump with her

behind, and George Marsh hits the bass drum twice, real quick.
All of which illustrates why Clara is persona non grata, but her
host hasn't noticed any of this and wouldn't have cared if he had,
because Keaton himself is ready to go on stage. He's broken out
his famous porkpie hat and sent one of the servants over to cue
Whiteman. Whiteman abruptly finishes off a number and alerts
the boys who watch as Keaton in the hat and carrying a tray
loaded with chops, cutlery, and a champagne flute carefully
climbs the long ladder to the high board. Then George Marsh
gets on the snare and gives him a big-top roll. Up on the board
Keaton leans at a precarious, impossible angle, the tray still perfectly balanced, then drinks the flute down and finishes with a
long, skyward flourish. Now his guests are all applauding, because
they've seen this act before, and so has Trotsky who begins to
bark. Upstairs in satined solitude with only her dozens of gowns
and hundreds of pairs of shoes for company, Natalie Keaton, too,
knows what's happening and what's going to happen. She hears
the drum roll, the building applause, the dog's frantic barking;
hears then the breathless pause followed by the thunderous splash
as her husband, that vulgar, compulsive clown, hits the water,
plate of chops still held level before him, heels together, knees out,
porkpie hat square. And then the applause once more as the hat
bubbles to the surface followed by its owner while the tray and
glass and chops slant swiftly to the pool's bottom where tomorrow
they will be retrieved and the soggy meat fed to Trotsky as a re-
ward for his part in the production.

When the long day's over, and a summer sunset has begun to
guild the westward windows of The Italian Villa and the band has
packed up and started home and the white-coated help is clearing
and cleaning, Joe Venuti, ripped to the gills, is speeding back to Los
Angeles when he swings wide around a bend and crashes head-on
into a car with two vacationing schoolteachers from Winnetka.

Both are badly hurt, Venuti's bowing arm is shattered, and Mario Perry, the band's accordionist, is instantly killed.

⚜

Agatha carries the somewhat battered postcard in her purse. It bears one of those heavily retouched photographs where flesh tones look like third-degree burns, the sky like a robin's egg, the sun an orange. On this one, mailed from southern California, smiling Mexicans under gold sombreros move among groves of paradisal lushness. On its reverse her son had scrawled an address and phone number, but when Agatha's repeated calls went unanswered she began to think he'd made a mistake, until one afternoon, after the operator had rung and rung and she was about to give it up again, the receiver on the other end had been lifted, fumbled, dropped, and retrieved, and a voice had mumbled something unintelligible. Eventually she came to understand that the voice belonged to a Mr. Cullen, Bix's roommate. Bix, Mr. Cullen finally managed, was out. Didn't know when to expect him. When she rang off, all of Agatha's alarm bells were ringing, for this Mr. Cullen had clearly been intoxicated. She thrashed in her bed that night, keeping Bismark awake with her anxiety, and by the following afternoon had decided she must go to Los Angeles to see about her wayward youngest and if possible bring him home with her. A rescue mission, then.

Los Angeles has all but paralyzed her: the scale, the sky, the sun, traffic, all those foreign faces. From the Alexandria Hotel she calls him twice within the first hour but gets no one. On her third try she raises Mr. Cullen again who this time seems sober and shortly fetches Bix. Now, it's his alarm bells that are sounding. He stalls her, telling her he can't see her today because they have a rehearsal and then the radio broadcast over KMTR, all of which is true. Tomorrow's no good, either: they have work to do over at the studio (not true). But the day of reckoning must come the day after that.

"Gee, Hoagy, you've got to help me out here," Bix tells him over the phone. Bix needs company, diversion, action up in Laurel Canyon, because Agatha has made it plain she wants to see just where he's living. And Agatha knows Hoagy a little from a visit he made to the house in the spring of '24. If he could pick her up at the Alexandria and bring her up to the house, do a little piano playing, reminisce about Davenport, maybe that would put her mind at ease and she could go back home and not worry. "Why sure, Bix," Hoagy says, amiable as ever. "Be glad to. Nice lady. I remember a wonderful meal we had at your home, and then afterwards, well, we got into a jug, and if I remember right we drove off to Bloomington with Esten Spurrier's horn in the back of that old Ford I had. And you remember how that turned out." Bix remembers, all right: how before dawn they'd rolled to a stop at an Illinois cornfield below Pontiac, gotten out, and then, hundreds of yards apart in the fledgling rows, had played to each other—Hoagy on Spurrier's horn—while the sun like a bloated red grape had arisen out of the swarming ground fog. But he's in no mood for reminiscences now and merely mutters, "Right."

When the dreaded day arrives Hoagy couldn't be more courtly in a folksy way and would have been entertaining, too, if the audience were any less formidable. But Agatha isn't buying, even when Hoagy sings a couple of his songs and plays a duet with Boyce Cullen, thinking to please her with a nineteenth-century piece of German band music that might remind her of home and family. Then he tells her that his tune, Stardust, is something he's stolen from her son. "See," he says, smiling his slab-sided smile, "he used this little phrase, and it kind of stuck in my head, don't you know, and so I just naturally had to figure out a way of doing a little something with it." He plays an eight-note sequence to show her how the phrase goes, then plays the tune and finishes by telling her how deeply indebted he is to Bix. She forces a smile, and Hoagy shoots a glance at Bix who's been shuttling back and forth between parlor and kitchen, bringing out iced tea and cookies that nobody wants, fetching refills, pretending to make an important call while his friends try to run interference for him. No good. Now Agatha says, "I've come for my son, Mr. Carmichael. I've come to take him home with me." Now Hoagy and Cullen fall all over themselves trying to get out of there, murmuring apologies for having intruded on a family discussion, taking up so much of her precious time out here. And Agatha waits through this, too, sitting on the couch in her dark print dress, gloves and hat next to her and the purse with the postcard curled inside it and the gingersnaps untouched on her plate.

Bix watches them leave like a marooned man might watch erstwhile shipmates shove off from a desert island in the longboat, and when they're alone he says he's worried that she might have hurt the boys' feelings. They only meant to be entertaining. But Agatha brushes that aside like the iced tea, the gingersnaps, Hoagy's piano and patter: what are the boys' feelings compared with hers, with the sleepless nights he's cost her, the anguished days, wondering where in the world her son was and what he was doing? How could a mother live with peace of mind when she feared her son was ruining his health with this . . . *nightclub* business, a word that, pronouncing it, makes her avert her face in distress? What he so clearly needs, she resumes, looking at him now in searching fashion, is wholesome food taken regularly, proper rest, regular hours. She wonders aloud what it was that got him started on this terribly wrong road that has brought him here, so far from home. Perhaps it was those dreadful recordings Burnie brought home from the war. But what could she and Bismark have done about that? Or the other mothers up there on the hill whose soldier sons came back so restless, so filled with strange ideas and habits and slangy speech? What could you do with boys who'd seen what they'd seen, been to all those places? And then the Hoffman boy—blinded. She shakes her head, dabs at an eye with a handkerchief. Bix, sitting across the room, elbows on thighs, head hanging motionless, looks up briefly at last and says quietly, "It wasn't that. It wasn't Burnie's records," though he thinks if it began at any one place, it began there. "No, no," she agrees. "It was before that, wasn't it. It was back when you had your first lessons, from Professor Grade." She's trying to catch his eyes, but he's back to staring at the floor in front of his shoes. "You were so gifted, dear, *precocious*—that's the word. Why, when you were five and crawled up on the piano bench at the Beckendorf's and picked out Mister Dooley, why, nobody could believe it. They put your name in the papers, and we engaged Professor Grade who told us you had a real gift. But he said we must be careful, careful just because of that. He gave us a pamphlet—I can still see it: 'Little Hands, How Will They Grow?'" She pauses, emits a long, deep sigh, mourning the way those little hands had grown. "And Opah hoped so much for another musician in the family, someone who could take the piano further than I'd been able. O, we had such high hopes for you, son. Such high hopes."

Looking up from under his brows he can see her wringing her handkerchief, the still-slender fingers he remembers moving over the keys of the parlor piano, playing the light classical German pieces of the last century, now twisting and pulling the lace-bordered thing until it has begun to lose its shape. He wishes he could think of something to say here but knows too well that the only thing he might say that would relieve his mother's anguish is the very thing he can't say: that he'll come back with her to Davenport. So the wringing and twisting continue while Agatha relives those piano lessons of twenty years ago, the high hopes, the training of the little hands, asking him if he remembers the lessons, and he mumbles, "Sort of," though in fact he remembers them with a hard-edged clarity. Remembers the look of old Grade as he came through the front door and stood by the fireplace, a small, spare man in square-cut, rimless spectacles, and the unrelenting somberness of his black suit with its shiny seat and elbows. Remembers the raw look of his gills as if maybe he'd shaved with a shard of glass, the mingled odors of soap and pipe tobacco as he sat close to him on the piano bench, the way Grade with his hard old hands would force his own little hands into the correct position on the keys: "Nein, nein, nein. Alvays you vant to play flat. Flat is for *pounders,* not players . . . *Zo.*" And Agatha's voice filling in again, telling of how the lessons got off to so promising a start because he'd learned so quickly, so effortlessly. She stops and a silence falls, and he sneaks a glance and sees the wringing and twisting have ceased, the slender fingers stilled in the taut tangle of the handkerchief, and then she recites the family's amazement when Professor Grade reported to them that the little hands were not growing as they ought, that their precocious child was actually a wayward one. "He told us," she says, still apparently shocked by the ancient disclosure, "that you knew your practice pieces, not because you actually practiced them, but because you heard Professor Grade play them—to show you how they went. He told us he suspected this, and so once he made a mistake—on purpose—and sure enough, the next time, you played it exactly that way, with the mistake. And not only that: he said you put in things that weren't there. 'His little . . . *improvements,*' is the way he put it. Do you remember that?" "Kind of, I guess." "Why was that, son? Why? O, your father and I have asked ourselves that question so often over the years. Why was that when all we wanted was the best for you—your father, Opah, everyone." Her voice has begun to take on a wearing, plaintive whine, amounting almost to a kind of keening. "Why was it you wouldn't study your lessons and learn to play just what was there on the sheet?"

The tone and direction of this have begun to get to him, down deep, beneath the guilt he feels at having caused her this distress, having been such a disappointment. "Don't know," he says now, shifting so that he can pull out his Camels and light up, still avoiding her searching eyes. "I guess I wasn't very interested in them once I knew how they went. I guess I must have wanted to play stuff I didn't know—I mean, stuff that I didn't know how it was going to sound." But he knows how these words must sound and instantly regrets having voiced them. Words have never meant that much to him, except in books where presumably the writer really meant them. But the rest—the endless, thoughtless chin music of daily discourse—what could they mean? But he had meant these words and wishes he could somehow reach out and grab them back, pull them into the dark void of the unspoken, the unarticulated, where they belonged, but it's too late, and he glances up and sees his mother regarding him with that well-meaning, uncomprehending look he remembers too well: the look she'd give him at the house on Grand when he'd flung down the stairs with his horn, late for a job and on fire to try out some new lick he'd mastered. His mind involuntarily skips back up those same stairs, to the closet at the top, and he knows now it's too late, too late for any attempt to explain himself, what he means, what he's meant ever since he sat on that bench with the raw-gilled old dictator. No. Not now, not ever. He leaps from his chair with an abruptness that startles both of them, and Agatha stares up into a face she's never seen before, paste-white, eyes popping, locks from the center part fallen on damp forehead, lips drawn back over teeth. He glares down at her in feral fixedness, as if to freeze her. "Son," she says, her hand reaching out for him, the bit of white rag fluttering floorward. "Son."

"No," he croaks. "No! I won't come back to Davenport." But with the utterance of the town's name it floods back over him: the high, stolid hilltop homes, the riverward flow of the streets, the long industrial brick façade of the high school—clock on the wall in the history classroom and the admonitory minute hand that never moved, time hanging. The river slopping at the levee. Stacks of raw, sap-seeping lumber, lumps of coal in the yard of his father's company where he could find steady work, forever. The family dinner table, grain of its polished surface, his father ponderously presiding. The limitless reach and stretch of the undulant cornfields behind town. "No! I tell you," his voice cracks with the weight of his determination, his terror. "I won't come back there—not now, not ever. I don't want to die in Davenport!"

Later, when there is no sign left of the cab that is taking Agatha down the winding road to the city, nothing except the tire tracks in the gravel drive and a last, faint crepuscular bruise of exhaust that dissipates into the late afternoon air, he stands in the deserted parlor holding a tumbler of gin and raises it, looking through its heavy clarity to the gold of the Pacific light with its first premonitions of evening gray. It would be dusk now in Manhattan, that time when the magic of the city emerged once again from behind its workaday disguise. In a hundred speaks they'd be shaking the shining cocktail shakers, and a piano would tinkle evening's first notes like ice cubes tumbling into a tall glass. The boys who were working tonight would be getting into their monkey suits, boiled shirts, hair slicked, ready to go on. Somebody's shoelace would break, and somebody else would laugh at that. The instrument cases would be snapped open, the shining horns assembled. Out in Davenport the shops would all be shuttered, except maybe the drugstore, and bluff businessmen and their wives plump as pouters in the fashions of five years previous would be well into their prime ribs and mashed potatoes and succotash at the Blackhawk. In an hour the telephone in the house on Grand would rattle and his father would go to it heavily and hear the adenoidal voice of the operator announcing a long distance call from Los Angeles.

He takes a long sip, wondering what Mother will say to Dad. He probably shouldn't have said that stuff about Davenport. That had hurt her, and there was no call for it. But, hell, she shouldn't have said all that stuff about coming home and steady work and well-balanced meals at regular hours. There is something about the very notion, the prospect of regular hours—knowing what lies there ahead of you, waiting—that makes him cringe. Lowering the tumbler, something catches his eye, and he spots Agatha's handkerchief lying by the couch, lonely-looking, a tiny standard of surrender.

≈⟡≈

The pool at the Garden of Allah is shaped like Ali Nazimova's beloved Black Sea. Nazimova has made good on her threat and left the new Hollywood for New York, turning her mansion into a hotel, though she still keeps a suite for herself. Other stars have also taken suites here at the foot of Laurel Canyon, Clara Bow among them. It's a strategic necessity for the It Girl. Home has become a menace. Despite her great wealth, Clara knows nothing of finances or even simple arithmetic, is far behind on her mortgage payments, and the house is peppered by termites. Her maid is someone she met by accident who reports to work in high heels and does no cleaning, her chief function being to keep the insomniac Clara company, playing cards all night or throwing darts. When Clara goes to work the maid goes to bed. But the greater problem at the house on Bedford is Clara's father, who's there far too much of the time. Always a tyrant, lately he's begun insisting others address him as King Bow. Back in his Brooklyn days King Bow—then just Bob—was a persistent visitor to Clara's cot, from the time she was eleven until as an eighteen-year-old she won a beauty contest and left for her amazing career in Hollywood. Out here the King keeps his hands off his now-celebrated daughter,

sheds are not on cue but come unbidden when she flees the lot at
noon, leaving cast and crew behind, pondering the possibility of
life without their meal ticket. The director of *Dangerous Curves* has
already privately suggested to Schulberg that they begin scouting
around for a replacement for Clara. So the parties she throws at
the Garden of Allah have become essential: these days Clara's got
to have noise and merriment around her, friends, acquaintances,
strangers even. Last night she threw a beaut here: guys and dolls,
jazz band, her broad-backed football friends from Southern Cal.
And on this sunny Saturday morning she's sitting by the stony
shore of the miniature Black Sea with the flotsam of the night before, Bix and Buster. Keaton's hiding out. Yesterday his boys caused
a fire at The Italian Villa when they dumped their liver and broc-
coli down a heating vent. Much of the dining room has been de-
stroyed and there's a lot of smoke damage. Natalie has run off to
Mama's, and the boys are bunking over at Tom Mix's where they're
dazzled by the sight of his name spelled out in huge electric lights
across the mansion's roof. As for Bix, he was simply too drunk to
go anywhere and spent the night in Clara's bed. Awakening there
alone, he has little idea of how the night ended: Keaton passed on
the sofa, the Trojan he-men gone back to campus, the last guest
arisen shining from the pool under the paling stars, and strewn
about, the detritus of vanished merriment—glasses and half-
emptied bottles and ashtrays overflowing with crumpled cigarettes
bearing the carmine lip-prints of glamorous women. He doesn't remember sitting at the rented baby grand playing Eastwood Lane
and some of his own sketches, nor recall either Clara taking his
clothes off and then trying to force his limp fish between her legs.

Clara still has this in mind. There's something about this
strange, shy man she thinks she's just got to have, but the way he
and Keaton are going after the scotch and seltzer it's beginning to
look like today's not going to be the day, either. She wonders

to be recognizable. Clara's still laughing, bent forward now, her globular breasts jiggling within her knit jersey top. "Ha-ha-ha-O-O-O," she laughs, helpless. "But you know what?" she gets out just ahead of yet another avalanche, *"Neither can I!* O-O-O." Bix doesn't know what to make of this, wonders fuzzily if it could be true. Strictly, it isn't: both stars can read a little, though neither could get through a Wodehouse book. Bix isn't so drunk he can't feel embarrassed by the situation and folds the paper closed and drops it back on the table, telling them he never finished high school and can't read music very well. "I have to get guys in the band to help me read my parts," he says with a smile and a shrug. Keaton takes no interest in this disclosure, but Clara wants to know how he can play all the stuff he did last night on the piano. Bix wonders what it was. "O, that's all just made-up stuff," he says quickly. "You don't have to be able to read to make that stuff up." Keaton reaches for the paper with a show of deliberateness and unfolds it, appearing to scan the front page. His hands lift slowly, the paper spreads wider, his face disappearing behind it, and his companions watch as his right hand clumsily attempts to turn the page. Instead, the hand catches several pages, pulling them outward, and by now Keaton's completely enveloped in the thing, captured by the flimsy, ephemeral sheets, which appear to be getting bigger by the moment, multiplying with modern life's mysterious inexorability. Now they completely consume their reader who slowly, silently tilts backwards under this smothering, slow-motion avalanche to fall spread-eagled beneath the billows onto the lawn. "Say!" a voice calls. It's the portly bather whose exertions have brought him to their lobe of the kidney-shaped pool. "Say! I saw Buster Keaton do that in *The High Sign* years ago. Damned fine impersonation! Damned fine!" Keaton receives this tribute in silence, motionless beneath the brittle pages that still seem to have a life of their own, lifting and rustling a little in the breeze.

A couple of hours thereafter Keaton's supine again, back on the couch, and Bix is asleep, too, in Clara's bed, and Clara and the maid are playing Parcheesi—not exactly what the It Girl had in mind for this afternoon—when the phone rings, and Clara says, "O, shit!" One of the things the maid will do—must do—is answer the phone. She listens into the receiver a minute, then says, "Hold it, willya," and covers the mouthpiece with a palm. "This is the same dame what called you this morning when you were out at the pool with them," she tells Clara, jerking her thumb towards the couch where Buster lies, breathing noisily on his back. "You know, that one from the studio . . . Helen. Says you just gotta talk to her." She sniffs her unconcern as she hands Clara the phone. Helen is an obscure extra who instantly won the star's affection some weeks back when she took Clara aside and talked to her at another bad moment on the set of *Dangerous Curves*. "Don't let them buffalo you with that stupid gadget," Helen had said, placing a strong, consoling arm around Clara's shaking shoulders. It hadn't helped much, but in that instant Helen had Clara's heart, and at the end of that awful day Clara had brought her home and had admired the efficient way this unknown girl had brushed off the King. They'd become pals, and Helen had sat up a couple of nights with Clara, playing cards and talking. Once they drove out to Malibu, watched dawn flood the placid sea, and matched stories of their hard-bitten girlhoods in the tenements of Brooklyn and Chicago. Now Clara hears this tough girl sobbing on the other end. "Ya gotta help me, Clara," Helen says, struggling to get through. "I got no one to turn to out here." And then manages to say that she's been attacked and is stranded over at California Hospital with no money either to pay her bill or get back to her apartment. "I'll be down ta get ya, honey," Clara tells her immediately. "You just sit tight till I get there."

Entering the long, echoing ward with its rows of white-painted metal cots, Clara's looking and looking, and there's Helen, way

down at the end, beneath a dull red EXIT sign, sitting on the edge
of a cot with the whole left side of her face below the eye covered
in thick bandages that reach under the jaw and back behind the
ear. Clara doesn't waste time asking what happened, just goes into
action, paying the bills, including Helen's cab fare down here, getting the doctor's name and number, arranging an appointment,
and in something less than half an hour they're in Clara's fire-
engine-red Dodge convertible, spinning out of the lot, and Helen's
beginning to describe what happened to her yesterday afternoon.

She'd been sitting on the Murphy bed in her two-room apartment behind Sunset Strip, rubbing her sore feet and wondering
about this movie business when the buzzer sounded and she'd answered it. "And there's this guy out there," she says, her voice con-
trolled enough in this part of the narrative at least, as her savior
whips the convertible northward on Grand, "big guy. And he's got
some kinda clipboard an papers, so I figure him for some kinda in-
spector or somethin—checking the gas, ya know. So I'm talking to
him in the doorway, just a minute, then—WHAM!" Clara glances
over, sees Helen ghastly in her bandages and pallor in the brilliant,
heedless sunlight, and wishes she'd thought to run the top up so
people wouldn't get a gawk at the poor girl. "Somebody's got me
from behind, up under here," Helen goes on, gesturing carefully
with the back of one hand to her throat, "an the big guy, he hits me
with something real quick. That's the last I know until I come to an
I'm—I'm just—." Her head sinks onto the chest of the hospital
smock Clara's just paid for and bobs brokenly with the motion of
the convertible. And when her voice sounds again it's lost its fragile
control, the narrative disintegrated into raw emotion, the air being
forced through a passage constricted by agony: "—soaking in my
own blood. They cut me, Clara—my face." "Well, what was it,
honey," Clara asks, reaching across and finding Helen's hands, one
balled tightly within the other, "a burglary? Did they get your poise

'n stuff?" "Must have," Helen says, looking away but seeing nothing. "I don't know—." She swings her savaged face back to Clara. "O, God, Clara! What am I gonna do? Where'm I gonna go? Can't work like this, can't—." A driver cruises up alongside the red convertible, the man leering at Clara. "Love your pictures, babe!" he hollers. Clara slams down on the gas, and the convertible bucks ahead, and when they've left the other car well behind she reaches for Helen's clenched hands again. "Tellya what we're gonna do," she says, squeezing. "You're gonna come over right now an stay at Clara's. We'll get your face fixed up, an we'll figure out what to do." Helen is fighting more tears as Clara, still holding her hands, swings wide and reckless around a tight curve. "Honey," Clara says, all the brass gone from her voice, "you was a friend ta me when I needed it—an that's a thing I don't forget: you'll have a place ta stay with me long as ya want. You can count on it."

On Monday Clara gets three of the Southern Cal pigskin heroes to go back to the West Hollywood flat and collect some of Helen's things, and they find the place curiously in order, all except for the blood everywhere in the two tiny rooms, the big drops dried almost black now, as if it had happened long ago, and the front door securely locked. The rear door is unlocked, but there's no sign of forced entry, which makes them wonder how the second mug, the one who maybe had the knife or whatever it was, got in, unless Clara's friend had left the rear door open. And the other thing that puzzles them, halfback Morley Drury tells Clara, is that they found a purse, right out in plain sight, on the table, strange if it was a burglary. Clara doesn't understand these things, either, but she says nothing to Helen, only turns over the suitcases to her, pretty nice ones, she notes: good leather, brass fittings, HLW in gold lettering.

That night the woman known out here as Helen Weiss sits on the edge of the guest room bed, staring at the two big suitcases that remain just where the backfield star had set them, silent, mute, oddly like pets that have strayed but found their way back to their owner. And in the beginnings of what will become a tic of her own, she runs her fingers lightly along the padded, gauzy surface of her bandages, wanting to feel her face's familiar contours but knowing she can't. The mystery of what lies beneath the mountain of tape and cotton plagues her every waking moment, pries beneath the eyelids of sleep, remanding her again and again to those first shocked and static moments when she'd come to in the molten stew of her blood and staggered into the bathroom. But when she'd tried to inspect the extent of the damage the blood was still pumping out of her face so fast—dark, heavy blood—that she could see nothing except the blood that seemed to be bubbling up out of a bottomless reservoir. And after filling hand towels and bath towels with it, rinsing them in the toilet and watching in horror as the bowl turned a cloudy red, she'd finally collected herself enough to call a cab for the hospital.

Still, the suitcases. If they were like pets strayed, they feel to her as if somewhere in their journey they'd acquired a strangeness, almost a whiff or whisper of menace, and so for long minutes that lengthen into a quarter-hour, a half-, she sits there, staring at them, wondering what about their once-familiar contours and matched color could be setting off some inner system of alarm. "Helen Louise," she mutters finally, hearing once again the long-silenced voice of her mother, "you open those goddamn things." She hefts one onto the bed, undoes the heavy buckles that always hurt her fingers, pries up the top that yawns like a jaw, and finds within the brutally jumbled nightgown with its fake fox ruff and some of the flashy gowns she must be more careful about now. The great, blunt hands of the footballers have also scooped up and stuffed in some lingerie and pink mules and a compact. She can hardly blame them for these clumsy efforts, the things they chose to stash. What the hell would they know about the clothes a woman wanted when what they wanted was to get them off her? She begins to hang the dresses, but stops herself short and turns back to the other valise, mouthing something as she does, and flings it up on the bed where it jostles the one already opened. And when she's undone the straps and buckles and pried up the lid, there atop blouses and sweaters and shoes, innocently aslant, is her purse. Her hand goes automatically to her face, fingering the heavy dressing. And she knows right away.

It was Jack.

And she knows something more in this same frozen moment, has known since that moment when she heard the news—that Don Murray's death was no accident. When she'd heard he'd fallen from a running board and hit his head, she'd instantly thought, "No." Whatever had happened, however it was he'd really died, it hadn't been that way. In the world she's come to know, the one she's running away from, there are no accidents. Mysteries, yes, but not accidents. Jack had found out where she was and who she'd been seeing.

He was funny, Don. Wild. They'd reminisced about that summer of '26, talked on and on about Bix. Don loved the guy, spoke of him as if he were already legendary instead of a living man, going about his life the same as everybody else, and it was only when they'd actually climbed between the sheets and Don had slid between her raised legs that he'd finally shut up about Bix and turned on his own steam. But then, the next time they saw each other, it was Bix all over again, Bix this and that, and so she'd said to him, half-kidding, what was it about that guy that had so many of his friends sounding like they might be kind of queer for him? And Don had taken it the right way and laughed it off, and they'd gone on to other things. But still, while she'd been seeing him she had always had this funny feeling that there were three of them, wherever they were, even in bed.

For about a week after Don's death, certain it was no accident, she'd waited, listening for something: phone call, letter, note slipped under the door of her apartment, footfall at night, a rustle outside the window where the bushes flanked the door, someone on the lot looking funny at her, someone she works with suddenly evasive. One night the phone rang, once, and she'd lain there, shaking, thinking, not "No," but, instead, "Yes, this is it." But then nothing happened, and finally, like a sentinel vainly fighting sleep, who knows that sleep is certainly more than Death's little brother, is Death itself, she had drifted slowly away from vigilance, borne on the quotidian tide, out into this sunlit world where people didn't think about mortal vengeance, where to stab someone in the back was common enough practice but was more a manner of speaking. And she knew that Jack was in jail, because in those days immediately following Don's death she had gone down to a Los Angeles phone booth and at two a.m. in Chicago had called Muriel Finch, who told her he'd been picked up on suspicion of involvement in the deaths of Scalise and Anselmi and the Hop Toad and that Snorky's connections weren't working very well because Jack hadn't been sprung—either that or Snorky had decided that Jack was expendable. But of course Jack in jail meant little since if he really wanted something done, he could probably figure out a way to get it done from in there. Unless Jack in jail really meant Jack was *out*. She stands there in her closed room, in which she seems almost to hear a clock ticking, the opened valises on the bed, purse untouched, and she doesn't even have to open it to see if everything's in it, because she knows they didn't come for her pitiful thirteen dollars and change, nor for anything else there. They came for her, to mark her, to blight her chances in the movies, and they've certainly done that. She thinks, remembering Joe E. Lewis, that this is all they'll do to her, and then the swift logic of the thought is completed before she can try to cut it short: and it will be enough. But still, there's the

Wolverines, years back. Chili Three Ways, the menu had it. He ate somewhat regularly back then, he thinks, seeing himself there at the counter in Nap Town, crumbling crackers into the thick chili and washing it down with coffee. "Okay," he finds himself saying to Clara, "if you want to make the drive. I don't have a car anymore." Clara says she'll be there within the hour, and when she arrives it's clear she has more on her mind than a bowl of chili.

They're in the kitchen, Cullen gone again in the violet Ford down to the airport where he and Tram are taking flying lessons. Bix hands Clara a drink, and she turns that high-wattage smile on him, and the next thing he knows she's astraddle his leg and breathing hard. He tries to retract the leg but Clara puts the clamps on, and so after a silent little struggle he says, "Gee, Clara, I like you, too, but I hardly know you." Clara lets out a hoot and relaxes her thighs and Bix disengages and takes a backward step. "That's a hot one," Clara laughs. "Must be maybe a million guys don't know me at all would like ta be where you're at now." Bix smiles back, face flushed. Forward girls have always frosted him, but this situation strikes him as very strange: the It Girl herself, throwing it at him in his kitchen. But there's an artlessness to her advances, a childish impulsiveness, a deep need to be loved at some level, that disarms him. Some. "Well, you know," he says to her, a small distance created between them and his drink held in front of his chest, protectively, "I'm really not much for this kind of stuff, Clara. If you want a lover-boy, there're plenty of hotter guys than me." She stands there looking up at him with a quizzical smile that says, "Yeah?" thinking that's just the point, but thinking at the same time that if she said that, he wouldn't get it anyway. "But," he goes on, "there are a couple of things I can do that maybe the lover-boys can't. Like me to play for you? That I can do." And smiles that boyish smile that somewhere in it contains a remoteness, as if it came from afar and included you only in a casual kind of way. And Clara, playing for time, says, "Sure," and they go into the parlor and the spinet, and he sits down and plays through a version of In A Mist, then Cloudy. He starts on Candlelights, then stops and looks up at her, leaning on the piano. "This isn't a finished piece," he tells her, and now he's fully present, connected, if not to her, then to what his words and his hands are trying to tell. "It's something I'm working on." The hands rest on the keys. The room is dim, the sun sunk behind the Santa Monicas and outside the house the flakes of fallen stucco begin to take on a strange phosphorescence. "It's kind of a story," he continues after a brief pause where he appears to be thinking something through. Clara might be feeling a bit beyond her depth now, except he seems so genuinely interested in communicating something to her. "What's it about," she asks, chin in hand, elbow propped, thinking of those bulky, typed screenplays they handed her, then had to help her with—until she found her character in them, and it was always the same one. "Well, not a story, exactly. It's more like a—well, a poem, a tone poem." He sees he's losing her. "See, I want you to get this picture in your mind. See what comes to mind when I play a bit of this." The hands begin to move among the slightly yellowed ivories, the dullish blacks, and he plays a bit of it, then stops and looks up into the eyes that aren't working now at some sort of artifice, simulating some emotion, but are just themselves as they have come to be, full of the burden of their secret history, eyes haunted and tragic beneath the dyed and flaming hair, above the Cupid's bow mouth with its heavy appliqué of lipstick.

What Clara likes is jazz, the faster and hotter, the better. You didn't have to think about anything much when a band was blasting. She doesn't want music that makes her think, puts pictures in her head, because the pictures that are likely to come to her out of the dark tangle of her Brooklyn childhood are the ones that keep her up all night, playing cards and Parcheesi and throwing darts until dawn with whoever happens to be available. "Well," she says hesitantly, "I dunno. It's kinda flowery-like . . . real nice. . . ." "Well, flowers are in it, yeah," Bix says, "but I'm thinking of a dinner party, friends gathered, you see, and candlelights, social drinking, just a warm kind of occasion. And the name, Candle-lights—that's where that comes from." He plays through the rest of the piece, skating quickly over the portion that remains provi-sional, that he can't seem to make come true, as if the picture he wants to create isn't something he fully understands but only yearns for, something he might once have glimpsed through a win-dow while he stood outside, in darkness. He drifts into a sequence of chords drawn from listening to Debussy and Ravel and Delius whose Over The Hills And Far Away Lennie Hayton has lately in-troduced him to. "Do you make this stuff up?" Clara asks when the chords tinkle out into separate notes and then come to a halt. "Well, yeah, sort of," he says. "These aren't really pieces; they're just bits of stuff I've picked up here and there." "I hoid ya played Sweet Sue for hours on ya horn at that whammer Dick Barthel-mess threw for himself," Clara says. "I love Sweet Sue—can ya play it for me on ya horn?" He rises quickly from the bench, making a short, backhanded motion. "Nah," he says, already moving to-wards the door, "there's something wrong with it. Gotta get it fixed. What about that chili you mentioned? Too late for that?"

Clara knows a place for chili, one that will stay open for her as long as she wants, and when they roll up to it Bix sees why, because the circular sign hanging above the now-deserted sidewalk says CLARA BOW'S IT. Clara's set it up for her father to run, to give him something else to do besides chase her girlfriends and make his unannounced visits to the Bedford house where he loudly as-serts the royal prerogatives. The lights are still on inside, but the staff is clearly putting the place to bed, and the only customer left is counting his change and putting his boater on. When Clara walks in the staff knows what to expect and are cheerful enough about it, and tonight at least she has company so they won't have to provide the chatter, and it's easy enough to rustle up a couple of bowls of chili and two mugs of coffee. They pull the shades and lock the door and go back to the chores of closing, and an hour later they leave the young woman and her young man still sitting in that far booth, their hands cupped around their thick white coffee mugs, the air above them blue-white with cigarette smoke. And in the kitchen, Thompson, the black cook, settles in with radio and newspaper and will lock up whenever the It Girl decides to call it a night. And while the mugs grow cool, then cold and Thompson in back begins to nod, Bix is telling Clara that he's begun to suspect that jazz might be a dead end for him, that it can't take him where he needs to go. Maybe if he was Armstrong and could spear those stratospheric Cs, it would be different. But he's not. And whatever this "King of Jazz" project finally turns out to be, he's already seen enough of Hollywood to feel that the movie's score will be merely more of the thing they're already famous for, that completely competent but vapid symphonic jazz. Here is something Clara can grab hold of, telling him she knows kinda what he's getting at because for more than a year now she's been pleading with B. P. Schulberg at Paramount for a dramatic role but can't get one because the flapper role she's created is so wildly successful that the only real competition for a new film of hers is the last one she's made, so that *Dangerous Curves* will compete with *The Wild Party.* Every time she goes in to talk about this B. P. simply points to the sacks of mail filled with letters to her from Selma and Salina, from Traverse City and Texarkana, all testifying to their love for her. When she appeared opposite Richard Arlen in a gangster film, *Ladies of the Mob,* the sacks of mail took on a different tone, the letters imploring, anguished almost, telling her they couldn't bear to see her suffer. "We want you to go on dancing and singing," they said. "We want you to go to parties and have fun." "I just wish I was havin half the fun she's havin," Clara sighs to Bix, speaking of her celluloid persona, its dominating, independent existence. She looks at him out of those haunted eyes and suddenly blurts, "I kin act! I kin *talk,* fer Chrissake! But they gotta give me a chance—and they're not gonna, not unless I can figure a way to make em."

Meanwhile, Clara thinks of a way she might be able to make Bix and brings him back to the house on Bedford. She says nothing about her houseguest because Helen keeps mostly to herself, in her part of the house, especially when there are visitors. The house is dark when they roll through the gates and up the sloping drive, and once they get past the panting, lunging welcome of Clara's chow they move through an almost funereal gloom, passing through a living room with a baby grand draped in an ornate Spanish shawl, Chinese rugs, a Ming lamp and leaning against it a giant teddy bear with some kind of ornament around its nappy neck. Past a bedroom, then into a room where there's no light at all until Clara flicks a switch, and a spray of green light comes up behind a larger-than-life-sized gold-plated statute of the Buddha, seated in the lotus position with one hand raised, showing all who could see it the flower of the field. Clara flicks another switch, and the Buddha's eyes light up, one red, the other green. "Wait here, honey," Clara says, her arm around Bix's waist, "and I'll get us something to drink," and glides off into the darkness. Bix, made a bit uneasy by the furnishings, the black and red lacquered wallpaper, looks about for something to occupy him and finds it—on a low table a dozen or more framed photos of stars like Valentino and Gilbert Roland and Tom Mix, all of them with inscriptions. He picks up one of a tall, broad-shouldered hero across which is written, "To Clarita, whom I love, whose beauty & life by day are as real as the sun & by night have all the mysteries of the northern lights with the softness

of a summer's moon. You are all that. I love you, Garyito." He's feeling a trifle guilty about reading this, like opening a door into an intimate situation and is about to replace it when Clara materializes
with a bottle and glasses on a tray. She sets it down, takes the photo
from him and carelessly puts it back with the others, though not in
its original position. "Scotch okay with you?" she asks. "Always has
been," he says. She pours and then settles herself at one end of a
deep leather couch, and he takes the other, their legs outstretched,
Clara's bare toes pushing against his shoe soles.

Bix drinks deep, settles into the couch's cushy depths. "That's
quite a collection," he says finally, another big slug of the scotch
put away, nodding in the direction of the photos. "Are all those fellows personal friends?" "Ya might say that," Clara comes back,
careless again about the glossy galaxy. "Who's Garyito?" Bix asks.
"O, him. That's Gary Cooper. Might be a star some day." Clara
shakes her head and gives a short giggle. "Biggest cock in Hollywood and no ass ta push it with." "Now, that *is* a shame," Bix says,
the scotch taking hold already. He's thinking, What the hell: Clara's
really a nice kid beneath the brass, and the evening's turned out to
be enjoyable. Clara hoots at his sarcasm. "Ain't it though. But what
about you, honey? Ya got what it takes?" "That depends, I guess,"
he says, and Clara, determined to solve his mystery, is already on
the move, sliding up the couch towards him, insinuating herself
between his legs, covering him with a body that is warm and small
and very vibrant, and despite everything he feels himself rising to
the occasion, and her bobbed hair looms close in murky silhouette
before his wan face, then obscures the spray of green light on the
far wall, and her dark tongue flickers into his mouth, and he tastes
the scotch in a new way, its smoky, boggy heft, and lowers his glass
over the side, his arms going around the girl, and Clara's pulled her
dress up to her waist and is astraddle him, reaching with practiced
hand for his belt buckle, and he lets her take over down below and

concentrates on the kissing, his own tongue now venturing tenta-
tively into her mouth, rather like a boy just entering a cave. His
eyes are closed on the garish light, on the Buddha's eyes that are like
Oriental traffic lights, Stop and Go, and he's waiting for what's
next when he feels Clara's tongue quit and her body go still and
then her drawing back, and he opens his eyes to find her looking
down at him as she says, "Honey, have ya ever done this before?"
and he only smiles, and whatever kind of answer Clara takes this
for, she places him then, and there's only one problem now and
that's for him to hang on with Clara riding high above him, her
hands slowly massaging her breasts, hissing through clenched
teeth, and when this furious gallop is done, she falls backward into
the couch, pulling him by the elbows, and they do it that way,
Clara doing the bucking, and it doesn't take much before she's arrived again and doesn't even pause to savor that one but just goes
again, holding him tightly while her hips are thrusting, slamming
into him, his pelvis stinging under the successive shocks, her legs
locked behind his. And when that one's over, Clara releases her
hold, pushing him deftly off, and he feels that shocking disengage-
ment, the air of the exterior world cold on his wet member, and
Clara is rolling out from under him and onto a bearskin rug,
and while he watches, dazed, defenseless, she kneels down there,
dress hiked high over her gleaming cheeks, and turns and looks
back at him, reminding him of that moment at the party by Buster
Keaton's pool where she'd turned and flashed that famous smile at
the band and wiggled her rear and George Marsh had hit the bass
drum pedal. Now she's switching it at him again, but he doesn't get
the nature of the invitation until she comes to his rescue, calling in
a husky voice, "Now, honey, you come down here and put your hot
dog between Clara's buns." And he, compelled, even while a part of
him—his mind—is aghast, does what she's told him, and he's
down there on the black fur of the dead beast's back, Clara reach-

ing up between her legs and placing him anew, and he grabs her around her waist, and this time finds himself doing the thrusting, and Clara is making a strange noise, but he can't hear it, and then at the end of a long, lunging thrust that really has no end, seems unending, something is yanked out of him from somewhere deep inside—bolt, arc, flame or shot—that kindles him from thorax to kneecap, and he feels everything cave in and falls shudderingly away from behind Clara, collapsing into the bear's bristly back, wanting dimly to cover his drooling, throbbing nakedness, but he's paralyzed, his hands rigid and clenched, and now he can make out the sound she's been making, and she's laughing, and he turns his head towards her, eyes opening, and sees her face lit by the green light, shining, mouth parted in laughter, and he thinks she must be laughing at him and covers his crotch with his hands. Clara lies on her side, her dress still up around her waist and her dark triangle merged with the bear, and he finds himself wondering if she'd slipped out of her panties when she went for drinks or whether she even wore any and had arrived at his place naked beneath the skimpy dress. He rolls away from her, fumbling with pants and belt, and while he's doing this feels her arm come around his shoulder and the amazing warmth of that small body snugged up behind him, and he holds still, and so does she, the two of them silent at the feet of the Buddha while a velvet calm comes over him and he decides Clara hasn't been laughing at him after all, that she's a small vessel for huge emotions that race through her in bewildering succession and almost without her notice, and after lying this way for some minutes he feels her arm relaxing in sleep, this sleepless star, pursued across the nights by visions that won't let her escape until daybreak when she can reenter the world of make-believe.

Slowly, quietly, he pulls away and her arm drops softly into the black fur, and he gropes his way back out to the living room to sit at the shawl-draped piano. He finds a very crushed pack of Camels in his pants' pocket and rummaging there feels again his wetness. He straightens a cigarette with thumb and forefinger and is hunting for a match when Clara enters, intersects with him, and produces what he needs. She sits beside him on the piano bench and asks to hear the one about the party, and he smiles at the dim keyboard and starts into it, more slowly this time, lingering on the keys, adding in a few small runs up into the treble, and he's thinking that maybe this more meditative tempo suits the piece better, evoking more of the emotional tone he's after, and coming once more to the difficulty, one of the three provisional, unsatisfactory bridges he's got and for none of which is there any notation, he finds that playing across it at this twilit tempo makes it sound better, and a sort of inner logic within it is revealed to him, like some night-blooming flower whose pistil—stigma, style, ovary—has persistently remained closed to him. Almost wonderingly his hands discover the barely seen keys, guided by some force that translates itself into faint yet distinct pressures, showing him where to press and release and move, the girl there beside him, silent, stilled, all her electric energies focused on what he's trying to do. And in this moment it feels to him that this is what he's needed all along, just this dim yet particular feminine presence, here, at this hour and this place. He's never sounded better to himself, never more at home, never closer to the realization of something he's been searching for since Hudson Lake and even before that—all the way back to Nick LaRocca. And there it wasn't what LaRocca played, he now sees. It was always what he was *going to play,* what *might* come next, what unheard, utterly surprising notes would suddenly be there, emerging out of the formerly familiar, the known, as now out of what he knows of Candlelights he finds the hidden direction for the way the rest of the piece must surely go.

He is suddenly aware of something else present, something intruding into the moment, and looking up from the keyboard finds at the room's entrance a white glimmer that hovers there. But he keeps playing, though now with an altered intent, willing with his hands, the notes they sound, the hovering presence to come closer, and it does, the white glimmer becoming more distinct, advancing with timorous indecision through Clara's strategic, Stygian gloom, until it reaches the piano's far side, and he can see it's a woman with a white shawl or veil over her face, and now Clara sees this as well. "Helen," she says in soft surprise. The presence comes closer yet, around the piano's curve, brushing the Spanish shawl, and now Bix can make out that the white something that glimmered from afar is a large bandage above which a great blue eye darts into his, and his hands freeze as he exclaims, "O my God! I know this girl!" And in that same instant the girl herself cries out, "O, my God!" and runs from the room, and then, seconds later, from an echoing recess of the house they hear a door slamming with the thunderous finality of a tomb. Clara is off the bench, listening, looking through the darkness while he sits there, hands still frozen, neck hairs standing out stiff as spikes.

In the kitchen Clara snaps on all the lights. Except for the ice tray sitting in a puddle next to the sink the place looks almost un-used because Helen has taken over the maid's duties and performs them with a shining scrupulosity. And so now she must quickly ex-plain to Bix the circumstances of the ghostly guest, and she's hardly finished with this before he's telling her he's got to talk to this Helen. She leads him down the corridor to her room, but when he gets to it he stands outside and doesn't knock or try the handle. He looks at Clara and she thinks he's waiting for her to knock and call out to Helen, but when she starts to move around him he holds up his hand, stopping her. Then: "Hey, in there," he says, his voice light, friendly. "It's me, Bix."

And the voice from within comes back, strangely muffled. "I know who it is. Get the hell away from the door and let me alone." A brief pause, and then the one other word, "Please."

Then Bix again and after another pause, as though he might have been improvising some sort of new appeal. "Aw, come on, now. You and me and Herman go too far back for that. I'm standing out here thinking about that wild party we had once, some place up in Michigan—or maybe it was Wisconsin, and you—"

"Wait a minute!" The voice is sharp, unmuffled now, and the listeners hear something being pulled away from the door, and then shortly the voice calls out to Clara. "Right here, honey," Clara calls back. "Clara," the voice says, "believe me I appreciate all this, but I gotta talk to this guy alone. Okay with you?" And Clara, looking at Bix, says slowly, "Yeah, sure thing, honey. You just talk to him long as you want. I'll be in the livin room if ya need me." And already she's turning, looking at Bix over her shoulder, and then moving off into the gloom, carrying back along the corridor her own long-kept secrets for which no listener awaits as Bix now awaits what the woman within has to tell him.

"Okay," comes the voice within, muffled once more by something Bix comes to understand once he enters the room and finds a figure lying on the bed, shrouded with a sheet from head to toe, the sheet arranged taut as a tent, its lines severely horizontal but up at the head quivering with life, with breath. He pulls the chair that had barred the door up near the head and when he's seated and a minute or more has passed the shrouded figure begins to speak, telling him that she's let him in only because she was afraid he'd spill the beans about Chicago and Jack and all that, and so far nobody out here has connected her with all that mess. Not even the producer who once made a pass at her when she was out here with Jack on Snorky's business: she's encountered him twice and he hasn't made the connection, probably because he was so drunk at that dinner when he told her she might have a future in pictures. And Bix quietly assures her he's said nothing to Clara, only listened to what Clara has told him about her accident. Then the voice tells him only a few things more about that, and when she's finished she lies silent, and only the shroud quivers and quivers. He sits in the chair, watching the shadowed suspirations, waiting. At last there's a long exhale, the sheet lifting in a constrained little arc, then collapsing, its horizontal tension resumed.

"So now ya know what's what," the voice says.

"Yes," he says quietly. "Now I know."

"And ya know my life's over—"

"O, I don't believe that, Lulu, not a minute. You don't know—"

"One thing I always liked about you: you were always such a boy. Only I can't use that now, understand? You're being a boy. I'm ruined, see? Jack, he knew how to fix me good. It's better than being dead, me this way. I can't be in pictures. I can't be no guy's fancy girl around town. Whattam I gonna do, ya know? Peddle my ass. I gotta girlfriend has to do that now—."

"Lulu." Bix's voice is full now, and its weight stops her. "Lulu," he says again, waiting for the next notes to come to him, but then he thinks maybe that's all he needs to say, just that and reaches with one hand towards the bed. The hand lies there at the shroud's stretched edge, like a bird, tentative and with flight in mind. And the minutes drop slow as blood here and his shoulder begins to ache from the reach he's making, and then from beneath the shroud and its taut, steady quivers, the in-and-out of life, the quick of it, a hand emerges and flutters into his and after a moment is quickly withdrawn.

❧❖❧

"I've just got to help her get back on her feet, is all," Bix tells Clara. They're sitting at Clara's kitchen table where she sometimes plays cards with the maid. From Clara's observations, he's not too steady on his own feet, but she doesn't say that, only says that Helen can stay here until she's better, if that's what she wants. He shakes his head. He's shoved his glass aside, trying to explain to her about Helen without revealing too much. "See, we knew each other back in Chi," he tells her carefully. "Through her brother, actually. He worked for Goldkette, and after we broke up Tram and I got him on with Whiteman." "Well, why don't he take over?" Clara wants to know. Bix shrugs, raises his eyebrows. "He quit. Last year, I guess it was, and nobody knows where he is." He looks down at the table, remembering some of it. "Great guy. I roomed with him." He swings his glance towards the double windows above the sink. "I miss him; he was a good guy to room with—very considerate and all." He pauses to straighten out another cigarette and light up. "Anyway, I owe it to Herman—that's her brother—to do what I can. He'd do it for me, I know." There are a great many things Clara doesn't understand in this world, her own experience having been so terrifically narrow: a succession of blackened Brooklyn tenements, a deranged mother, concupiscent father—her night visitor—no schooling. But if there's one thing she can instantly comprehend and respond to, it's succor, it having been in such glaringly short supply in her life, and so what Clara finds now in this strange guy she's just practically raped is that rare and precious thing—much rarer, she thinks, than his piano playing. "I'm there all day," he's explaining to her, "when you have to go down to the studio, and so if she needs anything. . . ." His voice trails off and he raises his hands and lets them fall. Clara asks if this is what Helen herself wants, and Bix tells her it seems to be. Actually, all Lulu had said to his proposal was that it didn't make that much difference to her one way or the other but that in any case she wasn't ready to go back to her West Hollywood flat yet. And so the next afternoon after another awful day on the set, Clara drives Helen up the Laurel Canyon road, Helen's stylish bags stashed in back and the girl staring listlessly out the window so that Clara gets the feeling she could drop her passenger almost anywhere. "Ya know ya got a room with me any time ya want, if this don't woik out," Clara says as she wheels sharply into the drive of the flaking bungalow. While Bix and Cullen tote the bags inside the girl sits there, not even glancing at her new surroundings, her blonde hair somewhat disheveled by the wind, the big bandage hiding half her face. "Yeah," she says heavily. "Yeah. And thanks." She steps down into the gravel turn-around and marches into the house, leaving the three standing there looking after her and then at each other in silence. Clara tells Bix to call her right away if it looks like Helen wants to come back down to her place. He nods. She wants to see him soon again, she adds, and he nods once more. "Sure," he says. "I'll call." Then there's nothing left for Clara to do but turn around and head down to her home with its dead trophies of fame and amorous conquests and hope that the maid is up for cards tonight.

Inside, the men have done their best to make this a home for Lulu instead of a hospital ward or a prison. Cullen has given up his room and moved in with Bix and they have bought so many bouquets the effect in her room is unintentionally funereal, the scents combining into a crushing compound that makes her weep once they've brought in her bags and left her to herself. She stays in there that night, refusing to come out for the canned soup and crackers Bix has prepared, not wanting either of them to see her disfigurement. But the next morning, the sun in the back window, the flowers opening out in their vases, she hears his voice outside her door, telling her he has breakfast, and relents, telling him it's okay to come in, and presently he does, bearing a tray on which there's a dangerously rattling cup of coffee and a piece of blackened toast smeared with jam. And even at this it's the first time in her life she's ever been served breakfast in bed by someone she knows, and so again she feels weepy and angry too at this uncharacteristic weakness, but takes the tray and looks quickly away without speaking. She feels him hesitant there at her bedside and then the sound of him moving off and the door softly shutting. The next morning it's the same routine, and the one after that she's waiting for him to say, "Lulu, I have some breakfast here for you," but this time she abruptly says she has to go to the hospital today to have her stitches removed.

In the violet Ford he's repossessed from Cullen he drives her down there and waits. And waits, until suspicion begins to replace concern and he asks the nurse, "What's keeping Miss Weiss so long?" The face beneath the starched cap returns a blank look to his question, then says, "O, that lady. She went out the back way long ago." "Show me where," he says quickly. "Show me the back way," and then runs down the indicated flight of metal steps, feeling the pain in his groin grab at him and shoot up into his belly. Outside, he comes to a baffled halt in a small garden where patients and their visitors sit on benches and palms wave high above them, indifferent to their suffering. No Lulu here. He gimps around the path and finds a high iron fence at the rear of the grounds and an arch above its open gate, spelling out the hospital's name. Beyond, the city begins again and, crossing the street to the corner, he sees her sitting at a bus stop bench, her fawn-colored picture hat tipped in a vain effort to hide the new dressing that courses down her cheek and under her chin. She doesn't look up, seems oblivious to his presence, and he merely slides silently onto the bench's other end. "Beat it, buster," comes the hard voice from beneath the hat brim. "Scram." "Hey, Lulu," he says quietly. "O," she says, still not looking up, "it's you. I shoulda known. No masher's gonna make a pass at me the way I look now. Jack was always a jealous bastard, but now he's fixed me up so's he don't have that to worry about any more." They sit silent in the sun, two feet of brown-painted bench between them until a bus belches up and its driver levers the door open and waits for them to make a move and when they don't he slams it shut and the bus moves off in a dense black cloud. When its roar is diminished by distance, becoming but a minor strain in the city's vast hum, Lulu says, "Aint we somethin, though. No place to go to." He says nothing, can't think of what to say, when suddenly something comes to mind and he grabs at it. "I know a place to go," he tells her, trying to make the idea sound more attractive than he feels it is. He tells her about a place Clara's been trying to get him to go, Guadalupe, on the coast somewhere north of the city, where De Mille filmed *The Ten Commandments*. "What's up there?" Lulu comes back, weary, contentious. "Well," he says, improvising, "I dunno. Never been there myself. But I think it'd be good to get away from here, you know, see some country." "I wouldn't be here now, only I don't have any place to go to." "You've got my place to go to, Lulu," he says, being perhaps the very boy she's said she can't use any longer. "C'mon." And he takes her arm, which is limp, resistless, and they walk back through the hospital grounds to the violet Ford shining in the sun.

Above Santa Barbara, after they gas up the Ford, he pulls a bottle from his bag. He starts small before promoting himself to deeper pulls as they whip along with the hulking San Rafaels on their right, Bix sitting straight behind the wheel, silent, only once in a while looking over at Lulu who doesn't return his glance but stares straight ahead or out the side window, except once when she happens to look over at the same moment he's glancing at her with that shy, removed smile of his. It takes her back suddenly to that summer night at the Indiana lakeside roadhouse when she'd heard him play for the first time, and there'd been something there that she felt she ought to have. Or was it, she now asks herself bitterly, that she was simply horny with Jack over there in Michigan? Well, now she probably could have it, whatever it was, except everything's too different even to think about it. And he's as different as she is.

By the time they get up there it's full dark, and they can't see much of the town, only some dusty-looking buildings huddled along the main drag and the streets empty except for a parked truck and a high-wheeled cart with its tongue plunged into the dirt of the road. The one gas station's still open, bedizened outside with ads for Gold Medal Flour, Camels, Texaco Petroleum Products, Fisk Tires. Inside, more ads for tourist cabins, hot meals, mechanical repairs. The kid hosing down the bays wears a soiled Texaco uniform and a rubber bow tie, his face as tired and dusty as the town, but he drops his hose and hops out to the tall glass pump. Then he busies himself around the Ford—tires, radiator, windshield—clearly admiring its newness while Bix asks him about places to stay around here. The kid tells him about La Misión Vieja about a mile north, tourist cabins he claims are clean and where some of the big wheels stayed when they made the movie here awhile back.

"We want to see that," Bix says. "Well, like I told you, you just follow this road north about a mile, and you'll see 'em," the kid says. "No, no, I mean where they made the movie," Bix says. "You can't see it," the kid comes back, "—not much of it, anyways. They covered it up with sand after they finished." "With sand? All of it?" "All they could. Sand's what we got plenty of around here: that's why they picked the place to begin with. We got as much sand as Egypt, I bet." He begins going over the Ford's brightwork with his rag. "O, you can still see some of the statues and part of the palace, I think. Haven't been out there in a while." Bix wants to know how to find it, and the kid tells him he has to backtrack out of town, past the cemetery, to a side road running west through the dunes. "It's back in there," the kid says, taking a final swipe at the Ford's spotlight, "and seeing's we got a good moon, you'll find it." He pauses, takes a step back from the car as Bix hands him a bill. "Road's rough, though. Now, if I had me a new Ford pretty as this one, I wouldn't take it back there myself."

Lulu says she doesn't want to see any old movie set. Right now, she's sick of movies, plus she's tired, and so they go out to La Misión Vieja and take a casita—whitewashed fake adobe, twin beds, rustic wooden table and chairs, tiny bath. When Bix brings in her bag he finds her standing by one of the beds, almost as if defending it, and he quickly drops the bag and says he'll be out on the porch, if she needs anything. In bed, she pulls the rough cotton sheet up around her neck and lies staring at the ceiling beams. Under the new dressing her wound itches and she runs her fingers over it gingerly. She's never seen it clearly, but she knows it's bad. She wishes she could escape into sleep but can't. If she were more of a drinker, she might ask Bix for some; she can hear him out on the porch, but he's drinking gin, and that stuff would make her puke, especially straight like he's taking it. Back in Chicago on nights when she was alone, she'd finger herself to bring on sleep, but when she slides her fingers between her legs she knows right off she's not interested. Helplessly, she turns to reviewing her situation, searching through the ruins of this crypt, her life, for some heretofore secret, unrevealed tunnel that would lead her out into a new place, and finds, again, nothing: can't be in pictures; can't go back to Chicago; might try to hook up with Herman in New York, but to do what there? Might try to work Clara's connections at Paramount for some kind of job there, but she's seen what's happening on the lot and knows that Schulberg and the others will tolerate Clara only as long as she's putting those asses in the theatre seats and not a minute longer. The way Clara's going now, she might be out of work herself pretty soon. The image of the theatre and its dark, plushy seats filled with Clara's devoted fans takes her back to those days when she was married to Tommy Rolfe and still working as a ticket taker, cashier, primitive bookkeeper at a theatre in Chicago, though Tommy kept telling her he'd soon spring her from that. And one afternoon Jack had stepped to the window and spotted her and then rescued her from that life. She pictures him as he was on that day, a chilly one and not much business for a Ramon Novarro film, time hanging for her behind the wicket, sneaking glances at the movie magazine in her lap. And here's this guy all in gray: gray hat with dark gray band, gray three-piece suit with white pinstripes, off-white shirt with dove-gray tie and pearl stickpin. Sharp as hell and with a cocky appraising leer to match: "Hey, toots, yer way too classy to be sittin in that cage, but inna meantime, gimme one for the matinee, and then we'll work out something about later." And she'd come right back at him: "Well, for your information, it so happens I'm busy for later, but if you got the dough, I got the ticket for the matinee." But even then in that brief banter she'd sensed Jack could be a guy who could really take her out of the cage, could dress her in style, drape her in those flapper fashions that were so devilish, so daring. How could she have known then, or even long afterwards, that Jack was such a murderous prick? And she hadn't wanted to know it until she'd literally stumbled over the evidence. And now, here she was, with this strange, sweet guy, who wanted for some reason to take care of her when he was probably as lost as she was. And here they were together, up in this nowhere town with an abandoned movie set swallowed up somewhere behind it. If it weren't so desperate, she thinks, it would be killingly funny. When she sees Herman again she means to ask him about this guy, what really makes him tick. That summer of '26 she had asked Herman that, but he hadn't known Bix very well himself and told her that as far as he knew Bix was all music, period. The rest of the time he seemed to sleepwalk through life enveloped in a haze of booze. It's hard for her to understand someone like that, with only that one, single interest. Even Jack liked different things: the fights, movies, dancing, going out on the town. She feels her face with her fingertips again. O, Jack, you *dirty* bastard, you really fixed me good.

and they still can't figure out what these might be, though they're quickly bearing down on them, and when they're almost on them Bix shoots through a gap in the line and slams to a stop, and they find they're in a long avenue of sphinxes, the great mythological amalgams lying atop pedestals, their leonine paws regally out-stretched above the human heads that stare across the avenue at each other with the simulated, sentinel vigilance of the ages. Some of them are all but obliterated by heaped sand, are only humps with maybe a paw, a haunch, the spiked tip of a headdress show-ing. Only a few are completely visible with the late moonlight ly-ing dully on their plaster surfaces. There must be twenty of them, ten to a side, and at the convergence of the lines, the vanishing point, a monstrous dune hundreds of feet high that obscures what must be the remains of the Pharaoh's palace. Bix slews the Ford around in that direction and drives, slowly now, down the avenue, the automobile tiny, tinny, incongruous, farting along past the blurred monsters looming above it on both sides until they've ar-rived at the base of the great dune and they can see that beneath it is the palace wall and its triumphal entrance, it too blocked with sand. They sit there, looking up at a pair of heroic legs carved in high relief on the wall, and after a while Bix cuts the motor and there's no sound or movement, only the moonlight, the sand, the thong-and-sandal legs in their arrested motion, and Bix is strangely reminded of a snatch of Runnin Wild: "Always goin, don't know where." Where in hell was that guy going? he wonders, reaching into the backseat for his bottle. Where in hell did they all think they were going? He snakes the bottle out of the tangle of shirts in his Gladstone and offers it to Lulu who has already re-fused it a couple of times. "That stuff makes me puke," she says now. "Too sweet." He nods, remembering that Herman had once said the same, so maybe it ran in the family—or didn't. "Maybe that's why I started on it," he tells her, "because it was sweet. You know how kids are. Plus, that was the stuff they had around then—that and beer, which fills you up pretty quick." He tilts the bottle, swallowing quickly, and when he lowers it, it's done for, and he shakes it, smiles, and drops it out the window, wondering to himself what the Egyptians did for drink. Once again, he turns and reaches back into the soiled tangle of the bag he hasn't bothered to take out of the car, this time bringing up a pint. Lulu watches this silently, wondering how much this guy can hold.

"I don't know that much about the Egyptians—I mean the real ones—," Bix says after a bit, settled back in his seat, knee propped against the wheel. He's begun working on the pint now. "I flunked history twice, once in Davenport and another time up in Lake Forest. I guess that makes me some kind of All-American, eh?" He smiles over at her, the smile looser now, his teeth showing. "That second time, up in Lake Forest, I had history first thing in the morning, and damn!—darn—a lot of times I'd been out all night, down in Chi, sitting in when they'd let me, and, man, by the time I got to history class I was *beat.*" Later, he tells her, he got interested in history on his own and read a lot about a guy who fought with the Arabs in the desert during the war. "He was a hero of mine for a long time—still is, actually—but he's kind of obscure now." Lulu knows nothing of this guy, whoever he was, and little enough about the war—mostly just the uniforms the guys wore around to the amusement parks and dancehalls in Chicago, and you didn't always know whether they really were sailors or soldiers or had merely picked the duds up in secondhand shops. But here at least is something else he seems genuinely interested in, and she asks why the desert fighter was his hero. "He just kind of appealed to me," he says after a thoughtful pause, and for a minute or so she thinks that's all there's going to be to that. But then (another hit on the pint), "I liked his . . . *style:* out there all on his own, no battle plans, instructions." He waves his hand out the window in a grand, sweeping gesture that includes the towering dune, the remnant portion of the triumphal gate, the heroic, guardian legs. "All the way out there, middle of nowhere, where he had to make it up, don't you see, nothing to guide him except"—he taps his temple twice—"the old noggin." Suddenly his speech is slurred, his words running together, and she glances over and sees his eyes widen and his Adam's apple working, and then he's turning around quickly, reaching back into the Gladstone and pulling out a shirt that trails up out of the back like a winding sheet, and he keeps yanking at it until he has it all over him and the door flies open and he falls out, the shirt around his neck, sprawled in the flat sand from which the moon now has fled, the wind blowing the shirt around him, and she can hear his muffled laughter. And while she watches from the Ford, he struggles up and begins a kind of shambling, weaving run toward the sphinx next to the palace wall of the most colossal movie set ever built, and reaching it starts to scrabble up the mounded sand at its base. She watches him working around the pedestal, still clutching the shirt, then with an astonishing agility fling himself astraddle the beast's back, and he sits there, tying the shirt's sleeves into a knot on his forehead, the wrinkled tail flapping down his back. The first rays of dawn now hit the edges of the sphinxes, lighting up a jaw, a blind, no-color eye, the moon still large but now a thin blue-pocked wafer, and something pulls Lulu out of the car and sends her hurrying across the intervening sandy space, calling up to him, "Hey! *Hey!* You're gonna get hurt up there!" But he doesn't look down, doesn't respond at all, astraddle the sphinx, his improvised burnoose flapping in the wind. He spreads wide his arms and holds them there while the new sun cracks up from the humped dunes to the east. "Nothing is written!" he hollers. "*Nothing is written!*"

At the base of the pedestal Lulu stares up, wondering how in hell she's going to get him down from there and what she's going to do if he does fall. The right half of his face is now shining in the new sun, his eye wide, staring off across the ruined avenue towards another monster that returns his stare, and then, in slow motion, his cruciform pose collapses, crumples inward, and with an easy twist, he slides off the monster's back and rolls down the mounded sand to come to rest at her feet, the burnoose flapping with each roll. Her hair, dyed platinum weeks ago and now mellowing, is incidentally retouched by the sun as she bends over him. "Hey!" she says. "Hey!" Then straightens up and looks into the sun. "Aw, Christ!" she hisses, at once alarmed and angry. "Aw, Christ!" She turns him onto his back, undoes the knotted shirt sleeves, brushes the sand from his face and eyes, watching him blink the grains away while a grin spreads over his face, the sand running along its creases, off the still-smooth cheeks, around the flanges of the nose, falling on his neck. He isn't looking at the bandaged face that leans over him, is looking somewhere past it. "Nothing," he murmurs, and then his eyes gently close.

⚜

It isn't until four days later that they pull into the drive at the Laurel Canyon bungalow and troop wearily in, Bix looking like he's been underwater for a week. "Jesus!" a worried Cullen says, "Jesus, Bix." Inside, Lulu right away feels an indefinably different air and then spots Cullen's instrument case in the parlor. Bix walks right past it and flops onto the couch while Cullen tries to tell him that the show's over out here, that Pops has finally made good on his threat to pull the band out of Hollywood and take them back to New York until Universal can show him an honest-to-God shooting script, something that Ferde can really work with. "Pops says they're already beginning to forget about us back there," Cullen says, avoiding looking at Lulu, trying to get through to Bix. "Heigh-ho," Bix sighs from the couch. Now Cullen looks to Lulu who's standing just inside the parlor, still with her overnight bag in hand, as if there's little point in even setting it down here. She'd known this was coming, just not this soon. "Bix," Cullen says, trying again, "what I mean is this: we've only got three days to pack up, settle with the landlord, and you've got to figure out something about your car. We open at the Pavilion Royale on the thirty-first." He stands there a moment, looking at the couple who have never looked to him like they belonged together, wondering where the hell they've been and what they could possibly have been doing there, then turns and goes into the kitchen, giving them some sort of privacy. Lulu looks at Bix, recognizing now that whatever it was he had to give her—his inarticulate and fumbling efforts at care— is over with. Now it's her turn, and she must do whatever is necessary to get him aboard that train back to New York.

Over the next days, while Cullen deals with the landlord, she does Bix's laundry, packs for him, and then cautiously drives them down to Union Station with their bags and instrument cases, mid-morning of the twenty-eighth, Bix patiently coaching her from the passenger's seat. Yesterday, he'd given her another lesson in the Ford, driving down the winding Laurel Canyon road before turning the wheel over to her at the Garden of Allah. He'd made her practice turning in traffic and parking, and after an hour of this she'd told him she'd had enough, and they parked outside the Roosevelt on Hollywood and sat there shaking, each for a different reason. "You'll be okay," he'd finally said.

"O, yeah," she said with sarcasm. "I'm gonna run it up to Clara's and let it rust."

"What'll you do there?" he asked.

"Clean for her, keep her company, nights. Try and straighten out her checkbook: I can do arithmetic. She can't." She shrugged and glanced over at him. "What about you?"

"O, I'll be fine. I've got a bunch of stuff saved up to read. I'll get some rest on the train and be ready to go in New York." She'd looked at him steadily, but he wasn't looking back, only puffing on his Camel and apparently watching the traffic's easy flow along Hollywood.

Now, down at the station she's looking at him again and still he's not looking back, is looking out at the Old Gold Special being loaded—instrument cases, grand piano, Whiteman's car, eighty-seven trunks. The first of the gang's gathered in small knots, smoking, shifting, a bit uneasy about the abrupt end of this strange, palmy interlude, watching Whiteman and his manager Jimmy Gillespie out of the corners of their eyes, Pops in an obvious foul humor. When Bix climbs carefully out, Whiteman glances over and sees him standing next to the violet Ford, talking with a blonde with a bandaged face, but he makes no acknowledgment: he's still steamed because Bix missed the last KMTR shot and Andy Secrest had had to play two parts. With her hand resting lightly on the warm curve of the fender she tries to look up under the fedora he's got pulled low over his face, his gaze on the brick pavement between them. Cullen has already cleared the car, carrying his own bags and two of Bix's.

Someone calls Bix's name, but he doesn't turn around. "Well, I guess it's goodbye, Lulu." Her name on his lips wavers off into their local silence before he adds that he's glad it worked out for her to move back in with Clara. He shifts, boyishly, hesitates, then bends stiffly from the waist, his lips just barely brushing her bandaged cheek. Then he turns with his bag towards the waiting cars, and she stands, watching his retreating back. Her face itches where he's brushed it but she checks the impulse to touch it. A tall man steps forward out of a small group, one hand extended in greeting towards Bix and an autograph book in the other. Lulu can see the others in the group have their books out as well and pens ready. Bix barely glances at the tall man, but stops, reaches for the book and signs it quickly, then moves resolutely towards the train, leaving the group behind, and she thinks she can almost see the molars in their gaping mouths at this brush-off. Bix slowly mounts the porter's metal footstool and the high, corrugated steps and then is gone.

An hour later, the violet Ford cooling and ticking in Clara's driveway behind barred gates, the Old Gold Special gathers itself, gives a shuffle and a puff, and then begins to haul out of the yards on what will not be some leisurely, triumphant procession such as it made coming out here but instead a fast nonstop to New York, rattling full-throttle through crossings with flashing lights, through sleeping hamlets, racing under the dappled skies of the Great Plains, over the broad rivers of the mid-continent where the tracks are joined by more and more lines, a denser network of iron roads, the hamlets of the west flowing into the towns of the midwest, and everything racing towards the cities of the seaboard. In his stateroom with Jimmy Gillespie, an uncharacteristically grim Whiteman maps strategy to make up for lost ground, the encroachments of other orchestras into territory he'd won and then vacated for this fruitless trip to movieland. His boys, he knows, are not in fit condition for work, Bix especially, and the loss of Bix, which he must now openly contemplate, would be critical to what he thinks of as his orchestra's full versatility, its unique sound. "Losing him," he tells Gillespie as they roll through western Pennsylvania, "isn't just that fourth-chair trumpet. Hell, I can pick up a fourth chair on a street corner in Altoona. Bix is the flame that lights up everything we do." Gillespie starts to say something to the effect that Bix has become too erratic to be worth it, that the flame has become a flicker, but he stops himself. His boss is hardly in the mood for debate, and it is just possible that getting away from the idleness of Hollywood might be good for Bix.

But the Pavilion Royale job confirms Gillespie's sense of the situation because on opening night Bix shows up in no condition to work. There's a large contingent of his fans, sun-reddened college men and their dates who've turned out for him, and they're puzzled, then angry when he simply sits at a side table and doesn't take the stand, and every time they holler, "We want Bix!" Whiteman's temperature inches up a notch. And when at the evening's end a few of the college guys hurl their napkins at the stand Pops is only one beat ahead of a fit. "Look," he tells a subdued Bix backstage, "this can't go on. You know it, I know it. I just hope to hell you aren't going out now with those kids, because you know they're going to ask you. Go home, Bix. Go home and get some sleep, for Christ's sake, and tomorrow night, show up ready for work." And then he can't help himself—it's Bix—he finds himself giving Bix a fatherly bear hug while the others watch, and one of them mutters, "I'd like to see him give me a hug if I'd shown up like that." And whether or not Bix follows Whiteman's directions and goes back to 605 of the 44th Street Hotel or whether he goes out with the boys, whatever he does in those dark hours that flow so swiftly to dawn, the next night he shows up at the Pavilion Royale without his horn, and Pops is wild. Lennie Hayton and Jack Fulton frantically scour the Valley Stream neighborhood for a horn and find a retired high-school music teacher who owns a beat-up cornet that looks like it's been up San Juan Hill, and Whiteman and the rest are amazed when Bix makes it sound like a well-conditioned Conn.

The next night they're in the WABC studios for Old Gold. The stock market has just closed at a record high, and in the confetti of buy slips on the exchange the rhetorical question once again is posed and roaringly answered: Is prosperity due for a decline? Why man, we've scarcely started! Most of the boys are in the market (on margin) and there's a certain amount of giddy self-congratulation going on as they talk about it: Isn't this thing an absolute *gas?*

Their new blues singer, Mildred Bailey, opens the program with Moanin' Low. The Ponce Sisters do Butterflies Kiss Buttercups Goodnight. Bix mostly sits around with little to do except an eight-bar break on When You're Counting The Stars Alone where he uses a mute. Afterward, he tells Boyce Cullen he feels like he's drowning here in New York and wishes he was back in California. "Can't get my breath here," Bix says, standing outside the hotel and breathing heavily, his face slick with sweat. He gestures weakly towards the stony walls of the canyon that surrounds them, that rise to those aeries of power and privilege where, so it occurs to him now, players like himself are a dime a dozen, hired help for a night, faceless, interchangeable, like parts on Mr. Ford's assembly line. "Fall's here," Cullen says, trying to be helpful. "Cooler weather and all." "It's not that," the other says and turns away.

Friday the thirteenth they're back in the studio, this time for Columbia. Warming up, Bix can't do anything, has trouble even getting the mute in the bell of the Bach, and looks almost dead on his feet. "Feel rotten," he mutters to an alarmed Andy Secrest as they get ready for another try at Irving Berlin's Waiting At The End Of The Road. Earlier in the week he'd ruined three takes of this number with fluffs or tardy entries. Now here it is again, and the black dots are dancing in front of him, and he has sixteen bars hidden in there somewhere and turns to Secrest. "Hey, kid," he says with a ghastly simulacrum of a smile, "kick me where I come in, okay?" Secrest nods. "Sure thing, Bix." Up front, Pops gives the high sign, the recording light glows, and they're off, and when it's time Secrest gives Bix's foot a good nudge. And there it is again— summoned up from somewhere—that golden thing, his sound, flickering like a firefly out of the dusk, sixteen brilliant, open-horn bars, strong, certain, almost to the very end before there comes just the slightest waver of indecision, but it's definitely a keeper, and everybody feels better when it's over. Smiles all around and the rustling of pages as they turn to When You're Counting The Stars Alone. Everybody but Bix, who now lurches to his feet and Andy

Secrest has to reach for him and looks up into a blank-eyed mask and watches the mouth work disjointedly. "Got to lie down," it whispers. "Can't make it anymore." Secrest helps him through the chairs and across the studio to the gloom in back where he arranges three chairs and Bix lies down along them. At a break Cullen and Jack Fulton go back to check on him and find him lying there with his eyes open. "Bix," Cullen calls, bending over him, thinking he's awake. "Bix." No response. The eyes show nothing, even when Cullen waves a hand above them, are like two pieces of glass. But the breath is regular enough. After a minute Fulton says, "C'mon, Boyce, let's let him sleep." They leave him there, with those two, depthless points of light, his eyes, staring straight up into the blackness. At the end of the session they discover that somehow he's gotten up and left.

Saturday's papers carry news of Italy and Germany. In Italy Mussolini has handed out seven new cabinet portfolios to his fascist henchmen. Germany, the papers report, has now borrowed almost as much money as it has paid out in war reparations. Macy's runs a full-page spread about what the smart sophomore, the suave senior will be wearing to the gridiron games this season. Beginning next week, Colonel and Mrs. Lindbergh will make flying visits to sixteen South American nations. And the *New York Investment News* runs an ad asking investors if they think it's safe to run a red light when all the others they see are green as go: our forty experts, the ad advises, are here to warn you of any impending dangers in the market. No one hears anything in 605, though the papers containing these items have at some point been silently retrieved from outside the door. Gillespie rings Whiteman to say that something's got to be done about Bix, and Pops roars into the receiver, "*Goddammit! Don't you think I know that?*" Slamming it down, Whiteman thinks again how much better everything would be if he could have talked Herman out of his impetuous decision to quit.

Herman knew how to handle Bix, and there wasn't any of this . . . trouble. Sure, Bix drank then, but, hell, they all did. Now it's no good, Bix by himself, without proper supervision, and Cullen has advised him Bix had gotten tangled up in something messy out there on the coast. Well, Whiteman thinks, angrily throwing on his clothes while trying to reach Lennie Hayton, then Jack Fulton, he himself had better get a handle on this or he's liable to lose another manager in Jimmie, and at this critical point that would be disastrous. He can't reach Hayton or Fulton either, so he enlists Kurt Dieterle and Cullen to go up to 605 with him. "I'm sending him home," he tells them, in the elevator, steeling himself, "back to Davenport. And none of this crap like there was in Cleveland. The three of us are going to put him on that goddamned train and sit there with him until it jerks."

⚜

Burnie's quickly out of the family Chrysler and lifting the bags from the backseat, setting them solidly onto the gray gravel of the drive's leisurely oval while his brother sits within the cab, motionless except for the hands that move together and apart as if feeling for each other. Bix looks at the high wooden ramble of the institute, its porches and porticoes, the discreetly drawn curtains of the inmates' rooms, but he can't work up more than a dull dread. When Burnie straightens and turns to him he stays where he is, only fiddling slowly with his fingers. Five hours ago they left Davenport, and he's done nothing but this, even at the stop where Burnie gassed up and went to the toilet. They haven't spoken a word and they don't now, only looking at each other, Bix knowing Burnie can't wait to discharge this embarrassing burden and clear out for home, and who could blame him? So now, slowly, shakily, he alights, deciding he's got to do his best to make this easier and stands there in the drive under a sullen sky, looking back down the drive to the street, past the institute's offices, to where the railroad tracks run atop a small slope, northeastward, to Chicago. The long-held moment, heavy as an old clock's pendulum, swings forward now on the dark flash of double doors opening under the portico, and then they see the forceful stride of a tall, muscular man coming towards them in dark pants, white shirt, and bow tie, wearing a set, professional smile of welcome. His entire being radiates a healthful, sober sanity, a nimbus casting a deeper shade over Bix. "He forgot the prune juice," Bix mutters, seeing the man is empty-handed. "Cut it out, Bix," Burnie says. "You brought yourself here." "No, no," Bix says, "you brought me here, Burnie." "What I mean is, you brought this on yourself," Burnie says quickly, out of the side of his mouth, not wanting the family linens aired any more than necessary; even being on the grounds of such a place is shameful enough.

Mr. Dalton introduces himself while giving the new inmate a quick, appraising glance, thinking he's pretty young for so bad a case, and then they go in, past the lounge with its arched brick fireplace, its medieval armored figure with sword and shield standing tall in the niche between windows, its upright piano. When Bix spots this something that might be hope if he had the energy to assent to it flickers inside him as he slowly follows Dalton and Burnie up the stairs and along the corridor to his room where, from the other side of those discreetly drawn curtains, he can now look down on the oval drive and the parked Chrysler. Bed, nightstand, wash basin, desk, wing-backed easy chair with footstool. On the desk, perfectly squared to the edges of the blotter beneath, lies a booklet explaining the objectives and methods of the Keeley Institute. He flips it open at random and reads, "The drunkard continues to drink because the craving for alcohol is a symptom of his disease." Seems simple enough, he thinks, closing it. Behind him, Dalton and Burnie are making the formal exchanges, and then

Dalton leaves the brothers, and Burnie turns to Bix and puts his hands on his shoulders. "Mother and Dad—we all want you to do well here, Bix and, uh, quit this stuff." Bix nods and smiles a little. Burnie drops his hands, finds Bix's right hand and shakes it, and then he turns his broad back and is out the door, and Bix can hear him going down the long corridor to the door at its end and then the door opening and shutting, the heavy handle turned and released and the tongue of the latch finding its grooved home. And in a few moments he can watch from behind the thin white curtains—Burnie in the Chrysler, swinging past the building, his coat sleeve resting on the edge of the car's opened window, and then he's gone in a crunch of gravel and the Chrysler's gassy gargle, and he's alone.

Not a sound in the place, and he wonders what they've done with all the others who've been sent here by parents or husbands or wives—whoever it is who decides which ones get to stay home and which are simply too much of an embarrassment or nuisance and so must be sent someplace else, some secret place where anonymous others can handle them. He starts to sit down in the wing-backed chair, then remembers the piano and moves quickly enough down to the lounge and sits at it. At his first touch he finds it in good condition, but his preliminary notes—a spread chord, a tentative tickle up into the treble—bring Dalton into the room, and the tall man, still with that set, professional smile, tells him this piano is reserved for evening hours only. "There's another one across the way in the clubhouse," he adds, "and you are free to use that at any hour of the day." "Sorry," Bix mumbles, "I had no idea . . . ." Dalton assures him there's no harm done and says he'd like to have an interview with Bix whenever he feels up to it. "We need some more background information, you see," he explains—"about your life, habits, and so forth. And by the way, Mr. Beiderbecke, what is your drink?" "My w-what?" Bix stammers, unbelieving. "Your drink: what form of alcohol is it you customarily indulge in? You see," Dalton continues smoothly as Bix stands beside the piano wearing a red look of violation, "here at Keeley we are careful not to inadvertently set off a shock to the patient's nervous system by instantly depriving him—or her, as the case may be—of all alcohol. We have found through more than a half century of work with thousands of patients that this retards the total healing process. So—" Dalton's professional smile widens just a bit as if in confidentiality—"we allow our patients an initial supply of their customary beverage, whatever it may be, so as to prevent that shock. Usually this is a gill, which the patient may take when so inclined, and for the first few days more may be supplied, as needed. But I can safely assure you, Mr. Beiderbecke, that after just a few days here you will find your craving for alcohol dramatically reduced." The smile now fades as Dalton moves on from the regimen to the cure itself and concludes by predicting that "after the prescribed course, four weeks generally, you will be entirely restored to a healthy life." His voice rises into the broad, public range. "So then, what shall it be?" "I don't want anything," Bix says hoarsely. "I don't need anything. What I need is rest. That's why I'm here. I need rest."

And rest is what he gets, so much at first that Dalton remarks to Dr. Oughten that Mr. Beiderbecke seems rather determined to sleep his way through his stay. "Get him up. Get him involved," Dr. Oughten orders. "Sleep isn't what his parents are paying for." Dalton passes the order on to Bix's attendant, a short, blocky fellow named Sam whose red, pocked face is in constant motion, eyes rolling, jaws working with a steady stream of patter. Sam sees to it that his man makes breakfast, attends the daily lecture, takes his constitutional around the spacious grounds in the afternoons, the two men walking beneath the steadily showering autumnal trees, along the green serpentine slither of the long pond created by the founding doctor, old Keeley, who made his reputation restoring G.A.R. drunks through a rigorous regimen of exercise,

diet, and daily deluges of Doctor Keeley's Double Chloride Gold
Cure for Drunkenness. Eventually Bix and Sam begin to move off
the grounds, along village streets lined with shade trees that are
still full but showing bare here and there, the squirrels hard at
their husbandry under mellow skies that only occasionally carry a
portent of the season's turn. And then they walk out beyond the
village on farm lanes, past shocks of corn stacked like teepees,
twists of smoke standing in the distance, tractors puffing over flat
fields, the patient for the most part silent but not sullen, and Sam
easily filling the void: talking of his boyhood in nearby Joliet, of
his brief stint in the navy, of a long courtship that failed because
the girl was Catholic and her parents disapproved of his casual
Protestantism. When the A's wallop the Cubs in the Series, Bix
has to sympathize with Sam's tragedy, and so for a few days roles
are reversed, and it's Bix who has to take Sam for these restorative
walks.

Bix plays some on the piano in the clubhouse, beginning once
again to work at In A Mist and exploring its potential thematic
connections to Candlelights. On the floor above he plays shuffle-
board, the game now in vogue among Floridians and the ocean-
going smart set. Dalton supervises basketball games, having once
been a star at nearby Eureka College, but Bix doesn't feel up to so
strenuous an activity. In the evenings after supper he sits in the
lounge, smoking a pipe—more healthful than cigarettes, so he's
been told—listening to a six-foot woman play Liszt and Schubert
and Chopin on the piano, and one afternoon in the clubhouse
reading room when she has laid aside Edith Wharton's *The Age of
Innocence* he works up his courage to speak to her, asking softly if
the book's good and what is it about, and Enore Skelton looks up in
wary surprise behind her heavy spectacles, her coarse complexion
framed by deep auburn hair, to find it's the young man she'd heard
once or twice fooling around with spread chords on the piano in

the late afternoons. "Well," she says, hesitant, defensive, alert for some cutting remark to come, "yes, rather good. I'll likely finish it tonight, and you may borrow it. If you wish." The next evening after supper she delivers the novel, and he disarms her with a shy smile and confesses he really wants to talk with her about music, about the piano—though he would also like to read Wharton. Keeley vigorously discourages fraternizing between its male and female patients, who are housed in separate grounds across the tracks, but surely it's all right for this so evidently mismatched pair to talk at the piano and exchange books.

Enore Skelton is a music teacher at a girl's school on Chicago's North Shore, down here for the cure, of course, though in her case it may be less an alcohol problem that has landed her here than that twice in the past year (most recently just after the beginning of this fall term) she has touched students in such a way that they have complained to the administration. After the latest incident, sparked perhaps by the nightly doses of Madeira she administered to herself in her dormitory rooms, Miss Skelton's patrician parents decided she might greatly profit from a few weeks at Keeley and then an extended trip abroad where she could have some intellectually and psychologically bracing contact with Old World culture. Contacts in Firenzi and in Paris with the well-known piano teacher Miss Boulanger have already been arranged. All she says to Bix is that she's here for the cure and then will have a European tour until spring. He volunteers even less about himself, and she doesn't ask.

He hasn't finished *The Age of Innocence* when he returns it one evening after she's been playing for an appreciative group and then walks with her out onto the portico. Enore Skelton pauses, feeling he's come out here with her for a reason, remembering too vividly obscure errands of her own where she'd found herself inarticulately positioned on the verge of some possibility. But when a minute passes in silence she says, "Well, goodnight, then," and turns to

walk up the drive towards her quarters across the tracks. "I wanted
to ask you something," he calls to her tall straight back in its heavy
sweater. She stops and turns, facing him through the falling
gloom. "It's a favor, really . . . I'd love to have a few lessons from
you, learn to read better, and so on. . . ." His voice trails off, and
she can hardly make him out there in the condensed darkness of
the portico with the vast bulk of the mansion above it. "I don't
know," she says at last, standing her ground. "I have only a little
time left here." She senses rather than truly sees his mute supplication, his obscure, evident need. "Well," she says at last, "let me
hear you play tomorrow afternoon, and then we might discuss
what could be done. Goodnight now." And after he does play for
her, she says In A Mist is really quite pretty. "But why do you rush
through it so?" she wonders. "Nervous, I guess," he tells her with
another of his shadowy smiles, not realizing that he has rushed
through it, because he's always played it just this way. Ever since
that day in '27 when he came in to the Okeh studios with Tram to
cut a recording of it. They'd tried a couple of versions that were too
long and a condensed version that was forty seconds too short, and
the producer was getting impatient when Tram said to him,
"Look, why don't we just let Bix *go* on it, and then when he's got
twenty seconds left, I'll tap him and you (looking at Bix) make
some kind of an ending." That's what they'd done, he hurrying
through his piece, wanting to get all its strains in, then improvising
an ending, and he'd played it the same way ever since, including
that night at Carnegie Hall, never hearing what Enore Skelton had
just heard. And why hadn't he? Why hadn't the others heard that
hectic quality?

Three days later Bix and Enore Skelton wander out of the lodge
after supper. Some others have taken over the piano and are trying a
four-part version of the institute's official song, The Keeley Cure,
with false starts and many stops and good-natured laughter. Walking

past the clubhouse they see the lights on in the billiards room where a small gallery of onlookers is just settling in to watch Mr. Marstens, a businessman from Cedar Rapids, demonstrate some of his trick shots. They walk on, leaving the buildings behind, following the graceful curve of the walkway that has taken on a luminescence in October's dusk and presently arrive in silence at the rear edge of the grounds where the brittle grasses, the trimmed shrubbery and pruned hardwoods leave off, and there's a sort of symbolic gate there without fencing on either side of it. A small, narrow path slants down from the gate into a harvested cornfield, the rows running, converging westward and only a few scattered cobs and stalks litter-ing the darkened earth and the sun already a wintry red, a disc har-rowing the tree-bordered horizon. They stand at the gate, looking, Enore Skelton in her heavy sweater, its shawl-like collar upturned against the settling chill, he with his suit coat collar up, hands plunged into its pockets, shoulders hunched. When he looks up into her face with its lines and old, effaced pockmarks the sun is making twin discs in her spectacles' lenses, and he can't see her eyes nor even much of her face now as the sun drops like molten shot through the far-off trees.

"What do you think I should do—I mean, with my playing, with these pieces?" he asks. "I don't know that I can help you there, Mr. Beiderbecke," she answers finally. "You already know too much: it's rather like the two-fingered typist, you see: that person is harder to teach than the true beginner." And he, quickly, with something in the center of his tone that makes her turn towards him, "But I want to forget everything I know!" "That will be very difficult for you," she says. "There's so little time." "Well, show me what you can, won't you?" Still that tone, and she wonders where it comes from, whether it comes from somewhere that's close to panic, whether it has an objective altogether different from im-proved piano playing. She sees now his hands emerging from his coat pockets, watches as he hesitantly extends them in her direction, as if this is finally what he's been moving towards in the weeks he's been shyly circling her. After a long moment she takes one of them between her own large, capable hands and holds it briefly, there in the not-light of the sun's final disappearance, and then lets it go. "What is it, Mr. Beiderbecke, that you aspire to?" she asks him gently. And in answer he turns from her to face once more the blackened field, its gleaned rows, the scatter of stalks, and, beyond, the inky clump of the far copse and says in a strangely altered voice, "I don't know." His hands make a small, brief offering in the direction of the field. "I don't know. This, maybe."

❧❖❧

On a gentle Friday morning he takes his now-customary solitary stroll down to the depot where he knows the papers will have been dropped and finds scare headlines in both the *Des Moines Register* and the *Chicago Tribune*. The grain markets and securities on the Board of Trade and the Chicago Stock Exchange have imploded in the wake of a disastrous dive on Wall Street. FORTUNES IN PAPER VALUES WIPED OUT IN REACTION TO WEDNESDAY'S WALL ST. SELL-OFF! PIT A TURMOIL! TREASURY OFFICIALS BLAME SPECULATION. He buys the papers and reads them at the café on the edge of town where the truckers stop and the farmers gather in their denim jumpers and wool shirts and caps, the talk buzzing around him as he reads over his oatmeal and coffee, some of it about the car ferry that went down in the lake just off Kenosha with all aboard apparently lost. But mostly about the wheat crash—a bushel down a nickel this morning—the role of the speculator, Wall Street Jews. He finishes his coffee with the last of the papers' inside items, leaves both papers neatly folded

on the counter, and walks out into the new-made morning, a thin
fog lifting out of the fields, great clusters of birds spreading like
black fans against a tardy sun. But now something tugs at his
sleeve, and instead of turning towards the institute—lecture, exercise, lunch, rest-hour—he takes the high road that runs between
St. Louis and Chicago, walking with hands in pockets, out into the
country and its limitless fields. And out there, surrounded, engulfed even, by the fields, whatever the impulse was that tugged
him this way, it dissolves in the presence of the fields and sky and
he turns back. And the morning following, he's at the café again,
hearing more talk above his newspapers, louder now, angrier, the
men still trying to digest the shocking news from the Board of
Trade, ruminating on rumors the Big Boys are gathering in New
York to rescue the markets, and who in hell is gonna look out for
the man who feeds the whole kit-and-caboodle and how disap-
pointing Mr. Hoover's turning out to be. After all this he turns out
of town again on the high road, not looking at the fields this time
but only steadily at the road ahead, refusing with polite smile and
wave the offer of a weather-roughened farmer who slows his trac-
tor and hollers at him above its blue, unmuffled roar.

Twenty minutes later he's at Marlis's Diner, a huddle of buildings
that has sprawled out from the original roadside stand and where
the long-distance drivers stop for their breakfast meat and eggs. In
here they're talking of the markets, too, and of the tragedy in the
lake, but not quite so angrily, because in here are men with wider
experience, more urban concerns, men whose travel takes them to
the great cities, and the longer he dawdles over his coffee, the more
he keeps hearing the word Chicago, until it comes to be a kind of
drumming refrain inside his head. The Big Town. It sends a shiver
down his spine, bristles the hair above his ears. He's known in
Chicago. There, if he showed up anywhere, they'd open their arms
to him. Back down the road, in the café where he'd read through

the dense agate of the *Trib*'s entertainment pages, he'd spotted a dozen familiar names, and now imagines himself walking unannounced into the stinking blackness of the Green Mill on Broadway, and seeing Wingy and Art up there on the stand and how when they picked him out their faces would crack into grins of affectionate recognition, and it'd be like old times. Here nobody knows who the hell he is, nobody cares, certainly not the chubby redhead who now intrudes her freckled hand with coffee pot just beneath his nose, pouring in a smoking refill. He looks up, but she's already moving on, seeing to the Joe on the next stool. Back at the institute they know him, all right: he's Mr. Beiderbecke, a man with a shameful problem his parents are paying them to solve. Even Miss Skelton didn't recognize his name; he was just a guy who pestered her for lessons, and yesterday she'd left without saying goodbye. His hand races ahead of his mind, reaches for his wallet and finds there a ten and two singles, surely enough for a train ticket to Chi, but he might just as easily catch a ride right outside the door and be up there by late afternoon at worst. And as for money, there were plenty of guys up there who'd put him up, lend him some dough. Krupa was in town. Hell, he'd stood Gene and his whole group to dinner once when they were stranded. But then—.

But then.

His mind flashes back to the garish interior of the Green Mill: Wingy up on the stand, black glove on his artificial hand; Art in his baggy suit, hunched over the keyboard, the spot making black blotches beneath his cheekbones; the special booth to the right of the stand, reserved for the Big Shot; and then the blue-white blaze of the spot, scything through the smoke-shrouded room, searching for him, finding him there at a table. They would want him to play. No, that wasn't it: they would *demand* it. Why the hell would he be in there if not to play? He can picture it all perfectly, and they're waving him up to the stage, calling to him, and the crowd too is calling for him, rising to its feet, the spot staying there on him, relentless, pitiless. He sits on his swivel stool at Marlis's, frozen by this imagined scene, unable to move an eyelid as the chubby redhead, moving back down the counter calling, "Coffee? Coffee? Coffee?" comes relentlessly on and reaches him, but she's much too busy to wonder what his problem might be or even to notice that he has one and moves on, leaving him behind where he struggles against the thought that keeps pushing itself forward, until it finally comes bursting into consciousness.

I don't want to play.

Never since he lifted that first scored and tarnished little cornet, felt it, tilted it, sighted along it to its brownish bell, loving every inch of it, never had he not wanted to play his horn. How many things had he sacrificed to it, foregoing outings with his childhood chums, with parents and family, foregoing girls, so much of the adolescent social swim, skipping school, begging Paul Mares to let him sit in with the Rhythm Kings and Mares laughing at the little cornet that he said looked like a coffee pot. Those hot tears he'd shed in front of all the others when old Kautz had failed him on the union exam and told him to go home and study for two years. And he had studied, too. Had been studying all along. Not the way Kautz had wanted, but, dammit, it was study nonetheless, thousands of hours of thought and practice and careful listening, trying to discover his own, authentic voice, seeking his personal sound amidst the weltering blare of this age, learning what he needed to leave out so that what he kept, the few precious notes he did play, would be as clean, as clear, as direct as a statement straight from the soul. How many nights after the others had passed out had he gone where the music was, playing his horn until finally even the last of the blue-hours jammers had called it a day? To play his horn—that was what he'd lived for, *all* he'd lived for. And now he'd admitted in a flash of insight and image that he no longer wanted to play it, that it felt now that he was through with it. Panicked, bereft of sole purpose, he lurches up from the swivel stool, staggering backwards, knocking cup and saucer from the counter but somehow in a miraculous feat of coordination catching them both before they crash. And so crouches there, coffee puddle on the floor, splashed on pants' cuff, the eyes of the others on him, and a great ruddy flush instantly emblazoned on his face and neck. Trembling, he replaces cup and saucer on the counter and turns to walk out when the redhead calls at his back, "Say, mister, you owe me for the joe." And then outside in the road, he begins to run, hard, back down the road towards town, feeling the surface hard and lumpy beneath his fleeing feet, his clenched fists pumping the empty air, chest straining against a sudden gust of wind, until he can't run any longer and shambles into a walk and then quits even this and stands in the road, bent, hands on knees, gasping, afraid he's going to lose the oatmeal and toast and coffee. And then the unmuffled roar at his back, and it's the same old farmer again, stopping and yelling, "Son, are you lost?" And he, gasping, "No . . . but . . . I . . . sure could use a lift to town." And Sam, coming from the clubhouse across the stretch of lawn and gravel to the main house, sees him turn in the gate, wild-eyed, hair flapping on sweaty forehead, and calls across to him, "Hey, Mr. Beiderbecke! Been looking for you everywhere." He says nothing in response, only flings lopsidedly up the steps, and later Sam will report to Dalton that Mr. Beiderbecke isn't feeling well and wants to spend the rest of the day in his room.

That evening, after billiards in the clubhouse and a slide projector presentation by a local man who has been to the Valley of the Kings, Dalton sits down with his tall, ruled ledger books to continue his weekly notes on patients, writing in his careful hand under the block-lettered entry, BEIDERBECKE, LEON, that the longer Mr. Beiderbecke has been in residence, the more moody and erratic his behavior. "Underscored by this morning's episode when he failed for 2nd consecutive day to appear for breakfast, was absent from morning program, and was subsequently observed by staff returning from town in a state of considerable agitation." Dalton turns back the pages, scanning quickly through the Beiderbecke entries, their references to signs of acute alcoholic poisoning—"enlarged liver tender to touch, tongue coated and flabby, eyes slow to retract to light stimulus, trembling hands, almost wholly illegible signature on the admittance form": yes, a bad case. But certainly there had been some improvement noted through the subsequent weeks. How then to account for this widening disparity between physical improvement and deportment? Dalton sits there, his pen poised to create the next entry. And then he makes it.

"It is possible," he writes, "that patient may be using his freedom of movement to obtain alcohol off premises. This might account for his moody behavior. As he has less than a week left here a relapse is to be considered a distinct possibility.

"Recommendation to family: some steady, undemanding sort of work in the home environment, perhaps into the new year.

"Prognosis for complete recovery must be considered as extremely guarded."

Dalton rereads his words, hand held to brow in concentration, and then turns the page to make the next entry.

In his old bedroom of the house on Grand he sleeps late or pretends to, sometimes stealthily reading in bed, hearing the sentinel tread of his mother as it approaches his door and pauses and then like Time moves onward. In the deepening seasonal interregnum, summer only a brown memory, temperature dropping a few degrees deeper each night, he can hear the way the house gathers to itself, and then on these mornings, lying between the clean sheets, he hears it expand in sunlight, its thews and tenons ticking and popping until at noon when he finally arises it has achieved its full dimensions once more. In the afternoons he sits at the piano and plays, though not very determinedly, and there are long silences in which Agatha, coming through from the dining room on some alleged errand, finds him sitting on the bench staring at the keyboard, his hands in his lap. He seems in these moments to be waiting but for who or what she can't imagine. He makes no calls, writes but one letter and that to someone unknown to her, in New York. Once, his old friend Esten Spurrier from riverboat days drives past and sees a figure muffled in some sort of blanket or shawl, sitting on the porch on the far side of its generous curve, away from the street, and when he later calls the house and gets Agatha she tells him, yes, Bix is home, but he needs his rest. And, yes, she'll tell him about the call. He has developed an aversion to the front door and the front portion of the porch since he made the sudden, incredibly belated discovery that the porches of the neighboring homes are perfectly aligned so that someone standing on their front porch five doors down has a straight line of vision through to the porch at 1934. So when he goes out, he uses the back door, and when he sits on the porch as he sometimes does in the afternoons it's around on the side. Most of the excursions he makes are nocturnal. His family doesn't discourage these almost furtive habits.

The night walks are his main outlet, more so just now than the piano, which somehow seems difficult, almost as if it's fighting him. He hasn't touched his horn since that day in the studio when he played a solo on the Berlin tune. After the evening meal, after Dad has remarked on the disheartening news of the days—markets continuing depressed, family financial cushion flattened, signs of distress in the community where some customers are beginning to ask if they might defer payment for their coal until after the first of the year—then he slips on his old blue overcoat to take what he tells the folks are his prescribed constitutionals. He goes out the back way into Walling Court and from there on a winding ramble without fixed course, changing from night to night as if following some subconscious impulse, his hunched, huddled progress taking him past substantial places just like his own: wide, furbelowed, tur-reted, deep of porch, narrow of window, though often enough all he sees are the broad sidewalk slabs laid down in front of them by Davenport Stone & Marble. Lights from the windows and porches beam mellowly onto small sloping lawns and short flights of steps leading up from the sidewalk. The new municipal street lamps shed a cold gleam through barren branches, and the old smoke of all-but-extinguished leaf fires wavers weakly from heaps in the gut-ters with here and there a spark winking through the ashes. Once in a while a man passes him, dog on leash, the animal's breath visi-ble as it strains against its collar. One night he walks the long hill down towards the river, passing his old high school that looks as if heaved up during the night of the earth, down to the fountain at the base of the hill where the gang used to gather in those days be-fore he found his way to the cornet and went his own way. He turns east along the levee, hearing the river slapping at the stones, on past his father's company, smelling the sharp, acrid dust of the coal, past the waterworks where the steamer used to dock. And then he's into a worn path that keeps company with the river to Bettendorf. The shin-high brittle grasses brush his legs, and a bird, startled from sleep, flushes with a squawk and is gone in the black-ness. A long barge pushes silently downriver, and he stands a few minutes looking after its cabin light as it slides along, until the light's gone and he's under the black, dimensionless lid of a starless night. He comes to the sign announcing the limits of Bettendorf and recalls playing one of his first dates there, a high school dance when he was still just learning his way around the horn but was somehow certain even then of a few things, just how he's never bothered to understand. It was as if he was searching on the horn for a way to make the sound he already had in his head—and certain that at some future point these two sounds, the real and the ideal, would meet and he'd be in that moment the player he was meant to be.

The path forks around a large double-trunked oak sunk almost to its lower branches in a nest of high grass, and he walks under it, fishes for a cigarette, and lights up. The real sound had never matched the ideal one, that much he now realized, nor would it ever for him, not on the cornet. And where now were all those alligators who adored what he did, who not very long ago had hollered his name in the fraternity houses and gymnasiums, the hotel ballrooms and cozy clubs with cater-cornered bandstands, plucking at his sleeve, begging him to come out with them afterwards and play till morning; the young marrieds with new money and time on their hands who at all hours banged on his door with gin bottles, wanting to be able to boast they'd "been up there with Bix," looking at each other in barely concealed amazement when he'd let them in and had gotten out the bottles and picked up his horn for them; the bankers and bond salesmen and stockbrokers who whisked him up to penthouses, telling him the place was his and everything in it for just a few more of those golden bars? Gone. All gone. Nothing here now but the relentless rush of the great river at his back, running south in the night to empty out below New Orleans. His mind returns again, as it has often on these night walks, to that moment with Miss Skelton, there at the edge of the institute's grounds in the last fiery wink of sunset, the question she put to him there, and his almost involuntary response: that little gesture out towards the darkened, harvested field. What the hell had he meant by that? Couldn't have been the cornfield: he'd been running away from cornfields ever since he found out where he was and how much more world there was left to discover. If he no longer wanted to play jazz on his cornet, what indeed did he "aspire to," as she'd put it, a cornfield symphony? A cornball symphony? What was it he was supposed to do now if he isn't going to play jazz anymore?

He's still circling around that moment and its question when he ventures out days later on an afternoon walk about the old neighborhood with his high-school sweetheart, Vera, who's in town visiting her folks with her baby boy. And as they pass the big hilltop homes, Vera letting him push the pram, the curtains are pulled aside to remark their passage, the strange Beiderbecke boy and Vera Cox who married Ferd Friedrichs and moved away to Des Moines. Vera finds him strange, too, oddly overweight in a pulpy, unhealthy way, wearing an unbecoming little moustache, and not at all the delightful, handsome boy she'd known and looked up to in school days. Even then he'd been quiet, of course, but this man's silences suggest to her he's withdrawn from the world into a dark place where he's unreachable even to himself, where he is captive to some whelming sadness, until at last, both uneasy and moved by the shadow of the old Bix walking next to her, she touches his hand on the pram's handle, lightly, quickly, and asks, "What is it, Bix? You seem so sad—." He turns his eyes towards her and she finds them frightened even while the moustached mouth beneath them is trying to work up a smile. He shrugs, and they walk on, reaching the intersection with Harrison Street down which her parents still live. "Dunno," he says there. "I kind of feel like life's passed me by somehow. Can't figure out how that could've happened." "O, come on, Bix!" she says brightly, touching his coat sleeve quickly. "You've done so much. Why, you're even *famous!*" He makes a quick, dismissive gesture. "Why, look where you've been—all those places—New York. We heard you were even out in Hollywood, making a movie." "Yes, well now I'm back here," he tells her. "But just for a rest," she coaxes. "A rest, yeah, that's it. But I don't know if I'll ever go back." She asks, incredulous, if he means he's thinking of giving it all up, all he's worked for, and he tells her he just might. "I've been to the top," he says tonelessly and stops to peer into the pram where the baby boy lies placidly, eyes open and bright among the swaddled covers. "Remember that time," he says, gazing down the street towards the Cox home, "when we got stuck at the top of the ferris wheel out at the fairgrounds, and we just sat up there—O, I don't know—a long time?" "Sure," she says, "worrying Mother and Dad wouldn't believe our story." He smiles. "They never really approved of me, and they were right." He shakes himself away from that digression. "What I mean is, the rest of the way is down, see. It's like that ferris wheel: when you've seen everything, it's kind of a letdown." She tells him he's still tired, that when he's really rested he won't be thinking this way: it must be a very hard life he lives, on the road so much of the time, strangers pestering him, no place to call his own. He nods, yes, and they roll on towards the Cox home, the whole scene as serene and unchanged as when they were boy and girl and he rode his bike down this street, no-handed, to show off for her.

"You play so beautifully," she says at last. "It would be just a terrible shame to give it up." Actually, she hasn't heard him play in some years, yet she carries with her an indelible memory of what he used to sound like, the overly ambitious things he'd try during school assemblies, which she didn't understand but liked anyway.

"I kind of feel like I've said whatever it was I had to say—on the horn, anyway."

"But you played piano beautifully, too. I remember that. Do you still play it? You could go on with that if you don't want to play your trumpet right now."

"I play it, sure. But nobody wants me as a pianist, Vera." He shakes his head. "I'm not good enough to go around playing solo;

I'm not even good enough to play with a band, really. I can only play in C." He looks down and shakes his head. "Besides, things are tough right now, and nobody seems to be able to figure out how to make them much better." Vera knows how this is: if there isn't any improvement soon she and Ferd and the baby might be forced to move back in with her parents. The baby begins to turn fretfully in his blankets, and Vera says she guesses she ought to take him inside for changing and feeding. "Sure," he says, quickly releasing his hold on the pram. Her dark eyes regard him with an old fondness. "This has been such fun, Bix," she says. "It's been wonderful seeing you again. My friends in Des Moines will be jealous." The baby lets out his first whimper.

"I kind of feel like I have something else to do," he says, not looking at her but glancing off down the lumpy, brick-paved street, "but darned if I can figure out what it is." She cocks her head and gives him her brightest, most vivacious smile. "You will, Bix," she says. "You've got so much to give."

IV

Sunnyside

They're in Plunkett's, on 53rd off Broadway where the elevated rattles black overhead, the few who have work and the many more who don't and for whom the weekend yawns soundless as a void, payless like so many weekends now. In these bleak days Plunkett's is more welcome and more necessary than it ever was in the salad days left so suddenly behind. In here, if a man's lucky enough to have some radio work or a college weekend to play, he's buying, and he keeps buying until he's out of work again, and then maybe the guy standing next to him will have work and will stand him to a few. Plunkett's isn't much to look at, but it's their clubhouse, home. A glass door painted a dead black faces the street, and inside of what used to be part of a warehouse is a long narrow room with a balcony running around the upper story. There's an old upright up there, used to hammer out new arrangements. Downstairs, a bar, tables and chairs, and a room in back where a man could change into his monkey suit or grab forty winks on the leprous couch or freshen up in the can. Big Frenchy and Owney are the suppliers so there's never any trouble with the cops. Jimmy Plunkett's usually behind the bar, a florid, barrel-chested Irishman whose father was well-connected at Tammany Hall. When the old man was around Jimmy was a club fighter, welterweight, but he wasn't going anywhere, and when the old man kicked, Jimmy hung up the gloves and took his place behind the bar. Jimmy knows every white musician in town and quite a few of the colored, too, though they don't come in here.

The topic of today's seminar is Bix, and when Jimmy hears that strange, electric name he quits rolling glasses through the sink of sudsy water and comes down the planking in his side-to-side gait, as if he'd once been a sailor not a boxer. Jimmy wants to hear this because he knows Bix is back, but except for two very brief sightings he hasn't seen him, and until he went away this was Bix's spot. Jimmy Dorsey's telling about Bix to a group that includes his brother Tommy, Red Nichols, Slick Condon, and a few others. "He told Whiteman to shove it," Jimmy's telling them. "Said he was fed up waiting all night for eight bars, and I—." "You're full of shit," Tommy cuts in, "but what's new, huh?" Jimmy gives Tommy that O-Christ-the-younger-brother-bullshit look, rolling his eyes at the others. The others look at Tommy. "I don't know what he said to Whiteman," Tommy says now, "but I do know this: Bix wouldn't say that. He loves Whiteman. Plus which, he's a gent, a real gent, which is more than I can say for some of the present company." Slick Condon puts his glass down long enough to smooth his already well-slicked hair. "I gotta go with that," he says, talking as always out of the side of his mouth, though at the moment he doesn't have a cigarette in it. "I gotta go with that. Beiderbix would never say that to Whiteman." "Well, I—," Jimmy Dorsey starts to protest when Frank Signorelli says Roy Bargy was there at the time and reported that what Bix actually said was that times being what they are, Whiteman should keep Andy Secrest on because Andy might have a harder time landing another job, whereas he, Bix, could always get work.

"That's Bix," Jimmy Plunkett says from his post and breaking the bartender's code, which is never to lead. "What I hear is he isn't sounding so hot right now," Jimmy Dorsey persists, "so maybe it might not be that easy for him, either." "You wouldn't, either, brother," Tommy says. "He's on the wagon." Jimmy glares at Tommy, and the others get set. The brothers have had it out often enough, even on the bandstand, and once Bix, the peacemaker, tried to step in between them, and Tommy landed one right on his jaw, and when the brothers saw Bix lying there with his eyes rolling like pinballs they'd laughed and made up. "Now, there's to be none of this funny business in here," Jimmy Plunkett says quietly. "You boys want to work out your upbringing, you go out there under the elevated where you can get in some real swings. This place is built for bantamweights, not sluggers such as yourselves." This is classic mixologist verbal strategy: you make your point and take the sting out of it with a bit of flattery. Tommy's taken his glasses off, but now he slams them back on. There's a kind of shuffling of bodies, glasses lifted, a refill called for. Then Red Nichols says Bix has a girl-friend. They look at him in something close to shock. Red is a Bix alligator to the least inflection, has his style down, all except the tone, which nobody can get, maybe not even Bix anymore. And Red is starting to make pretty good money doing Bix, too. Some of them resent this a little, but times being what they are, it's hard to begrudge someone who's making it. "Does Bix know this?" some-body asks, a reference to Bix's famously absent manner. Laughter all around, including from the edgy brothers who are now over it. "Big T met her," Red reports. "What's she like?" Frank Signorelli asks. "You mean, what does Big T say she's like?" Red says. He imitates Teagarden's slurring Texas drawl that is just like his trombone style: "Sweet ass, short in the Tits Department." Then in his own voice he adds that Big T said she was a blonde with a long scar on her face, like maybe she'd been in an accident.

They don't know what to make of this. The Bix they knew played beautiful horn and strange piano and drank. That was all. Still, Red's report kind of fits with what little they do know these days: that their boy isn't himself since he's been back. "We need to go around to cheer him up," Slick Condon says finally. "I'm going to cheer him up, all right, if I can put this Princeton date together,"

Tommy Dorsey says. "Me and Jimmy are going to take a band down there week after next, and of course they want him. The kids are trying to get the scratch together. And we have another possible date up at Williams. He'll get work." Jimmy Dorsey doesn't want to use Bix; he'd rather get the hot new trumpet star Bunny Berigan who can burn the house down. But he knows as well as his brother does that the Princeton kids will accept no one else, regardless of talent, regardless of how Bix sounds these days, and he knows, too, that after a couple of numbers it won't make any difference whether Bix's lip's in good shape or not: they'll holler their heads off for him, then get drunk and dance and try to get in the girlfriend's pants, and except for a small cadre of alligators the kids won't care what any of the players sound like. They want noise, pep, and the Dorsey brothers can certainly provide plenty of that.

When Tommy approaches Bix with the Princeton plan Bix isn't wild about it. He doesn't think he sounds so hot these days, either, and doubts his ability to get through a college campus weekend, so Tommy has to do a lot of coaxing, telling him the band won't get the date at all if he's not with them. Finally, he tells Bix he'll bring along Big T's kid brother Charlie as an extra trumpet, in case Bix can't make all the parties. They drive down in two cars, Bix with Tommy, Bud Freeman, and Joe Sullivan, and he's so silent, huddled in the back seat, that it casts a pall over them and it's a relief when they get to campus and meet up with Jimmy, Benny Goodman, and young Charlie Teagarden. They jump out, laughing so loudly you'd think they'd bumped into each other in the middle of Kansas, and the jugs come out there in the parking space behind one of the eating clubs. Bix stays in the backseat, door open, smoking, smiling at the others once in a while when they try to include him, throwing a remark, a reference his way. It's a perfect early autumn weekend, the football team opening against Lehigh, a game they should handily win, the girls in from Vassar and Sweetbriar around there with Don Murray. He made it a point to read the better books, which he imagined he'd have been exposed to in the classroom, but had found that the college men pounding him on the back and pouring his glass brimful either didn't know what the hell he was talking about when he brought up Dos Passos or Sinclair Lewis or T. E. Lawrence or else weren't interested in talking to him about books. They were there to hear him *play*, to get ripped with him, to laugh. So he was left to conclude that either college was some sort of vast, empty joke or else a *really* secret society within which the college men discussed literature and philosophy and history only among themselves. And now the old seductions of campus life, the very lawns and ivied walls and angled walkways he looks out on here have vanished for him like smoke, leaving in him an awful clarity in which he sees just how far outside all this he really is and must always be. And while the others are getting primed to go on and provide the background noise for the kids' sophisticated mayhem, he sits in the backseat of the sedan, dreading it, all of it, including the hollow acclaim that will inevitably come to him, those first cries of recognition that will arise from the floor when they see him up there, sandwiched between the Dorseys. He knows Doc and Squirrel and Zero, that bunch of amateur tootlers who graduated a couple of years ago, will be down for the weekend, and they'll be all over him, leading the cheers from the floor, wanting to jam with him after hours, wanting to show off their friendship with him to a new crop of undergraduates. And they will call for all the old numbers he's made his famous improvisations on through the years, the numbers he no longer wants to play, no longer believes he can play. Sacred to them, his solos were never more to him, he thinks, than simply the best he could do then. And now, even those old inventions feel beyond him—as he learned back in Davenport when it became clear to him that the only way out of there was to pick up his horn again and do the best he could with it.

It had been after a mostly silent Thanksgiving dinner, and he'd gone up to his room and taken out the Bach and sat with it in his lap, feeling it smooth and solid beneath his fingertips, knowing in that moment that he could stay there in Davenport and drown in a bottomless pool of respectability or he could take this thing up again. And so he'd gone downstairs and called Esten Spurrier to ask him if he thought he could arrange some dates with local bands. By Christmas week he was back on the bandstand with Trave O'Hearn's Blackhawk Band, playing a fraternity dance, getting by with the second trumpet part when O'Hearn had called for Singin' the Blues, the number he'd made an instant jazz standard when he recorded it back in '27. And right in the middle of it Ed Sidebotham had snatched away his lead sheet and dropped the first trumpet part in its place. "Your solo," Ed had smiled. "Take it, brother!" And he'd looked down at those crazy notes he was supposed to play, gripped by a paralyzing panic. The rhythm section kept steadily on, the reeds laid down their background figure, and he stood soundlessly up, his fingers frozen on the valves as eight bars pulsed by, then sixteen, the dancers whirling, O'Hearn smiling encouragingly, and then he'd finally managed something, though it was certainly not the immensely complex score Ed had so suddenly saddled him with. Only at a break when he'd asked Ed what the idea was did he find out that first trumpet part was a note-for-note transcription of his famous recording. "That was *yours,* Bix!" Ed had laughed. "I tried to tell you that." And then they'd all had a good laugh about it, but then he'd had to ask them not to do that again, that his lip wasn't real strong yet.

Now, here he is again in the same situation, and so he calls from the car, asking Tommy once again what they're going to open with, and it's Dinah, and that's safe enough. Nobody knows any famous licks of his on Dinah, and after that it's If I Could Be With You, and then The Sheik Of Araby. And that's how it goes, and he finds he's doing okay in the ensemble with the brothers and Benny and Bud doing the heavy lifting and the kids getting quickly oiled, and he's beginning to think it's going to be okay down here, playing the hops at the Colonial Club, Ivy, and the Tiger Inn. But then he hears it, that first call from the floor, and pretends he doesn't, and they're done with the Sheik and with Margie, too, and Tommy's turning some pages, and he stands there, back to the crowd, trying to make conversation with Stafford, the drummer, who's heard the call too and is wondering why this guy is nervous enough to try to chat with him now, and he's still clinging to the desperate hope he won't be noticed, hoping Tommy will go ahead and call something quick. And then Tommy does and it's After You've Gone, and Tommy counts off and looking out into the crowd he sees Squirrel and Doc and Zero and the others, their smooth, assured faces beaming adulation at him. And he knows. And when they finish After You've Gone it begins to build and they're calling his name, and Tommy looks at him and he tries not to look back, leans over to say something to Benny but Benny's no help, either, and says, "Sounds like they want you, Bix," and he answers something back but neither of them hears what it is and it doesn't make any difference anyway, and he feels himself going down in this cauldron of sound, the chant of his name now augmented with rhythmic handclapping and stamping, and he looks at Tommy with mute appeal—Don't do it, Tommy—. But what can Tommy do except call for one of the oldies? "Tiger Rag," Tommy says and then points to the soloists in order: first Benny, then Jimmy, then, pointing to his chest, me, and then his finger points at Bix. And, of course, down here at Princeton they have to love Tiger Rag, and when at last it's his turn there's a high, raucous sound in the big room that rushes towards the bandsmen and overwhelms them, and he plays into it, finds himself playing LaRocca's solo, note-for-note, knowing here at least what comes next, not having to think, his lips and fingers finding their ways into the old grooves LaRocca laid down so long ago, and who cares now:

they're all hollering and most of them have never heard the original, never heard his inspired improvements on it, and some of them hardly know who he is, except he's somebody special they're supposed to holler for, and they're certainly up for that, and isn't it a gasser, being here tonight with Sally and with Corinne from Chappaqua and, boy, we are going to have ourselves a hell of a weekend and if everything goes right, maybe she will. In the meantime, Hell *yeah,* we want Bix! And they want him afterwards, too, the gang of grads and the upperclassmen who remember, sort of, and the underclassmen who don't and who, up close to him, are wondering what really is so special about this slightly puffy guy with the funny moustache and shrinking manner. But the big guys, the grads and seniors, are falling all over themselves just to shake his hand or reach over the backs of others and pat his shoulder, the top of his head, and the trombone guy's kind of laughing off to the side with the clarinet player, watching all this, and so there's obviously something here they need to be up on—don't want to be left behind here—and so find themselves reaching for him too and pushing in, holding tight to the girl, pulling her along into the midst of the moiling mass. And most of them don't get to shake his hand or even so much as touch his sleeve as the big boys form a sort of shield and take him off with them. And one of the girls, brushing a shining strand off her perspiring temple, says to her date, "Gee! He's so shy!" And the weekend boyfriend says, "O, that's just Bix. Have to know him." In the upstairs suite overlooking the secluded lawns and walks they pile in, Bix lost among them, and Doc has a couple of bottles of Lamplighter gin, straight from London, and the first of these is quickly emptied into tumblers while the high hilarity courses like a current through the room, and he's handed his and Doc hollers, "Down the hatch!" and he takes it down, just like that, and it's like a lightning bolt through his shriveled and desiccated system, frying everything in him down to his scrotum and into the tips of his toes, and in the sudden aftermath of that glassful while they pour their adulation over him he tries to keep his head from wobbling off his shoulders, and somebody calls for quiet to hear what he has to say, and he gasps, "What the hell," just like old times, and that sets them off again into gales and whoops, and Doc is already tearing the neck wrapper from the second Lamplighter, and Tommy and Jimmy are brought in just in time to get the top of the new jug.

And the next morning he has a pitiable hangover, his face the color of a dead toad's underbelly, one eye half out of its socket, his body a quaking bog of tremors, and twice he has to be taken quickly to the bathroom. When he'd awakened, he'd thought that he shouldn't drink any more this weekend, that last night was a big mistake, but now he's got to have one, and Tommy goes on a hunt for something—anything—because clearly he can't go on this way at Ivy for the pre-game jam. And Tommy comes up with some scotch that he has to feed to him because he can't hold the glass. Watching this, Bud Freeman shakes his head and says to Benny that this isn't funny anymore. Benny says little. A guy's behavior off the stand's his own business, and if this is what it takes to get Bix ready to play, well. . . .

He does make the Ivy appearance and is awful, can't play a lick. They do their best to hide him in the ensemble, asking little, and, mercifully, the kids don't ask much, either: everybody's a little sleepy and hung over. After the game, at the Tiger Inn, that's when things will really begin to jump. But they can't find him for the Tiger Inn spot, and Charlie Teagarden sits in for him, and Doc and Squirrel are pissed when they hear some undergrads took Bix riding with them during the game, nobody knows where. Later, one of the kids confesses they'd taken him riding around town in an open convertible with a couple of jugs and that after a while he'd gotten down on the floor in back with his horn and made loud moose farts through it when they'd stopped at intersections.

"We'd roll up to the crosswalk," the kid tells Squirrel, eyes runny with hilarity, "and Winston's at the wheel, see, and he gives Bix the word when some old biddie is crossing: 'Got one, Bix!' And Bix lays on that horn—real loud, see—and that old biddie jumps a foot and probably wets her drawers. O, it was killing!" But then that had come to an end when they encountered a cop and Davis had to quickly smother Bix and had accidentally jammed the horn against Bix's lip and the lip was slightly swollen and Bix had a false tooth up front that had gotten a little loose, and they'd dropped him at Cottage, and that was the last they'd seen of him. This news makes Squirrel and the rest of the acolytes furious. Didn't they know who they were dealing with?! Didn't they know Bix was supposed to jam with them this afternoon? Davis, the guy who had to kind of smother Bix with the cop just across the street, gets a bit huffy himself. Davis is on the varsity heavyweight crew and doesn't feel like taking a whole lot of crap from these guys just because they've graduated and are friends with this crazy drunk. "Hey," he says to Doc and Squirrel, "you guys can go take a shit in your hat, far as I'm concerned. We didn't *kidnap* the guy: he said he wanted to go for a spin, for Christ's sake, and we took him."

So Bix misses the post-game jam and the date that night as well. Nobody knows where he is until the small hours when a kid at Cottage, seeking out a secluded spot where he can put the blocks to his date, stumbles over a body sprawled on the floor of the library. This ruins the kid's plans because the girl's spooked about making it in the same room with this stiff and eventually word gets back to Tommy, but by this time the weekend's long over with. Doc and Squirrel and Zero have left campus, and Benny's taken the train back to New York for a Monday date. Bix tells Tommy and Bud he's going to stick around on campus for a couple of days; there's a literature class he says he wants to attend. And so they leave him behind. The next day, midmorning, he stumbles out of

Cottage with a pint he's gotten somewhere, his stained shirt hanging over his rumpled pants, holding his horn by the bell, and takes a long, swaying, gurgling hit while some passing students stop to laugh. But a professor happens by and angrily asks who this fellow is and what he's doing here, and then he tells the men at Cottage that they must do something about this and quickly, too, and so that afternoon a corporal's guard gets Bix down to the station and puts him aboard a train for New York.

～◆～

When she finally gets another call from him Lulu's surprised. She's been in town for many weeks now, but after hunting him up at his hotel she's hardly seen him. At that first meeting he was almost comically ill-at-ease and made a point of surrounding himself with cronies—loud, leering guys who could only talk music and dames and drinking. Even under those circumstances, though, it was obvious Bix was a different guy from the one she'd said goodbye to in L.A.: dry now and determined to stay that way, he said. And apparently he was being as elusive to his cronies as he was to her, because they kept asking him where he was keeping himself these days. When she thought about it later it almost seemed to her he was hiding out from someone or some thing, though she couldn't imagine him involved in anything shady. She wondered fleetingly if he'd been put off or embarrassed by her scar but then dismissed this. He hardly seemed to notice anything, anyway, she thought. So it must be something else. Then he'd called, and at their second meeting in a cafeteria around the corner from his hotel he told her he'd quit Whiteman. The only people she knows quitting their jobs these days are on the lam, either that or nuts. The rest are out looking for work, like she is, but she doesn't ask why he's quit, and he doesn't volunteer, not looking at her and making a big deal out of loading up a pipe—something else different about him.

"What about you?" he said finally, the pipe going now. He stowed the narrow can in his jacket pocket, and then she told him, briefly, almost curtly, that Clara had taken on a manager whose first act was to clean house and put the clamps on Clara's spending. Even the King had been cut off. So, she was out here, looking for anything and meanwhile sleeping on Herman's couch in his west-side apartment. He looked up at her at the mention of Herman, and she thought she saw a little light come into those shadowed eyes, and so then she had to be evasive, turning aside his eager questions about Herman, because Herman had made it clear he had no interest in having any contact with Bix, didn't even want him calling the apartment. "You have to handle that, Hellie," he'd told her, "that's your red wagon." He'd started to say something else but then with an almost visible effort at self-control had stopped short and turned abruptly away. When he turned back it was only to add, "Me, I have enough on my hands like it is." So all she said then was that Herman was working for Big Frenchy and kept odd hours. "I hardly see him," she told Bix, "except if he happens to leave the bedroom door open and I see him asleep on my way out." Bix nodded and fiddled some more with the pipe that she could now see was neither an accessory nor a mere affectation but was instead something he needed to keep his hands occupied. And when finally they'd said goodbye outside the cafeteria and she'd begun the walk uptown in the beginnings of a drizzle, she thought the chances of seeing him again any time soon were very remote. Anyway, she'd told herself, she had more immediate, pressing concerns—and so did he. She had to find work, and she had to find a room of her own: Herman had introduced her to a woman in the building, a big, broad-shouldered blonde from Minnesota, and it wasn't hard to figure he had been entertaining Clementine in his flat—until his sister had moved in. But then through Clementine she'd landed a maid's job with a family on Sutton Place and left that number with the desk at his hotel, and after a few days he'd called back. "I can't talk now," she'd told him. "But I can call you Sunday, from Oyster Bay."

The Whartons can still afford Sutton Place, the house at Oyster Bay, and live-in help, too, because Sam Wharton had gotten out of the market in the spring of '29, alarmed by some doom-ciphering Daniel from the Yale economics department who said he could read the writing on the wall. Not so his son, Sam Junior, who'd stayed in and gotten crushed in the crash and who had vanished in the vast wreckage of Black Monday, the last known sighting of him down by the old Customs House at the Battery, wearing an improvised necklace of ticker tape. That left Mrs. Wharton Junior with no husband, no money, and two small children, and when she subsequently moved in with her in-laws there was an obvious need for another pair of hands in the Sutton Place household. Shortly, Clementine, one of the maids, brought around the sister of a friend, and while Helen Weiss didn't have the sort of references the Whartons normally required—only a strangely worded note from some person in pictures—these were hardly normal times. So Helen now has this job and lives up under the eaves at the Wharton home while Clementine takes care of the children—and the mother as well, who does little these days but sleep and then begin her nipping at noon. On Sunday afternoons the Whartons visit their Oyster Bay neighbors or else play host to them, and on this particular Sunday they're out and Lulu gives Bix a call at his hotel and is just about to tell the operator she'll call back when he finally answers. His voice is weak and wavery, and after the initial exchange it's clear he doesn't remember having called her earlier in the week. "You said you needed to see me," she prompts at last. "I get Monday afternoons off—that's tomorrow."

"O, right, right." Trying to recover.

"We could have coffee, a show, something." She can hear him in the silence that trails behind her words, breathing short and shallow.

"I'm not feeling so hot these days."

"You want me to stop by?" she asks shortly, and he says he guesses that would be okay, and they set a time, and when she sees him, she's shocked at the changes, though it's evident he's made an effort: shaved, hair in place, orange-and-black striped four-in-hand, shirt wrinkled but clean enough. He sees himself in her eyes and is eager to divert her attention to his new acquisition, a piano his next-door neighbor has loaned him, a big upright he's wheeled into a bathroom longer by half than the area that combines kitchen, sitting space, and bedroom. "Looks kind of funny in here," he says as they stand at the bathroom's threshold, looking at the blond Wurlitzer. "I get an echo effect in here—off the tiles, must be. Want to hear it?" "Sure," she says, her practiced eye running around the bathroom where it's also evident he's made some effort: stuff stashed in corners, a tie wadded into a ball on a shelf, mirror smudgily wiped, but a buildup of soap lather filming the sink. On the edge of the tub there's a draped towel with something dark staining its folds. She wonders how long it's been since the maid's been allowed in here, but her wondering is interrupted by the touch of his hands on the Wurlitzer's keys, and instantly she's borne back to those notes that came so mysteriously to her, drifting down the darkened hall at Clara's, calling her out of her room and into the dim, melodramatic living room where she'd blundered into him and then tried to escape. But he hadn't let her, had pursued her, and after he'd left California and gone back to New York she'd wondered from time to time, doing the chores around Clara's house, what might have happened to her had he not offered her his gentle, impractical help. The memory of her despair is still vivid enough, but she doesn't recall contemplating suicide. She'd known a couple of girls in Chicago who'd done that when their gangster boyfriends jilted them and sent them back into the life, but it had seemed a shameful thing to do, somehow.

Now here are his notes once more, bouncing off the black and white hexagonal tiles, and she stands there at his left shoulder and looks down on his oddly defenseless neck, at the sharp and almost juvenile jut of his ears, thinking she's never seen him like this. And just at that moment his hands stop and stay where they are, plunged in sudden silence among the blacks and whites and his shoulders slump. She can't be sure from where she's standing what he's doing, whether he's pausing before going on or looking at his crotch or what, but then he starts to speak, mumbling as if to himself. "I can't hear ya," she says. "What're you talking about?" The mumbling ceases but the head stays down, the hands still plunged into the keys, motionless as stone.

"I had this dream," he says then, the voice up some but not much so that she has to move yet closer, bending over him, so close now she can smell his mingled odors and learns then at least part of what's been happening to him and why he looks the way he does. "I was somewhere, I don't know where, but some place open, and there was this fellow, across the grass, or whatever it was, and he had this tiger on a leash—really a big one, huge. And I was thinking, 'That guy doesn't look to me like he really has that thing under control.' And when I looked into the tiger's eyes I could see that if it ever got away from that guy, it was going to come for me. So, I was thinking, 'Hold that tiger! Hold that tiger!'

"But he didn't hold it. It got loose—snapped its chain—something—and, sure enough, it came for me, and it bit me, here." He moves a hand, slowly, as if still back in the dream, and points to his forearm. "Not too bad, but bad enough to draw blood. And the fellow—the owner—he said, 'O, boy! Now we've got trouble because he's smelled blood, and there'll be no stopping him.' So then I figured I better get out of there. There was this tree nearby, in the field, and I ran to it and tried to climb it, but I was, uh, I—somehow I'd lost all my clothes, and the bark was really smooth, and I was having a hard time climbing up the branches, and the tiger was coming for me and I—and I. . . ." The voice chokes off and he slowly turns his head into her hovering body, into her lower belly and begins to sob, and after a few hesitant seconds her arms reach out, encircling his head, cradling it, drawing it into her. And through his sobs, muffled by her body, he tells her of Princeton and Williams after that and Middlebury after that—the blind succession of lost weekends and blank weeks and drained bottles that have led to this slate-blue Monday afternoon. "O, Christ, Lulu," he sobs, "I didn't hold that tiger. *I didn't hold him!*" And she, bending there above him, holding his head into her, feels as much as she hears the voice humming into her lower belly, and despite what the words are telling her, the bleak, blasted litany of drink and drifting and despair, the ghastly mornings when he couldn't remember what started all this, the fears of where it must lead—despite this, the hum of his voice is sending another sort of signal, and she knows this isn't right, isn't the right sort of response, but she can't stop what the muffled hum is doing to her, lighting a bonfire down below, the flames licking up inside her, down her slightly parted thighs, and she can't remember the last time she's had anybody but herself but thinks fleetingly of a grip guy at the studio and they did it standing up against a makeup table in a tent. And she remembers now with perfect, sharp-edged clarity the first time she ever laid eyes on this man who now has his face buried in her and is making the front of her skirt wet with his tears while under her skirt other things are getting wet as well: the warm languor of that long-gone lakeside afternoon and her boredom and restlessness broken by the call from Joe Batters, telling her to expect a package from Jack by messenger, and then the polite, soft knock at her hotel room door, and she'd had time to do a few things to herself, had brushed out her hair a little, put on fresh makeup and a canary-colored dress with the top two buttons left carelessly undone and looking at herself in the bedroom's full-length mirror had thought, "You know, honey, you aint bad, not bad." And then there he was, a not very clean oatmeal-colored sweater draped over his shoulders: a kid, really, his face as open and unmarked and guileless as a high-schooler, and looking at him out of her own terribly wise eyes, she thought she'd never seen anything more strangely beautiful in all her life and wished in that moment she hadn't had to learn all those things she'd had to learn to land in this cushy suite at the Edgewater Beach and could maybe merely walk out of here with this kid, his arm through hers, just a boy and a girl, strolling along the lakefront with the Loop's big gray and brown buildings towering in the distance and the day spread out before them, theirs. But she'd only asked him in, and he'd smiled, sunny, and she'd offered him something and he'd said sure, and she'd made them both highballs with some of Snorky's best scotch, not the crap they sold the suckers, but the real McCoy. And then they'd sat there with the wind off the lake blowing the curtains in on them like white blossoms and she thought, listening to the few things she could coax out of him, smiling at him in her most artful, arch fashion, her hem hiked high on her glossy flank and the ice cubes crackling in the tall glasses, "This has got to be just about the most beautiful moment of my whole goddamned life and what is it about this kid that has me so goddamned lit up—or am I just horny? But, Jesus, I'd love to get those pants off of him." And then, looking at his pants, saw the package there in his lap and realized she hadn't remembered to take it from him and so did that now but didn't open it. And when he'd finished the highball, which was quick enough, too quick for her, he'd said he guessed he ought to be going, didn't want to miss his ride. "But, say," he said at the door, turning, the light behind him out of the high hall windows making a nimbus around his head and shoulders, "you ought to come out to the club some time. We've got a band that's really hot." And she'd said, languorous, seductive, careless, "Yeah, maybe I'll just do that." And then he was gone and she'd walked into the bedroom and flung herself spread-eagle onto the bed and whipped up her dress and skinned down her panties and made fierce, brief love to the image of him, his face and its sunny smile.

And now here was that same face, buried in her belly, but how changed, and her face is changed too, forever, but still she's smoothing the top of his head with increasingly long, rhythmic strokes and he's stopped sobbing and his shoulders heave in a profound and wracking sigh, and now she reaches for him, gently, pulling him up from the chair and into her and with her thumbs brushes the tears from his cheeks, flinging them aside and leans into him, kissing him full on the lips once, then again and longer this time. "Come on, babe," she breathes huskily and takes his hand, leading him out of the bathroom and to the bed in the other room, and he doesn't hang back, is willing to be led though not to lead. They lie down facing each other, and she opens him up from collar to fly but he makes no move, and so she says, "Ya gotta help a little," and while he does so she's off with her sweater and blouse and skirt and panties, not bothering with her slip and he's looking at her with an expression she can't fathom, his member lying flaccid and lifeless along his thigh like Adam's awaiting God's inspiriting touch in Michelangelo's mural. She slides downward along his body and pushes lightly against his up-thrust hip, turning him on his back, taking him in her mouth, noticing as she closes with him a long, annealed scar that travels down his groin into the darkness of his crotch. Under the proddings of her dexterous tongue he begins to grow inside her mouth, and then quickly she slips him inside her. And despite the terrible all that has intervened since that sunlit, windy Chicago day and this one—half a continent and another age away—this now feels like all she's ever wanted, just this, just this, just this. But then she feels him begin to die within her and pulling her face from his sees again that unfathomable expression, his eyes wide but with no particular light or spark in them, and it occurs to her that he isn't a part of this, not any of it, that he's still back there at the piano or maybe still entangled in the dream of the tiger, and seeing this, feeling it, her own fire is swiftly extinguished in a shower of sadness, and she rises from him and pulls down her slip and slides over next to him and thinks of saying something, like "What the hell?" but something stops her, and after long minutes of silence she asks, not what the hell, but, "What is it?" He's looking straight up but at her words turns his head towards her and simply shakes it. So, it's over, for whatever reason, and then they arise and turn from each other in sudden, intense privacy, buttoning and fastening and smoothing with a haste that seems somehow shameful.

But afterwards, when they've recovered a little, he tells her he wants to take her somewhere, and she says okay, and now he's collected again and courtly in his way, telling her he has the money for a cab, taking her arm out in the street, hailing a cab with the other, telling the hackie they want to go to 205½ West 53rd. When they alight there's a wind whistling along the street under the black elevated, and she sees nothing here but a dull-painted door, but he knows what he's doing and pulls open that door, and inside the gang's all here—Tommy, Big T with his owlish eyes, Jimmy McPartland, for whom Bix once bought a new cornet when Jimmy replaced him with the Wolverines. Lulu looks at him, silently asking, what about Princeton and all those other places? But he winks at her, wading into the midst of the back-slapping bunch, holding on to her and steps to the bar where he tells Timmy the substitute bartender that he'll have a straight seltzer and asks her what she'll have and she says the same. Then he introduces her as his girl and they all smile and somebody on the upright hits the opening notes of the wedding march and there's laughter all around, and he stands there, surrounded, squeezing her hand so tight she thinks she can't stand much more of it, swirling the seltzer in the thick tumbler, nodding, smiling that elusive, down-looking smile, and she thinks maybe she's the only one who can see how much of an effort this takes. One glass of the fizzy, empty stuff, a half-smoked pipe, and that's all he can stand of Plunkett's, and then they're outside in the hard gloom that's closing like a fist around the city, and he asks her if she has time for a sandwich and she does, and they end up at the Willard on 6th where they sit with others at the long, metal-wrapped counter. She has a fried egg sandwich and he toys with a plate of hash, and under the harsh lights she can see even more clearly what the fall has cost him, hear it too in the tittle-tattle of his cup against his saucer, and when he tells her he has more of these college dates lined up ahead of him, it's like he's talking about an empty road leading nowhere. "If I could just stay in my hotel and work on my music, maybe I'd be okay," he says, looking into her eyes a moment. "But I can't. I need the money." She asks about going back with Whiteman, whether that might be better, and he shakes his head. "I can't go back with Pops: he's had to cut the band in half and they do five shows a day. I can't take that now." He smiles briefly, telling her Whiteman's keeping a chair open for him, just in case he changes his mind. But then the smile's gone when he says, "I'll never go back. I can't."

"What'll you do then?"

"Try and work on my piano music. Go out to the colleges. What else can I do?" He pushes the fork against the mound of hash, moving it across the cracked white surface of the plate, making a small margin against an edge.

❧❖☙

He writes her at the Whartons where they don't mind Helen getting mail:

Dear Lulu,

Well, we had that session that I told you about at Victor—Hoagy, me, Benny, Bud, Tommy, Eddie, Venuti—a lot of the old gang. + Bubber Miley who used to play with Duke up at the Cotton Club. I sat in with him up there awhile ago. Krupa was on drums—and say, he can really ride 'em. Anyway, Bubber showed up with Fats and so you know how that went. We got to fooling around in the studio and only cut 2 numbers and only one will be released because on Barnacle Bill Venuti sang Barnacle Bill the s–head and you could hear it plain. But, here's the good news—have landed a job on Camel Pleasure Hour, Weds on WJZ, so if you have a radio up there you can catch yrs truly at 9:30. Bill Challis is arranger so you know I'll have plenty of good spots. This is the break we talked about at the Willard because I won't have to travel so much to the colleges that are n.g. for me these days.

Believe I have the 'old tiger' on the leash right now—you know what I mean and trust you are keeping yourself well too.

Your friend,
Leon Bix Beiderbecke

And a week thereafter:

Dear Lulu,

Well, that probably wasn't the most thrilling afternoon of your life, I know, but gee it was great to have you up there @ Bill's—meant the world to me, honest. So now you know what I'm up to with my piano pieces. Also Bill who's going to help me with them. Can I talk you into another date up there? Afterwards we could have dinner somewhere.

Bix

P.S. Bill's kind of gruff. But he liked you.

Actually, Bill Challis doesn't know what to make of the girl who starts out by correcting Bix when he introduces her as Lulu up at Challis's Riverside Drive apartment. "It's Helen," she says shortly. Yet throughout that afternoon and the ones that follow Bix always calls her Lulu and she doesn't bother correcting him. Challis is happy to call her Helen but there's little conversation between them, the girl sitting in a corner of the big, airy living room, flipping through the magazines she brings along.

From the outset Challis sees she knows nothing about music and doesn't care about it, either, taking no visible interest in what Bix is trying to do with his piano sketches, and when he talks it over with his wife Challis wonders aloud if the girl knows who Bix really is—or was. But when Connie asks if he's thinking she might be a pickup, Challis says no, even though Lulu or Helen or whatever the hell her name really is certainly looks like she's been around the block a couple of times: tough, and with that hard-sealed finish a certain sort of woman acquires. And when he looks at that long scar down her cheek—a rip really—he thinks that's the kind of ritual marking a pimp would put on a whore who'd held out on him. Still, he knows there's got to be something more here, because he goes back with Bix to Goldkette days and had seen the way the guys in that band—and Whiteman after that—would scramble to make their arrangements for women, even in the smallest of towns, one-night whistle stops where maybe the best you could do would be the flaw-faced waitress who served you the locally famed fudge cake in the fly-specked café, and if she happened to have a sister or cousin or roommate, then maybe your sectionmate might score, too. Before he and Connie were married Challis himself had had a few of those hit-and-run encounters and once, in considerable need, had gone with Venuti to the local body shop where you paid for it. And in all that time he'd never known Bix to engage in any of that sort of activity, and of course they'd all wondered about that. The guy was so unbelievably popular with the younger crowd, and the girls just gushed over him, wanted to mother him, cuddle him, protect him somehow from the hurly-burly of this garish world they shared. And they knew through Tram that there'd been a girl in St. Louis Bix had seen a lot of, and it was even said he'd had a kid by her, but that was just rumor and nobody but Tram had ever laid eyes on her or knew her name. They all knew he'd dated Ruby Keeler—that got around, all right—and Boyce Cullen had told Challis once that Bix had had something going on out in Hollywood, but the reference was cryptic and brief. So Bix's love life was a mystery none of them had ever penetrated, not even Herman Weiss who'd roomed with him.

Yet as Challis thinks about it he finds himself wondering why this should be any different than any other aspect of the guy who'd always been remote and elusive even in those clubbiest of circumstances when the bottle was going around and for that moment anyway everybody was your brother. All the boys had allowed Bix that dreamy and impregnable space he inhabited, and Challis had too. But then there'd been the scene in the Cleveland hotel room, the enforced convalescence in Davenport, the disaster of Hollywood, and by the time they'd come back to New York nobody was reaching through to Bix, who seemed more the prisoner of that interior realm instead of its architect and voluntary inhabitant. Challis finds it hard to imagine that this girl who cares nothing about music is reaching through there. "Maybe she's a tiger between the sheets," Connie says, rolling her eyes, but Challis says that would be just the sort of dame who would send Bix in the opposite direction. "Well," Connie says, "do you think *he* might be helping *her* in some way?" But Challis says no to that speculation too because whatever is going on it's clear to him that Bix keeps bringing the girl along on these Monday afternoon sessions because he needs to have her with him—talisman, worn rabbit's foot, lucky stone with that striation down its face—. Anyway, she's unobtrusive, sitting in her corner, flipping through her magazines, or simply staring out the windows at the sky and its flitting, evanescent show of clouds and sun and snow. When she gets restless she quickly puts on her coat and goes out for a walk, and then Challis notices that Bix's concentration wavers until she returns. On the days she doesn't come—Thursdays generally—Bix seems moodier and Challis gets the feeling that something's missing.

With the girl or without her, though, the going is tough. Because what Bix is bringing uptown these winter afternoons— arriving empty-handed, shadow-eyed, ringing the buzzer and Challis finding him there, bowed with invisible burdens—are the fragmented messages from that interior space he's been living in all these years: unwritten, uncharted, randomly gathered, fleetingly caught, some of them all but wholly lost and only the last whisper or scrap or strain saved: melodies that have come to him as far back as Davenport school days and from Indiana and Chicago, St. Louis and Hudson Lake, Manhattan and New Orleans and east Texas and Oklahoma, in the hours that like blue notes can't be located on clocks or charts, that fall into the unfathomed slot chasms between waking life and dream, night and dawn, the last round of the night watchman and the first clank of the milkman, between the last silent swoop of the owl and the rooster's raucous salute: songs without words, without notes, without beginnings or end-ings—flashing, fleeting, partially occluded glimpses into realms beyond what he consciously knows, fragments accumulated in his unsteady passage through his appointed time and place. And it is these that are bringing Bix up here, on time, all the time, despite what Challis can see and sometimes smell have been long nights. These are what Challis now understands it is up to him to rescue.

He finds himself surprised there's as much here as there is. Surprised, too, by the beauty of so much of it, and the contrast between these fragments and Bix's current cornet playing is nothing less than astonishing to him. When Bix had joined the band for the Camel Pleasure Hour Challis had wanted to spot him on cornet as he had of old but learned quickly it was no longer possible: the golden tone was gone, coarsened to bronze or even copper and often just as dull, the execution stiff, hesitant, lacking in that old assurance that had never truly been devil-may-care-what-the-hell, but instead a brilliantly intuited sense of what chances could be taken at the given moment: that inimitable risky phrasing; in, out, around the melody with that preternatural ability to understand on the instant what he needed to keep of it and what discard or reinvent. All that gone now, somewhere, leaving Bix the cornetist merely mortal and sometimes even less than ordinary. So that Challis has had to turn to the Dorsey brothers as players around whom he can build arrangements, and in doing so he almost feels Bix is relieved to be just another man with a horn. And now Challis understands why.

He remembers hearing him in person for the first time that fall of '26, the Goldkette band poised just outside Boston, getting set to take on New England and then the big time, New York, and how unprepared the recordings had made him for how marvelous Bix really was. Hearing him in the attic rehearsal room of that country hotel, he had instantly understood that here in the flesh was the answer to what weren't even dreams because he'd never dared to imagine a player so superbly equipped to execute ideas he hadn't even fully formulated himself. But that day up in the attic, all the windows wide, the roof cooking under the Indian Summer sun, he heard in Bix's first notes all manner of possibilities—for that same tight, funny little half-smile he'd worn at the riverside barn, that lopsided look that was both grin and grimace and that said to the others, "Let's not get into a sweat over that: they've had their best shot; now it's our turn." And then he heard Tram talking to them all while he, Challis, stood off to the side with Goldkette himself and Herman Weiss, and Tram was explaining the strategy of a decoy and about how it might be nice to kind of sucker everybody with their first number, play something sweet, even slightly schmaltzy, and his little grin cracked open just a bit more when he said Valencia, and then they all got it, got the spirit of the thing, the essence of the ploy, which could only be ventured if they *knew* the power they had in reserve, and they had it all right, and they had the kid with the cornet. And when they'd struck into the sedate 6/8 tempo of Valencia a sound came to them up from the floor, the mingled sound of surprise and disappointment and the negative satisfaction, too, that was the crowd's response to a challenge unanswered, and there were smiles all around out there and nowhere broader than over on the adjacent stand where the Henderson boys settled into their chairs and relaxed, and a couple of them even laughed: cute guys, they aren't gonna take us on straight. They're gonna try and slip our punch. Cute white guys. And the applause after Valencia was good, generous, because they'd played it well, you had to give them that. Still. And then Challis had heard Tram call Baby Face, one of Challis's best and hottest, and Tram had told them not to take down but to go from Baby Face right into Blue Room and not to stop there, either, but to keep on going, right into My Pretty Girl, and by the time they reached My Pretty Girl the smiles were gone from the boys there on the adjacent stand, and Joe Smith was staring over at Bix and saying something in Rex Stewart's ear, and Stewart was turning his cornet in his hands like it was something he wished he could hide somewhere just now, and the crowd was hollering and the penguins in their boiled shirts and tuxedos were laughing out arrivals, maddeningly unpredictable performances. But still he keeps coming up to Riverside Drive, though now always alone, wordlessly flinging aside his shabby coat, cracking his knuckles a few times, sitting down at the grand, coughing deeply (always the cough now), then working hard with Challis on Candlelights and In The Dark and Cloudy from his early Indiana days. And he can't help it if he plays these pieces differently on a Thursday than he has only two days before, which makes Challis's work of transcription that much tougher. One day they have it out when Challis points out that he now has three different versions for a passage from In The Dark. "Goddamn it, Bix!" he says. "You've got to stick to one of these— settle on it!" remembering as the last syllables are out that this is the man who'd had words with Tram back in the Whiteman days because he wouldn't stick to his rehearsed portions of their chase choruses, telling Tram he no longer felt the same as he had when they'd worked them out. And Tram had looked at Challis, mutely asking, "Bill, what are we going to do with this guy?" Nor had Challis known then, either. Later, when Andy Secrest had joined the band, Bix had blithely turned aside his question about a certain passage Challis had left open for improvisation. "Play it your way, Andy," he'd said, when what the earnest newcomer had most wanted to know was how *he* played it. "That's what's nice about jazz," Bix had added in a loquacious burst: "I don't know what's going to happen next, do you?" Secrest had looked around for help like a man afraid of going under and had found Challis's eye, but Challis had merely shrugged, raising his thick eyebrows, as if saying, "I don't know what to tell you, Andy." So now, having spoken out of exasperation, he immediately regrets it, hearing the long futility of it. The composer sits there at the grand, looking down at the keys, then looks up sharply to face Challis. "Well, dammit, Bill, this is better than the other ways I thought of. I mean, why are we here if it isn't to work out these things?" Challis thinks of three responses all at once, but he says nothing, only puts the pencil and notebook down with exaggerated precision. "I'll make us a pot of coffee," he says, buying them both some time, and when he returns he finds Bix at the long bank of windows, staring out over the river's steely seaward sweep. A ponderous silence sits on the room, and thinking Bix hasn't registered his return he rattles the notebook and sniffs. The aroma of the fresh coffee begins its bitter invasion and still the figure at the windows remains motionless. "You want to get back to work?" Challis asks at last, but Bix doesn't move. "Coffee?" The figure shrugs, and Challis has to take this as a sort of assent, going to the kitchen for it. When he comes back Bix is gone, the door left open behind him.

When he doesn't show the following Monday Challis phones the hotel but gets no answer, and it's the same on Thursday, and then the week following Challis hears Bix has been out on a short tour of New England colleges with the Dorsey brothers.

Challis isn't a Plunkett's regular. For one thing he's married and wants to lead a more regular life than those guys. For another, he thinks some of the Plunkett's bunch are a bad influence on Bix and doesn't want to encounter them. But he drops by there late one afternoon, thinking maybe he might intersect with Bix and talk him out of his sulk. Instead, he hears about the Dorseys' college tour from their drummer Johnny Morris, and it isn't good news, Morris reporting that Bix was terrifically withdrawn and blue, though playing a competent enough second trumpet to Bunny Berigan. At first, Morris tells Challis, they all thought it was Bunny who'd set Bix off. Handsome as a matinee idol, as outgoing and effervescent as Bix is now moody and withdrawn, Bunny has become the brassy man of the moment, putting the former star into a deep shade. And yet at the Amherst senior hop weekend it was Bix they'd hollered for, and they kept on hollering for him while he continued to tell the Dorseys he wasn't going to solo. "Finally," Morris tells Challis, "it got so that Tommy said Bix had to take a turn, and he did his thing on Riverboat, and, by God, it was terrific! I didn't know he had that in him. So then Tommy calls Jazz Band Ball, and he rips that baby up, too—better, maybe, than Riverboat—and he has this funny look on, and Tommy says, 'Well, why not give 'em Tiger Rag?' and Bix goes, 'Well, why not?' And that's the way it went the rest of the night: he played out front the whole way, and they just lapped it up, and Bunny, he thought it was funny, too—you know Bunny. Best we sounded the whole tour. But then, the next day"— Morris spreads his hands—"same deal: blue, wouldn't talk hardly." Challis buys Morris a drink and then steps out into the niggardly sunlight of a mid-March day where in the shadows of the buildings it still feels like deep December, walking Broadway's angle south, the air filled with grit and whizzing wads of debris. Against the lowering light the grit looks like spangles showered broadcast from above by some benignly indifferent hand that overlooks the street-corner apple sellers; the men shuffling along, beating mittened hands behind sandwich boards advertising pathetically modest services; children manning cookie carts; pickets protesting; a man stirring a tall, blackened cauldron whose steam almost entirely obscures his face. Passing, Challis hears him explaining to a potential customer, "No soup. Garbanzo. Chick-pea."

On Bix's floor of the hotel Challis can hear the Wurlitzer down the hall, hesitant, intermittent. As he raps, a Ravel-like sequence ceases and silence descends like evening. He raps once more and listens to sounds within, some sort of interior rearrangements being made. He waits, feeling the other in there, waiting, too, probably intent on out-waiting. "Bix, it's me, Bill." No answer. Waits. "Bix, for Christ sake, don't be a jerk. Let me in." More silence. "Look, I know you're in there because I heard the piano, so open up." Then, inspired, he adds, "Besides, I'm thirsty." There's a laugh on the other side, and the door opens, and there's Bix in a stained sweater, unshaven, his right eye popped, and a kind of smile that contains a shadow of his former self. But then the smile's gone like the sun behind this day's quick-scudding clouds, and he turns away, leaving the door ajar, and Challis enters a desperate squalor. Newspapers everywhere as though flung by the wind, clothing dropped on available surfaces, plates of congealed, uneaten food on the kitchen counter and table, a hamburger warped with age and grinning greenly from the kitchen windowsill, the bed like an ongoing nightmare. The smell is like a fist in the face: rotting food, soiled clothing, body odor, the thin acridness of dry newsprint, and something vaguely medicinal Challis can't identify. "Jesus!" he wants to cry out but doesn't, hearing then the characteristic coughing and glancing at the bleared windows that look as if they've been battened so long they couldn't be opened with a crowbar. "This is all I got," Bix says, coming in from the bathroom with a full glass and a half pint of gin. Challis shrugs okay, and Bix has to hunt through the kitchen midden for another glass for his visitor and runs it quickly under the tap. "Maids on strike, too?" Challis asks, smiling, and Bix manages an answering smile and says he doesn't want to be disturbed. They stand there in the kitchen area, looking at each other, the visitor in his heavy overcoat, gloves in one hand, glass in the other. "Well," Challis says at last, looking at his glass still wet from its cursory cleansing. "Well," Bix comes back and with a show of defiance raises his glass and drains half of it. "Smashing," he says in the fake Wodehouse British Challis recalls from Goldkette days. "Simply smashing, what?" "Yours looks kind of yellow—what the hell's in that?" Challis asks, indicating the other's glass. "Lemon drops: I put 'em in for health, don't you know." The fake accent saves nothing, only adds its pathetic bit to the pain of the moment. "Ready to go back to work?" Challis asks, breaking an ensuing silence he senses could last until he left. "Sure," Bix answers, his face masklike, immobile, "why not. Got all the time in the world now: last night I got canned at WJZ."

When Challis asks him what happened, Bix says he's not sure, and he really isn't. He knows only what a couple of the guys later told him: that during the broadcast when he stood up to take a solo no sound came out of his horn, and Charlie Teagarden had to jump up and take it, and afterwards the director had given him the pink slip. He remembers nothing more until Charlie and Tommy were taking him home in a cab. Telling Challis this, he seems unable to attach any particular feelings to the episode. It's as if it happened to somebody else, somebody he only distantly knows and he's merely recounting what he's heard. And then, as though this were only of minor consequence, he goes right on to tell Challis he'll be around sometime next week, that he's working on something he's calling Flashes. When Challis tries to pin him down, Bix ducks, says he's not feeling like laying out a strict schedule for himself, wants to work some more on the new sketch before letting Challis hear it. Challis sets his half-empty glass on the cluttered sideboard, nudging aside haphazardly piled plates and glasses, a desiccated sponge, and turns towards the door. His hand on the handle, he turns back to Bix. "Why not bring the girl up with you?" he says. "Seems like she was good luck." And Bix tells him he can't, that the family she works for has taken her and the rest of the household to the south of France or maybe it's Spain and won't be back until late spring. Then Challis is gone, and Bix retrieves the unfinished glass and dumps its contents into his own. He walks woodenly to the Wurlitzer in the white-and-black tiled bathroom, relieved if not glad to be once again alone.

⌘

"We must flee this place." So he says, tonelessly, while she stands surrounded by a wreck worse by some than what Challis had walked into weeks ago. It's summer now, and the stench in 605 is so stunning she wonders why those in the neighboring rooms haven't complained to the management. She marches to the kitchen window, unsnaps its latch, grasps its handles and strains until with a sticky, two-note *pop* the thing comes loose and she heaves it up. And then she's across the room, moving quickly past the bed, hand to her mouth, and at the window over there, but it won't budge, and so she tries its fellow, which does, and he's still sitting there at the little kitchen table, muttering, "O, we must . . ." Then she's in the bathroom where she sees the Wurlitzer's gone, the black-and-white tiled space seeming suddenly immense, empty, and at the tub throws open the cocks and draws him a bath, standing above the rising, steaming water, smoothing her platinum hair while her upper lip begins to bead with perspiration. When the tub's full she retrieves him from the kitchen area, taking his hand in hers and bringing him to his feet. In the bathroom he turns to her, motioning at the Wurlitzer's ghost, and says, "Pat had to take it back." "Yeah, sure," she says. "Now you get in there and give yourself a good soaking, and then we'll figure out what's next." When she hears the reassuring plunk of his feet in bathwater she begins a sort of triage on the disaster of the place, using shopping bags and newspapers to gather up decaying scraps of food and bottles and emptied packs of cigarettes, emptying the refrigerator of its curdled bottles of milk and some now unidentifiable vegetable mass, working furiously, tumbling dishes, saucers, glasses into the sink, running water over them, finding some Lux beneath the sink. All the while she's listening for sounds from the bathroom, and before she takes the garbage down the hall to the service stairs she calls out to him, "Ya all right in there?" "Yeah, sure," he responds weakly, and on her way down the hall she thinks, "Yeah, sure," and wonders what the hell is coming next, because it's for sure she can't take care of him, mother him, nurse him through another of these bats, get him back to his music. She hasn't the time, and this is Wednesday and so she's had to ask Mrs. Wharton Senior for a couple of hours off to see a sick friend, but that's all she's got. And this guy's so sick and lost he needs the kind of round-the-clock care Clementine gives the Wharton brats who aren't sick but who are lost without their vanished father and their disintegrating mother.

She'd gotten the story of how bad things had become through Clementine, who had it from Herman. And Herman himself wouldn't have known if he hadn't happened into a sudden, shocking glimpse of the man. He'd been pinch-hitting for another driver because the fool had slugged a cop over a traffic ticket and was in the cooler—where a disgusted Big Frenchy said he could damn well stay. And that was how Herman had found himself inching the delivery truck through two narrow right-angle turns of the blind alley behind Plunkett's, perfect for concealed deliveries but hell to get into and out of. While he was lugging and stacking the cases in the basement, Timmy, the relief bartender, had come down to help him and asked if he wanted a snort when they were through, and Herman had grunted maybe a glass of beer. Then when he was finally finished he'd shouldered his way up the ladder to the trap door behind the bar and had just emerged when he'd heard the wide, whiskeyed whoops of laughter and somebody slamming a chord on the balcony upright and then the bleat of a horn, empty of all art—a wavering, off-color jumble of half-notes and somebody hollering, "Hey! You gotta give us more than that fer a double—don't he boys!" And looking up to the balcony then, he'd seen what he'd seen and shot a glare at Timmy, and Timmy, glancing up towards the merrymakers on the balcony, had merely shrugged and said sometimes it got loud in here and what about that snort or was it a beer he'd wanted. And Herman hadn't said anything, had only turned quickly and gone down the ladder into the blackness of the basement, hounded by those awful sounds, putting his hands to his ears until he was out again in the alley with its black cinders, black fire escapes, black-painted window casings—all of it black, the world suddenly gone black at high noon. And for some moments he'd stood there, panting, thinking about going back up there and making some sort of rescue, belting a couple of those bastards grouped around the upright. But for what? *For what?* he'd asked himself in a fury. You can't rescue nobody. He hadn't been able to rescue Bix years back when he'd seen what was happening, and now it had happened. It was too late for anything, even for regret. So, he'd only said something to Clementine, who'd passed it on to Helen.

And now Lulu stands in the middle of the room, thinking she can't rescue anybody, either, that maybe all she can do is clean up the room some and get him to clean himself and that will be about it. She starts to make the bed but finds the sheets so terrible it's pointless. So she turns to the little telephone table by the windows and begins sorting and stacking papers and books piled there and on the floor beneath it in random drifts, dropping the yellowing newspapers into a dusty pile, the records of events long dead and forgotten—WOOD DRIVES BOAT 102 MPH. GRAND JURY TO SIFT CRATER MYSTERY—. She exhumes a letter to his folks with only the salutation and a half-composed first line— "Dear Folks, A long time since I hear from you—." And beneath that a hat check with Bill Challis's name and a number under it, and she seizes on that as though it were a splintered oar drifting past after a shipwreck and dials the number and miraculously it is Challis's, all right, and he answers.

That's how the work with Challis begins again, but it's different now when she takes him up there those Monday afternoons. He's weaker now and this seems to have heightened his sense of urgency so that the least delay makes him anxious to the point of anger: if Challis has to go to the bathroom, it upsets him, and he paces the room, coughing, running his hands through his hair. If

Challis wants to break for a cup of coffee, he shows impatience, waving the proffered cup away. She stays out of it, parked in her corner with her magazines, trying not to look at this tense show, hoping Challis won't snap. But he has his limits, too, and one warm late June day Bix, working through something he's calling Brooklets, snaps at Challis, "Dammit, Bill! Haven't you got that yet?" And Challis flings down the notebook, and his pencil bounces high off the piano's polished surface and clatters to the floor, and he barks back, "No, Goddamn it! I don't have it yet! You think I'm some goddamned *stenographer?*" That's all for that day.

Bix has been saying for some time now he can't live at the 44th Street Hotel any longer—too many distractions there, he claims. In fact, hardly anyone comes around these days, and even the Princeton alligators leave him alone since he snarled at Squirrel when Squirrel tried to play the famous Singin' The Blues solo on Bix's Bach and Bix had asked why the hell he was trying to play that moldy crap. So Challis and Lulu find a place for him over in Queens, Sunnyside, a brand-new building with ornate Moorish entrance, and Challis has his late sister's piano taken out of storage and hauled over there and they somehow cram it in, practically next to the bed. Bix sits down at it that first day, and it's hot as blazes in the little first-floor flat, but he's cold, he tells Challis, and anyway he can't compose with all the noise off 46th Street flooding in, so the front window's got to stay shut, and Challis sits on the bed while Bix tries out the piano, riffling over the keys, then moving into a passage that belongs to something Challis doesn't recognize: crepuscular, woody, putting him in mind of something he can't place, from years ago. And when Bix leaves off, it comes to Challis, and he says that reminds him of Eastwood Lane, and Bix turns and gives a half-smile and nods doesn't it and says he must have had Lane's Adirondack Sketches in the back of his mind when working on this, had always loved them, and that he now wants to combine the sketches they're working on into something like that. "Dusk," he murmurs, but Challis doesn't quite get what he means. "Dusk," Bix repeats. "I'm thinking of dusk here—the last of the light, on the fields, maybe. Maybe the whole thing—all of 'em—would be called that: Dusk, An American Sketch." He shrugs. "Anyway, that would be something to be remembered for, not that . . . other stuff."

Not many days in the new place, though, before the building's super, Kraslow, begins to hear from the other tenants, first one, then another: someone down on the first floor is playing the piano late at night. The complaints, though, aren't really that, are made in such ambivalent fashion that Kraslow doesn't know what he's supposed to do about them. Because what the tenants are telling him is that this is music such as they've never heard before in all their lives, coming to them on the hot, still air of the city night, beautiful music that sounds unrehearsed, unpremeditated. And even if it does keep them awake—as it does—it might even be that the sleep they lose when the invisible player begins is made up because his playing eventually makes them sleep more deeply when they do drift off on notes struck by ghostly hands. All they know is that in the morning's light the music's gone like a dream, displaced by the sounds of the workaday world within which they must struggle.

None has knowingly seen the player. Kraslow has, though not often. He's seen the girl, too, once, when she took him out to sit on a bench down by the corner, her face shrouded by a broad-brimmed sort of sunbonnet with close-fitting crown of the type Kraslow's noticed in the fashion ads. One afternoon late he knocks diffidently on the door of 1G, and Bix lets him in, invites him to sit, but Kraslow has to explain about the neighbors. And before he can quite finish, glancing over Bix's shoulder to the piano—as if to reassure himself there is a substantial reality to all this, that it's not some strange sort of collective fantasy—Bix is stammering out his apologies: fearfully sorry, had no idea, etc. So Kraslow finds his errand changed in character, trying to help Bix through this, suggesting finally that maybe it might work out better if Bix could wait until well after midnight. Thereafter, the tenants don't hear that music on the stifling air of this blast-furnace summer—unless they're lying awake and staring into the blackness above the bed because they've already lost their job or there are new rumors of general layoffs, or have read in the morning's paper of a man so despondent he took poison in church on Fifth Avenue and dropped dead right there in full view of the congregation, and they know too well how he felt, and nobody knows how to stop this thing, apply the brakes, throw the emergency switch halting the elevator plunging through space as sickeningly deep as the Grand Canyon. Governor Roosevelt says he has some ideas about how to stop this thing and is thinking of throwing his hat into the presidential ring, and surely he couldn't be any worse than the guy they're stuck with, whose hands are frozen on the controls. And so, if they are awake, thinking these things, staring up into blackness, then they do hear the piano, the notes like smoke finding their ways down marbled corridors, around corners, under doorsills, up through the flooring, the hands invisible, the piano strangely unimaginable. And so this late and accidental audience, lying in the sweaty sheets of seventy Sunnyside flats, overhears the inmost passages of the player's soul, what Bill Challis has only fragments of, what Lulu doesn't understand but can only feel as something the player is struggling to get out of himself.

Kraslow never hears any of it, living at the building's other extreme, but like Challis and Lulu he too gets the feeling that Mr. Beiderbecke believes he's working against a deadline. When Kraslow has an afternoon errand to run in his car, he takes to stopping by 1G to ask the man if he'd care to ride along, and the man usually says okay. Then, for the most part he's silent, sunk deep within himself, sometimes nodding off and awakening sweaty, disoriented, talking wildly of things Kraslow can't follow—places and

song titles and people all run together. One afternoon Kraslow's errand takes him all the way over into the forties in Manhattan
where his passenger suddenly glances out the window and mutters,
"This is Roseland," and as they swing past Bix sees a bunch of colored guys hanging out on the fire escape in back—sharp guys in
suits and spats—and he suddenly sits straight in his seat and says,
"Quick! Stop the car!" And Kraslow, thinking maybe he's going to
be sick, yanks the car out of the stream of traffic and over to the
curb, and Bix jumps out. Up on the landing the sharply dressed
men are smoking, laughing, the stage door ajar so they can maybe
make a little breeze, and looking down to the sidewalk they find a
white man waving up at them and ask each other, casually, who
that cat might be. Nobody knows. But the longer they stand there,
looking down on him, the more frantic he becomes, waving his
hands high in the air and even trying to jump, but from where
they're standing it looks like only his heels leave the pavement
while his toes seem embedded, and then the guy yanks off his hat
and waves that at them, and he's hollering something, but they
can't make it out. Then one of them says, "Hey, somebody wave at
him, looks like he's way off shore and headin out to sea," and so
they all wave at him now, big, flashy smiles, exaggerated gestures.
And the man down there quits trying to jump and smiles back at
them and gives a valedictory wave of his hat and turns back towards the waiting car. And then he hesitates, as if thinking of one
thing more he wants to convey, some further long-distance emotion, and half-turns towards them but then ducks into the car
where Kraslow waits, having seen only half of this strange pantomime. Glancing at him now Kraslow finds an animation on
those pasty features he's never seen before. "They all know me,"
the man pants, "they all know me," adding that they're the
Fletcher Henderson band, and Kraslow knows neither the Henderson name nor why it should be so important that these colored
men—a circus troupe maybe?—would know his passenger. And

maybe they really don't, and this is just another of the man's sad delusional states. He'd known some like this, after the war: you couldn't tell what was going to set them off, maybe only the sudden memory of a shell screaming over the trench or the eye of a dead horse, staring up into the smoky infinitude.

※❖※

Like most of them, Hoagy is scuffling these days, plugging tunes, working as a session man in the studios, a little radio work when he can get it, demonstrating pianos at a Seventh Avenue music shop. Still, he does his best to stay in touch with Bix, cheer him up with a phone call, invite him to a studio session, though after the one with Benny and Bubber he thinks he can't use Bix any more on recordings: it's just not there now. Hoagy doesn't know what to make of the move out to Sunnyside. He hasn't met the girl and wonders whether she might be trying to fence Bix off from his old friends. But when he gets Bix's new number from Challis he asks him to bring the girl around for dinner at his place—nothing fancy, maybe just spaghetti and some good talk.

When Bix shows with the girl Hoagy's almost stunned by his appearance. Not that he looks anything like the guy he knew when they were helling around Indiana, and he's still got that bad cough. But he does look better than when Hoagy'd seen him early in the summer: shaved, hair in place, clean shirt. One end of the bow tie is quite a bit longer than the other, but this detail is endearingly reassuring, and the face above it does have a kind of life to it, muted, yes, and haunted as if by some deep sadness. But at least the guy is looking at you when you speak to him and answering too, even if in half-whispered short sentences, two at most. And so right away Hoagy's for the girl, figuring her as the agent of these changes, though like Challis he can't figure her out as Bix's girl with her tar-

years and yet you wouldn't know it because you hear his voice every day, it seems like, and maybe it doesn't make as much difference as you thought whether you're alive or dead, because now they have all these ways of preserving what was really important about you—your art or whatever it was you wanted to call it—and so maybe being alive, breathing, was kind of overrated. Hoagy doesn't like the trend of this line of talk and tries to get Bix off it by talking about Ted Lewis, but it's no good because Bix dismisses Lewis right off as near-beer and seems to want to talk about Don, and Hoagy says wasn't it a damned shame how Don died and who in hell would ever have thought Don would go that way—maybe jumping out of an airplane or falling off a horse, something like that. But a normal sort of pedestrian accident—no. And Bix says, looking closely into the inky circle of his coffee cup, maybe no death is truly accidental, and Helen practically jumps up and goes into the dim little kitchen where she's not wanted to ask Carolyn if there's anything she can do, and Carolyn says sure, that the stuff's ready to go (though it's not), and in a few minutes they're seated around a card table with their underdone noodles and overdone meatballs in a thin, acidic sauce, but Carolyn's thinking Hoagy's not asking her out because she's Aunt Jemima, and somehow they get through it. Bix spends most of the time pushing his food around his plate and coughing into his napkin, and things seem like they're sliding from the merely awkward to the purely disastrous when Hoagy jumps up from the card table and tells Bix he needs his help, and Bix almost laughs at that until Hoagy explains that it's a musical matter and leads Bix over to the piano. "See," Hoagy says, sitting down to it, "I got this little strain here—" he plays it. "Been runnin around and around in my head, for *years,* seems like. I forget about it, then some morning I'll wake up, and there it is again. You have that kind of thing ever?" "Lots of times," Bix says softly, standing by the piano, looking down at his friend's long, slab-sided face that used to remind him somehow of their midwest but doesn't now. "Well," Hoagy goes on, "I get it on my brain, and I'll come over here and sit down with it, try to tease something more out of it, don't you know. But damn. . . ." The characteristically melancholy set of his features breaks into a grin as he reaches back for a memory. "Remember the old janitor at the Fiji house—always wanted to play your horn, and so one day you let him?" Bix shakes his head. "Well, you did, and he tried to play it, and then he handed it back to you? You don't remember what he said?" Bix shakes his head again. "He said, 'Nothin won't come out.'" Hoagy chuckles and Bix nods, whether actually remembering or not what was for years a shared joke. "Yeah," he says slowly. "I know how that is." But Hoagy hurries on, afraid of losing him again to some blue fugue. "Well, that's it, see: I can't get any further with the damn thing, and I'd let it go, don't you know, only it won't let *me* go." He laughs and shakes his head in exaggerated rue. "Play it again—what you've got," Bix says, solemn, and Hoagy does, but Bix says nothing, only stands there, looking down at the keys, and Hoagy can't tell whether he's thinking about the strain or has drifted off again into that unreachable place he seems to slip into so much these days. Sensing another vortex of silence, Hoagy beings to play something else, talking over his playing, explaining that this isn't really new but something he's been working on. In the background, Helen and Carolyn clear the table and put the dishes in the sink.

And then it's over. There's nothing left, no further topics Hoagy can think of to introduce, none that Bix seems likely to supply, the dishes washed and dried, not even any coffee left in the pot. The girl comes into the front room and looks at Bix who turns towards her and nods. At the door of the flat Bix turns back slowly, a small smile on his moustached lips. "O," he says in afterthought, "try this," and he whistles something, something brief but beautifully right, and Hoagy instantly knows it's the next strain in the song that won't let go of him, the one he's been trying to tease into being, and he grabs Bix by the sleeve, pulling him back from the threshold, towards the piano. "Do it again!" he says tensely.

"Whistle it!" And while Hoagy grabs a pencil and scrap paper Bix does, and Hoagy scribbles the notes. "Again," he says. "Once more." But Bix tells him he can't, and so Hoagy plays what he's got down, and Bix tells him that's close enough. Then Bix confides softly that maybe he'd better use the can before he goes—so much coffee. While he does Hoagy speaks to the girl. "If he gets sick," Hoagy tells her earnestly, holding a pinch of her thin cotton sleeve, "Call me right away, will you? I'm in the book." She gives him an odd, blank look in return, as if she's not quite getting it. "Okay?" Hoagy asks. "You'll call me?" And then slowly she nods. "Yeah, sure." And then here's Bix out of the can, walking right past Hoagy, his eyes on the girl, and they go out the door, and Bix is starting carefully down the stairs to the street when Hoagy calls after him, "Bix!" But Bix doesn't turn back, just waves with his free hand, the other one clutching the girl, and then they're gone, and Hoagy turns to Carolyn who's picking up an overflowing ashtray from the deal table and asks her what she makes of that, and she asks what part of it: "Your friend or that ninny of a nursemaid?" And later that night, lying next to Carolyn, hearing the sound of her untroubled sleep, its steady systolic suspiration, Hoagy wonders whether Helen knows who Bix is and in that same instant wonders whether he does either.

❧❖❧

The doctors Haburski—John and his wife Ruth—are not among those who've spoken to Kraslow about the night music. They've heard more of it than anybody else, though, because their flat is directly across the marbled hallway from 1G, separated by staircase and wide end-of-hall window. They've never said anything to Kraslow because they've fallen deeply in love with the music. Before she began her medical studies Ruth Haburski had studied piano and still carries within her an abiding love of Chopin, her Frederic the Great. And this is what comes to her the first time she hears the nocturnal notes from 1G—Chopin and his nocturnes. She thinks she must be dreaming of him and for some minutes lies there, trying to disentangle Chopin, dream, and this moment in which these are blended by a piano being played somewhere close to her. She nudges her husband awake and whispers to him, "Jay, do you hear that?" and Jay, awakening, turns onto his back, listening for a long while. "It's marvelous, isn't it," he says finally. "What is it? Do you recognize it?" She doesn't, though by now it's obvious it's far too modern to be Frederic the Great. The next night they hear it again and the one after that, and by this time they know where it's coming from. Neither has ever seen anyone going into or out of the apartment across the hall, and when they leave in the morning for their clinic they look searchingly at that closed door that seems so silent and barred. In the evening, returning together or separately, they find it the same. "Ghosts," Jay says playfully, and they speculate about the unseen player, whether man or woman, alone or in company, young or old. Ruth finally decides it's a solitary man, living a rich, intensely interior existence, one they must not attempt to intrude into. So in these summer weeks the doctors fall asleep in anticipation of the night music, sleep towards it, and when it commences—one o'clock, two—their hands slide towards each other in the close, heavy darkness, the fan doing what it can, as they attend the most private recital possible, one in which the mysterious, unseen artist dreams aloud, and Ruth Haburski comes to believe that all the divagations, the reiterations and single-note hesitancies, have a strange sort of architectonic coherence.

Then one day she sees him.

Beginning of August. No relief in sight from the heat and the papers carrying news of drought and crop failures in the western states. Kraslow, moving with feather duster about the Moorish columns of the lobby, his undershirt gray with sweat, says hello to the lady doctor as she comes home with her small black bag and a sack of groceries. "Isn't this just terrible heat, Mr. Kraslow? I think of the babies and little children in the tenements." Kraslow nods yes it's terrible, making a sweaty swipe with his hand across his brow as the doctor passes wearily out of the lobby, turns down the corridor, and at its end is startled to find the door of 1G ajar. She knows she mustn't pause there, must respect the privacy of someone simply trying to get some cross ventilation from the window opened in the hall. But she can't help herself, is compelled to stop and peer within—and sees the artist, sprawled on a sheetless bed with a sweat-slick arm hanging white and lifeless over the edge. Next to the bed two tiny fans are propped on chairs and rattling noisily. The stillness of that arm, its dangling fingers: she raps sharply on the door and there's no response. Raps again and on the sound marches in, clutching her groceries and the little black bag that gives her a sort of right of entry, past the low counter that divides kitchen from bedroom, past the piano that takes up most of what space there is beside the bed, the keys of its upper register disfigured by multiple cigarette wounds. "Sir!" she exclaims. "Sir! Are you all right in here?" She's about to identify herself as the doctor from across the hall when the wet, white face turns its huge eyes to her but seem to be staring just past her, so that she turns about to look but finds nothing there except the piano. "Excuse me for this intrusion," she says, standing behind the chairs with their rattling fans, her backside almost touching the piano's keyboard. "I'm Doctor Haburski—from across the hall." But the eyes don't appear to register this, are still looking past her, and then the dangling hand comes up and points to the piano. "Up there," the voice croaks. She turns again to try to find what he means. "Up there. On top." On top of the piano she finds a package of cigarettes and a claim slip from Kim-Lee Cleaners & Dyers around the corner. She holds the slip towards him mutely. "If anything happens, call that number," he says, and now she knows he's delirious. She feels she needs to wait for her husband, and then together they could make an examination, and so she says, "Sir, you look very ill. I'll just step across to my apartment, and when my husband comes in, then I think we ought to have a look at you—you certainly seem to need some attention." He says nothing, and she stands irresolute, then crosses the hall to wait for Jay.

But it's much later when he finally arrives, much later: after the figure in the bed has sunk into a restless sleep, the feet twitching, fingers clenching like claws that would grab hold of something; after the doors along the echoing corridors have ceased to open and slam shut as the last of the latecomers trudges across the threshold into the closed cauldron within; after a burdened dusk has settled on Sunnyside and the lights come up in buildings and on street corners: then John Haburski himself trudges home to find his wife pacing the hall between their flat and the open door of 1G. And then he arouses the man in the sheetless bed and together the doctors make a swift examination and determine the man has pneumonia and needs immediate hospitalization, something he refuses as adamantly as he can.

And still later the man himself arises from his clammy mattress and stands there, swaying in the pathetic breeze of the rattling fans, dimly aware that someone has been in to see him and maybe has even wished him well when what he needs now are not well-wishers but a drink, but he doesn't have anything around, has just two days ago taken the last of a pint of gin and defiantly shaken it down the drain and stood there above the sink's blank, medicinal white, sweating, smelling the sweet last of the utterly vanished stuff, muttering through clenched fangs, "You bastard, you *bastard!*" And so now is dry and hot as the Sahara and thinks about trying to make it down to the corner and up the half-block to the blind tiger he has so often visited but doesn't think he can, and anyway maybe this is the time he can kill this beast that's been stalking him through all these years, though already the room is beginning to get a little funny, and he's almost certain things have moved around some from the way he remembers them. But the pattern of the wallpaper looks stable enough, and he remembers that much from Cleveland, and so maybe he can somehow make it through this, and the thing to do—waiting until it's late enough to get to the piano again—is to get on the phone, call a few friends. He thinks it might have been last night or the night before when he tracked Tram down in Chicago, at the Edgewater Beach, though he can't remember what they talked about, but maybe it was that he told Tram he was really close to finishing something good. If he could call Lulu, he would, but at this hour, whatever hour it is, it's out of the question: the phone would ring in the Whartons's bedroom, and that would surely get Lulu in Dutch, and, anyway, what he wants to talk about now is music, and he can't do that with Lulu and so rings up Red Nichols and instead gets Red's wife, Bobbi, because Red is playing a job at the Park Central.

Like some others Bobbi has always had a little thing about him, which sometimes makes her feel funny listening to Red practicing Bix's stuff. Bobbi is used to Bix's odd and sometimes disjointed way of talking, but this is different, and she's finding it hard to follow him as he switches from present to past, from one name to another, coughs interspersed throughout. At the beginning of a sentence he's in St. Louis, and by the middle of it he's on the South Side, and then she's completely lost and doesn't know where he is and thinks he doesn't either, and then there comes a kind of clearing with something consecutive as he recalls when they jammed at the Bronx Zoo, and there was a guy there dressed in an ape outfit doing the Black Bottom outside the monkey cage, and the monkeys were all excited, and the guys couldn't play because they were laughing too hard, and she tries to keep him there because it seems like a happy memory while the rest of this is so desolate, but she

can't, and he's already on Don who he says was murdered, and if
only Don were here he could call him, and Don would come over
and at least just sit with him, for Christ's sake. And Bobbi tries to
get in here and ask him what's wrong but it's too late, and he's already moved on to other guys—Bill and Fred and Howdy—and
how not one of them would give him a quarter now if he asked for
it, especially Tram who was out there at the Edgewater Beach, and,
hell, Tram wouldn't come out to help his old friend: too busy at
that fancy place, and he'd been there many a time himself and long
before Tram, for that matter, and now Bobbi knows he's truly
jumped the track because he's calling her Lulu and talking about a
time they had together in her room at the Edgewater Beach and
how smashing he thought she was, having no idea she was really
Herman's sister, and what a surprise it was to learn that. Then
there's a pause followed by a long coughing fit, and she says over it,
"Bix, honey, this is Bobbi. What's bothering you? Are you in trouble? Are you sick? Want me to call a doctor? Bix?" And then on the
other end she hears him gasping and saying he doesn't need a doctor, that what he needs is a friend, for Christ's sake, and after all
the guys he's bought drinks for and dinner, too, you'd think just
one of them would be here now, with him, when he's got to have a
friend to help him out, but she's a friend, he knows, and did she
ever think it could work out for them to get married, maybe not
right away, but later, after he's gotten himself straightened out here
a bit and has some steady work again. Tram was married, Red. And
she's trying desperately now to intervene, stop this terrible torrent,
saying she knows he's sick and won't he, for God's sake, let her call
a doctor and she and Red will pay for it, and he says it's too late for
that, that they're all asleep and anyway things are changing around
so fast now that it's hard to keep anything straight—you look for
something where you left it, and next thing you know it's moved
someplace else, and anyway, even if she did get hold of someone,
how could they find him way over here, wherever it was, when

everything is changing so fast. She wants to keep him on the line, all the way till Red gets home, if need be, and he's asking her if she couldn't please just come over here for a little while, maybe just till sunup, but she tells him her kids are asleep, and he just says, O. She asks him to hang on while she brings a chair over to the phone, and he says fine but before she gets back with it she hears a scream, and the chair falls clattering from her hands and she lunges for the receiver but drops it too as if it's alive, a live wire filled with screams, and each one of them sends a huge spasm down her spinal chord, but she wills herself to grab the swinging thing and tries to scream back, to get through the little black, one-way muzzle, but its screams won't let her, and then between her own screams she hears a woman's voice, sharp, imperative, "Sir! Sir!" the screams now shaping themselves into words impossibly high above falsetto, he who had always played within the singer's best range: "*There! There! Under the bed! Its tail!*" And then a crash, a glottal click like something being swallowed, a buzz, a droning silence, and then on her end the sounds of the city coming in—the rattle in the corridor, radio blaring in the next apartment, auto horn, once, the murmurous rustle of one of her kids, dreaming perhaps of his new tricycle and Mommy and Poppy following him along the paths of the big park with the pigeons making their brief, fluttering escapes before his rushing wheels. And on the other end of the broken line Ruth Haburski struggles to guide the writhing man back towards the bed, making little shuffle steps against his weight when suddenly all that anguish ceases, he stops fighting, and she sees on his glistening face a strange, small smile, the eyes half-shuttered, downcast, and his arms reach out to her, gliding gratefully around her while his forehead finds the hollowed haven between her neck and shoulder, and he murmurs, softly, confessionally, "Lulu," and on that last two-note breath is whirled elsewhere.

V

Davenport

The tapping on the glass shatters the dream he's having of Hellie, and he lurches out of it, eyes wild and unfocused, glaring at a face craned close to his car window, its eyes wide as well but not wild, the features squinched into quizzicality, a face he comes slowly to understand he recognizes by sight though not by name. The man has been tapping with a key, and Henry Wise can see beyond the craned head broad daylight aloft and shimmering in the oaks and pines. "Hey, old-timer!" the man is hollering. "Hey! You all right in there?" From his side of the glass he nods back, not really sure he is or even, just fleetingly, if this is only another room in what feels like a large, dark suite of dreams he's been wandering through for years. But in that same instant he knows this is no dream because the man is making broad pantomime motions, insisting he roll down the window, and he does so, the morning rolling in as the glass vanishes smoothly into the chassis: bright, fresh air, bird calls, the man's voice—the harsh, nasal sound of quotidian reality—asking him what he's doing here and whether he wants any help, a doctor maybe. And Henry Wise has to explain that he must have fallen asleep at the wheel and spent the night out here. And then the custodian-groundskeeper tells him that isn't allowed but since nobody has noticed he guesses it'll be all right this time, adding that everybody has to clear out at sundown—too many weirdos these days, and then you never know what college kids will do.

Henry Wise's body is a minefield of small, sharp aches, each of which he discovers when he shifts in the seat, and if he could, he would get out and try to stretch and get the blood flowing back into bodily sectors that feel long abandoned, but he can't because the man's leaning on the door, and meanwhile he's realizing new urgencies by the second, the chief of which is a badly bulging bladder, and so with only a half-wave he turns over the ignition key, and the engine's immoderate roar drives his inquisitor back a few steps, and Henry Wise, looking neither right nor left and certainly not at the gape-mouthed man who now stands aside, drives up the lane, past the Beiderbecke family plot—Bismark and Agatha, Burnie and Bix—and on up the hill and down its westward slope and out into the city, moving fast for a coffee shop on Brady where he can take a leak.

Sitting at the counter, relieved but still dazed, he rinses his mouth with coffee, feeling the stuff hiss like the river of Hades through the worn gaps of his teeth and then snake its molten way into his innards. When the waiter wonders if he wants a refill he looks up at him from beneath the shaggy hedges of his eyebrows and nods and into the beige plastic cup comes another shot of hell, which he stirs with a spoon, his old mind fumbling backwards to that moment when he'd been awakened out of a dream by the insistent tap-tapping of custodial keys.

He never dreams of her, though whether this is because she's stuck so far back in his past or because he's willed himself never to visit that place is a question he doesn't ask himself. What he allows himself to understand is that he has never knowingly laid eyes on her since that morning when, moving along the blade's edge between some sort of duty and hysteria, she'd marshaled the grim necessities in the Sunnyside flat and gotten Bix ready for the undertaker and for Agatha. After which she had simply vanished. Two days after the mother and brother had brought the body back here the estranged Clementine had slipped a note under his door: "Where is Helen. Whartons want to know." And he had no reply to make, though he then began to make inquiries. But the underground network available to him was dry, empty, blank, no least rumor. In those early days of her disappearance he'd thought

*back on that morning in Sunnyside, searching through his visual rec-
ollections for some clue, something she'd done or said, that might lead
him to her, if not to her precise whereabouts, then at least to some sense
of reassurance—that she had gone somewhere, for reasons of her own.
But the clue hadn't turned up even though he continued to go over
those hours they'd spent together in the flat, cleaning up death, and he
kept at this for months, remembering how the doctors across the hall,
without a clue to the next-of-kin, had accidentally come across a laundry slip on the other side of which they'd found Hellie's name scrawled
next to the Whartons' number. Nor had there been any clue left in the
small, neat chamber she'd occupied under the verdigrised roof of the
Whartons' mansion. Her clothes were there in the closet, but who was
to say all of them were? A couple of suitcases, too. But no scraps of paper, notes, timetables, matchbook covers. Even the labels in the clothes,
souvenirs from her days with Jack, had all been carefully removed as
though left behind by one determined never to be traced. He waited
vainly for a phone call, thinking of other times when they'd been out of
touch for months, even a year once.*

*Then—it was October and a somber fall was turning into an early,
threadbare winter—he got a call from a mid-level man with Big
Frenchy, telling him they had a lead, that his sister had been spotted in
Chicago. But a week went by while he waited, and Thanksgiving came
and went, and there was nothing more. Frenchy's man had nothing else
for him, and Chicago seemed another dead end.*

*His life chugged on. People openly scoffed at Prohibition and its en-
forcers, and when the cops padlocked a couple of speaks in Manhattan
a large crowd gathered to jeer and throw garbage at them. Roosevelt,
running against the hated Hoover, was rumored to favor Repeal, and
it was easier and easier now to move supplies around the city, but there
were fewer and fewer who could afford to buy the stuff. The handwrit-
ing, though, was on the wall, and those in his line of work were thinking hard about what to do when Repeal did come. Out in Chicago the*

boys were having to get used to changes, too, with the Big Shot doing a stretch in a federal clink for income tax evasion. In New York Madden and others of the older generation were getting out of the business altogether while the younger guys like Lucky Luciano and Costello were moving smoothly into narcotics, pimping, labor racketeering, slots, and policy wheels—all lines Mr. Big had charted years earlier.

"So, what'er you gonna do?" Big Frenchy had asked him. Late afternoon, the day after Thanksgiving, and they were sitting at a back table at Jack Dempsey's in midtown. Above the bar, still innocent of liquor but with the taps newly installed and all the other materials in place (shakers, swizzle sticks, napkins), a broad white banner proclaimed in green lettering, THE BALLOON GOES UP DEC. 5. BE HERE!! Somehow, with the imminence of Repeal Big Frenchy looked diminished in some indefinable way, less menacing of mien with a cloud of autumnal melancholy sitting on his burly shoulders. Herman had shrugged his own wide shoulders and said he didn't quite know yet. "Seems like it's either runnin hop up to the jigs in Harlem or breakin legs down on the docks," he said finally, "and I don't know as I'm exactly cut out for that kind of stuff. What about you? What'll you do?" Big Frenchy looked up at the hovering waiter and nodded, and the waiter stepped forward with his gleaming coffee pot and poured Big Frenchy a refill. Big Frenchy snapped a sugar cube in half and plopped it in. "This'n that," he said, and then with the waiter safely away, he added, "I got a piece of the Preem, for one, but you know the dagos aint gonna let you have too much of that: they got the big hunks." "He can't fight worth a crap," Herman said. "I could probably whip him." "You probably could at that," Big Frenchy said, looking into his coffee and stirring it slowly, "but you'd never live to collect if you did. All his fightin's done for him ahead of time." "Well, I'm not looking to get into the ring anyway," Herman said, "and I got some time to figure it out." He threw a glance toward the premonitory banner above the bar. "I've been pretty careful. I got some put by." "Sure

artist—people would do anything for a buck these days—, this definitely had all the earmarks of a bump-off, and what was his interest, anyway? And he'd said numbly that maybe it was a girlfriend. Then the man, wearing a slight sneer, had fished for the card he had on the corpse and silently slid it across the desk and settled back into his swivel chair to enjoy Herman's reactions. There wasn't much on the card. Name. blank. Address. blank. Location Where Found. Catherine St. Pier. Date. Time. By Whom. Police cruiser. #. Personnel. And the description: blond female, 5'3¾". w. 138. age, b/w 35–50. subj showing considerable trauma to head. Decomposition consistent w immersion in water @ least 1 week, considerable abrasion around upper torso, ankles, consistent w heavy cordage bound around subj @ these pts. Remarks. blank. Disposition. Hart. Reading through this, he'd been aware of the man's eyes on him and was trying to show him nothing, and then there'd been a squeak from the swivel chair and the man asking from far away, "Sound like your girlfriend?" He heard himself saying could be, and then the guy again, "Wanna look?" and they'd descended through several levels, each one colder, darker than the last, until they were underground where they kept the stiffs that had washed up here and the guy was talking to him all the way down, about the surprising things you found down here, about the stiff they had thought might be Judge Crater, only it wasn't, about how they'd already set a record for suicides in the city and the year wasn't even over yet and you could always expect a rash of them over the holidays, but in this here case he guessed it wasn't a suicide, now was it? By this time the door of the cooler had rung open, and the guy was handing the attendant the file card and telling him they wanted to have a look at that thing there, and the floor was sucking at his feet like it was made of mud or blood or something, but the sound was that of the attendant's rubber-soled shoes, and then they were at the locker, and that thing his guide had demanded came roaring out on its casters into the dim, orangish light and the rough sheet was whipped off, and there, sure enough, was that thing.

There were ways to tell if it was her or not, ways he hardly had to rehearse, and he thought he was ready for the fact that the face wouldn't be one of them. And it wasn't. There was no face nor even a jaw line or slope of forehead, only a grayish-white tangle out of which some few teeth protruded and what once might have been part of a nostril or the septum and some dried, matted substance that was like the weeds of a field that had long been buried under winter. And maybe the file card had it right and she had been blonde, once. He had an indelible memory of two small, dark moles just above the left armpit, and he looked quickly for them, but there was no armpit, either: the long chafing of the heavy cordage the file card mentioned had worn this area down almost to the humerus. And so that left him with those other markers, the ones he knew too well, the ones he had no proper right to know, the ones he'd never been able to forget. But there weren't any breasts left, either, only flayed gray flaps. Then, the region beneath the bellybutton, towards which his eyes darted, then flicked away. It was shaved, grotesquely naked and frozen-looking between the pulpy, waterlogged thighs. "She aint much to look at now, is she?" the guy was sneering now, and Herman who had been forced early in life to learn how to keep a governor on himself at all times had felt in that instant a feral impulse to seize this shitheels by the throat and press his thumbs up through the voice box. But he hadn't, had only turned away and walked swiftly from the room, up the stairs, running now, and then out into the narrow walkway between the waiting room and morgue, and it had felt as if there wasn't enough air in all the great, wheeling city to fill the lungs he hadn't realized until then were bursting, and he'd stood there with the uniformed personnel blindly passing him, his eyes glaring like the holes of some infernally fueled lantern, his mind reeling and shouting, No! No! No! But then the countervailing shout, like that of a wide-open freight running under a midnight sky—Yes! So he'd stood there, paralyzed by hope and dread, half-wanting to charge back down into that awful place and confront the ripped, ravaged gorgon, to pry into it, if he had to—

anything to learn its truth. And the other half, the half belonging to the man he'd spent a lifetime becoming, the cautious man, the one who wouldn't rashly expose himself to harm or mischance, the prudent, skeptical guy always alert to danger and damage: this half saw the folly of that descent: the shitheels still down there with the flunky, doubtless having a grim chuckle over his alarmed, sudden retreat, probably, too, making easy anatomical jokes about the body on the metal slab: the violent encounter certain to ensue out of that; and then the hopeless new confrontation with that body—mute, mangled, mysterious—which would leave him with every one of the questions and none of the answers. And so at last he turned out of the passageway into the flow of the city and back to Union Square and his duties there: driving for Jimmy Hines, running the errands of Hines's fantastically involved and intersecting lines of interest: Tammany politics, charities, bribes, kickbacks, sub rosa retainers, protection, the holiday deliveries of turkeys and coal to the needy, horse racing, boxing, realty management. He did routine mechanical maintenance on the limos. Once in a while he might be deputized to take somebody's kids to the Polo Grounds or a bowling alley for a birthday party. As ever, he lived alone, took his meals alone when he could, had no close friends but many acquaintances. He found his solemn sexual relief in a succession of hatcheck girls, cigarette girls, cocktail waitresses, ticket takers, the receptionists he encountered on his Tammany Hall runs. He polished the brightwork on the La Salle limo while waiting for Jimmy Hines, looking up to see the cop clopping past on his big bay horse or the cop on the beat, walking by with a wink at the illegally parked car, tapping his leg with his night stick. He sat in the boxes along the first base line, behind the birthday party kids, watching Bill Terry's Giants but mostly keeping an eye on the constantly moving kids, signaling the hot dog man, the peanut vendor. Nights, he went to bed with the lay of the day—no fancy stuff here, just delivering the goods in a straight-ahead fashion. And in any of these places or moments, then like a thief a

thought of Hellie might steal through the careful order of things bring-
ing with it an image from the morgue, and he'd have to move to cut it
off quick: engage the passing, winking cop in a bit of banter; signal the
hot dog guy ("Hey! Hey! Four red-hots, here, huh?"); find some least
thing to say to the woman who lay next to him in the tangled sheeting,
her eyes on him and an unspoken question on her lips.

Then one night early in '36 he heard the other shoe drop—or
thought so, anyway. The talk of the day was about the death of the
king over in England, and about Hauptmann who was about to get
the hot seat for the Lindbergh thing. But the ongoing talk, the talk
that was everywhere present in his world, was that the heat was on for
Jimmy Hines and also for Luciano, who now ran all the families and
who the brash new D.A., Tom Dewey, had up on a prostitution
charge. This night Hines and Waxey Gordon and the bunch had been
to the fights at St. Nick's, and when the evening's duties were con-
cluded Herman was in Lindy's with Headly Hanlon and his brother
Alf who worked for Waxey in laundry and coal. Headly was a big,
blond-headed guy who wore an eight-and-three-quarters hat and
talked incessantly. Some of it was entertaining, occasionally even use-
ful, but Herman had formed the habit of filtering much of Headly's
steady stream, taking in only a little of it. Now as they sat in Lindy's
with their mugs of coffee and corned beef and kraut the talk turned
again to Hines and Luciano and the trouble Dewey was causing them,
and Headly said the dumb whore what had turned Lucky had come
up missing, that there was no point in looking for her to testify before
the grand jury, that she'd been seen to for certain, and any cunt dumb
enough to think the D.A. could protect her was dumb enough to talk
to him in the first place. It was like that dame out in Chi years ago,
the one that ratted out Machine Gun Jack, and where was she now?
Nobody's seen her since. That one had been dumb enough to think she
could just skip on Jack and hide out here, and that was her second mis-
take. "McGurn had long arms them days," Headly concluded with a

*wag of his cannonball head. And by that point Herman's own head
had felt like it could explode, too, and while he usually discounted
much of what Headly passed off as the straight goods, this rumor had a
peculiar resonance to it for him and while he heard Headly's voice, still
rambling, he heard behind it the roar of that metal slab on its casters
at Bellevue.*

*He was too careful a man to ask Headly his sources—and anyway,
the chances were Headly wouldn't remember them accurately—but he
knew the network well enough to figure out who they might be, and
within a week he'd found a guy who said he'd heard something like
that, though it was a while back, and then Herman had had to listen
to a lot of collateral stuff about Charlie Lucky and how Dewey's case
had blown up without the whore's testimony, but that Jimmy, he
looked like he might have a bit more trouble. Herman thought it over,
and the more he did so, the more the tattered old pieces of the puzzle
seemed to fit. If Jack had set those goons on Hellie out in Hollywood,
why would he stop at that when everybody who had ever known Jack
knew him as the pathologically vengeful guy he was? If he'd found her
out there, why couldn't he have traced her here? And if Hellie was
alive, she would surely have let him know somehow and long ago.
Then there was that poor thing on the slab that he hadn't wanted to
believe in. . . .*

*When he finally told Jimmy Hines he had to attend to some family
business that couldn't be put off any longer, Hines only smiled and
asked how long he'd be gone. If there was one thing the micks and dagos understood, it was family business. Then Hines had patted him on
the back and said if there was anything he could do, Herman had only
to ask. On the day he took his leave, Hines handed him an envelope
and insisted he open it on the spot. Inside were two crisp fifties, and
Jimmy winked at him out of that wide, cheeky face where the grin
wrinkles ran all the way from just under the eyes to beneath the jut of
the jaw—the enduring evidence of decades of benevolent expressions to*

friends, associates, crowds, the neighborhood needy. He'd mumbled his thanks and that early evening had boarded a coach through to Union Station in Chicago.

Stepping stiffly down into the station's dim light with one of Hellie's good leather grips, he shouldered his way through a sparse crowd of passengers, red caps, station personnel and two men up near the huge, hissing engine looking at nothing, missing nothing, either, and whom he instantly made as railroad dicks. Still inside the terminal, he could feel the deep cold of the city, smell it even. He hadn't been back since '29, yet outside on Canal everything was completely familiar down to the accents of the newsboys on the corners. Then he took a cab up to a clean, cheap hotel on West Diversey where he could quietly make his plans to take Jack.

Jack had come down in the world since February of '29, his work on Anselmi and Scalise and the Hop Toad only a temporary reprieve. He'd missed Bugs in the action on Clark, and that was unforgivable. Then with the Big Shot away and Greasy Thumb as well Jack had no constituency in the Outfit. Joe Batters, who ran things for Capone and Guzik and now went as Tony Accardo, had never had much use for him and spread it around that when Jack was in the ring he'd been yellow against guys who could really take a punch. Marked, too hot for use in any serious work, Jack had slipped towards the edges of the action, and it hadn't helped his reputation any when his blonde wife had skipped on him.

But he wasn't on his uppers, either. He still had some action with the cleaners and dyers, had a dame or two working in the Cicero houses. He was a successful sports gambler, a crackerjack backgammon player and bowler. But no more Edgewater Beach for Jack. No more big-time nights on the town where he'd flash into a joint and command a ringside table. No more brilliant blonde on his arm, dripping furs and jewelry. Now Jack lived low-key in Polack town, at a respectable residential hotel on North Milwaukee with his current companion, Delores, a good-looking

Mexican woman who managed a restaurant in the area. And though somewhat reduced, Jack still cut a figure, the hair still slicked back, the suits close-fitting, the slightly passé spats immaculate. His silk ties still came from A. Sulka on Michigan—marvelously flashy things featuring flowers and fruit. No more acrobatic stunts, though, like walking a city block on his hands or doing a backflip from street to curb: the Gusenbergs had seen to that. When he walked the bounce was gone, and the pigeon-toed boxer's gait was a trifle slower. Still, there were times after he'd cleaned out a sucker at backgammon or bowled a 200 game when Jack would shoot his cuffs and crack that fuck-you grin, just like the high old days. For the most part, though, the olive-brown features wore a slightly bemused look, as if the violently unphilosophical man had been forced by time and fortune to ponder some of humankind's more puzzling matters.

It hadn't taken Herman long to learn that this new, more subdued Jack had become a man of wonderfully regular daytime habits. His nights were less predictable and seemed to depend in part but not altogether on Delores's work schedule; other nights Jack rode off in his car alone, and when the watching Herman would give it up at last well after midnight, Jack still hadn't returned. Herman thought he might have a room down in Cicero. But every day it was the same. At eight sharp, the newsstand at West Fullerton and Western. Breakfast at a Polish place on Western between Milwaukee and North. Sometimes a meeting there in the back booth. Forty minutes to an hour of phone calls from the manager's office. Back to the hotel. Early afternoons, Jack walked four blocks up Milwaukee to Chick's 12-Lanes where he spent the rest of the day, bowling, talking with associates in the café-bar, or using the office phone. Jack had a 188 average, plenty good enough to play professionally, but he wasn't even in a local league, preferring to freelance, taking on all comers at Chick's, waiting to shark some sucker who strutted in there with his own ball and shoes. Jack would watch such guys from the shadows, fingers to his mouth, and after taking their measure would signal Chick to arrange the contact. Chick was Chick Gandil of the Black Sox, a big, long-armed guy, defiant of his role in the fix, happy to host Machine Gun Jack and give him the use of the office phone for his business calls.

When Jack had wiped the boards with a sucker, he'd go into Chick's office for his suit coat, then disappear into the bathroom at the other end of the place, emerging at long last washed and powdered and pomaded, every hair in place and the suit coat carefully draped over an arm. Over several days Herman took notes on all these habits: walking by Jack's hotel; passing by the Polish place and taking a window seat at another diner diagonally across Milwaukee where he could watch Jack's comings and goings; averaging out the times in the stubby schoolboy notepad he'd bought; waiting thirty or forty minutes after Jack had entered Chick's 12-Lanes before drifting into its café-bar for a sandwich and coffee; then moving off into the hangar-like hall with its broad expanse of gleaming yellow hardwoods, the twelve lanes brightly lit but the seats shadowed and even weekday afternoons busy enough for him to avoid notice. After a few days it became obvious that the bathroom at Chick's was the place to take Jack, and he'd found a muted sort of surprise in himself at how simple it seemed to him in prospect, how confident he was of his ability to carry it out.

He'd never killed before. He'd never even pulled a trigger, though there'd been that long, silent stand-off out on Long Island when it seemed clear he'd have to kill and would probably be killed himself. That experience had only served to strengthen his determination not to let himself get placed in such situations if he could help it: it was pointless because he'd seen early on how interchangeable the parts of any gang's machine were and how easily disposable. He'd attended a few send-offs of former colleagues and knew that score: the vulgarly showy floral tributes and the waxy effigy in the casket who'd died for nothing. Even in his early days with the Big Shot he'd told Hellie that he wasn't about to shoot it out for a load of watered sauce, and she'd rolled her blue eyes at him in sardonic disbelief. Of course, to work for Capone you had to carry a gun and know how to use it and maintain it, too, and at some point Greasy Thumb Guzik had deputized Blue Island Artie Sena to give him some lessons with a .32, which Blue Island Artie thought lacking in heft but said, what the hell, if that's what you're comfortable with, we'll work it that way. And they had, going out to the dump behind a Blue Island factory on a couple of Saturdays where Artie had shown him a few things: how to take your time because you always had a little more time than you thought, and the guy in a hurry was the guy who fired wild anyway. "This aint the Wild West," Artie had said with a tight grin on his handsome, unmarked face. That and to remember to extend your arm in the direction of your target and try for a mid-body hit. Artie set up targets for him, all of them at close range, where any shooting would be done, and he found, to their mutual surprise, that it was easy enough for him to pull the .32 from his waistband, clearing his coat, and squeeze off an accurate shot. On the second Saturday of their tutorial Artie had shrugged after Herman had knocked up some horsehair stuffing from near the top of a derelict chair on which Artie had placed a bottle. "Close enough," Artie had said. "Youda hit him inna kidney, maybe, which would take him down." Then he'd looked at Herman, raising his eyebrows. "Ya know, kid," he'd said appraisingly, "you're gonna be okay out there. Okay." Not many months later, he'd looked down into Blue Island Artie's professionally composed features as he lay in state in a South Vincennes funeral parlor while his wife and mother stifled their grief in long lace handkerchiefs. And for what? Who outside of his family gave a crap that Artie had shot it out with Bugs's boys and lost?

Nor did the risks of this rub-out seem great to him. No doubt Jack went armed; a man with his reputation would have to. Yet at Chick's 12-Lanes he could hardly bowl with a pistol, and Herman thought he must leave it either in his overcoat in Chick's office or possibly in his suit coat. *If it was the latter, that would explain why Jack carried the coat to and from the bathroom, but while he was washing up and primping Jack wouldn't have the gun instantly accessible. Herman figured he'd wait in the wings until Jack finished a game and went for the suit coat in Gandil's office. Then Herman would go to the can, enter a stall, and wait for him. There was, of course, the possibility others might be in there as well—at the sink or the trough, in another stall—but he'd been around enough to learn that bystanders at a shooting were always para- lyzed by fright and afterwards virtually useless as witnesses. Blue Island Artie claimed that when he was doing a job he was actually more com- fortable with others around because they constituted a distraction that made his escape a bit easier. Besides, he said, there was something a lit- tle creepy about doing somebody all by your lonesome.*

The night before he was to make his attempt Herman took his soli- tary dinner in a chop suey joint on Ashland, forking up the grayish goop speckled with fried noodles but not tasting it, then walked back in swirling snow to his hotel. He settled his bill with the night clerk, packed his few belongings and sat down with his weapon. It was a snub-nosed Iver Johnson .38—plenty of heft here, especially at close range. He'd had it since his days with Big Frenchy and knew it was cold. He checked its action, dry-fired it a few times, then loaded the greasy slugs into its chambers.

In the morning mirror his face looked strange to him in the harsh yellow light of the unhoused bulb in its horizontal socket: the long up- per lip blue with stubble, the eyes red and narrowed under the heavy brows, the short hair bristled with sleep. It was almost as if he'd never given it close inspection before, never had either time or need to do so. Yet now he did and shaved with more than ordinary attention, too. Outside, it was evident winter wasn't about to release its grip on the city, the wind lashing along the street off Diversey Harbor, bits of news- paper and wrappers skittering before it, pedestrians mittened and muf- flered against the biting cold. It felt too cold to snow. The entrances to

*Union Station were manned by apple sellers advertising their wares
and distress in equal measure. He broke one of Jimmy Hines's crisp
fifties and bought a coach ticket on the evening 6:06, stashed the grip
in a locker, and entered the terminal's café for breakfast. Yet scanning
the dingy menu with the thumbprints of nameless predecessors stamped
around its margins like castaway medallions, he discovered his jumpy
stomach, damp armpits, clammy brow, and went out again into the
wind's gray cut, buying an apple from the nearest vendor and storing it
in his overcoat pocket. Walking north on Canal towards Milwaukee, he
was conscious of the .38 snug against his belly. At a corner he bought a*
Tribune *from a kid whose pimples had turned purple in the cold, then
lingered long over coffee and a sandwich until he saw Jack striding past
on the other side of the street, heading for Chick's 12-Lanes. He forced
himself to go through the paper once more, digging deeper into its ad-
vertisements, its movie listings, neighborhood news of the Near North,
watching the jerk of the minute hand of the Bulova strapped to his
wrist. Then it was time.*

*Entering Chick's 12-Lanes, the customer came through a kind of
corridor with the office on his left, the windows of the café-bar on his
right, and the lanes spread out before him under the dramatic lights.
Herman noted the drawn blinds in Gandil's office and saw the owner
himself down at Lane One talking to a couple of pin-setters—tall,
slump-shouldered and with a potbelly flumping over his striped pants.
Down at the other end a man and two women were bowling and
laughing at the lane nearest the bathroom. No sign anywhere of Jack.
Through the open entry to the café-bar Herman saw two of the three
booths occupied, and in one of them two men in bulky overcoats and
cloth caps sat over coffee, not saying anything, just looking into their
mugs. Behind the small half-circle counter the bald, square-shouldered
colored guy was frying up a hamburger and onions on the grill. Herman thought he must once have been a fighter because of the shiny scar
tissue above the browless eyes. "Be with you directly," the colored guy*

until one of the gunmen wheeled about and slammed full force into him, knocking him sideways, the .38 flying one way and he the other, and then in the next moment the men were fleeing down the short corridor to the street door, and he was trying to get to his feet and looking vainly for his gun. He saw Jack, his shirt-sleeved arms wide spread, and knew he was dead and saw in that same instant the whole frozen tableau before him: Chick Gandil, half-turned from the pin-setters toward Jack, his mouth open in an oval of awe; and the black guy crouched by the open office door, holding Gandil's still-hot lunch plate. Then the tableau moved again on the flash of the street door, and righting himself he saw that his own path to that door was clear, and he raced to it, the skirts of his topcoat flying. Down Milwaukee to the corner and around it at a precarious angle, hearing his shoe soles sliding on the cement, cutting across the street through traffic, hardly hearing the blare of a horn behind him, heading for an alleyway on the other side. The alley might have been blind and thus a trap, but Herman felt he had to take the chance, and running into it he saw that it was blind but that halfway down it a delivery door stood wide open and waiting with a dolly propped against it. When he reached it he shot a glance within to find the stock room of a hardware store and no one in sight. Beyond that, he could see the flood of daylight from the store itself and ducked into the stock room and slumped against some shelving, trying to get his breath. His hat was gone, and there was an artery slamming in his neck like a piston. He reached into his back pocket to pull out a wadded handkerchief and heard voices from the storefront and then the front door shutting on the cheery jingle of bells and then nothing but silence. Mopping his face and neck, he waited for the clerk to return to the stock room, but he didn't, and finally Herman stepped slowly out into the back of the store, moving with feigned concentration along a narrow aisle filled with a jumble of things he couldn't comprehend. At the end of the aisle he peered cautiously around a bin and saw the clerk wiping his hands on a towel and then looking up to find that while he'd been in the bathroom he had somehow acquired a rather disheveled new customer.

So that was how he hadn't killed Jack—the arch way he thought about it once the fear of arrest had gradually receded. But that was much later, and at first he'd been plenty worried that he'd be nabbed as one of the assassins. Especially at the station when he saw the late papers that day with their headlines: **CAPONE TORPEDO TORPE-DOED. Police Seek 3 Killers in Bowling Alley Slaying.** *And beneath the picture of Jack, spread-eagled and the floor pooled dark beneath him, the story, which he read, waiting anxiously in his seat on the 6:06, willing the train to back out into the yards and carry him away from all this:*

Machine Gun Jack McGurn, one-time gunman for Al (Scarface) Capone and long rumored to have been central to the 1929 St. Valentine's Day Massacre, was shot to death this afternoon at a north side bowling alley. The murder, gangland style and coming on the seventh anniversary of the massacre, is thought to be a much-delayed act of vengeance in the protracted blood feuds that have plagued this city.

Of course, the papers on the other end of the line had the story, too, when he got off in New York, but there the murder of Machine Gun Jack wasn't front-page news, though one of the tabloids did run a photo of Jack with his wife, Lulu, the two of them coming down some courthouse steps, Lulu's face mostly obscured by her hat. And it wasn't long before the McGurn story faded out of even the inside pages, old news quickly becoming no news at all, and by the end of that summer Herman felt certain that whatever investigation was ongoing out in Chicago, it was a pretty leisurely thing, basically buried in the bulging file of Good Riddance.

But with him, the file stayed open a while longer, even if it wasn't exactly active, because Jack's murder was like a story that didn't have an ending. Not only had he not been able to avenge Hellie, but he had begun to question his earlier conviction that Jack was behind her disappearance and wonder whether it hadn't been rash and ill-considered. Her long silence said to him she was probably dead, even if it hadn't been her he looked at in horror that day at Bellevue. And there were some things that did seem to point to Jack. But the more he thought about it, the more he found that the pieces of the puzzle that once had seemed to fit together didn't quite. And his original source for the story, Headly Hanlon, was hardly reliable. He began thinking that his own deadly mission to Chicago might have very nearly been a deadly mistake. Shortly after this he found he'd begun to take a strange, oblique sort of comfort in the very inconclusiveness of it: only a witness to Jack's murder instead of the agent of it. And so, finally, he closed the file on Jack, stashing it down in that dark, capacious place in his mind where he kept some other matters he no longer wished to consider.

❧❖❧

One day, driving Jimmy Hines up Broadway, his life began a swing back in an old direction on a chance remark Hines muttered from the solitary darkness of the back seat. Hines was alone more and more these days, whereas before he'd always been surrounded by jocular, cigar-smelly cronies, laughing and talking with energetic earnestness as they were whisked to one function or another—political rally, official dinner, testimonial, funeral, sporting event. Not now. And Hines, who'd begun as a blacksmith in the last century and still went at things with a smithy's clatter-and-bang conviction, found himself in a wholly modern era in which he looked suddenly archaic. Tom Dewey, the same inoffensive-looking little chap who had Charlie Lucky by the short hairs, now had him there as well and was trying to nail Hines for having provided protection for the Dutchman. Jimmy could hardly protest, even through any least exposed part of you—nose, ears, wrists; the wind off the lake in summer, too, when some errand would bring you onto the Outer Drive, coming up from the inferno of the South Side maybe, and you'd feel it and crank down all the car windows to get the full effect. And then for a few blessed minutes anyway you'd feel the marvelous position of the city and be glad you lived there and of its winds and of the tall, somber, high-standing town, dyed black and gray with soot and cinders, crime and cow's blood. He dreamed of the faces of the tough guys he'd had to learn to live with, the ones who talked always out of the side of the mouth, cigarette bobbing on the clipped words, the mouth held always small and hard and the eyes opaque, unfathomable. And the more such images came to him in dream, the farther back they took him until he was back in the world of his lost, truncated childhood and recalling his mother, her face early seamed with work and care, and how, briefly, she'd done what she could to protect him from part of life's bruising onslaught: put iodine on his knees after he'd opened them up in an unskillful leap from a garage roof; listened to his complaint when one of the sisters had wrongfully whacked him in parochial school. In one dream he saw her sitting on the edge of the bed he shared with Hellie (or did until Hellie got her period and after that he'd slept curled in the big chair in the front room), singing songs from some old time and place. But most of the time his mother had simply been too tired for such attentions, and what mothering he got, he got from Hellie. And then his mother had been taken off in the great flu epidemic, and that had been the end of his childhood. He saw also, fleetingly, mostly effaced, some of the west side rooming houses they'd moved through after his mother's death—cheerless, graywarped places around Ashland and Halsted, one way out on 47th. And the more he dreamed of these things the more it seemed he needed to go back there. There were only the shadows of the past back there, of course, but they were at least his shadows, not those of Jimmy Hines or anybody else. Here in New York it was he who was a shadow, and the world he'd shared with Hines and his cronies was passing swiftly away. He could let it go, even if Hines couldn't. So when Tom Dewey finally sent Jimmy Hines to Sing Sing and Hines's successor Carmine De Sapio asked Herman to stay on, Herman simply said no thanks, that he had an opportunity down in New Orleans, a place that had always kind of appealed to him.

He arrived back in Chicago as Henry Wise, a man too old to fight in the war against the Axis Powers but of considerable value in a defense plant where they built the engines for the gigantic flying fortresses that rained death on the cities of the enemy. Then, the war over, he'd easily found adjacent work at the Tucker plant near Midway where they were building the Car of the Future and where eventually he'd come to the attention of the chief engineer who was so impressed he wanted to send Henry Wise to engineering school. But while he was making up his mind whether at his age he wanted to take so drastic a step, Tucker had folded, and so that decision too had been made for him—as in another way an earlier one had been at Chick's 12-Lanes. Instead of going to school, he'd gone into business with another guy from the Tucker plant, operating a small fleet of cabs, both of them doing the mechanical maintenance, dispatching, and even some of the driving. Henry Wise found himself most at home behind the wheel, especially at night. The night runs reminded him of his youth, and the cityscape was so profoundly familiar he sometimes had the feeling he could negotiate any of the turns, detours, or shortcuts around the Loop, or down in Berwyn and Cicero, blindfolded.

Once in a while his work brought him into glancing contact with someone from the old Outfit, though not often: most of those he'd known back then were dead or dispersed. At a cabstand outside Comiskey Park after a night game he recognized a black guy who once cooked alcohol for Capone, but he'd never known the guy's name and was certain the old cooker had never known his. So, they'd merely signed each other with their eyes and gone their ways. Tony Accardo, who might have recognized him, had moved to a densely barricaded splendor up on the North Shore. The Big Shot was dead.

One summer night he picked up a fare at the Drake—two young couples, the girls giggling in the jump seats—for a jazz concert in Grant Park. There, under the bandshell, was a Dixieland outfit augmented with a reed section and a couple of mellophones, and out in front of it the cornetist Bobby Hackett who he remembered hearing in the Village years ago when Jimmy Hines had wanted to hear some jazz. Dropping his fare, he'd found a spot and parked to listen a little. Jazz was part of a past he wanted to forget. But he couldn't, and so now he found himself drawn in by Hackett's notes. Warm night and the breeze like balm, whispering off the dark expanse of the lake, blowing to him from Michigan on the other side, and with Hackett's horn memory came unbidden to him of that time they'd driven up from Hudson Lake to play that dago joint for the Big Shot, and Hellie had been fooling with dynamite, flirting with Bix all the way up. That was his first close exposure to a jazz band, and what with Hellie's dangerous flirting and the mayhem that was busting loose just behind his driver's seat he was having trouble keeping his mind on the road. He'd been pretty sure that strange kid, Bix, had no idea what he was getting involved in—or even realized he was getting involved, but he at least could see the looming danger ahead, and so when he'd stopped the bus to gas up he'd motioned to Hellie when she'd come out of the toilet. "Do you know what you're doin?" he said tersely, standing by the bus's opened hood, a smoking rag in his hand. "We get up there, right off Jack's gonna see—." But she'd cut him off with the same remark she'd made once before, out at the Blue Lantern: "Jack don't— Jack doesn't—own me." And he'd said sure, sure, and then turned to her. "Listen, sister, we're both of us owned." But she had the bit in her short teeth that Jack had paid the dentist to fix, and she bared them at him then in a slightly stagy smile and patted him on his swart, sweaty cheek, leaning forward just a bit, not wanting to get dirty, and he could smell her through the hot grease, that heady mixture of perfume and powder and glossy flesh. Then he'd looked over at Bix who stood in the greasy cinders of the nameless little filling station, talking earnestly with Tram, and he'd have bet one of Capone's sawbucks Bix wasn't talking about any girl but was talking music.

Now while he began to mentally sidle around the question—Bix and women, Bix and Hellie—looking for something else to attach his mind to, he heard Hackett cutting through the drift of reminiscence, and it was I'm Coming Virginia, Bix's legendary solo, Hackett playing it note for note. From his darkened cab he could see a bit of Hackett through the shifting silhouettes of the throng, his face behind the bright, slightly bobbing horn. But more: he could hear what maybe few in the park could hear: the love that was going into the recreation of Bix's notes, the profound reverence there in the phrasing, the slightly percussive attack. And he knew, too, and thought Hackett himself must know, that there had been many other versions of I'm Coming Virginia than the one laid down in a New York recording studio, who was to say just how many? Versions invented on cut-down bandstands and lavish theatrical stages, on temporary platforms in college gyms and dining halls, in fraternity houses where the band would be all but engulfed by kids, and if they had a trombone player in the ensemble, then that player might have to somehow find his positions over the shoulders and between the waving arms and clamorous hands of the audience. And among those uncounted, uncountable, lost versions there was no telling how many were superior to the legendary one now wafting over the crowd on the darkened lawns of the park, seated in the roseate spangle of the lighted fountain, because he knew that back in those fizzing days of 1927 Bix had just been on fire, tossing off solos so incandescent his peers would have given lifetimes of effort to have achieved just one of them. But as for Bix himself, so what? What was one solo—or a hundred? Tomorrow, something even greater would happen. Tomorrow there'd be another recording session, another jam,

*another prom where they'd all get hot and lift each other to heights
theretofore unreached. It must have been around that time, he
thought, that Bix had said to somebody that what he loved most about
jazz was that you never knew what was going to happen next—only
that it was bound to be more exciting than ever, better than ever. So,
he never cared to repeat himself. Why should he when the next time
around he might suddenly discover a wholly new way of taking the
same passage, some way into it and out of it that would make it a new
and shining thing never heard before. Always the new thing, the thing
unheard, that had been waiting for someone to find it and give it
voice, once. As the number ended and the applause rolled over the
darkened park toward where Hackett stood, bowing with appropriate
modesty, Henry Wise found himself thinking for the first time that
maybe it had been that impossible, unattainable aspiration that really
had killed Bix, not the booze, or whatever else they thought it might
have been. How, he wondered, could you live that way, always unsat-
isfied with what you'd done, certain that you were destined for something far greater, finer, something that in all the long, dim history of
the world had never been heard before? He shook his head and permit-
ted himself, perhaps for the first time, just the shadow of a sorrowful
smile, thinking that it was no wonder the guy couldn't bother to get
the ends of a bow tie lined up.*

❧❖❧

*That night in Grant Park, he now can see, had been the first step in
the final journey, the one that had brought him here to Davenport
and his obscure life on the fringes of the Bix phenomenon that every
year grew larger, more elaborate, so that by now it had taken on a life
of its own. He doesn't think even the insiders understood quite how
this had come about and sometimes imagined he saw that puzzlement
on their faces while they made their plans for the annual festival that
had outgrown their grandest hopes for it. What was it really all about,*

after all? Asking himself that same question again, his mind skips back to that night at the Blue Lantern on Hudson Lake when he'd first heard Bix and asked himself that, standing in the shadows of the hall, where those notes came from. And he remembers again the dawn-hours conversation in the hallway of the 44th Street Hotel when he'd been trying to get rid of the tipsy violin player so he and Bix could grab a little shut-eye, and the guy wouldn't go quietly but wanted to talk to him about those notes, those beautiful notes that, so he said, fell all over Broadway: where did they come from, the violin player had wanted to know? He hadn't answered because he wanted to get the guy on the elevator. But, living around here and bearing his silent, secret witness to the Bix phenomenon, he'd been forced to pose the question to himself so often he'd come to believe the question itself might lie at the heart of this whole thing: the Society, all its activities, the festival and its bands from all over the world. Where had the notes come from? If he could know that, he could maybe understand everything. But you couldn't know. Not now, anyway.

"Something the matter with that?" The waiter behind the counter cuts through his numbed musings, and Henry Wise glances up, almost blindly. The waiter's face is out of focus for a moment, though Henry Wise can see the big wall clock above the grill well enough, its lower portion smudged with ancient grease spatters. He's still trying to bring the face into focus when the waiter decides the geezer needs a little prodding and so jabs a thick forefinger at his plate. "That," he says flatly. "Your omelette." Henry Wise looks down to find that at some point he has ordered a Denver and hash browns that are untouched and beginning to show the metallic signs of congealing. "Nothing," he mumbles, "only I guess I wasn't as hungry as I thought." He fishes out a ten and places it next to the beige plastic plate, and the waiter slides it off the counter and turns away to the old-fashioned cash register.

Back in his car he heads down Brady's steep slope, passing the choco-late-colored pile of the old high school Bix once told him he had night-mares about, glimpsing below him a sliver of the Mississippi, shining between buildings. Then, at the bottom of the hill he hesitantly, jerkily makes the dogleg necessary to cross over the railroad tracks, then swings behind the station where they brought Bix back that last time, seeing in his mind's eye the coffin being canted out from the black hell of the baggage car into the Iowa sun, Burnie standing there supervising and Agatha in the shade of the station roof's overhang, veiled, gloved, silent—O, he'd gotten that part of the story, all right. He turns down the frontage road now called Beiderbecke Drive towards the shrine and park opposite it. Behind him a white municipal truck bumps slowly over the grass on its way to clean up around the shrine and the bandshell. As he slowly emerges from the car he sees that one of the replica steamboats used for gambling is still doing a good business with festival folks who've stayed over to have a few yanks on the slots or try their luck at blackjack. There are a few festival fans around the shrine as well, snapping photos of it and of one another posed beside the silent head, its bronze blackened by sun and snow and flecks of verdigris beginning to show along the part of the hair, the wings of the bow tie. The faces of the living laugh and freeze into photogenic smiles, and while he watches a young woman removes her "Bix Lives!" cap and places it atop the head where it looks small, cockeyed, comical. Noticing the old man standing off and staring at the disfigured bust, she giggles nervously, wishing her husband would hurry up and find the focus button. When he finally does, she snatches the cap back and darts a glance at the old man who continues staring at the head as if nothing at all had happened. And for him, it hasn't: he isn't thinking about the woman's innocent little joke, any more than yesterday he was paying attention to the innocent, jolly tootlings of the Natural Gas Jass Band here. Instead, he's wondering again just where it was the sculptor had gone wrong and why it's so hard for him to put his finger on it. Somewhere along the way the real Bix had slipped away, just as he had in everything else that went into the making of the legend: the tales about him jamming all night, then catching the morning

train—and the time he missed and caught a plane instead; the vener-
ated artifacts he left behind—the Bach in California, cufflinks in a
New Orleans museum, the few letters his family still keeps with their
schoolboy spelling, the random evidence of a life improvised on the
run. Nor was that elusive man really present in the reverent reminis-
cences of those who'd played alongside him, who loved him, were mys-
tified by him, grieved him. Nor in the films, the steady stream of books
and articles about this aspect or that of what was so brief, really, that
it was more like the outlines of what a career might have been than a
full-fledged career itself. He was not really there in the recordings that
furnished such fragmentary and partial evidence of his greatness, of the
beautiful notes that fell everywhere. None of this, he thinks, touches
the real Bix who was always elsewhere, beyond all of them. Behind
him he hears the cleanup crew at work and above them a young voice
saying to him cheerfully, "Man, he must have been something to
know." It's the fellow who took the shot of his wife with her cap
perched atop the bust, and she's there beside him. They're holding
hands, and she's blonde, plump, pretty and reminds him of someone in
the news, only he can't think just who.

She smiles at him, pert, friendly, her "Bix Lives!" cap fetchingly
placed on her blonde hair, and tilts her head into a quizzical angle.
"Could I ask you something?" she says, her voice light as air, musical,
and before he can respond she says, "Are you from around here?" He
nods, and she continues. "Well, I was just wondering if you were—I
mean, did you by any chance, uh, know him?" "No," he hears himself
answering, and thinks he needs to add something, some sort of grace
note to that and so says, "but I would've liked to." "O, me, too!" she says
with a fresh and untroubled enthusiasm. "Me too!" There's a pause
then, the sounds of the cleanup crew filtering in, and then she asks with
her bright, blonde smile, "What exactly did he die of?"

He thinks of an instant answer: booze. But he doesn't say that be-
cause right along with the word he thinks of the terrible stuff Bix

drank, the lethally toxic crap that would be prohibited everywhere these days, deadly stuff that could blind you if you happened to get into a bad batch, and so maybe you'd have to explain that part of it, too, have to go into the specifics of a business he knew a bit too much about to discuss with a stranger. And then maybe you would have to say something about the way they'd lived then, in those years between the end of the war and the crash, and nobody he knew had ever called them the Jazz Age or the Roaring Twenties, but still, tags aside, there had been no doubt among any of them—alky cookers, doormen, rum-runners, drummers, dancers, the cop on the beat—that they were living in crazy times, unprecedented times in which nobody knew what was going to happen next and few seemed to care. He thinks finally of those doctors who lived across the hall in Sunnyside—his final audience and maybe his most perfectly attentive—discussing the cause of death while they stood over the fact of it—the body itself—and agreeing the certificate ought to read "Lobar Pneumonia," the wife particularly adamant about that in a way familiar to him of old: they all wanted to take care of Bix, even at the very end. So, when you added all these things up, what answer could you give somebody who hadn't lived along on that shoot-the-chute ride? He's still mutely wondering what to answer when he glances over to find the husband towing away his plump, pretty wife with short, insistent jerks of his hand, saying something earnestly in her ear. She retreats reluctantly, turning to look over her shoulder at the stooped old man in his John Deere cap who's looking after her as if he's finally thought of something to say, the answer to her question. And when she turns one last time and he catches her eye, he calls out to her, his voice like an aged raven, "Everything!" he calls after her. "He died of everything!"